REMEMBER ME

MARY McCARTHY

D0766967

POOLBEG

Published 1996 by
Poolbeg Press Ltd,
123 Baldoyle Industrial Estate,
Dublin 13, Ireland

A catalogue record for this book is available from the British Library.

ISBN 1 85371 610 3

Cover photography by Michael Edwards
Cover design by Poolbeg Group Services Ltd
Set by Poolbeg Group Services Ltd in Garamond 10/12.5
Printed and bound in Great Britain by
Cox & Wyman Ltd, Reading, Berks.

ACKNOWLEDGEMENTS

My thanks to everyone who has encouraged and supported me in the writing of this book:

To Patricia Scanlan, who set everything in motion and changed my life! Thanks, Patricia.

To my editor, Kate Cruise O'Brien, whose expertise, kindness and unfailing support saw me through. Thanks for everything, Kate.

To Philip MacDermott and all the team in Poolbeg, who've been so enthusiastic.

To my family: my brothers, sisters-in-law, nieces and nephews. Thanks, Loretto, for listening to my moans on the phone!

To my late father, Denis McCarthy. I miss him.

To my friends, who are always there for me.

To my colleagues at work, for their friendship and loyalty. I couldn't imagine working anywhere else.

To my pupils, past and present, for keeping me on my toes!

A special word of thanks to those who've given me advice and help with the research: David Cox, Cynthia Maher, Susan Corrigan, Pauline Gallagher, Cathy Murray, Jennifer Rickard, Mary Hayes, Assumpta Broe, Edel McAteer, Frances Clarke, Eddy O'Brien, Donal Byrne, Ronnie Atkinson, Des and Niall McCarthy. Thanks for your generosity and your time.

ABOUT THE AUTHOR

Mary McCarthy was born in Dublin in 1951. She studied English and French in UCD from 1969 to 1973. Since then she's been teaching in a girls' secondary school on the north side of Dublin. This is her first novel.

DEDICATION

This book is dedicated to three very special people.

To my son, Dara, who has filled my life with happiness.

To my mother, Emily, the kindest person I know.

To Pauline, a friend in a million.

PART ONE

CHAPTER ONE

Sheila Crosby was terrified. She was dreading this moment but there was no way of avoiding it. The rain pelted down and her shoes and socks were sodden. This weather did nothing to dispel her downcast mood. What if it were true? No, it couldn't be. She'd be feeling different, wouldn't she? She'd be able to feel something. She opened the gate and made her way up the path, her legs shaking. Gingerly she opened the front door and went into the waiting room. Nobody there. God, she'd be first. She picked up a magazine and idly flicked through it. She couldn't concentrate. The words made no sense, no sense at all. The door opened and Sheila's heart skipped a beat. It was a mother with a small child. The little girl looked frightened. Sheila could empathise. Her stomach was in bits. The door opened again. This time it was the receptionist.

"Who's first?"

Sheila stood up and followed the girl into the surgery.

"Hello, Sheila." The doctor smiled.

This was it. She'd know all in just a minute.

"Sit down, dear."

Dr Hanley was a glamorous woman in her mid-fifties. She was perfectly groomed and soft spoken but this did nothing to assuage Sheila's fear.

She consulted her file and took out a letter.

"Your results are back. You are pregnant."

Sheila was dumbstruck. She tried to say something but the words just wouldn't come. The doctor smiled sympathetically.

"I know this is a shock, Sheila."

Sheila nodded vacantly.

"Try not to panic. It's not as bad as it seems at this minute."

Not as bad as it seems. Who the hell was she kidding? Was she for real? It was all right for her to sit there in all her finery and mouth some silly platitudes. What had she to lose? How in God's name could she know what it felt like? Pregnant. Christ, she was going to have a baby. Here was this elegant sophisticated career woman telling her not to panic.

"Sheila, are you listening? I know this seems like the end of the world to you now, but it isn't. You're young and healthy. There are a few options open to you, but this is not the right time to discuss them. You are naturally distraught. For the present we'll concern ourselves with your physical well-being. When you get used to the idea of being pregnant, we can discuss what you're going to do. All right?"

Sheila did not respond. She seemed paralysed, rooted to her seat. Dr Hanley was doing her best to be kind. It was vital that she said the right things. She had seen such misery before and it was all so unnecessary. Why had this girl, like so many others, had unprotected sex? Why take such a risk? Was she obeying the restrictions of the Church on the one hand while disobeying them on the other? Ludicrous. No point in dwelling on that now, the damage was done.

"Do you remember the date of your last period?"

Sheila had to think. "Somewhere around the middle of December. The 18th I think."

"Have you any idea of when you might have conceived?"

"Yes, it was only the one time, you see," Sheila replied softly. Her voice sounded different, the voice of a stranger. "December the 31st."

New Year's Eve. Typical. The girl had probably too much to drink at a student party. It wasn't her job to pass judgement. She had to help this girl through what would be the most difficult time of her young life.

"Get on the scales, dear."

Sheila went through the motions, zombie-like. Her weight was recorded and her blood pressure checked. Sheila felt removed from the scene, like some disconnected spirit looking on. She could pretend this wasn't happening to her at all.

"If your dates are right, the baby is due around the 21st of September. I want you to have a blood test done. We need to establish a few things; your blood group, your immunity to rubella, your iron level. No need to worry, strictly routine."

Sheila tried to smile back at her, but a lump was rising to her throat.

"I'm giving you a letter for the hospital. Have the test done as soon as you can and I'll see you again in two week's time. Have you had any morning sickness?"

"No, nothing like that."

"You're lucky so."

Lucky, thought Sheila, yeah bloody lucky. The doctor hesitated. This was a sensitive area but she had to ask the question.

"What about the father? Have you said anything to him?"

"No, no way. I didn't honestly think it could be true."

"Will you tell him now?"

Sheila was mortified in spite of the doctor's tact. She tried to stifle a sob.

"No, I don't think I will. There'd be no point."

"I see."

No, she didn't see. How could she see? Sheila had no intention of getting herself into a worse mess. It wasn't that Sheila was afraid of rejection. He might turn up trumps, but she had no desire to get trapped in a relationship that was going nowhere. She couldn't help herself, she started to cry. Dr Hanley took her gently by the shoulders.

"That's right, love. Have a good cry. It's better not to bottle up your feelings. I want you to go home and try to think about all this as rationally as you can. It might be better not to tell the father, if you're not seriously involved with him. It would only complicate things and make your decisions even more difficult."

Sheila nodded. The doctor continued gently.

"Will you tell your parents?"

"No way, it would kill them." Sheila shuddered at the thought.

"No, it certainly will not kill them. But maybe it's too early to say anything at this stage. Anything could happen yet."

What on earth did she mean by that?

"The timing isn't too bad. You can finish out your year in college at least."

Sheila couldn't believe her ears. The timing wasn't too bad. Bloody wonderful. Here she was, nineteen years old, single and pregnant. The timing couldn't be worse. How could she sit for her degree next year? What would her mother say when she found out? If she found out? Her whole future was up the swanee and this woman honestly expected her not to worry, not to panic. It was laughable.

"Are you feeling any calmer?" Dr Hanley prompted softly.

"Yeah, lots. I'll see you in two weeks. Thanks." She almost stumbled out the door.

Sheila left the surgery and headed down Dorset Street. The rain was still bucketing down. She was soaked. There was a queue at the bus stop. Was she imagining that they were all staring at her? The bus came at last and she tramped upstairs. She lit a cigarette and stared out of the window. The bus was crowded with damp bodies and the smoky air made her feel hot and sticky and claustrophobic. She wanted to bawl and scream. She wanted to die.

She was scared stiff. What was she going to do? Maybe this was just a bad dream. Yeah. She'd wake up in the morning and laugh about this nightmare, wouldn't she? Wouldn't she?

She got off the bus in Rathmines, the rain still falling. Her shoes squelched on the hard pavement. She reached the bedsit at about 9 p.m. The light was on in Mary's flat next door. Would she tell her? She had to tell her. She had to talk to someone or she'd burst. She could hear the strains of the "Help" album, George Harrison singing "I need you." The irony wasn't lost on her. She knocked. Mary, her hair wrapped in a towel, let her in.

"Hi. Come in. God, you look awful, Sheila. Are you OK?"

That was it. The dam burst and a flood of tears followed. She threw her arms around the flabbergasted Mary. After numerous fags and coffees, Mary succeeded in calming her a bit. Mary was a brick. The best friend anyone could have. She didn't make judgements and she didn't criticise.

"Well, are you going to tell Don? He'll have to be told."

No answer.

"Christ Almighty, it's his baby too. He's responsible. Well, he's bloody irresponsible when I come to think about it." Mary was really angry. "It makes me puke."

Sheila said as little as possible. There was no point in blaming him. It was her fault too.

"I'm not going to tell him, I've made up my mind." Sheila was adamant. "He's doing his finals

8

this year. He has no money and no job. How on earth can he help?"

"He can marry you. That's what he can do."

Sheila looked aghast at that idea. "Married? I don't want to get married. I've no intention of getting married for years, if at all."

Mary was horrified. What was Sheila thinking of? She had to get married. There was no other way out of this. Holy Catholic Ireland in 1967 . . . You couldn't have a baby and not be married. It was out of the question.

"Are you thinking of going to England?" Mary was almost afraid to ask.

"Oh God, no. I wouldn't dream of that. No. Of course I'll have the baby."

Mary was relieved and a little ashamed of what she had thought. She could have kicked herself. She was supposed to be helping. She was really mad with Donald Fagan. She'd never liked him. He was too handsome, too smooth and too bloody wrapped up in himself. In her opinion he used Sheila. It was always his problems, his worries and his studies. Sheila was too considerate, a pushover. Sheila was so gorgeous, with her auburn hair and her beautiful skin. She could have any fella she wanted. Why put up with him? She didn't seem to want him at all now. Mary couldn't fathom it. Maybe Sheila was right. Would it be easier if he didn't know? He hadn't the gumption to support her emotionally, never mind financially. He'd probably be a liability.

"So, what are you going to tell him?"

Sheila stared determinedly at her friend. "I'm going to finish with him."

There was no point in Mary saying anything more. Sheila had made up her mind. There was no use arguing with her.

The following morning Mary sat in the crowded Great Hall, trying to pick out the relevant details from Bradley's criticism. She was preparing an essay on the tragic flaw in Shakespearean heroes but her mind wasn't on it. She spotted Don Fagan out of the corner of her eye. He was chatting up a blonde from his third year tutorial. Where the hell was Sheila? She was supposed to meet Mary after her lecture. Maybe she'd chickened out. No, there she was now coming across the aisle. She looked beautiful in her jeans and black polo. God, she'd look terrific in sackcloth and ashes.

"You're late." Mary scolded. "I thought you weren't coming."

"I skipped my lecture. Is he here?"

"Yeah. Don't look now. He's seen us."

Sheila started to fidget in her case. She took out a text and pretended to be reading it.

"What's he doing?"

"He's talking to a girl from his class."

"Shit! What am I going to do? Will I go over?"

"No need. He's on his way over to you now."

"Oh God, Mary. What'll I say?"

"You can't talk to him here. Suggest a coffee or something."

Don Fagan stood beside them. His blond hair

was dishevelled. His eyes were bloodshot and he stank of stale beer.

"Hi, girls. Swotting away, huh?"

Mary ignored him.

Sheila tried to keep her voice calm. "Don, could we go for a coffee?"

"Can't see why not. I could do with a coffee. I'm feeling a bit delicate this morning. I was in Sinnot's last night with the lads."

Sheila nodded.

"We all got totally smashed. I'm suffering today, I can tell you."

Mary saw red. He was still thinking about himself. He had a ruddy hangover, God help him! She could bloody strangle him. He hadn't even noticed that Sheila was worried about something. Anyone could see that she wasn't herself. Such a selfish pig.

Sheila put on her jacket.

Don peered over Mary's shoulder. "Very impressive. Shakespeare, no less. I admire your application. Model student, what? Very commendable. She'll put us to shame yet, Sheila. You need a break from it though. Do you want to join us?" he asked pleasantly enough.

"No thanks," Mary replied coolly. "I've got to finish this."

"Righteo. Don't let me disturb you so." He smiled ingratiatingly at her.

"You don't," was her sharp retort. "I'll meet you back at the flat, Sheila."

He put his arm around Sheila who looked decidedly uncomfortable as they left.

They went around to Newman House for coffee. It was a lovely old building, full of charm and character. Comfortable and familiar, like a pair of old slippers. Don went up for the drinks and Sheila lit another cigarette. Her fifth today. God, she'd have to give them up. They must be doing damage to the baby. The baby. Oh dear God, there was a baby growing inside her and its father was a few feet away, totally ignorant of its existence. Should she tell him? Had he the right to know? Would he want to know? Doubtful, very doubtful. He wouldn't be able for it. It would be too much of a shock. He couldn't cope and she couldn't cope with an adverse reaction at this stage. She was trying to get used to the idea herself. He came back with a tray.

"Are Mikado OK?"

She nodded. Mikado. That's what he had on his mind. Mikado and coffee and a hangover. She couldn't give a fiddler's fuck what biscuits he'd chosen.

"Cripes, it's not worth it. I'll have to stay off the booze. There's a hammer beating in my brain."

Sheila searched for words. "Don, I've been thinking."

"Sounds ominous," he interrupted. "I try not to do that too often."

"Be serious for a minute, will you?" She was losing patience. "I need to talk to you."

He looked at her blankly. "What's up?"

"I think we should stop for a while."

"Stop what?"

"Seeing each other." She stirred her coffee and avoided his eyes.

"Is this a joke?"

"No."

He seemed genuinely perplexed. "Why?"

"I just think it might be a good idea. We both have loads of study to do and I'm finding it hard to concentrate lately."

That bit certainly was true. She couldn't think about anything but the baby. When she opened a paper there were ads for nappies. If she walked out the door, she saw nothing but pregnant women. She'd even crashed into a pram on her way into college. Babies everywhere and one particular baby inside her. She fought back the tears.

He was lost in thought.

"Don?"

He coughed. "This all seems a bit sudden. Is there someone else?"

Yeah, there was someone else now but he was way off the mark.

"No. Don't be daft. There's nobody else. I simply think we should cool it for a while. Anyhow, you're going away in the summer, aren't you?"

"Yeah, I've got my old job back in Smedley's. A few of the lads are going over to Peterborough. The work is lousy, but the pay isn't bad. This'll be our last year of freedom. Next year, hopefully, I'll be able to get gainful employment. After the H. Dip., I mean."

The mind boggled at the thought of Don standing in front of a class.

"There you are, then. We wouldn't be seeing each other much anyway."

He pondered that for a while. She was right. Things were getting a bit heavy lately. The lads were always slagging him about the amount of time he spent with her. What was the point? He'd no intention of getting tied down yet. He'd other fish to fry. That girl, Doreen, from his class. She was a bit of all right. Not as pretty as Sheila of course. Still, maybe she was good in the sack. Sheila wasn't exactly the forward type, was she? He'd never got far enough with her. Except for that one night and then she was sloshed.

"Right. If that's the way you honestly feel, we can break it off for a while. We'll see how it goes for the summer. We can always get back together next year, if we want."

"Yeah," Sheila agreed. "We can take a rain-check when college starts again."

No earthly way would Sheila be taking a rain-check. It was over. She had to wipe him out of her mind if she was to survive the next six months.

* * *

Mary went with her to the hospital that afternoon. Sheila really needed moral support. The waiting-room was crowded so they had to wait in the corridor. Sheila wished she was anywhere else. She'd always hated injections and the last time she had a blood test she was bruised for a week. Mary chatted incessantly in an effort to keep Sheila's mind off what was going to happen. It didn't work. Sheila gave the shortest replies to her questions. She didn't really want to talk about what had happened with Don this morning. She wanted to forget all about it.

"Next."

Mary tried to go in with her, but she was firmly turned away.

"Only the patient, please." The nurse said gruffly.

She sat Sheila down first in order to take the particulars.

"Name? Mrs Sheila Crosby."

"No. Miss. Miss Sheila Crosby." Sheila winced.

Nothing was actually said as the nurse filled out her chart but Sheila could sense the disapproval. She was humiliated. To think that a private act between two people could become so public. She'd made love once in her life and this was the result. A total stranger was asking her for personal and intimate details.

"Address? Telephone number? Doctor's name and address?"

Sheila felt like a disembodied statistic. She went inside and rolled up her sleeve as she was told to do. The phlebotomist was big and brusque. She shot the needle into Sheila's arm, making her flinch. Her arm hurt like hell and she was hot and flustered.

"Your doctor will have the results in a few days. Next."

"Stupid old bag," muttered Mary on their way

out. Sheila faltered. She was light-headed and dizzy. Mary took her arm to steady her.

"Come on Sheila, let's go for a drink. You deserve one."

"I don't know, Mary. I don't feel like it. Would you mind if we went straight home?"

"You're the boss."

They walked on, towards O'Connell Street.

"Mary, I don't know how I'm going to get through all this. I can't see how I'm going to cope."

"You have me. I'll be with you every step of the way."

"You're fantastic, Mary, you really are. But you can't hold my hand forever. You'll have to go away in the summer. Aren't you going to stay with Joanne?"

"Yeah, I have to earn my fees. But Sheila, you can't stay in the flat all summer on your own. Would you not go home to Galway?"

How could Mary ask her that? There was no chance of her going home, not till the whole thing was over. Her mother would be spared the shame at least.

"I can't go home."

"What about Seán? I know he'd help." Mary persisted.

"I'll think about it. I might tell him the next time he's in Dublin."

"He's your brother. He loves you. He'll help, I know he will."

"You know what, Mary? In a way it's all a huge fuss about nothing. I'm pregnant, so what? I'm going to have a baby. It's the most natural thing in the world."

"Of course it is," Mary agreed.

The most natural thing in the world if you're respectably married, Mary thought to herself. How could Sheila bring up a child on her own? How would her parents react? How would any parents react? It was considered a moral disgrace to have a child out of wedlock. Where would Sheila go when her condition became obvious? What was going to happen to the baby? She hadn't mentioned the word "adoption" yet but surely it had crossed Sheila's mind?

"I'm going to start to think positively about this." Sheila interrupted her thoughts. "After all there are more babies born to married couples who should never have had them. Kids are being abused and neglected every day of the week in this so-called Christian country. Who are they to criticise me? I'll make a very good mother, just wait and see."

God, this was heart-rending. Sheila was in a fool's paradise.

"I feel better already. Will we walk home? The air and the exercise will do us both good." Sheila was nearly euphoric. Mary decided to keep her trap shut.

* * *

The euphoria didn't last. Sheila went through huge mood swings in the next few days. She started to miss her lectures and her practicals. She stayed in the flat all day, drinking coffee and chain smoking. Mary was terribly worried. Anyone would go nuts cooped up in that bedsit all day. It wasn't healthy. It wasn't natural. Sheila had lost weight too. She picked at her food. Her humour was erratic and Mary never knew how she was going to find her. At one stage, Mary was afraid that Sheila would do something really drastic. Would she be that desperate? There was just no knowing. Mary felt out of her depth. She needed to talk to someone but she couldn't. She'd promised Sheila to keep the news to herself. That was the important thing; keeping the whole thing secret. She had to do something though. She had to jolt Sheila out of this depression and lethargy. How could she get her out of the flat?

When she was coming out of her English lecture one day she noticed a poster for the debate in the L and H. Mary remembered Sheila telling her that she used to captain her debating team in school. Maybe she'd agree to go on Saturday night? It was worth a try. Jim Ryan was chairing it. That was a bonus. Mary had fancied him for ages. Mary hadn't a clue what to do next if Sheila wouldn't go. Sheila needed to see the university counsellor. That was one sure thing. Her GP was fine, but Sheila needed more than the usual advice dished out by doctors. She needed psychological help.

Surprisingly Sheila agreed to go. They went back to Earlsfort Terrace on Saturday night. The hall was crowded as usual. The teams came in and took their seats. Jim Ryan looked terrific. He really was a fine thing! The motion was a contentious one: "The Church in Ireland has too much influence."

The only female taking part was Anne Nolan and she was on the opposition. She spoke very well but Mary was disappointed with her right-wing views. She'd probably end up in politics. Her rebuttal was brilliant. She could mange to keep a cynical tone without stooping to sarcasm. Mary noticed that Sheila wasn't listening. She kept shifting around in her seat and the odd time she'd let an involuntary sigh. Mary, on the other hand, was riveted. These students were so articulate, so self confident. Many of them would no doubt end up in public life. Mary envied them their guts. When Jim opened the discussion to the house, Mary suggested that they go for a drink. Sheila was relieved.

They went over the road to O'Dwyer's. They managed to get a seat over in the corner near the stairs. Half the clientele seemed to be from UCD. The next thing, Jim Ryan appeared. Mary nearly had a stroke. Thank God she had her leather jacket on. He nodded to them and Mary prayed he would make a move.

"Go on up to the bar and get the next drink." Sheila prodded her. "Go on!"

"I can't. It'd be too obvious."

"Would you go on, for God's sake, before he moves off," Sheila insisted.

Mary shuffled up to the bar trying to look nonchalant. He smiled at her and she was in heaven.

"Here, let me carry the drinks," he offered politely. "It's impossible to get by in this throng."

19

Mary didn't argue. He came over to their table and sat down. "Do you mind if I join you?"

They assured him they didn't.

"So, what did you think of tonight?"

Mary racked her brains for something intelligent to say.

Sheila came to the rescue. "I've been to better ones, I must say. Some of the speakers tonight have very right-wing views. They're much more conservative than I'd have thought."

"Yeah," Jim agreed. "It kind of proves the motion was right, doesn't it?"

"What's Anne Nolan studying?" Mary asked for want of something better to say.

"History and politics, I think." Jim gulped down his pint. "Can I get you both another?"

"Thanks." Sheila accepted before Mary could object.

He went back up to the bar.

"Jesus, Sheila, we shouldn't have let him do that." Mary didn't like it at all.

"Cop on. If he gets us a drink, we'll be here longer. We can buy him one back then."

"I never thought of that."

"You're hopeless!"

Mary laughed. Sheila was in much better form. This was great.

Jim came back. "I was just chatting to Peter Morris at the bar. He said the same thing as you did, Sheila. He was horrified."

"By the conservative thinking?" Sheila lit a cigarette.

20

"Yeah. Gas, isn't it? This country is hilarious all the same."

"What do you mean?" Mary asked him.

"You know, the way people think. They have a queer notion of right and wrong."

"For example?" Mary egged him on.

"Well, for example, tax evasion. That's a cause for celebration. People go to any lengths to avoid tax. Plumbers, carpenters, electricians, all sorts of tradesmen do nixers. That's perfectly acceptable to everyone. Industry suffers every Monday morning when staff are off 'sick'."

"That's exactly what my father is always saying," Sheila agreed.

"Yeah," Jim continued, "Middle-class morality. You can get away with anything in this country except the big S." He downed his pint with a flourish.

"What's the big S?"

"Sex, of course. Don't you remember all the sermons you got at school?"

"Yeah," Mary laughed. "They used to warn us about impure thoughts. I didn't even know what impure thoughts were."

"Precisely," Jim warmed up. "We were warned about you lot!"

"Us? Do you mean women?" Mary asked provocatively.

"Yeah, I do mean women." He laughed. "Occasions of sin. That's what we were taught ye were. Occasions of sin."

"My God!" Mary grimaced. "Can you credit it? It's unbelievable."

"My only complaint about you is you don't give us enough occasions." He seemed to think that that was a huge joke. Mary was very conscious that this conversation would be uncomfortable for Sheila. She tried to change the banter but Jim carried on regardless.

"Like I said, we're some little country all right. Sex is the only sin."

Sheila could feel her cheeks burning.

"And even sex is OK so long as you don't get caught." Jim was totally oblivious.

Mary nearly collapsed. Why had he said that? You'd think he knew. But he couldn't know. He'd never be that insensitive if he did know. She had to put a stop to this immediately.

She stood up abruptly. "Why don't I get us another round?"

She was off like a light. Oh God, poor Sheila. This was turning into a farce. What was he saying to her now? She had to get back to the table fast before he made matters worse. Where the hell was the barman? Why was it taking so long to get a drink? Finally she managed it. She peered over, but she could see no sign of Sheila. She must be in the loo.

Mary hurried back to the table. "Where's Sheila?"

"She left."

"What?" Mary gasped.

"She got up suddenly and said she was leaving. I couldn't understand it."

"Oh my God. I'll have to go after her." Mary grabbed her jacket.

"I'll come with you," he offered.

"No, no, you stay here and finish your pint."

"Did I say something to upset her? I didn't mean to." He felt responsible but wasn't sure why.

"It's all right, Jim. She's not feeling well. It's not your fault."

She was about to leave when he stopped her.

"Can I see you again?"

This was what she'd been waiting for. She'd have been delighted if she hadn't been so concerned over Sheila.

"Sure. Here's my phone number. Give me a ring."

She scrawled her number on the top of her cigarette packet and handed it to him. She rushed out. Jim was left sitting, wondering how to figure out women.

CHAPTER TWO

"Sorry, he's not here right now. He's on his rounds, Mrs Brogan. Can you wait till the morning surgery? Grand. Not at all. Bye."

Caroline didn't particularly mind acting as his secretary if he'd give her credit for it. Like everything else she did, he took it for granted. "Come on you two. Bath time."

She gathered up the twins in her arms and whooshed them into the bathroom. Seán didn't like to come in to the sight of dirty nappies on the floor. She grappled with Colm who insisted on wriggling out of her arms whenever she tried to undress him. Ciara meantime found her lipstick and proceeded to draw on the newly papered wall. This time of the evening was dire. Chaos. She heard his key in the door.

"Hi. Your dinner's in the oven. Be out in a minute."

Seán Crosby could hear the excited squeals and the splashing of water. He took his burnt casserole out of the oven and poured himself a glass of red wine. He was tired. It had been another rough day. Afternoon surgery had been packed and he had two extra house calls this evening and a flat tyre in the middle of nowhere. Blooming flu epidemic. He was in foul humour. He wondered if he had done the right thing, having his practice on his home patch. He was owed money and he had his own bills to worry about. Times were tough. There was a lot of unemployment in the district. These people were his own, but that had its disadvantages. Familiarity did breed contempt or, if not exactly contempt, a mild aversion to paying his fees. He wished he had gone for paediatrics. He could have had a cushy number by now in the Regional. The arrival of the twins put the kibosh on that.

"Is the dinner OK?" Caroline handed him the evening paper.

"Fine," he muttered between mouthfuls. "Fine."

Actually the meat was as tough as old boots but he knew better than to hang himself. Ciara crawled up on his knee, spilling the wine in the process.

"Shit." He put her gently on the floor and she promptly started to howl. Caroline gave him a scathing look. Colm put his arms around his sister. It amused Caroline to see how they looked out for one another. Colm stared defiantly at his father.

"Shit," he sang gleefully. "Shit shit shit shit shit."

"Stop it," Seán warned him sternly.

"Whose fault is that?" Caroline asked smugly. "Say goodnight to Daddy."

He kissed them both. "I'll be in in a minute to tell you a story," he relented. He'd have to watch his tongue. He knew that. She was cool when she came back. He put on the radio and handed her a glass of wine. She joined him on the couch.

"New skirt?"

"Do you like it?" She got up and did a swirl. He could see her knickers.

"God, if they make them any shorter they'll do as belts."

She ignored that. "How did today go?"

"Don't ask."

"Like that, was it? My own wasn't much better."

There was no answer to that. She hadn't a clue. What had she to do all day except mind the kids? She certainly hadn't spent much time doing the housework. The place was filthy. He didn't particularly like living over the surgery, but one mortgage was definitely enough. He had a woman in to clean downstairs. It was vital to have his place of work spick and span. That only left their living quarters upstairs to Caroline. She could make more of an effort.

"Your Dad called in. They had a phone call from Sheila."

"Oh? Wonders never cease."

"She can't come to the party apparently."

"She can't come? What do you mean she can't come? It's his seventieth birthday." Seán got angry.

"She's busy, Seán. She has a lot of study. Second year chemistry can't be easy."

"It's a damn sight easier than medicine. She's only doing three subjects; chemistry, biochemistry and botany. She has months before the end-of-year exams."

"She said something about a project."

"Rubbish," Seán retorted. "She just can't be bothered. To think of the way Dad dotes on her."

26

"Look, there's no point taking it out on me. Speak to Sheila if you feel that strongly about it."

"I bloody well will. I'll be in Dublin next week for a conference. I'll give her an earful."

"Calm down, Seán. It's not as if Sheila had to worry about your parents. She knows we're here."

"That's the shagging point. It's fine for her. She doesn't have to bother about anyone else but herself."

Caroline gave up. His language was going to the dogs. For a supposedly educated man he was often vulgar. Maybe his medical studies made him crude. He used to refer to the cadavers as "Mabel on the table." She certainly wasn't leaving her body to medical science!

This evening he was in one of his martyrdom moods. She suspected he was jealous of Sheila. There was a ten-year gap between them and Sheila's arrival must have been a huge change to a boy who was used to being an only child. Mr Crosby idolised Sheila and Seán was still suffering from sibling rivalry, in her opinion. Time he grew up. Anyhow, didn't his mother think the sun shone out of his arse? She got up to do the dishes. His patients thought he was God. So did he, when it came to it.

"What about the story for the kids?"

Christ, he'd forgotten all about it. "I'm on my way," he moaned.

That's big of you, she thought. The cooker was crusted with grease. Ah, she'd do it tomorrow. She dried the dishes and put them away. She was glad

27

he was going away for a few days. It would give her her own space. She knew he worked hard, but that was no excuse for his constant irritability. He thought she did nothing all day. He had no conception or idea of how much energy it took to look after two-year-old twins. Although his job was hard, at least he was meeting people, other adults. She felt that she was turning into a vegetable. Normal conversation would be beyond her soon. The kids were great and she adored them but they didn't exactly provide intellectual stimulation. She missed her job.

She missed the excitement of meeting new clients, getting new contracts. Although the advertising agency had been small, they were kept very busy. She'd loved her job as a graphic designer. She'd resented having to give it up when she got married. Why was it the woman who had to make all the sacrifices? Seán couldn't understand her annoyance. He didn't realise how unfulfilled she felt. He thought she had a great life. Comfortable. Secure. She loved being a mother, but she could be that and so much more. A married man was a good candidate for any job. Marriage suggested responsibility and steadiness . . . in a man. For a woman it meant having babies and absenteeism, according to the powers-that-be. It didn't have to be like that. But Seán didn't want her to work outside the home. There was no necessity for it, he said. She took her gratuity, left the world of work and tried to settle into the cosy lifestyle of the doctor's wife.

Now they were strapped for cash. He hated to admit that. She'd love to have their own house, not to be living on top of his surgery. If she were working they could manage it. He refused to listen. He said it was his responsibility to support his family and hers to look after the twins. Bullshit. She thought of her mother. The woman had devoted her whole life to her family. What had she got now? Her children had grown up and gone and she was left a widow. Bingo was now the highlight of her life. Sure, Caroline was in a better position. She went to functions and receptions with Seán. She dressed herself up and was wheeled out on these occasions. She was the token little woman behind the great man. She couldn't content herself with that. Why should she?

* * *

Mary O'Callaghan was in love. She was walking on air. She'd been out with Jim six times now and the more she got to know him, the more she liked him. He was kind. He was thoughtful. They laughed a lot together. The dates consisted mainly of going for walks, or for a drink. They'd been to the pictures last week. *The Graduate* was brilliant. She loved Simon and Garfunkel. Already she had managed to pick out "April Come She Will" on the guitar. Dustin Hoffman was terrific. He reminded her of Jim. They were both a bit gauche. Jim was like a little boy in some ways. When he rang her he'd never ask her out directly. He'd say: "Are you going into town tonight?" She'd say "maybe" and he'd say "I'll be in Neary's at about nine". He was a scream.

Sheila said that would drive her mad. But Mary liked it. She thought it was kind of sweet. He was gentle too. She loved the soft feel of his lips on her mouth and his arm around her. She felt protected. Joanne rang her last night and she was all into it. Joanne loved romance. She was living in London now with her husband, Brian, and three children.

Mary missed her sister. She was looking forward to staying with her in the summer. Brian had fixed her up with a job in the hotel where he worked. She'd miss Jim though. He was staying in Dublin to study for the autumn exams. Some day he'd be a successful architect and she saw herself as his wife. Wasn't she cracked to be thinking like that after only a few dates? She just couldn't imagine going through life without him. She felt they were right together, that this was meant to be. Guys were different though. If he knew she was thinking like this, he'd probably run a mile. She'd have to keep cool and play a bit harder to get. Impossible. She was mad about him and she wasn't into playing games. Sheila told her not to worry, that she was sure he was nuts about Mary from the way he looked at her. Oh God, being in love was torture sometimes.

Her mother used to say that she wouldn't die happy till her children were all happily married. Her parents were great. They were really united. They'd lived in the same house in Drumcondra since their marriage. Joanne was the eldest and then came

Paul. He was a civil servant like her father. Mary was the youngest and, everyone said, the pet. Growing up in that house was wonderful. As children, they were always encouraged to do well in school. Their mother genuinely believed her children were prodigies. She praised them constantly. That was a terrific way to bring up kids. Her father was a religious man and she remembered with fondness his insistence on the family rosary. It wasn't as reverent as it might have been, with Paul making faces at her behind their parents' backs when it came to her decade.

The girls both did music. Her mother could see a potential Shirley Temple in Mary's head of black curls. Mary took up the violin when she was eight and Paul despatched her to the bathroom to practise. It was the only room in the house where he couldn't hear the wailing, strident scrape of the bow. She persisted in spite of him and he had to admit she came in handy when they had visitors. She'd be brought into the sitting-room to play for the guests, accompanied by Joanne on the piano. Paul would take advantage of the situation. He'd be in the kitchen smoking rolled newspapers up the chimney. She gave up the violin when she was fifteen and her mother gave the instrument away to a nun who had arthritis, to exercise her fingertips. So much for her musical career!

She enjoyed strumming away on her guitar now. Jim kept asking her to play for him, but she was too embarrassed. She wondered if she should bring Jim home with her to meet her folks. No, it was too soon yet. She didn't want to scare him away. She'd better not mention him to her mother either. The poor woman would never be satisfied till she saw a ring. Mary stared down at her notes. She was wasting valuable study time mooning about her love life. Ah, sure wouldn't it help her to appreciate Browning? She got up to stick on the kettle when she heard knocking on Sheila's door. Who could it be? Christ, she hoped it wasn't Don Fagan. No. It couldn't be. She'd seen him last week with the blonde. He hadn't wasted much time. Creep. Naturally she didn't mention it to Sheila. The knocking continued. She'd better go and have a look. A man she faintly recognised stood on the landing.

"Hi. Can I help you?"

"I'm looking for Sheila. Sheila Crosby."

"She's not here. She should be back soon though. Can I give her a message?"

"I'm her brother."

"Seán?"

"Yes. Do I know you?"

"I'm Mary O'Callaghan, Sheila's friend. I've seen you in photos."

They shook hands. Mary was thrilled he was here.

"The key is over the door. I can let you in."

Seán walked into the bedsit and was happily surprised. It was much nicer than the one Sheila had last year. Her bed was in an alcove and there were lots of shelves and a table and a chair. She had a galley kitchenette and it was spotless. The green carpet looked new. The walls were freshly painted and there were nice chintz curtains on the big window. The room was bright and airy and smelt of furniture polish.

"This is nice." Seán was impressed.

"Yeah, Sheila keeps it lovely. She's very organised. You'd want to see my place. It's like a pigsty. Sit down and make yourself at home."

He looked a bit uncomfortable. "I hope I'm not disturbing you?"

"Not at all. Any excuse to get away from the books. I was just making a cup of tea, can I get you one?"

"No, thanks all the same. I'm grand. Do you know what time Sheila is due back at? Is she at a lecture?"

"She's gone to the doctor." God, that slipped out. She hadn't meant to say that.

"To the doctor? She's sick then?"

"Yeah, some kind of a virus or something." Jesus, why did she say that?

"I hope she's looking after herself. Girls in flats tend to neglect their diet."

A bit pompous, wasn't he?

"I can check her out. I'm a doctor."

"I know." Mary felt idiotic. This conversation was awkward in the extreme.

"If she's not well, perhaps she should come home with me for a few days. I'm driving back to Galway tonight."

"Ah no," Mary blurted out. "She's not that bad. I can look after her."

33

"A virus you said. Was she vomiting?"

This was impossible. What was keeping Sheila?

"I think she was getting sick, yeah."

"Any pains?"

Mary couldn't go on with this. Lying never came easy to her.

"Look, it's not my place to be telling you this, but I think you should know. Sheila is pregnant."

His face turned a ghastly colour. "Pregnant?"

"Yes."

Silence.

Mary wished the ground would swallow her up. Sheila would kill her for this. But he had to know. He had to. He had to help. He was family.

"Pregnant? My God. I can't believe it. What is she thinking of? This is disastrous."

Mary looked at him in horror. What did he mean, disastrous? Disastrous for whom?

"We'll have to keep this quiet. Who else knows?"

"Nobody. Just me. Now you." What was he getting at?

"Thank God for that. I think I can fix it."

"Fix it?"

"An abortion. It'll be difficult, but I know people."

"Sheila won't hear of that." Mary was furious. "She won't hear of it."

"She doesn't have much choice. How could she have been so stupid as to get herself into this mess?"

"She didn't exactly plan it, you know." Mary couldn't keep the rage out of her voice.

"Whose is it? Who's the silly bastard who got her pregnant?"

"That's none of my business. Or yours," she added pointedly.

"Does she even know who the father is?"

Jesus, he was some tulip. Her own brother. He could fuck off. Mary was mad with herself for having told him. Some help he'd be. Bastard. If he behaved like this with Sheila, it would finish her.

"Seán, Sheila is very vulnerable. You can't imagine how frightened and alone she feels. We have to help her as best we can. She certainly doesn't need a lecture or your disapproval."

This mollified him somewhat. "You're right. I'm sorry. It's just such a shock."

"I know," Mary agreed. "It's more than a shock for Sheila. She has to deal with it."

"Yes." He had the decency to look embarrassed.

"I wouldn't mention anything about the baby's father either." Would he take that hint?

"No, I won't say a word. I'd love to get my hands on him, all the same."

"What's done is done." Mary stared at him.

"What are her plans?"

"Plans? She hasn't got any plans. She's up the walls. She can't think straight. What plans is right. She's in no fit state to make plans. Jesus." Mary was shouting by now. "Your sister is in deep shit. Can't you understand that?"

Seán was taken aback. He wasn't used to being addressed like this.

"Where is she going to go for the summer?" He

tried to keep his tone civil. "She can't come home, obviously."

"Why? Are you worried about the neighbours?"

"Among other things, yes. But I'm more worried about my parents."

"They're Sheila's parents too."

"Exactly. She wouldn't want to cause them any hassle, surely."

"Oh God forbid," Mary drawled sarcastically.

Seán could see this was getting nowhere.

"Look, let's call a truce. I was only trying to help. Sheila will have to have somewhere to go for the duration of this pregnancy. How far is she gone?"

"About three months. She's not showing, if that's what you're worried about. She's like a rake in fact."

"She won't be showing for weeks yet. She could come home with me for a while."

Jesus, he was so fecking condescending. Mary couldn't get over it.

"She could stay with my mother," she announced unexpectedly. Why hadn't she thought of that before? Her mother would be perfect. Her parents would be fantastic with Sheila.

"I thought you said nobody else knew."

"They don't know, but I could tell them. They'd be more than willing to help. They like Sheila." She hoped that hit home.

"No, let me think for a minute."

He could think as long as he bloody well wanted. Still . . . Maybe he did really want to help? She'd give him the benefit of the doubt.

"I have an idea. Is there a phone here?"

"Down on the first floor, by the hall door."

"Back in a minute." He left.

Mary was drained. She was guilty of betraying a trust. Would Sheila understand? Would she forgive her? She lit a cigarette and inhaled deeply. Footsteps on the stairs. That was quick. But it wasn't Seán who burst into the room, it was Sheila.

"I've just passed Seán in the hall. My brother, Mary, my brother Seán is here. What'll I do?"

Mary put her arms around her. Then Sheila spotted the coat on the back of the chair.

"Jesus, he's been here. You've been talking to him. You didn't say anything, did you?"

Mary spoke quietly. "He knows."

"Oh my God!"

"Sheila, I had to tell him."

Sheila sat down slowly. She was trying to take this in.

"He knows." Her voice was a whisper.

"Yes."

"How did he take it?"

Mary's face said it all. Sheila was stunned. The door opened. Suddenly he was there, standing before her.

He moved closer. "Sheila."

Sheila flung herself into his arms and wept.

"Shh, shh," he crooned into her ear. "It's all right, Sheila. It's all right."

"I'm so sorry, Seán. I'm so sorry. I didn't mean to cause all this trouble." She sobbed bitterly.

Mary crept out of the room. They needed to be alone.

Seán sat her down on the bed and folded her in his arms. He was dismayed. There were no recriminations or accusations. His heart went out to her. She was his little sister again and he wanted to shelter her, to make her safe. He could kill the bastard who was responsible. They sat there for a long time, locked in an embrace.

"Sheila," he said softly, "I think you should come home with me for the weekend. Caroline would love to have you."

"No, no, I couldn't. I don't want to see Mam and Dad."

"The change would do you good. They needn't know anything. I won't even say it to Caroline, if you don't want me to."

"I couldn't face them. I couldn't pretend that everything was normal. I couldn't." She dried her eyes in his handkerchief.

"How did you get on with the doctor?"

"She gave me this." Sheila handed him a bit of paper. It was screwed into a ball. He unravelled it. The name and address of an adoption agency.

"I'm not going, I'm not," Sheila said defiantly.

"We can talk about it later," he pacified her. "I've just talked to a friend of mine."

"About what?" She was alarmed.

"About the summer. You can stay with him."

"Stay with strangers?" Her tone of consternation unnerved him.

"He's an eye specialist and his wife works too. They have two young children. Their au pair is going back to Germany."

Sheila stared at him. "Where do they live?"

"Howth. They're very nice, Sheila. They'd be good to you. I can come up from time to time. So can Caroline."

Sheila nodded. Her mind tried to absorb this news. It might be an idea.

"They'd pay you, of course."

That had been the furthest thing from her mind. But she'd need money, naturally.

"What do you think?" he asked hopefully.

"Yeah. It's a good idea. Could I meet them first?"

"Of course. I'll give you his number. You can arrange to meet them whenever you like."

"I have to leave this flat at the end of May," Sheila thought aloud.

"That's fine. It's nearly April now. Are you going to stay on in Uni?"

"Might as well. I'm not brain dead yet." She smiled.

"Why don't we go for a meal? You could do with some good food, by the look of you."

"God, you're a carbon copy of Mam, do you know that?"

"You get yourself dolled up and I'll pop into Mary. Maybe she'd like to come out with us? She's a lovely girl, Sheila, very loyal. She said some hard things to me, but she was right. I deserved a telling-off. She's a good one to have on your side."

"Who are ya telling? I wouldn't say she'll come with us though. She has a new boyfriend. It's the real thing."

Mary politely refused the invitation. She was staying in to study and anyway she thought they'd be better on their own. With any luck, Jim would call around.

"Thanks for putting me straight, Mary. I was a bit of a pain."

"No, you got a fright. You weren't thinking. Is she all right?"

"Yes, but she's upset with the doctor. She got a note for an adoption agency."

"Oh God, that's all she needs."

"She'll have to consider it, Mary. It's awful but she'll have to think about it seriously."

"Yeah. I don't envy her. You know she wants to keep the baby."

"I guessed that. It's out of the question. You can see that, can't you?"

"Yeah." Mary was on the verge of tears. "It doesn't bear thinking about."

"You might talk to her about it?"

"Seán, I couldn't. Who am I to be advising her?"

"Will you at least give it some thought?"

"Right. But I couldn't be responsible for persuading Sheila to do anything she might regret later."

"There's going to be regrets whatever happens," he said ruefully.

CHAPTER THREE

June was sunny and warm. Sheila had settled in well
with the Regans. Philip was an extremely successful
eye specialist with private rooms in Merrion Square.
He was easy going and mild mannered. From
everything she saw he was a model husband and
father. After a gruelling day, he found time to play
with the kids. He took out the bins, did all the
gardening and generally mucked in. He joked that
his mother had trained him well. Sheila couldn't
help comparing him to Seán. Philip maintained that
since they were both working, they should both
share the home jobs too. Not your typical hubby.
Seán would probably think he was a sissy.

They wouldn't let Sheila do any heavy work at
all. She was only asked to look after the kids and
do light housework. She'd bring Tom to Montessori
school and do a bit of hoovering and polishing
while Julie had her morning nap. In the afternoons
she'd bring them for walks or to the playground.
She adored them. They had short fair curly hair and
were the image of their mother. They resembled the
little cherubs on holy pictures or, as Sheila thought,
the Bobbsey twins.

Susan worked part-time in a travel agency off Grafton Street. She was gorgeous. She had a trim figure and looked cute in her mini skirts. When she went out in the evenings, she wore elegant evening dresses. Their house, on the hill of Howth, was truly spectacular.

They had a huge kitchen, two fabulous reception rooms and a spacious hall with a cloakroom downstairs. Their five bedrooms were tastefully decorated, each having its own colour scheme. Sheila's was pink. She loved it with its views of the sea and Ireland's Eye. Aware of her need for privacy, they had installed a television and a radio for her in this room. She appreciated their thoughtfulness. She was beginning to enjoy this life of luxury. Although she should have been an employee, she was treated like one of the family.

Susan became her friend and her confidante. Sheila depended on her as she missed Mary so much. She lived for the weekly letters from London. Mary was working as a chambermaid and she hated it. Cleaning had never been Mary's forte, she would be the first to admit. She missed Jim, but she enjoyed being with Joanne. Sheila envied her having a sister. Seán was good, but it was different. He was much older too, a different generation.

Sheila told Mary all about her new life in her letters. She assured her she was in good form and was being treated like royalty. She was free most evenings, but she didn't go out. She was keeping a low profile because of her condition. It wouldn't do for her to be seen by anyone from home. She was in no mood for socialising anyhow. *The Fugitive* was enough excitement for her now! She was in her twenty-second week of pregnancy. She had a little bump, but otherwise had put on no extra weight. The Regans were always trying to fatten her up. She had managed to cut down on her smoking for the sake of the baby. She had felt the first faint movements. "Quickening," the doctor called it.

Sheila was enthralled. It was not an unpleasant sensation, like moth's wings fluttering inside your belly. Sheila felt and looked well and healthy. Susan said she was radiant and that pregnancy suited her. Susan gave her a manual and she read it avidly, fascinated by the changes going on in her body. At this stage the baby was developing hair and had eyebrows. Its little eyelids would still be completely fused. Sheila was amazed by the diagrams in the book. The baby was a real little human being. Sheila no longer felt the overwhelming need to pee all the time as she had in the first weeks. Susan told her this would come back with a vengeance in the last weeks of pregnancy, but Sheila didn't want to think about the last weeks. For the moment she had her baby safe and warm inside her.

She'd sit basking in the sunshine in the back garden while her charges played happily in the sand pit. She was happy. She thought of how her father would love this garden with its red and yellow rose trees and hydrangeas with their pretty blues and pinks and mauves. The thoughts of her father saddened her because of the lies. Seán had thought it better if her parents were told she was in

London with Mary. When she wrote to Mary, she enclosed a letter for her parents which Mary then posted back to Ireland. Sheila hated this subterfuge although she knew it was a necessary evil. After supper one evening, Susan came to her room for a chat. She brought Sheila a glass of wine.

"Do you think I should?" Sheila was a bit anxious.

"Oh, one won't do you any harm. How are you feeling this evening?"

"Fine. I get a bit tired at this time of the day and my ankles swell, but the doc says that's normal."

"It is. Sheila, Seán rang me at work today."

"Oh?" Sheila said defensively.

"He mentioned something about the adoption agency."

Sheila's face turned to stone. She sipped her wine in silence.

"I said I'd talk to you." Susan was walking on eggshells.

"There's no need for you to concern yourself, Susan. You've been too kind already."

Susan had to go on with this. But it wasn't easy. Sheila was clearly in no mood to discuss it.

"Will I put on the telly?" Sheila asked. "Do you want to see the news?"

"I'd rather talk." Susan wasn't going to be put off. "There'd be no harm in making an appointment."

"Where?"

"With the adoption agency. They could help you."

"No. I have all the help I need. You and Philip are here for me. Seán and Caroline are on the other end of the phone when I need them."

"But you need advice, Sheila. You need to discuss what you're going to do."

"I've already decided. I'm going to keep the baby."

How could Susan get through to her?

"Couldn't you go and meet them anyway? They might be able to give you practical help."

"They'll just try to get their hands on the baby. That's all they want."

"I could go with you," Susan offered. "There needn't be any pressure."

"Why go? I'm going to keep the baby. That's that."

"To please me? To please Seán?" Susan pleaded. "Philip thinks you should go."

They were all ganging up on her. They wouldn't let it go. Even the doctor kept on and on at her. Maybe she would go to shut them all up. She'd go once and put an end to all this haranguing.

"Right. I'll ring the agency in the morning. Now are you happy?"

"Oh Sheila," Susan groaned, "this doesn't make me happy, believe me."

She stroked Susan's arm. "I know," she replied gently. "I know."

* * *

Her legs felt like lead as she walked upstairs to the counsellor's office. The room was shabby and didn't inspire confidence. The counsellor was young and gracious.

"So Sheila, this is your first visit."

"That's right," Sheila said stiffly. First and last visit, she thought.

"There's no need to be frightened. I'm Betty. I'm here to help you."

"Well to tell you the truth, I don't think you can. I've been bamboozled into coming here and there's really no point. I'm going to keep my baby, you see."

The counsellor nodded. Let her continue. She obviously needed a listener. There was no rush. Let her get it off her chest.

"I decided ages ago that I wasn't going to give up my child. Why should I? A child is entitled to have its own mother, don't you think?"

Sheila was becoming argumentative. Her tone was defensive. Betty had to tread carefully.

"When's the baby due?" She decided to ignore Sheila's pointed question.

"The last week of September. They tell me a first baby is often late." Her breathing was laboured. Betty gave her a glass of water.

"Thanks. It's palpitations," Sheila lied. "All part of the condition."

Betty smiled. "So you want to keep the child."

"Oh I'm going to. Definitely."

"That's good. Where will you live? Are you going

home to your parents? You come from Galway, I see on your form."

Sheila was taken aback. "No, I'm going to settle in Dublin."

Betty nodded again. She was taking notes now and this aggravated Sheila.

"Why are you writing this down? I told you I won't be coming back here. You're wasting paper making out a file on me."

"Following procedure."

That smile again. Sheila felt like hitting her. Maybe she didn't mean to be smug?

"So you have accommodation in Dublin?"

"At present I'm staying with friends in Howth."

"And when the baby is born?"

"I'll get a flat."

Betty couldn't believe it. What planet did this girl inhabit? Where in God's name would she get a flat with a new baby? Landlords weren't too keen on renting to married couples never mind a single woman with a child.

"That mightn't be easy. I see you are a student. Will you continue at college?"

Sheila wanted to shout at her that it was none of her damn business. Who the hell did she think she was?

"No." She managed to control herself. "I'll get a job."

"A job? What sort of a job?"

"I don't know, in an office or something." She was losing patience with this woman.

"You have shorthand typing I presume?"

Sheila had to admit she hadn't. She felt idiotic.

"Sheila, I have to say you're in a very precarious position. You haven't a hope of getting an office job without secretarial qualifications. Have you any experience at anything else?"

Sheila acknowledged that she hadn't, except for shop work in her holidays.

"The best you could hope for would be hotel or shop work and quite frankly I can't see how you'd manage. Babies are expensive little items."

Sheila was about to protest that babies weren't items. They were human beings, flesh and blood. This baby was her flesh and blood and she wasn't about to abandon it. She didn't like thinking of the baby as *it* either, but she didn't know whether she was carrying a boy or a girl. She secretly called the baby "Buggins". She talked to it and sang to it when she was on her own. Did other women do that?

"Who'd mind the child when you were at work?" The third degree continued.

God, she'd never even considered that. All her great notions were floating away like so much jetsam. The others were right. She was a fool. She hadn't been thinking clearly. But there must be a way. There had to be some way of keeping the baby.

"Look, I know you must think I'm insane. I haven't planned it all out yet, but I will. I'll work out something. I'll manage somehow."

Betty was waiting for this moment.

"Sheila, you love your baby, don't you?"

"Of course."

"You want the best for your little son or daughter?"

Sheila nodded through her tears.

"Do you honestly think you're in a position now to give the baby the best?"

"No. Not right now. But I will be some day. I will."

"Some day? Somehow? Don't you think it's a bit vague? We're talking about a child. What's best for the child? Surely you can see that a baby needs a good start in life. Can you give the baby that?"

Sheila couldn't answer. She was choked up. She hated this woman. She detested her. She wanted to strike out at her. She hated her because she was right. Right. But who knew what the future held? How could this woman or anyone else say for sure what was best for her child? "A loving mother is best," she said coldly.

"I agree. A loving mother and father."

That stung. It really did.

"Lots of women have to bring up children on their own. Widows or deserted wives have to cope. Not every child has the luxury of two parents," Sheila retorted.

"I agree. They have no choice. But you do."

"Some choice," Sheila said bitterly. "Not every marriage is all it's cracked up to be either."

"Our couples are screened very carefully," Betty replied in a low voice.

"I'll bet."

This was not going the way Betty intended. She had to bring this interview to an end before things got out of hand. She didn't mean to upset this girl, and above all she didn't want to alienate her. She'd have to be gently cajoled. The baby came first.

"Will you at least keep an open mind?"

Why the hell didn't this condescending bitch keep an open mind? That's what Sheila would like to know.

"There's also the social dimension." Betty fiddled with her ring. Would that sink in?

"You mean I'm not married?" Sheila challenged her.

"Yes, I'm afraid that is what I mean. Illegitimacy is a heavy burden to impose on a child."

This was the first time anyone had said it out straight. Sheila had to admire her honesty. Betty had the guts to say it like it was. She made no attempt to argue with her. Betty was right. Again. It was irksome in the extreme.

"It wouldn't be you the finger was pointed at," Betty emphasised.

Sheila was getting a headache. She was running out of arguments. She was dying to get out of there. Her mind was in a whirl.

Betty was aware of her discomfort. "Why don't we leave it for today? You could come back to see me another day when you've had more time to consider."

Sheila breathed a sigh of relief. "All right." She'd agree to anything just to get out of there.

"You'll come back in a fortnight?" The counsellor stood up and shook her hand.

"Yeah," Sheila agreed too quickly. She was out the door in a flash.

Betty Byrne sat for a long time in silence. She hated this part of her job. That poor girl was overwrought and Betty's heart went out to her. She could only try to understand what Sheila was going through. She couldn't imagine how anyone could give a baby away. Life was so unfair. Every other day she interviewed couples who wanted to adopt. They were happily married, had good careers, lovely homes and financial security. They had everything except the one thing they wanted; a child of their own. It was tragic. Then there were the Sheilas of this world who got pregnant accidentally. Of course a lot weren't like Sheila. Some couldn't wait to get rid of the child, to get shut of the problem and get on with their lives. This girl was not in that category. She wanted the baby. Betty couldn't see any way Sheila would be able to keep the child. She consoled herself with the thought that one day Sheila might get married and have other children, but she knew, in her heart, that Sheila would never get over losing this one. She also knew that Sheila would eventually be persuaded to give up the baby because love for the child would demand it. This girl was not selfish. The baby would come first.

* * *

Sheila sat on a bench in Stephen's Green. She clutched her stomach protectively. She still had her baby, secure in its little cocoon. She felt a kick. It was as if her child was trying to communicate with her. Her eyes brimmed with tears. What now? She was utterly confused. Everything that woman said made sense to her, but she couldn't accept it. She couldn't. Marriage seemed to be the only way out of this. Should she have told Don? Would he have proposed? Would she have accepted? Did she want to marry him? Was it right to marry someone just because you were pregnant? No. That would have been a worse disaster.

Sheila tried to imagine the baby living with an adoptive mother and father. Who were the loving couple out there who could give the baby a happy life? A secure life? A life without shame? But how would she know the baby was happy? When she took her first steps? What childhood ailments she had? How would she know her little girl or boy was thriving and growing? How would she know how he or she was getting on at school? What the birthday parties were like? What friends came around to play? How would Sheila know? She wouldn't know. That was the problem. She'd never know. She'd be in the dark. She'd be cut off totally from the child. What would the baby think of her? Would she feel she had been rejected? Would she wonder who her real mother was? What would they tell the child about her? Would they say that Sheila was dead? Or would they tell her that her real mother had given her away because she loved her? Sheila would never know. She left the Green and joined the crowds in Grafton Street. She was sorry now she had agreed to meet Susan in Bewley's. If Susan quizzed her about the agency she'd scream.

* * *

July and August crawled by. Sheila got through
them with the help of the Regans. Julie and Tom
filled her days with their joyful antics. The closer
she got to these children the more she dreaded
parting with her own child. Part with it, she must.
She had finally resigned herself to the fact.

At her second visit Betty explained the entire
adoption procedure to her thoroughly. They would
choose a couple who were right for the child. They
would take into consideration height, colour of hair,
religious background, social class. In Sheila's case
they would look for a professional couple who
could give the child a good education. They would
even try to match the baby with a woman who had
auburn hair. Sheila was fascinated and appalled at
the same time. Could they honestly do that? Betty
assured her they could. They had many couples on
their books who would fit the bill perfectly. Sheila
found the whole business weird. Philip said that it
was funny, but he knew adopted children who
were the image of one of the adoptive parents.
Sheila asked if she could name the baby herself.
Betty told her that she could, but there was no
guarantee that the couple would keep her chosen
name. So now she wouldn't even know the name of
the child.

Philip and Susan talked to her time and time
again about her fears. They even offered to adopt
the baby themselves. Sheila thought that would be

worse. She'd be able to visit and see the child growing up. She'd be Aunty Sheila or something like that. No. That would be unthinkable. To see the child and know her and never be able to have her as her own. At this stage Sheila was convinced that the baby was a girl. She had picked out a name for her. Karen. That's what she would call her. It didn't matter what the couple called her because for Sheila, the baby would always be Karen. Philip remarked that a boy child would have serious difficulties going through life being called Karen. Sheila laughed, but she wouldn't change her mind about the name. She knew her baby was a little girl. Instinctively she knew. She was now fairly big.

One night when she was playing with Tom, he asked her could he feel the baby. Sheila put his little hand on her stomach and he felt the baby kick. "Get it out. I want to see it," he shouted excitedly.

"I can't. She's not ready to come out."

"Is she not cooked yet?" He screwed up his tiny three-year-old face.

Sheila had to grin. He was so cute. She'd miss them when she had to go. She'd miss Julie who demanded her bedtime story every night. She'd miss Philip and his comforting chats. Most of all she'd miss Susan. She had fitted in so well with this family. Perhaps it was living with them and seeing how happy their kids were that finally convinced her of the baby's need for a similar situation. She tried to imagine herself happily married with other children.

Would she ever fall in love? Would she be the happy housewife bringing up her family in suburbia? Hardly likely. This pregnancy had changed her. This baby would always have a special place in her heart. She couldn't simply forget and go on to produce other children, could she? You couldn't replace a child the way you replaced the family pet. How could she rear other children without telling them they had a brother or sister somewhere? How could she marry someone and tell him she had given away a child? How could a man understand that when she didn't fully understand it herself? She didn't see how she would ever want another relationship.

What did she really want? She wanted this baby. She wanted to bring the child into the world, to love it and cherish it always. They said it wasn't on. Were they wrong? How could they all be wrong? These were the people who cared about her. Seán did care about her and about the child. He mightn't be the most diplomatic person in the world, but he did care about her. The counsellor knew what was best for the baby. She experienced this situation all the time. Susan and Philip were like family and they thought adoption was the wisest choice. Even Mary, her best friend, could see no alternative. Mary had never mentioned the word adoption, but Sheila knew how she felt.

How could Mary feel otherwise? She had no idea what it felt like to be carrying a baby. She didn't understand how you got close to the little being that was now a part of your body and your life. No, none of them could see any way that Sheila could keep the child. They couldn't all be wrong.

And yet her gut instinct told her it was wrong. There was such a thing as maternal feelings and there was a bond between herself and the unborn child. She felt it. It was stronger than any other feeling she had had before. There was a binding force that existed between Sheila and this child and nobody . . . nobody could explain that away. All the logic and reason in the world wouldn't change that. It wasn't a matter of right and wrong. It was an undeniable fact. They could take the baby away from her, but they could never destroy the natural link. It might be the right thing to do to give her child to a couple who could rear her well. But it wasn't the natural thing. Mother and child together, that was nature's way. Sheila had to fight her natural instincts, ignore what her inner voice was telling her. It went against the grain. But she couldn't see any way out.

When the 1st of September arrived, Sheila's mood got worse. She felt like a prisoner on death row, counting away the days. Susan tried to keep her busy. They went into town on Saturdays. Philip took her for a drink in the local. They had a barbecue in the garden. Caroline came up on her own for a weekend. She was the only one who didn't lecture. When Sheila begged her for a solution, Caroline's only remark was that the answer was inside Sheila. Did Caroline secretly believe that she should keep the baby? Sheila thought she did. Caroline had her children, so she could understand Sheila's grief.

The doctor gave her a pelvic examination and confirmed that the baby's head had dropped into the pelvic cavity. Sheila had known this herself as she woke up one morning relieved of the pressure under her ribs. But now she felt pressure on her bladder. Once again she was bursting to go to the loo. She was going to the hospital now for weekly visits instead of fortnightly. She broke down on the last visit. The doctor told her she must convince herself that the baby was dead.

Sheila was fit to be tied. This woman expected her to pretend that the baby was dead. Dead. The doctor obviously thought that it would be easier for Sheila to get through the trauma if she thought of the baby as dead. Some psychology. Sheila had heard about women who gave birth to stillborn babies. It must be horrific. How could the doctor say such a thing? It might be understandable for a friend to say something like that, but for a professional it was inexcusable.

Philip was hopping mad when he heard about it. Why were people so bloody insensitive? Had they no cop on at all?

Sheila lived in terror of going into the hospital. She was dreading labour, but not for the usual reasons. Pain didn't frighten her. For others, labour meant the end of pregnancy and the beginning of a new life as a mother. That's not what it meant for her. Sheila's pregnancy would end. But she wasn't going to be a mother. She wouldn't be bringing her little angel home from the hospital to a loving home. She wouldn't be feeding the baby, changing the baby, having friends and family in to admire the baby. She wouldn't be waking in the middle of the night to the sounds of crying. For Sheila, labour meant the agony and pain of separation. For her, it was not a beginning. It was the end.

CHAPTER FOUR

It started as a twinge. Sheila was sure she was in labour and, if it hadn't been for Susan, she'd have insisted on going to the hospital. The pain came from her side and went into her abdomen. It was a bit like a bad period pain, but it wasn't too unbearable. It only lasted half a minute. Susan told her to give it time. The next one came about twenty minutes later. Susan rang the office and told them she wouldn't be in. This was the beginning of real labour, Susan told her, but she had hours to go yet. Sheila was agitated, she kept checking her hospital bag. Mary had bought her two beautiful night-dresses from London, but Susan advised her to wear an old one for the birth.

"I can't believe it's started." Sheila was panic-stricken.

"Sheila, I was sixteen hours in labour with Tom. It mightn't be the same for you, but you may as well be prepared for a long wait."

Another contraction engulfed Sheila and this time it was much stronger and lasted a minute. God, this wasn't getting easier. When she went to the loo the next time, she noticed the "show". Susan agreed that it was time to get going. Sheila was worried even though Susan knew that there was no hurry. Ignorance was bliss, Susan reminded herself. Sheila could be in labour for at least another twelve hours. Because she was three days late, Sheila seemed to think the whole thing would happen fast and furiously. It would be furious all right, but not as fast as Sheila believed.

Susan rang Philip at his rooms and told him they were going. She would ring him again when there was any news. It was now nine o'clock in the morning and Susan knew they were in for a long day of it. Her mother had come over to mind the kids.

Julie hugged her goodbye. "When you be back?" she asked, wiping her eyes.

Sheila gulped. The poor little mite didn't understand that she wouldn't be back at all. Sheila squeezed her tight in her arms.

"Will Buggins be back with you?" Tom wanted to know.

Susan hurried her out to the Cortina. This was far too emotional.

The car ride made the contractions seem worse. Every pot-hole jolted Sheila. The pains were now coming every fifteen minutes and were much stronger. Sheila sweated with fear. She didn't want to make a fool of herself. She clamped her stomach muscles as tight as she could. It didn't help. She gripped onto the door handle and tried not to gasp. Susan told her not to fight them.

"Shout all you like in there. They're used to it."

The traffic wasn't too bad. They reached the hospital and parked. Susan carried her case. Sheila walked up the steps like a lamb to the slaughter. Once she walked in that door, there was no turning back.

They took Sheila off for her examination. Susan sat in the crowded waiting-room. She had luckily brought a magazine with her. She couldn't help hearing the conversation next to her.

"That was on my fifth. 'Now, Mrs Boyle,' says he, 'I'm just going to give you a few little stitches.' A few little stitches, I ask ya. Ya know yerself. 'Ah Jaysus, doctor,' says I, 'ya can sew the whole bleedin' thing up."

The other woman tittered. "Them doctors are a howl. They think we're bloody fools."

"They'd be right too. Jaysus, if a man had the first one, there'd be no more after, wha'?"

"True for ya."

Susan had to smile. These were some pair. Typical Dublin wit. She gathered that the intrepid Mrs Boyle was in to see her first grandchild. She was a character. The nurse came back and told Susan she could go home. There was no question of her being allowed to stay. Strictly against hospital regulations. Sheila was going to have to go through this ordeal alone. Susan thought that this was abominable. Couldn't they make an exception for once? No. Nobody was allowed to be with the woman in labour except for hospital staff.

"Could you please give her this newspaper and tell her I'll be back after the baby's born." Susan's tone was curt.

* * *

Sheila was back in the ward, sitting in an armchair. She was in a state of shock. She felt lousy. They had bombarded her with questions. They gave her an internal and then they shaved her. It was gross. She felt like a plucked chicken. As for the enema, Sheila had never been so humiliated. The doctor told her she was three fingers dilated. She felt like giving him the two fingers for what he put her through. She was mortified. They poured antiseptic cream inside her. On the way back to the ward, when she thought the embarrassment was finally over, her waters broke in the corridor.

Nobody had told her this was going to be easy. But nobody had told her it was going to be as horrific as this. Why didn't women tell each other the truth? Was it a conspiracy of silence? Maybe women didn't want to frighten the wits out of their pregnant friends? Still, Sheila would have preferred to have been informed. The manual hadn't prepared her for this at all. The baby's head had moved deeper into the pelvic area so the pressure on her bladder was desperate. One thing she was sure of. God was definitely a man. She wished Susan was with her. She felt abandoned.

By six o'clock that evening, Sheila was in agony. She didn't want to make a nuisance of herself and she thought the nurse was a bit offhand with her. She wished she had painkillers. She hung on as long as she could. The pain was excruciating. She begged for something to ease it. She was given pethidine by injection into her thigh. Twenty minutes later the pain dulled. Sheila wondered how African women gave birth in the fields.

Sheila's mouth dried up, but she was refused liquid. They moistened her lips with a sponge. It was a wonder it wasn't vinegar. The nurse came in to check her at regular intervals. The day was endless. She felt like a specimen under a microscope.

Finally at about eight o'clock that night, the nurse told her she was fully dilated and it was time to go into the delivery ward. This was it. Sheila was petrified.

The atmosphere in the delivery room was clinical and cold. Sheila was helped up on the table in a dismissive way. The doctors saw the women only as mothers. They had no individual identity whatever. The women were simply an inconvenience, it occurred to Sheila. Their sole function was to produce the goods. She was furious, but she was in no position to argue. She was too bloody scared. The birth would be difficult enough.

Glaring lights burned her eyes. The antiseptic smell was overpowering. The doctor was formal and efficient. It was as if he had never seen her before. And after all those hospital visits. Did he no longer see her as a person? She knew that he was not sympathetic to the fact that she was single. Not so long ago, they used to put women like her into institutions and throw away the key. Sheila did what she was told. With every contraction she took in big breaths to fill her lungs with air. She held her breath and pushed down as hard as she could. It was worse than trying to go to the toilet. Much worse.

Embarrassment had given way to fierce determination. She desperately wanted to push the baby out. She was breathing in from a mask beside her. This also helped to numb the pain. She had a few moments to relax between contractions. Sheila felt she had never worked so hard in her life. She was aching all over. She had become a machine. "Push." "Don't push." "Hold your breath in. Push." "Don't push." "Bear down." Would it ever be over? It seemed like hours before the doctor announced he could see the head. Sheila was exhausted, but her work wasn't over yet. She was sweating profusely from all the pushing. It was worse when they told her not to push. The baby's head stretched her to bursting point. She felt her whole insides were about to explode. Another huge contraction engulfed her.

"Push, push," the nurse encouraged her. Sheila pushed with all her might. The veins throbbed at her temples. Her face was contorted and her eyes bulged.

"I'm going to do an episiotomy," the doctor said to the nurse.

Sheila remembered from her book what that was. A small cut. To prevent jagged tearing. She was past caring. She was too tired to be scared. The crucifix on the wall did nothing to comfort her. She felt she had been through her own Calvary.

"One last push, love. We're almost there." The nurse smiled.

Sheila summoned up every last bit of energy she possessed. She pushed harder. The muscles on her neck stood out. The pain seared up from between her legs and shot through her entire body. She couldn't take any more.

She didn't even feel the prick of the needle in her arm.

CHAPTER FIVE

Sheila was woken by the clanking of the breakfast trolley. Her eyes were in the back of her head. She was groggy after the anaesthetic of last night. Last night was one vast blur. She remembered having her feet up in the stirrups and being asked to bear down. Ludicrous. How was she expected to push down when her legs were up in the air? Then, at the last minute, her arm was punctured by the needle. Oblivion. The nightmare of labour was wiped out. She slept the sleep of the dead.

But she didn't feel rested now. She felt wiped out. She was so sore down there. She tried to sit up in the bed, but she was too weak. She gave up the struggle. She hadn't seen the baby. She had decided yesterday that she didn't want to see her. It was hospital policy anyway to take away the babies who were up for adoption. Maybe it was kinder like that. How could she bear to look at her child and then abandon her? Sheila wanted to cry, but she couldn't. There were no tears left.

She was nothing now, just an empty shell. She glanced down at her tummy under the bedclothes. Flat. There was no outward evidence that she had just given birth. It was as if the baby never existed. But her breasts were aching, the nipples painfully sensitive and tender. They were a constant niggling reminder. They were engorged with the milk that would never feed her baby. Her eyeballs were stinging, red hot pokers burnt through them. It would be a relief to cry. But no tears came.

The screens were pulled back.

"Morning, love." It was her breakfast. "You must be famished."

Sheila struggled up into a sitting position. She thanked the woman and stared down at the lumpy porridge. She'd always hated porridge. What did that matter? Who was feeding the baby now? Where was she? Down in the nursery with some other little waif? Oh, Christ. She sipped her tea gratefully. She was parched. She didn't remember ever being so thirsty. She pushed the trolley down the bed and lay back. Every movement was a huge effort. She closed her eyes and started to drift into a fitful sleep.

"Miss Crosby? Are you awake?" The doctor stared down at her.

She blinked up at him.

"You gave birth to a healthy baby girl."

Sheila kept staring.

He looked uncomfortable. "How are you feeling?"

How did he think she was feeling? Shitty, that's how she was feeling. She mumbled, "Fine. A bit weak." Her voice sounded different.

"The nurse will be in shortly to take you out to the toilet. We must get you back on your feet."

He was damned abrupt. What was so important to have her back on her feet? What? Nothing mattered now. She did want to go to the loo though. But she was so sore she wanted to put it off. The doctor patted her arm and left. Sheila felt bereft. She needed human contact. Even talking to the doctor was better than lying there thinking. She could hear hurried movements outside. The screen was pulled back again and a young nurse rushed in.

"Hello. I'm Laura. We have to get you up. Are you OK?"

Sheila did her best to manoeuvre herself to the side of the bed.

"I'm in agony," she confessed to the nurse.

"You had a lot of stitches," Laura explained gently.

A loud booming voice interrupted her. "What's this, nurse? Why is this mother still in bed?"

Laura cringed. Did she have to call every patient "mother"? This girl was giving her baby up. "Mother" was hardly appropriate.

"She's a bit weak after the anaesthetic." Laura seemed genuinely terrified of the matron.

"She'll be a lot weaker if you leave her languishing in that bed," Matron scolded. "Get her up immediately."

She turned on her heel. Sheila might as well not have been present. She'd been totally ignored. The matron was an ignorant bitch.

"What time is it?" Sheila slid herself down to a standing position, leaning on Laura.

"Seven-thirty."

"God, you're not serious?"

Laura was about to reply, but Sheila butted in, "Don't tell me. Hospital regulations."

The young nurse laughed.

Visiting time was a horror. Sheila was painfully conscious of the husbands. Happy families. Susan and Mary came in that afternoon. Susan hadn't been let in the night before as Sheila was out for the count. Susan thought it was shocking that they gave single women an anaesthetic at the last moment to prevent them from seeing their babies.

The visit was a disaster. Sheila tried to make it easier for them but the painful silences were awkward and embarrassing. Mary and Susan were terrified of saying the wrong thing. The other families were busy cooing and billing at the babies. There was an empty space beside Sheila's bed. Neither of them referred to the baby. They couldn't even ask Sheila how she felt. When Sheila asked about Tom and Julie there was a huge lump in her throat. Mary chatted on about college; who was back after the summer, who had to repeat exams, when her lectures were starting up again. She'd found a new flat in Donnybrook this year.

"Would you consider sharing with me?" she asked Sheila tentatively.

"No, thanks Mary. I've decided to go home."

Susan gave Mary a surprised look. "Mary means after that. When you come back to Uni next month, after your few weeks resting at home," Susan explained.

"I won't be coming back to UCD. I'm staying in Galway."

Mary was dumbfounded. "Not coming back?"

"No."

"But why?" Mary should have bitten her tongue. She shouldn't be pushing Sheila.

"What's the point?" Sheila said wearily. "I've lost interest in it. Maybe I picked the wrong subjects."

"But you were doing brilliantly. Your grades are always top notch." Mary was shocked. It had never occurred to her that Sheila wouldn't be coming back. The pregnancy was no longer a problem and Sheila could take up where she left off.

"God, I don't know. Maybe you should think about it," Mary suggested feebly.

"That's all I have been thinking about as I've been lying here."

Susan was not going to interfere and she nudged Mary to shut up. Sheila smiled at her gratefully. "I'm dying for a smoke."

The three of them went out to the corridor.

The next four days passed slowly. Sheila hated every moment of them. Her mood swings were chronic. She'd expected the "third day blues," but her depression went on all the time. She was numb. The woman in the bed opposite was getting on her nerves. Sheila nicknamed her the Earth Mother. She had enormous swinging breasts and bared them at every opportunity to suckle her fretful infant. Her baby cried incessantly. She nagged the other unfortunate woman in the bed beside her, about the vital necessity of breast-feeding. The screaming baby did nothing to prove her case. She'd look over sympathetically at Sheila from time to time. Sheila ignored her. At family visiting, she could hear her telling her family about the "poor" girl in the bed opposite.

The hospital routine was monotonous and, in Sheila's view, crazy. They were woken at an ungodly hour every morning. This suited the mothers, who were naturally anxious to feed and cuddle their babies. What about Sheila? They were given dinner at eleven-thirty. Pure madness. They were expected to sleep in the early afternoon. Sheila couldn't even sleep at night. They lay there from two to three pretending to sleep because Laura would be in trouble with the matron if her mothers didn't get their proper rest.

Sheila had bad constipation and also painful haemorrhoids. She was made drink molasses in hot milk. It was thoroughly disgusting. They took out her stitches on the fourth day. The physical discomforts were nothing in comparison to her mental state. Every day she spent in that ward was torture.

"Sheila?" A familiar voice wafted through her dreams. She opened her eyes. Caroline was sitting by her side. The relief of it. She threw her arms around her sister-in-law.

"Sheila, oh Sheila." Caroline sobbed on her shoulder.

Finally someone understood. Sheila felt the tears

pricking her eyes. She started to cry softly at first. Soon she was weeping bitterly. Her body was wracked with sobs. Hot tears scalded her face as she clung on to her sister-in-law. Caroline hugged her and whispered endearments to her. It was the first warm human touch since the birth. Sheila would never forget this kindness, this understanding.

"Congratulations. Well done," Caroline said. "I'm so proud of you."

Somebody had said it at last. Caroline wouldn't sit there and pretend that nothing had happened. She was the only one who was behaving normally. She'd actually congratulated her. Sheila was so thankful for this recognition. Caroline was proud of her. She was proud of herself. She'd given birth to a healthy baby. She'd given the gift of life to her daughter.

"I signed the first papers today. She's gone." Sheila groped for her hankie.

What could Caroline say? What words could possibly give comfort? She gripped Sheila's hand and said nothing.

Sheila wanted to talk. She had to tell someone. "I never saw her, Caroline. I never held her in my arms. I couldn't."

Caroline stroked her hair.

"I'll never know what she looked like. I'll never know where she is. How can I live with not knowing? Never knowing?"

Caroline was bursting to tell her something. She'd wondered if she would tell her, but now she knew she must.

"Sheila, I have something for you. She opened

her handbag and drew out an envelope. Sheila opened it curiously. It was a photograph. She stared in wonder at the picture of a beautiful baby, sleeping peacefully. Sheila's face lit up as she looked inquiringly at her sister-in-law.

"It's Karen." Caroline beamed. "Isn't she gorgeous?"

Sheila couldn't believe it. "How did you manage it?"

"I rang Susan and got the name of the nurse who was looking after you."

"Laura?"

"Yes. Then I rang her and asked would she do it for a favour?"

"Laura took the photo?" Sheila was stunned.

"Yes, Sheila. She couldn't deal with the way you were being treated. She knew what you were going through."

"How can I ever thank her?" Sheila held the photo to her breast.

"There's no need. You have to keep this a secret. Laura could get into serious trouble for this."

Sheila thought of the matron. She knew too well that this was a grave breach of hospital regulations.

"It'll just be between you and me," Sheila assured her.

"Seán doesn't know either. I thought it better not to tell him."

Caroline was right. Seán wouldn't understand and certainly wouldn't approve.

"It's the best present I ever got in my life." Sheila couldn't stop looking at it.

"You'd better put it away. Seán will be in in a minute. He's talking to your doctor."

"Oh?"

"Ah, he knew him years ago or something. Never mind that. We're bringing you home tomorrow."

Sheila smiled for the first time in weeks.

She was up, breakfasted and showered by eight the following morning. Laura was delighted with her patient's good spirits.

"I can never thank you for all your kindness." Sheila hugged the nurse.

"It was nothing."

"Don't say that. You were the only human being I met in this horrible place," Sheila said bitterly. "You saved my sanity."

"Give yourself time, Sheila. You've been through a hell of a trauma. You'll have some bad days ahead."

"I know that. But I have the photo, thanks to you. I can look at it whenever I want. It's something to cling on to. It's something real."

"I'm glad."

Laura thought it was desperate the way Sheila had been handled. It was cruel to knock these girls out at the moment of birth, she thought. They went through an agonising labour and then there was nothing. Nothing. It wasn't normal and it wasn't right. She knew that Sheila hadn't wanted to see her daughter and she could understand why. In her opinion though, that wasn't right either. She thought it would be more natural for single mothers to be allowed to look after their babies while they were in the hospital. It would make leaving them more difficult at the time but, in the long run, Laura thought it would be better. They'd have some memory of the child. They'd be glad that they'd fed the babies and bathed them and fondled them. They'd be able to remember these moments in their times of depression. Sheila was in high spirits now because she was going home. But this mood wouldn't last, Laura was convinced of it. What would happen in a few days? In a week? In a year?

Sheila was not typical. Other girls might be able to obliterate the memories, but Sheila would find that impossible. What had she to hang on to now? A black and white photograph. It was pathetic.

Would times ever change for these women? Would doctors and so-called specialists ever cop on to the needs of single women who gave birth and then were expected to forget? You didn't have to be a psychologist to know that Sheila was devastated. Who was going to help her back in Galway? Her parents? They weren't even aware of what had gone on. How was Sheila supposed to heal? Thank God she'd her sister-in-law. Laura liked her. She was down-to-earth, but she was sensitive too. The brother meant well, but he was a typical doctor. Laura knew all about doctors. There was no doubt that Sheila had received the best medical attention. But that was all she'd received. On the human level, she was ignored. If it wasn't for the photo, there would be no proof for Sheila that the baby ever existed. While it was bad now in the sixties, it was worse years before. Laura was glad that she'd done something to help. She just wished she could have done more.

* * *

Seán put her cases in the boot of the Cortina. Sheila got into the back. Caroline handed her a cigarette.

"You're not smoking in the car?" Seán growled at his wife.

She gave him a withering look. He wisely held his peace. It would be a long drive. Caroline didn't try to start a conversation. She knew that Sheila needed silence. Sheila must be feeling relieved to get out of there. She must also be feeling empty. Caroline couldn't imagine what it felt like to leave the hospital after giving birth and have no baby to show for it. She'd never moan about looking after the twins again.

"Sheila, we'll have to get the story right for the folks," Seán said suddenly.

"Leave it, Seán. We can discuss it later," Caroline hissed.

"That's OK, Caroline. We have to sort it out. Seán's right." Sheila leaned over and pressed Caroline's shoulder. "I'm all right."

She had to say that for Caroline's sake. But she was far from all right.

"Your doctor thinks you may not be yourself for a while." Seán glanced at his sister in the rear-view mirror.

So he had noticed then? The doctor had actually noticed that she was upset. He'd certainly never given her any clue. He'd treated her methodically and clinically, but he hadn't given her any sympathy. He hadn't encouraged her to talk. He hadn't offered any opinions. He'd explained everything to her medically. He'd done a good job there. He was a highly respected gynaecologist, but his bedside manner left a lot to be desired.

"I didn't like him." Sheila was blunt.

"That's neither here or there, Sheila," Seán retorted. "You got the best treatment available."

"Did I?" Her tone was sarcastic.

Caroline felt like clapping her on the back. She was showing some spirit, thank God.

"Anyhow," Seán ignored her insinuations and continued, "we had to come up with some illness which would take a long recuperation period."

"Well, you were right there," Sheila agreed ironically. "I don't know if recuperation is possible at all. It wasn't my appendix they took, you know."

Hear, hear, thought Caroline. Bully for Sheila. Her husband and that doctor were unfeeling chauvinists. Seán cursed at a woman driver who pulled into his lane without signalling.

"Sheila, you will get over this in time. You'll have to." Seán was firm.

"Maybe," Sheila said softly.

"There's no maybe about it. You'll have to pull yourself together for the sake of the folks. You can't go upsetting Mam and Dad. They're both too old to take on this kind of hassle."

77

Sheila could see that, all right. She'd no wish to upset her parents. They didn't know about the baby and she'd no intention of telling them. Her mother would freak. Her father would be more sympathetic. Her father always took her side in family disputes. It was he who had encouraged her to get away to Dublin for her college years. He'd be disappointed that she didn't finish her degree. But her mother . . . her mother would go stark raving mad if she knew about the baby. She couldn't take the shame. Seán would want to come up with a good story.

"What illness have you and the doctor decided on?" The question seemed lunatic.

"Glandular fever." His tone was self-congratulatory. "It can take months to recover from that."

"What symptoms am I supposed to have?" Sheila asked bitterly.

"It's caused by a virus." Seán was in his element. "You'd have a fever and a sore throat. The lymph nodes would be sore and swollen."

"Wonderful. How am I supposed to manage that?" Sheila looked at Caroline.

"No problem. I'll be the one treating you. I can take charge of your medication." Seán had it all sewn up. "It's dead lucky."

If anyone else mentioned the word lucky, Sheila would go mad.

There were huge delays approaching Leixlip. Seán got hot and bothered. He had no patience when it came to traffic jams and this one started at the sharp bend by the bridge and extended through the town. He gritted his teeth and swore. Caroline tried not to laugh. He was taking this as a personal affront. Sheila, in the back, held her tongue. They could be stuck here, by the Salmon Leap Inn, for an hour. Friday was the worst day for travelling. Pity Seán wouldn't take a leap in! The scenery was lovely, the river glimmered in the autumn sunshine. This wouldn't be the right time to point this out to Seán, Caroline knew. He was in one of his moods. Fifty minutes later they were held up in Maynooth. Sheila was fed up too by now. They finally got out onto the open road and Seán put the boot down. They stopped in Athlone for lunch. Now they were less than an hour from home.

CHAPTER SIX

Pat Crosby was worried about his daughter. She'd been back home now for the last six weeks and there seemed to be no improvement. She slept most of the time. Seán told them not to worry, sleep was a necessary part of the recovery. Rita was anxious too, though she said very little. Unusual for her.

Rita had gone into the city with Caroline to shop. What would he do without Caroline? She was terrific. She got Rita out from under his feet. Since his retirement from the gardaí some years ago, he often felt hemmed in by his wife. God bless her, she was the best in the world, but she took far too much interest in things that didn't concern her. Seán had warned her to go easy on Sheila, not to be nagging her about giving up college. Sure Rita wasn't worried about Sheila's education at all. She'd thought sending a daughter to university was mad in the first place. No, it was Pat who was disappointed. He'd no wish to push either of his children, but he believed that, if they showed ability, they should be given a chance. Sheila was a clever girl. It was a pity she'd decided so adamantly to give up her studies.

He crept into Sheila's bedroom. She was still fast
asleep and it was gone twelve. Should he wake her
with a cup of tea? Better not. Leave her to rest,
that's what Seán had advised. He'd take this
opportunity to do a bit of gardening, now that he
had peace and quiet. He loved this house with its
view of Galway Bay. He adored Galway city, it was
his home town. He knew every inch of it. He knew
everyone in all the shops, pubs and restaurants. It
was a compact city and yet it had its own
cosmopolitan atmosphere. The view from the front
of the house was spectacular. He liked living by the
sea. Salthill was only a mile away, but he didn't like
it in summer. The Dublin yahoos came down in
legions. In his sergeant days, they had caused him a
lot of grief. They were notorious for their cider
parties and their late-night revelling. It wasn't his
worry now, thank God.

He delighted in his front garden. The air out
here was pure and fresh. He breathed it in,
expanded his lungs and exhaled again. He was
pleased with his progress. He'd built a rockery in
the right hand corner, his *pièce de résistance*! He'd
planted his border shrubs last spring and they were
doing nicely. Gardening was a real pleasure. Funny
how he'd only discovered it this late in life. What
used to be a chore was now his best method of
relaxation and contemplation. His garden was also a
secret retreat, a sanctuary from his wife's garrulity.
He loved her dearly, but the woman never shut up.
She'd opinions on everything. He'd do some
weeding before lunch-time. Rita and Caroline were

having lunch in town, so that gave him a couple of hours grace.

Sheila was not asleep, as her father thought. She'd pretended to be for his sake. She didn't want him any more upset than he already was. She couldn't sleep properly, even at night. The hours of darkness crawled by. Endless hours of dark shadows and dark thoughts. She sobbed into her pillow every night. Her feelings of isolation and emptiness were worse than any physical pain she'd ever known.

She wanted her baby. She wanted to hold her in her arms. She wanted to cuddle her and protect her and love her. She needed her child with her. She imagined how her soft skin would feel against her own. How her tiny fingers would grip. She wanted to hear her make the little gurgling sounds that all babies make. Karen. Her daughter. Sheila's arms longed for her. Her breasts ached. Her whole being cried out for her baby. She felt as if her guts had been ripped out.

The drugs Seán prescribed were useless. They forced her body into a false sleep for a few hours at a time. But that sleep brought no rest. Only appalling nightmares. She saw herself running down never-ending corridors searching for her daughter. Doctors and nurses, horribly transformed were laughing . . . laughing at her. Every door she opened lead to an abyss . . . Misery engulfed her. She saw a baby crying in a cot, crying for her. But when she got there and tried to pick the baby up, she froze. The baby had the face of a devil . . . it spat at her. Sheila screamed so loudly that night, that her mother ran in to wake her up. No. Sleep was no solution.

She dragged herself out of bed and pulled back the curtains. It was a nice day for the beginning of November. She saw her father busy with his trowel. What time was it? She glanced at her watch. God, she'd have to get up. Another day to get through. She put on her dressing-gown and lit a cigarette. She knew this was bad before she even had breakfast, but she didn't care. She picked up a ragged teddy bear. He must be fifteen years old. Her shelves were filled with cuddly toys and favourite old books. Sheila didn't like throwing out anything. The Beatles posters on her walls were a reminder of her schooldays. Happier times. This room held all the memories of her childhood. It was weird to be back.

Her mother had left her clean towels in the bathroom. She couldn't be bothered to wash her hair or to shower. She splashed cold water on her face and caught a glimpse of herself in the mirror. She looked dreadful. She was as white as a sheet and big dark circles framed her eyes. How was she going to endure another day? She'd have to, for her parents' sake.

She went down to the kitchen where Moses was snoring loudly in his basket. She patted him gently, but he'd no wish to be disturbed. He was getting on now, must be eight or nine. She remembered well the Christmas Dad had brought him home. Her mother nearly had a fit. Funny to think of that when she doted on the dog now. He was a beautiful animal with his shiny black and white coat and his big ears and mournful eyes. There was something very sweet about cocker spaniels. She put on the kettle. It was too late for breakfast. She'd prepare a light lunch for her father and herself. It was about time she did something. She must be driving them mad with this moping around. She couldn't shake off her apathy, much as she had tried. She found some sardines in the cupboard. She'd make a nice salad to go with them.

"That was lovely, Sheila. I really enjoyed that." Pat licked his lips appreciatively. "I was always partial to sardines."

"Not exactly haute cuisine, but I enjoyed it too," she lied.

"How did you sleep?"

"Grand." Why bother him with boring details? What could he do about her nightly horrors? She knew she disturbed her parents as she tossed and turned in the small hours.

"I got a load of weeding done. That should see me through till next spring."

"Great." Sheila stood up to do the dishes.

"No, let me do that. You got the lunch."

"Dad, don't be cracked. It's not as if I was slaving over a hot stove all morning. You've done far more work than I have. You go into the front room with your crossword and I'll bring you in a cup of tea."

"Sure?"

"Of course. I'm not an invalid, you know."

He settled down to the cryptic in the *Independent*. He loved his crossword. It kept him mentally active, just as gossip did his wife. He didn't like that remark of Sheila's. Of course he didn't think of her as an invalid, but she had been very sick. Today she'd perked up a bit, but she was still far from her old self. He hadn't realised that glandular fever could be so debilitating. The depression that went with it was desperate. Seán said it was part and parcel of the illness and that he was treating her for depression too. Pat suspected that there was something that they weren't telling him. He wondered if a broken romance might be the cause. Mind you, Sheila was far too sensible to lose her head over some boy, wasn't she? Four down: Thy cat talks too much. Six letters. Ah ha! Pat grinned as he wrote out the answer. Chatty. Rita sprang to mind.

"Dad, I think I'll take Moses out for a walk on the beach."

"Good idea. He's getting fat and lazy."

"I'm getting lazy myself." Sheila replied as she went to get the lead.

Well, she certainly wasn't getting fat. She was far too thin, skin and bone. She had no colour in her cheeks. He was delighted she was going out. She'd been cooped up in the house for much too long. Maybe she was beginning to turn the corner. Just as he was about to solve three across, he heard the Cortina in the drive. No peace for the wicked. He prepared himself for the onslaught. He'd have to hear all the "news". God almighty, Caroline was driving off. He'd have Rita all to himself, which meant he'd actually have to listen and perhaps answer . . . So much for his afternoon of peace.

It was chillier than Sheila had thought. She walked briskly on the hard sand. The tide was miles out. Moses was getting a good run. He loved the freedom of the beach where he was allowed to run free, unhampered by his lead. He sniffed and investigated everything before cocking his leg. Sheila sat on a rock and stared out to sea. The faraway waves danced and glittered in the sunshine. This was the mildest winter she remembered in a long time. She picked up a few sticks to throw for Moses. He hated giving them back so half the time, he'd bury them. His little nose was covered in sand. He looked comical.

Sheila closed her eyes, letting her mind wander. Seán was mad to think that she could put all thoughts of the baby out of her mind. Why should she? She had every right to think about her child. Sheila got angry. They had taken Karen away from her. They had forced her to give up her flesh and blood. Your children are not your children. They are the sons and daughters of life. Bullshit. A man must have written that. What would a man know of the joy you felt as a baby grew inside you? What would he know of your astonishment and wonder as the baby developed week by week in your womb? Your inner core. Your womanhood. What did he know about wombs? How would he understand that all the years of menstruation, of "the uterus weeping", were a long preparation for the day the woman gave birth to her child? How would he know how you craved the child? How you yearned to see this little being who had developed with and in you? Flesh of the flesh. How you needed to cherish and nurture? How your breasts filled up with milk to feed your own? How would any man know that?

They had controlled her. They had allowed her to produce her offspring. Offspring. What a funny word. Product, outcome, result, seed, spawn. What was the outcome for her? Nothing. They had taken Karen. Taken her away from her life source. Cut the umbilical cord. Broken the connection. How could they break the connection? They couldn't. Karen would always be a part of her. Always. They couldn't change that. Sheila felt some comfort at that thought. Karen would always be hers in the most fundamental human way. That was outside their control. And so were her thoughts. They couldn't control her thoughts.

Where was Karen now? Was she still in Dublin? Was her hair red? Were her eyes blue? She would be seven weeks old in two day's time. What were her family like? Her parents? What were they like? Had they a good marriage sanctioned by the Church? Had they a nice home in a good area? Had they financial security? Probably. But they didn't have the same blood running through their veins. Karen would never have their genes. She was made flesh . . . but not by them. She'd never truly belong to them. Never. Had she a brother or a sister? When would they tell her that she had a real mother somewhere else? Questions, questions, questions . . . and no answers.

"So after our shopping, we went for a cuppa. Do you know who I met in The Skeff?"

Pat saw no need to ask. He knew he'd hear the answer in the next breath. Rita always asked you a question, but she never waited for a response, she just waffled on.

"Mrs O'Halloran, you know, the vet's wife. That poor woman is a martyr to her veins. Her right leg looks like the map of Ireland with all those blue lines running up and down it. God help her!"

"Would she not go and get it done?" Pat asked in as concerned a tone as he could muster.

"Get it done? Are you stark raving mad? Sure she got the other one done and it nearly finished her altogether. She had to walk miles every day and she in agony. No, no, she's better off putting up with it if she can. God love her."

Pat went back to his crossword. He could hear her putting the messages away in the kitchen cupboards.

"Cup of tea?" she shouted in.

"No thanks. Sheila made me lunch an hour ago."

"Oh, is she up?"

"Long ago. She took the dog out for a walk."

Rita came back with a cup of tea for him. Did she ever listen? He'd better drink it for the sake of peace.

"Should you not have gone with her, Pat?"

"She's a grown woman, Rita. She needs time to herself."

"She does not. She spends more than enough time by herself in that bedroom. I don't like it. She needs company, that's what she needs. I might invite that girl, Jean, over. Remember her? Sheila and herself were great friends in school."

"I don't think that's a good idea. Sheila hasn't seen her for ages. They've lost contact as far as I know."

"So? The company would do her good."

"Why don't you ask Sheila then? You can't go making arrangements that mightn't suit her," Pat warned.

"Jesus, Mary and Joseph, you'd need the patience of Job with you! Sure if I ask Sheila, she'll say no. I'd rather give her a surprise."

"Rita, it's obvious that Sheila's in no humour to socialise at the moment. Leave her be."

"Leave her be? That's lovely, that is. You like to ignore everything and hope that the problem will go away. Your daughter is pining away in that room and all you can say is, 'Leave her be.' Well I bloomin' well won't leave her be."

"If you don't listen to me, you might listen to Seán."

"Seán doesn't know everything. He's a good doctor, but he's not a mother. I can see that Sheila needs someone of her own age to talk to. Medication is all right, but it doesn't solve every problem. We both know that Sheila's depressed. I think she might have had a breakdown of some sort. She should never have gone up to Dublin to that college. She wasn't able for it. What's the good of it anyway? All that education's wasted on a girl. She should have done a shorthand typing course and got herself a nice little job here in town. She could do that now, as a matter of fact."

Pat didn't argue back. Rita had very old-fashioned ideas on how women should behave. She'd like to see Sheila in some dead-end job with no prospects because she really only wanted her daughter to get married, settle down and bring up children. Nothing wrong with that, if that's what Sheila wanted too. Pat didn't think it was what she wanted.

"Rita," he sighed, "Sheila is bright and ambitious. She needs something stimulating to do."

"Stimulating, that's a good one. What did I ever have to stimulate me? All I thought of was you and the children. I brought them up as well as I could. I was a good wife to you, wasn't I?"

"Yes," he agreed wholeheartedly.

"Well then? That's all the stimulation I ever got or needed."

"Sheila's different," he insisted. "Times have changed."

"Some things never change," she said mysteriously. "Anyhow I won't ask Jean over if you're dead set against it."

"It's not up to me. Ask Sheila what she wants."

"Pat, what do you think is really wrong with Sheila? Peggy Moran up the road had glandular

fever a couple of years ago. I remember visiting her.
She was washed out for a while I admit. She spent
weeks in bed and she'd no energy, but I don't think
she was as down in the mouth as Sheila is. I think
there's something else. Do you?" Rita was genuinely
worried.

"I don't know," Pat said sadly. "I wish I could do
something to help her."

"Would you not talk to her? I mean seriously talk
to her? She's mad about you, always was. I think a
little chat would do her the power of good."

"I don't want to pressurise her."

"You don't have to. Just a nice little chat. You
could take her for a drink in O'Connor's tonight.
What do you think?"

"I'll ask her when she gets back."

"Good man. God, these bottom teeth are a
killer." Rita took out her false teeth and plonked
them on the coffee table. It was a bit off-putting. He
remembered wistfully how fastidious she had been
during their courtship. Now her bottom set of
pearlies sat glumly on the table, grinning . . . no,
grimacing at him.

The pub was quiet which suited Pat fine. In the
high season you'd never get a seat here. It was one
of the most popular pubs in Salthill and attracted a
mixed crowd. Rita hated it. She preferred hotels. Pat
liked the buzz normally, but tonight he was glad of
the peace. He brought his daughter a glass of beer.

"You look very nice tonight, Sheila." He lit his
pipe.

"Thanks. I finally washed my hair, it was very greasy after all the wind today."

His daughter was a beautiful girl, even if he thought so himself. Her hair was a very unusual shade of red. Auburn really. His sister had red hair too. Sheila reminded him of his sister, Bridie, in many ways. She'd emigrated to the States forty years ago and never came back. They exchanged Christmas and birthday cards. But she was more American now than Irish. Pity the way families lost touch. It was inevitable in Ireland with all the emigration.

"Penny for them, Dad?"

"Ah, I was just thinking about your Aunt Bridie. You never met her. Funny, isn't it? I never met her family either."

"Yeah, it's sad. I remember Uncle Denis though. He was great."

"Aye. Denis was the eldest. He's twelve years dead now, imagine."

"Why did he never get married?"

"There's the question now. I don't know for sure. He stayed on the farm. A lot of eldest sons did that."

"What happened to the farm?" Sheila asked.

"I sold it. Sent half the money to Bridie. The rest is in the bank for a rainy day." He puffed his pipe contentedly. He enjoyed his smoke away from Rita's nagging. "Your mother doesn't know how much there is but, I can tell you, it's quite a considerable sum."

Sheila laughed. Her poor mother. She thought she ruled the roost, but that was far from the truth.

It didn't say much for partnership in marriage, though. Her father went up to get another drink. Sheila was glad she'd come out. She was easy in her father's company.

"That was Liam O'Flaherty I was chatting to up at the bar. He was asking for you."

"That's nice," Sheila remarked. She hoped he wasn't going to join them.

"I told him you were feeling a lot better. You are, aren't you?"

Sheila smiled. She wished he would talk about something else.

"Sheila? You are a bit better? Your walk today did you good?"

"Yeah, Dad. I do feel a lot stronger."

"You can't beat fresh air, I always said it. Now if you could only put on a bit of weight. You're like a skeleton. Anyhow, Liam asked me if you'd be interested in a job."

"A job?"

"Yes, in his chemist shop. If you're still dead against going back to UCD."

"I am. But O'Flaherty's? Oh God, Dad. I don't know." She didn't like the notion one bit.

"Not right now, of course," her father went on. "In a few weeks, when you're completely back to yourself. After Christmas, maybe?"

Sheila couldn't look at him. She stared down at the floor.

"Sheila? What's wrong? Have I upset you?"

"No, no. It's just that I don't know when I'll be back to myself. I don't know if I'll ever be."

"Nonsense. Of course you will. Seán says you'll be fine. Fine."

"Seán doesn't know everything," she blurted out.

"That's exactly what your mother said. Sheila, is there something you want to tell me?

He took her hand gently. Sheila bit her lip. Could she tell him? Could she say the words? Could she bear to hurt him?

"Lies," she whispered. "You've been told nothing but lies."

Pat was shocked. What was his daughter trying to tell him?

"We didn't want to worry you, you or Mam."

"Sheila, I love you. If you told us untruths, I'm sure you had good reason. Lies are not always a bad thing. Not if you're trying to protect someone."

"That's it. I was trying not to hurt you." The tears glistened in her eyes. His heart melted.

"Sheila, Sheila, what is it, girl? Nothing can be so bad that you can't tell me. Don't you know that?"

Sheila broke down. Her father was so good, so kind.

"Was it something that happened in England?" He was grasping at straws but he had to get to the bottom of this.

"I wasn't in England."

There. She'd said it.

"I don't understand. Didn't we get letters from you every week?" He was utterly confused.

"My friend Mary posted them."

"But why? Why? Where were you all summer if you weren't in London?"

"Dublin. I stayed in Dublin all summer."

He breathed a sigh of relief. "Well that's all right. I can understand that. You didn't want to come home. Sure that's perfectly understandable. Your mother would have kicked up, so you lied to keep the peace. Don't worry girl, I can understand that perfectly."

"That's not the reason, Dad. It's much more complicated than that."

"Yeah, I know. You decided to give up college and you thought I'd be annoyed. But I'm not, Sheila, I'm not, honestly. You must do what you want. It's your life. You must make your own choices."

That did it. Sheila couldn't stop herself. "I had to leave college. I didn't have any choices at all, Dad. I couldn't face going back after what happened."

"After what happened? I don't understand, Sheila." He spoke as softly as he could. He could see her great distress. Sheila opened her handbag slowly. She handed him the photograph.

"Her name's Karen." She held her breath as her father examined the photo.

"She's beautiful." He was overcome. "She's my granddaughter, isn't she?"

Sheila smiled at him. Then the tears came.

"Where is she, Sheila?" he asked simply.

"Gone. I've lost her, Dad. She's been adopted."

She was trying to stifle her sobs now. He steered her out of the pub and into the car. He hugged her for a very long time. He held her to him and tried to comfort her. He said nothing at all. Words would be useless. He was heartbroken. His little girl had lost her child. His grandchild. He had lost Sheila too. She'd never be the same carefree girl she'd been. His little girl who made him laugh, who played her guitar on summer evenings, who went to local dances and gave him blow-by-blow accounts of the goings on, who made him apple tarts and lemon meringue pies, who was naïve and simple and fun-loving. He'd lost her. That girl was gone forever. Now he understood it all. Sheila would never be herself again. Pat wanted to cry for her, for himself and for the baby he'd never see. His granddaughter.

CHAPTER SEVEN

Pat didn't sleep a wink. He went over and over the story in his mind. He couldn't believe it. What must Sheila have gone through? Yes, he knew she would be censured for her behaviour, if it were known. Sex outside marriage was a sin. That's all Rita would see. As a Catholic you obeyed the rules of the Church. QED. Sex outside the sanctity of marriage was a mortal sin.

What would really bother Rita though? Would it be concern for her daughter's soul or would it be what the neighbours thought? Was he being too hard on Rita? No, she was one of the first to ballyrag young Margaret Riordan last year. The poor unfortunate was married off before you could say Jack Robinson. That particular incident fuelled the gossips of the town for months. People could be so cruel. Sad to say, Rita was one of the chief offenders.

And what about him? Did he see Sheila as a sinner? Could he criticise his daughter for disobeying the moral law? Women, throughout history, were cast out of society for having illegitimate children. He had heard horrific stories of women and young girls going to terrible lengths to get rid of unwanted babies. One young girl from the next parish had given birth in a field and then buried the baby. That was twenty years ago but he'd never forgotten it. He was at the scene when the body was found. She'd committed murder to avoid being found out. What desperation would drive a girl to do that? What did it say about society? No, he wouldn't blame his daughter for what happened. She'd made a mistake. She'd been foolish but not evil. And what about the man? Sheila had not got pregnant on her own. Men got off scot-free. Sheila didn't need criticism and censure. She'd suffered the worst punishment possible. She'd lost her child. He felt nothing but compassion for her. He felt her pain.

Rita, beside him, snored on. She sounded like the ferry coming into port on a murky morning. Whoever said that women didn't snore? Although she was next to him, he felt cut off from her. Isolated. The rise and fall of her breast, her heavy breathing, her snoring, all irritated him. He knew he was being irrational, but he felt annoyed. Betrayed. How could she sleep so soundly while he was wide awake, worrying? She mustn't be told. She must never be told. She wouldn't handle it properly. She wouldn't understand. This was a very delicate issue. Sheila's mental stability hung in the balance. He wasn't sure that Seán had handled it well either. He'd have to talk to Caroline. He trusted his daughter-in-law's judgement. Dawn was breaking and he couldn't get back to sleep. He might as well get up and make some tea. He'd call over to Caroline this morning. They could have a decent chat while Seán was in the surgery.

* * *

Ciara crawled all over him as Colm pulled his trouser leg to catch his attention.

"Ga Ga, look."

Pat duly admired the drawing. "That's a lovely car."

Colm was disgusted. "It's a train," he pouted.

Caroline laughed at her father-in-law's discomfort. She plucked Ciara from his knee and handed him a coffee. "This pair can go down soon for their nap and then we'll have peace," she assured him.

"No hurry. I love to watch them playing. They're great at this age."

"You must be joking! The terrible twos. I can't take my eyes off them for a minute. This morning Colm poured an entire packet of washing powder over the bathroom carpet."

"I told you you were mad not to put lino down." He laughed. "Now you two, who wants a piggy-back to the land of nod?"

This was greeted with the usual screams of delight. He deposited them, one after the other, into their new beds. Within minutes he was back.

"How do you do it? They bawl when I put them to bed every morning." Caroline was amazed how he always managed to get them down so easily.

"Nothing to it," he boasted smugly. "I sing a few bars of 'The Teddybears' Picnic'. Guaranteed to send any child off to sleep. Especially the way I sing it."

He lit his pipe and accepted a second cup of coffee. "Sheila told me everything last night."

"Everything?" Caroline echoed. What did he mean by everything? She'd have to go warily. "What did Sheila tell you exactly?"

"All about the baby." He watched her expression carefully.

She was trying to disguise her astonishment. "She told you about the baby?"

"Thank God she did."

Caroline was amazed, to put it mildly. How had this come about? Hadn't they done everything to keep the baby a secret?

"So, how are you feeling, Pat?"

What a stupid thing to say. She told herself to cop on. Wasn't it obvious that the poor man was distraught.

"Relieved," he confessed. "I feel relieved."

That was the last thing she expected to hear. He didn't look relieved. He looked worn out and old. She'd never thought of him as old until now. He'd aged overnight.

"I'm relieved that she confided in me," he admitted. "We were always close."

Caroline couldn't bear to see him like this. He was trying to keep up a brave face, but the tears were forming in his eyes. There was something pathetic about such a big man close to tears. He fumbled with his tobacco pouch.

"I want to thank you for everything you've done for her. Sheila told me she'd never have got through it without you."

"I didn't do much. It was awful, Pat. The day we left the hospital was . . . awful." She looked hard at him. "I didn't think she'd ever tell you."

"I'm honestly glad she did. I'd do anything to make her feel better. Anything. I can imagine how you felt too. Sheila said it was the worst moment of her life. She felt like Judas. I didn't know what to say to her last night. Today isn't any better. She's my daughter, but I don't know how to help her. I feel inadequate."

"That's exactly how I feel. What can we do? I suppose all we can do is listen to Sheila. Give her support and love."

"Yeah, we have to listen to her. She only has us to talk to about it. And Seán of course."

"Seán? He refuses to discuss it, even with me. His attitude is that the baby's gone and should be forgotten."

"Forgotten? He expects Sheila to forget?" Pat couldn't believe it.

"Yeah. He thinks that Sheila will have to accept it and put it behind her. He tells her to get on with her life."

"Easier said than done."

"That's for sure. He means well but sometimes I think he hasn't a clue."

"He was always like that, even as a child. He approached everything like that. Identify the problem, consider the options and then decide.

That's Seán's way." Pat tapped out the ashes into the ash-tray.

"Unfortunately, not everything in life has an easy solution," said Caroline.

"No. I wonder will Sheila ever be the same after this?"

"How could she be? But we'll have to do something. We can't let her ruin the rest of her life. I know it sounds callous, but she'll have to find something . . . something else to focus on."

"I couldn't agree more. Liam O'Flaherty has offered her a job."

"I heard."

"How did you hear? It only happened last night."

"Seán organised it." Caroline smiled. "To be fair to him, he is trying to help Sheila. He thinks a job would occupy her mind."

"Well I think he may be right. She can't go on the way she is. She's not ready for it yet, though. I suggested after Christmas."

"That's another thing. Christmas will be a nightmare. It's mainly about kids, after all. We want you to come over here for Christmas dinner. How do you think Sheila will cope with the twins?"

"Oh God, Caroline. Sure she idolises those children."

"I know that. All the same, she's bound to be upset. She'll be thinking of her own baby and wondering where she is."

"It's cruel. What about that friend of hers? Mary, isn't it?"

"Yeah, she's very good. Maybe you should invite

her down for the New Year? Would Rita agree to that?"

"No problem. Rita is demented about Sheila. She genuinely would do anything to help. But we'll have to stick to the glandular fever story. Definitely."

"I agree. I'm glad Sheila told you everything. Secrecy is not in her nature."

"I'm glad too. I'm glad she knew she could trust me. I'm sorry I didn't know all along."

"What could you have done, Pat?"

"I don't know," he confessed. "Maybe nothing at all."

* * *

A chemist's shop. Sheila couldn't imagine it. What would she be doing serving in a grotty little chemist's shop? O'Flaherty's was dark and dismal. It was depressing. Liam O'Flaherty was a nice enough man, but the shop was the pits. What alternative did she have? None. They weren't exactly queuing up to seek the services of a drop-out chemistry student. She'd give it a try. At least it would get her out from under her parents' feet. She was half sorry she'd unburdened herself to her father last night. It wasn't fair to him. He'd been terribly upset for her. He knew how she was feeling, how she was suffering. Why make him suffer too? She hadn't meant to do that. But she just couldn't go on deceiving him either. He deserved the truth. What about her mother? Should she confide in her? No. Her mother couldn't accept it. She'd die of shame and mortification. She'd be aghast at the thought that her only daughter had actually had sex and conceived a child. Sheila was disgusted herself. One moment of weakness and look at the trouble she had caused. But she couldn't call her baby an unwanted pregnancy. Karen was wanted. She may have been unplanned, but she was wanted.

Would she ever know that? Would she feel loved and cherished? Would she ever know that her mother had loved her and had wanted to keep her? Would she grow up a happy child? Endless questions. Sheila would have to stop thinking like this or she'd go raving mad. Some day she'd find Karen. She was determined.

Until then she'd have to make a go of her life. The job in the chemist's wasn't a great prospect, but she could use it to get experience. She was nearly twenty and had her whole life ahead of her. She'd take the job and that would be a start. When she was feeling a bit better and more positive, she'd do something else. She wouldn't waste her life. She'd get a grip and get organised. She owed that to herself and to her daughter. She'd make a success of her life and some day she'd find Karen. That would be her goal. Where there was life, there was hope. She'd tell nobody about her plans. She'd plod on and get her act together. Things wouldn't always be like this. Some day she'd have money. She'd work hard and do well. Some day, she'd make Karen proud of her. But she had to start somewhere. She'd tell her father tonight that she was going to take that job.

CHAPTER EIGHT

Sheila cursed silently. These damn lights, every year it was the same. One set always went on the blink. Reluctantly, she unplugged them. Having two sets on the same plug mightn't be a good idea after all. She methodically checked all the bulbs. Everything seemed to be in working order. She couldn't fathom it. Blast it anyway! Maybe Seán would be in later. Yuletide. The season of peace on earth, goodwill to man . . . cheers! She swallowed a mouthful of hot whiskey. She turned on the radio. Jesus, that's all she needed. Bing Crosby singing "White Christmas". Rita came dashing in from the kitchen.

"Great. I love Bing. Do you know your father took me up to Dublin to see that film in 1942. Could you credit it? Twenty-five years ago. You weren't even born. My poor mother, God rest her, took Seán for the night. We stayed in the Shelbourne."

Sheila wasn't remotely interested, but her mother carried on regardless.

"*Holiday Inn,* that's what the film was. Bing was lovely, wasn't he?"

Sheila thought he looked like a dried prune, but she said nothing.

"And Fred Astaire, now there was a great dancer. I love those old Irving Berlin tunes. 'White Christmas', such a lovely song, but it's sad too, isn't it? It's sad for those who are separated from their loved ones."

"Yeah," Sheila agreed.

Separated from loved ones. If her mother only knew. Sheila was depressed enough without listening to some melodramatic blast from the past. These songs were real tear-jerkers.

"Now your father loved Cagney. He was great in that one about the GIs. What do you call it?"

"Yankee Doodle Dandy."

"That's it, George M Cohan. Ah, you can't beat the old songs. Not like that muck they're singing now."

Sheila handed her mother a hot whiskey. "Will I bring one up to Dad?"

"Better not. Seán is calling in after his evening surgery. He says it wasn't a real stroke, he called it a TIA, whatever the hell that is."

Sheila tried to explain it to her mother again.

"TIAs are little strokes. Transient ischemic attacks is the medical term."

"Transient what?" Rita was baffled.

"Ischemia. It causes hardening of the arteries, Mam. The passage of blood is restricted. It's very common."

"Well I don't understand how your father got it. Sure he was fine a few weeks ago."

"Seán says he'll be fine again. He just has to watch his cholesterol intake."

"I never gave him fatty food." Rita was on the defensive.

"Nobody's suggesting this is your fault, Mam. He'll have to stop smoking too."

"There, I knew it. Amn't I worn out telling him that? It's killing him, that pipe. They say strokes run in families. You know his older brother, Denis, died of a stoke?"

Sheila didn't confirm that family history did play a part. But Sheila also knew that hypertension was another factor. Had she, in fact, contributed to her father's illness? She prayed to God that she hadn't been responsible for bringing this on. Why hadn't she kept her mouth shut? Seán said it had nothing to do with it, but she knew he was annoyed with her.

"Seán told you that with rest and the anticoagulants, he'll be as right as rain again." Sheila tried to sound positive. "They'll give him more tests when he's up to it. Just to make sure."

"But what about the dizziness? And his speech?"

"His speech is nearly back to normal, Mam. Remember that he lost the feeling in his left side? Well that came back, didn't it? His speech will come back too."

"I still think he needs physiotherapy," Rita asserted.

"Leave it to Seán, Mam. He knows what he's doing."

"Right, love. I'm so glad you're better. I couldn't cope with the two of you sick."

Sheila smiled at her. "I'm fine. Now relax and listen to your programme. I'll go up to Dad."

"Thanks, love."

Her father was sleeping. He looked old and frail. She sat by his bed and prayed. She willed him to get well. She hated this Christmas . . . truly hated it. What was it all about? Nothing but rushing around, buying presents nobody wanted and pretending to have a good time. Christmas was for children. It was fine if you were in a happy family, but what about people who were lonely? What about the poor? The elderly living alone? The season to be jolly. Grand, if you'd something to be jolly about. What about her father? He was very ill.

She tried not to dwell on the past, but the images came unbidden, against her will. Christmas long ago, when they were kids; Rita stuffing the turkey, the smell of the puddings boiling on the stove, early morning Mass, her father stacking up the fire, presents under the tree, the arrival of Moses. Were things really that good or did the past take on a magical quality? Did memories distort reality? No. They were happy then. She was a happy child.

Look at her now. How could she pretend to be happy? She was in mourning. She thought of Karen every single day. Missing her was a physical ache. A longing. Now, her father. He had to get better. God couldn't be so cruel.

He opened his eyes slowly. He tried to speak to her. She took his hand and caressed it.

"Shh, Dad. It's all right. Don't try to talk. Just nod if you understand me. Are you warm enough?"

A nod.
"Would you like a cup of tea?"
Two nods.
Sheila hugged him.

The Christmas tree glowed brightly in the darkened room. Sheila had to hand it to Seán, he was a fixer. Her mother snoozed in the armchair. Christmas day was all arranged. Caroline insisted that she'd do the cooking and bring the dinner over to their house. There was no way Pat could be moved yet. Sheila didn't look forward to it, but she put on a brave face. The twins would bring some laughter and joy into the house. Tonight she'd go to midnight Mass with Mam. She'd get up early in the morning and make a big breakfast. There'd be no fry for her father, though. He was going to miss his fries, not to mention his smokes. Seán said he'd let him have a small cigar after the dinner. It was Christmas after all. She wondered if Karen would get presents for her first Christmas. Today was the twenty-fourth. She was exactly three months old.

Sheila looked again at Mary's Christmas card. It was a typical Dickensian scene, not at all like Christmas in Ireland. Mary's message cheered her up.

Season's greetings, kiddo! See you on the thirtieth. Hope you've something good planned for New Year's Eve. Here's to 1968. Love and cuddles, Maro.

She had something planned (thanks to Caroline). She and Mary were invited to the Great Southern for a massive New Year's Ball. Seán, as the local doctor, always got free tickets to these occasions. It came with the territory. Mary would enjoy it. She loved dressing up.

* * *

Sheila was slightly merry from the wine and the champagne. There were eight at their table. Caroline and Seán were chatting to Brian and Annette, Seán's golfing partners. Brian's brother, Peadar, had brought a friend called Terry. He was a bit of a twit but Peadar was a nice guy. He asked Sheila to dance and she accepted out of politeness. It was a slow dance, but he kept her at arm's length, which suited her fine. It was a long time since a man had held her and she could feel herself stiffen. She wasn't comfortable. She saw Terry ask Mary up. They glided over to them and Sheila was relieved. Terry was a bit jarred and the expression on Mary's face was a hoot.

"I'm going to get drunk, myself," Mary whispered as she waltzed by. "See you back at the table."

"Would you like to dance the next one?" Peadar asked pleasantly.

"I'd rather sit down, if you don't mind." Sheila was polite but firm.

"Grand. Maybe we could go into the foyer? It's more comfortable and not as hot."

They took their drinks with them. The foyer was huge and beautifully furnished with large armchairs and long mirrors. They took a seat near the window overlooking Eyre Square.

"You look beautiful tonight," Peadar said shyly.

Oh God, Sheila thought, I'm not in the mood for this. "Thanks." She smiled.

"You're studying in UCD, aren't you? Chemistry, I believe."

"No, I chucked it in."

An awkward silence followed. Sheila sipped her wine. Better put him out of his misery. "I wasn't well."

"Oh? I'm sorry. I didn't mean to pry." He was obviously embarrassed.

"That's OK. I'm better now. How about you?"

She wasn't really interested in what he was doing but she thought she'd better make some effort. He was a friend of Seán's and manners didn't cost anything.

"I'm a biochemist," he answered quickly. "I'm lecturing in UCG."

"Do you like it?"

"Yes, I do. I like dealing with young minds."

Sheila laughed. "You're not that old yourself."

"Comparatively speaking." He was quite serious, she realised.

"I was very interested in plants myself. I preferred botany to my other subjects," Sheila told him.

"I'd be interested in the healing property of plants." He was enthusiastic now.

She hoped he wasn't going to launch into a lecture. Mary swayed out of the ballroom.

"Oh ho, you two. Caught in the act!"

True to her word and to Sheila's chagrin, she was drunk.

"Mind if I butt in?" She plonked down beside them on the sofa.

"Not at all," he said graciously, but it was obvious he was disappointed. "May I get you ladies another drink?"

"Mine's a G and T," Mary mumbled thickly. "Sheila would love another drop of the grape, wouldn't you, honeybunch?"

Sheila tried to keep her face straight. "That'd be lovely, thanks."

Peadar bounced off eagerly to do the honours.

"Jesus, this is hilarious. It's great crack altogether. Yer man Terry brought me out the back for some air, if you catch my drift." Mary giggled.

"Mary O'Callaghan, I can't leave you on your own for one minute. What on earth did you get up to? Your hair's in a right mess."

"Nothing. Absolutely nothing. It was freezing out there, the air was icy. Anyway, I wouldn't touch yer man with a barge pole."

"What's so funny then?"

Mary was now in convulsions. "Wait till I tell you." She was laughing so much she couldn't get the words out. "Gerry or whatever his name is . . ."

"Terry." Sheila laughed. "His name's Terry."

"Whatever. Terry or Gerry, who bloody well cares? Anyhow, he lunges at me and guess what?" More hysterics.

"What?" Sheila was in stitches too.

"I leapt out of the way, naturally. He was so drunk, he staggered over and his top teeth fell into a barrel."

"He had false teeth?" Sheila gasped.

"Yeah." Mary sniggered. "The joys of rural romance, what?"

"Shh, Peadar is coming back with the drinks. Where's Terry now? Did you dump him?"

"No need to. We came back to join the party and just as he was proposing, he slid under the table. I left Seán to sort him out."

"You're gas, Mary. You really are."

"Let me out of this madhouse and back to my little Jimmy." Mary hiccuped. "Hi Padre, thanks." She took the proffered gin and tonic. Sheila nearly died. Had Peadar heard her? Sheila hoped not. But it was funny. Peadar was so earnest, he could have easily been a priest. He was a gentleman though, and Sheila wouldn't hurt him for the world.

"I'm sorry, I have to leave," he apologised. "My friend, Terry, is a bit under the weather, I'm afraid."

"Under the table, you mean," Mary joked good-naturedly.

Peadar went scarlet. "It was very nice to meet you." He shook hands with Sheila and left hastily.

"God, he really has the hots for you." Mary offered her a cigarette.

"The poor guy. You gave him a hard time, Mary," Sheila scolded.

"Do you like him? Janey, I wouldn't have said anything if I thought you were interested in him. I didn't think he was your type. Too short and squat."

"I'm not interested in him. And I don't have a type," Sheila insisted.

"Get away out of that. You do so. Tall, blonde and handsome, that's your type."

"Not any more." Sheila was emphatic.

Mary, though drunk, knew better than to say any more.

The following morning, Seán arrived over with a post-mortem of the night before. He had met the receptionist from the Great Southern on his rounds. Apparently, one of the barmen had discovered a set of false teeth frozen solid in a barrel of ice and vomit.

Mary and Sheila howled with laughter. Seán was mystified.

Mary stayed until the fourth of January. She was facing back to a lot of study as her degree exams were this year. She intended to do her teaching practice in her old school in Drumcondra. Sheila was due to start work the next Monday.

"At least you'll be earning a few bob," Mary said enviously.

"I know. I don't intend to stay long there, but it'll tide me over until I figure out what I want to do."

"There's no way you'd go back to college?"

"No way," Sheila said. "I might do a course in shorthand typing or something."

"Mr O'Flaherty seems to be nice." Mary stuffed her clothes into her case.

"Here, let me do that. You're creasing everything." Sheila placed Mary's blouses carefully one on top of the other.

"You're as fussy as ever," Mary teased her. "A place for everything and everything in its place."

"I know, I can't stand messes. The shop will drive me nuts. Did you see the state of it? It wouldn't exactly entice customers."

"Does he do a good trade?"

"Not really. Mostly the old dears from around here who need prescriptions filled. He's very friendly with them and he's full of knowledge. Some of them trust him with their symptoms and don't bother with doctors at all."

"Seán must be tickled pink."

"Ah, he has enough patients to keep him moaning." Sheila laughed. "They get on very well. To be honest, that's how I got this job. Liam did it as a favour for Seán."

"Nothing wrong with that."

"I don't know. I'd like to think I'd be of some use."

"You will, Sheila. You're a brilliant organiser. You could get that chemist's ship-shape if anyone could."

"Yeah. It might be a bit of a challenge. I wonder would he agree to modernise it?"

"You can always ask him," Mary encouraged her.

Mary was thrilled that Sheila was showing a definite interest in something at last. She'd been in good form during the past few days. Mr Crosby was on the mend and was now sitting up in the armchair in the sitting-room. He was able to talk now, although his speech was still a bit hesitant. Mrs Crosby fussed over him like a mother hen.

Sheila hadn't mentioned the baby once. Mary knew that Sheila was trying very hard not to spoil the holiday for her. She had great guts. It couldn't be easy.

"I'll pop into the kitchen to say a few words to your Mam before I leave."

Mrs Crosby was making sandwiches.

"Now Mary, these will keep you going on the train back."

"Oh Mrs Crosby, you shouldn't have. You're a terrible woman. Sure I had a huge breakfast."

"Young girls should eat properly. I'm always saying that to Sheila, but you might as well run up the wall and tickle the bricks!"

Sheila's mother had wonderful expressions, Mary thought.

"I want to thank you for all your kindness to me during my stay."

"It's me who wants to thank you. You've done Sheila a power of good. She's lucky to have you."

"That cuts both ways, Mrs C, I'm going to miss her when I go back."

"Can't you come down again, at Easter perhaps?"

"Yeah, or Sheila could come up to me."

"I wonder would she? She seems to have gone off Dublin for some reason."

Was Mrs Crosby fishing? Mary wouldn't blame her if she was, but this time she was giving no information away. Sheila blamed herself for her father's stroke. Sheila's mother had to be kept in the dark.

Caroline arrived to drive Mary to the station. Sheila hugged her friend affectionately.

"Good luck with the job," Mary shouted out of the passenger window.

Sheila and her mother stood waving them off till the car drove out of sight.

"She's a lovely girl." Rita put her arm around her daughter. "Is she doing a line?"

"Yeah, she is. She's going out with an architectural student."

"That's nice."

Sheila could sense her mother's reaction. If Sheila had got such a good catch for a boyfriend, Rita would be on cloud nine. Mothers, they were a different breed.

CHAPTER NINE

Mary's fifth-year class were a howl. They were very bright but not uppity as some A classes could be. She had a great rapport with them, probably because she was only a couple of years older than the students themselves. Last week one earnest student asked her why Hamlet had jumped into Ophelia's grave and it took all her self-control not to answer: necrophilia. They were revising the Anglo-Irish poets at present for the approaching summer tests. One bright spark suggested that Yeats was depressed because Maud was gone. Mary obliged them with a sarcastic retort.

"Tonight, go over Kavanagh's 'Stony Grey Soil' and, when you're discussing the mood, kindly avoid the notion that the poet was stoned when he wrote it."

The bell ran before they could retaliate.

Mary sat with her usual gang for the tea break. Some of the older teachers looked worn out and were eagerly awaiting the summer holidays of '72. Mary sympathised with them. It was fine for her, she knew. She'd only been teaching for three years now and she was still full of energy and what they called idealism.

"Any exciting plans for the weekend?" asked Margaret O'Brien, the science teacher.

"Not really." Mary was forced to fib. "I'm going out with Jim. Probably just for a drink."

"Young love, enjoy it while you can." Margaret was married with five children. She said she dreaded the weekend more than the school week.

"I've the third years next. We're acting out scenes from *Julius Caesar*. I better go and get the key for the choir hall." Mary sprang up long before the next bell.

"I envy you your youth and enthusiasm, Mary," Hilary Brogan said dryly. "I'm having another cigarette before I face the little monsters."

"She's great, isn't she?" Margaret remarked to Hilary after Mary had left the staffroom.

"Give her time. We were all like that when we started." Hilary was in no rush to get to her second-year Latin class.

Mary spent hours getting ready. She tied up her long black hair in a French roll, decided she looked like a matron, and then brushed it all out again. She hated her curls. Straight hair was all the rage. Every night she wrapped it around her head, but every morning the curls came back with a vengeance. She took out the iron and spread out her waves on the ironing board. This was a tricky business, she thought as she ran the iron over them. She should really have covered her hair with brown paper. It was vital not to singe the ends. She could imagine her mother's horror if she knew what Mary was at.

119

There, that was better. She looked like Judith Durham of The Seekers.

After her shower, she laid out her clothes on the bed. Wait till Jim got an eyeful of this! Navy hot pants, white blouse and navy knee-high boots. This was a change from her jeans or her sensible school skirts. She slipped into her new clothes and immediately felt sexy. The long mirror on her wardrobe door gave her a good view. She examined herself from every angle and was pleased. The boots looked terrific. She had long legs and good thighs, she might as well make the most of them. Her maxi coat would cover all until she swept it off in the pub. Very dramatic! Well, it wasn't every night a girl got engaged.

Jim was waiting patiently at Clery's main door. They kissed briefly. He didn't like shows of affection in public.

"You're late." He put his arm around her. "Come on, before the shop shuts."

"This is a bit corny, isn't it? Did we have to get the ring there?"

"Corny? Not at all. 'The Happy Ring House by the Pillar.' It's dead romantic."

"Hope it's not a bad omen," Mary said gloomily.

"What do you mean?"

"The Pillar is gone," Mary sighed.

"You're a right weirdo, do you know that?" He laughed at her wistful expression.

"Come on, after the jeweller's we'll go for a few jars before dinner. That'll settle your nerves."

"Dinner? You never said anything about dinner."

"I've booked a table in the Gresham."

"You're not serious?"

Jim smiled smugly. "I've another reason for celebrating." He held the door of the shop open for her. "I've been promoted. You're looking at the new junior partner."

Mary was over the moon.

Mary sheepishly handed in her coat at reception. Jim's face was a picture.

"My God. You look sensational."

"Not exactly suitable attire for this place," Mary apologised. "I thought we were only going to the pub."

"It's a knockout. Guaranteed to keep the waiters on their toes." His smile was lecherous. "You're giving me all kinds of salacious ideas. I'll be needing a cold shower tonight."

"You could have one at my place." She grinned boldly.

"Is that an invitation?"

The maitre d' was not impressed by Mary's dress sense. For a minute she thought she would be asked to leave.

"Could you give us a nice table?" Jim asked politely. "We've just got engaged."

That seemed to soften him up.

They got a lovely table for two in the corner. The candlelight made it very intimate.

Mary looked at the ring. Its three diamonds sparkled brightly. "I think it's time, don't you? We've been good for long enough."

Jim tenderly took her hand in his. "I love you," he said softly.

Those three little words melted Mary's heart.

The Chicken Maryland was delicious. For dessert they had meringues and cream. Mary finished off with a Cointreau. Very sophisticated.

"When will you tell your folks?" Jim wanted to know. "I'm going home tomorrow to tell mine." Jim was from Wexford. "Can you come with me?"

"Great. Could we ring my Mum now?" Mary was all excited. "I can't wait till the morning."

"I've a better idea. Why don't we take a taxi out to Drumcondra?"

"Jim Ryan, you're a dote. Are you sure? What about our night of passion?"

"The night's young yet! I'll take your old lad for a drink in the Cat and Cage."

"You will not. We're going to start as I mean to go on," Mary assured him in no uncertain terms. "You can take my mother and me as well. I'm dying to tell Sheila and Joanne. I'll ring them both tonight."

It was one in the morning by the time they left O'Callaghans. Mary's parents were thrilled with the news, especially her mother, Emily. She really liked Jim Ryan and she knew he'd make a good husband. His promotion couldn't have come at a better time. Now they could get married in the late summer, instead of postponing it till next year. Emily O'Callaghan didn't believe in long engagements. Hadn't she and Maurice met and married within a year? Mary and Jim had been going out now for five years. No sense in delaying any longer. Mary spent ages on the phone to her sister and to Sheila. Everyone was delighted with the news of the engagement. Emily was busy already, mentally planning the wedding. Iona Church would be a beautiful venue.

* * *

The sun streamed through the flimsy curtains, waking Mary from a delicious dream. The ring sparkled on the bedside table. She couldn't believe it. They were really engaged. Jim lay asleep beside her, his hair tossed on the pillow. She noticed one or two grey hairs, sprinkled among the brown. A few more at his temples would make him really distinguished looking. She truly loved this man. He was generous to a fault. He was thoughtful and caring. He was ambitious. And he was hers, all hers! She hoped he wasn't disappointed about last night. They'd intended to make love but, when it came to the crunch, Mary changed her mind. They kissed and fondled and both were very excited. He knew just how to pleasure her. She could still feel the touch of his thigh on hers, his lips on her breasts. Suddenly, she asked him to stop. She knew it wasn't fair to him, but she couldn't go through with it. The image of Sheila was vivid in her mind. Sheila and the baby. What if she got pregnant? That thought scared her out of her wits. It wasn't worth the worry. Their wedding was to be in three months

MARY MCCARTHY

time and she didn't want anything to spoil it. Jim
was really good about it. He'd kissed her and told
her not to worry, he could wait.

Mary decided two things this morning. First, it
wasn't a good idea to let Jim sleep over. It was too
frustrating, too unsatisfactory. Secondly, she'd tell
him about Sheila's baby. He was to be her husband
after all. Sometimes he was a bit harsh about Sheila.
He tolerated her only because she was Mary's best
friend. Sheila would be their bridesmaid, along with
Joanne as matron of honour. It was important for
Jim to like Sheila. Her friendship meant everything
to Mary. If Jim knew about the baby, perhaps he'd
be more sympathetic.

The smell of sizzling sausages woke Jim. Mary, her
back to him, was breaking eggs on the pan. He
crept up behind her and grabbed her around the
waist. He kissed the back of her neck. This always
sent shivers through her. She turned and kissed him
full on the mouth.

"God, you're sexy," he moaned, nibbling her ear.
He was so handsome standing there in his jeans.
His chest was muscular and hairy. Mary resisted the
urge to pull him back to bed.

"Sit down and eat your fry." She pushed him
onto the chair.

"My, you're getting rather violent. I like a bit of
rough," he joked. "I'm famished. I could eat a horse.
Where's yours?"

"I've no appetite," Mary sipped her coffee and lit
a cigarette.

Jim tucked into his meal with relish. She could see he was in great form.

"Jim, I'm sorry about last night." She was embarrassed.

"No need to be," he mumbled between mouthfuls. "Last night was great. You were terrific."

"No, you know what I mean." She wanted to discuss it.

"Mary, I love you. I adore you. I wouldn't want you to do anything that makes you uncomfortable, OK? Sure, I love to touch you and kiss you and fondle you. Sex is great, but it isn't everything. We've plenty of time. The rest of our lives."

The way he said it was so sincere. Mary jumped onto his lap and hugged him.

He kissed her again. "Get off me, woman. I can't guarantee that I'll be able to control myself if you sit on top of me."

Mary laughed. "How will your parents take our news?"

"They've been waiting for it for ages. They'll be delighted. Mind you, my mother will probably be a bit emotional. An only son is a bit precious."

"Yeah, a bit spoilt as well."

"That's inevitable. Well, it won't happen with us. We're going to have at least six kids."

"In your dreams." Mary giggled. "Two is my max."

"Not at all. I can picture you dropping them all over the place. No trouble to you. A baby a year and you tied to the kitchen sink. Marital bliss."

She gave him a clip on the ear. "On the subject of babies, I've something to tell you."

"Oh yeah? You want to start one right after the wedding?"

"Not on your nelly. We're going to wait until we're both ready."

"I'm only messing. You're right of course. I think we should wait till we have a decent house and a few bob saved. That little house in Ringsend will do the pair of us for a while, but children need a garden."

"I agree."

Jim had bought a cottage in Ringsend last year. It was small, but Mary thought it was a palace compared to her bedsit. He was living in it now and doing it up. But they planned to save like mad for a bigger house. His promotion would speed things up, but Mary was quite content to live there for the first few years.

"Timing is very important for having babies," Jim said earnestly. "Let's wait for a while. Is that what you wanted to say?"

"Not really. I wanted to tell you about Sheila."

"What? She's going to have a baby? The immaculate conception?" He sneered.

"No. She had one five years ago. A little girl."

Jim was stunned. "A baby?" He gulped. "Sheila had a baby?"

Mary nodded. "It was awful."

"Where is it? What happened?"

"She gave her up for adoption."

"Oh God, that's pretty grim. Why didn't you tell me before?"

"I couldn't. What could you have done? It's different now because we're getting married."

"That's why she left college that time." The truth dawned on him.

"Yeah. Jim, I know you always thought that Sheila was a bit of a wet blanket, but now that you know the story, you can see why."

"God help her."

"Last night, on the phone, she was telling me she was at the twins' Communion. She found it very hard. Her little girl is five now and she's never even seen her," Mary said sadly.

Jim was abashed. He admired women, he really did. What misery had Sheila gone through, forced to give up her own child? And Mary? She'd kept this from him for all these years. What loyalty women had for each other. He couldn't understand why people said that women were bitchy. In his experience, they always looked out for each other, confided in one another. Men didn't do that. He was slightly jealous of their total commitment. Maybe that was it.

Was he jealous of Sheila? Her friendship with Mary was a genuine and honest one. They were fiercely loyal. They were open with each other. They weren't afraid to express their feelings freely. They shared problems and analysed everything. He'd his friends too, but it was different. He socialised with his colleagues from work. He'd his tennis mates. He'd even kept up some of his Uni friendships, but the way they talked was utterly different. They stuck to safe subjects, sport and their careers when they were going well. When did they confide in one another?

127

When had he ever talked about his troubles to any of them? When he had something on his mind, he went to Mary. Jim rarely heard his friends discuss their wives or girlfriends, except in a flippant dismissive way. Yet they were basically nice guys, so what was the problem? Was it upbringing, he wondered. "You're a big boy now, don't cry." Such crap. Why shouldn't they cry if they felt like it? Men continually moaned that they'd never understand women. Women weren't logical or reasonable. Perhaps life wasn't logical or reasonable. Jim was certain of one thing: when it came to caring and concern, women had the edge.

"I'm glad you told me, Mary. You're absolutely right, I was too hard on Sheila. I know how much you love her and I'll make much more of an effort in future."

"She's my best friend, Jim. I'd like you two to get on."

"She has great spunk, I'll give her that," Jim said quietly.

CHAPTER TEN

Liam O'Flaherty wondered what he did before Sheila came to work for him. She had totally revolutionised his shop. She'd doubled his takings in the first few months. She was a real gem. To think that he'd only taken her on as a favour. This girl was a treasure.

She'd persuaded him to invest money in a complete overhaul three years ago. He did it reluctantly because his wife nagged him too. She agreed with Sheila on everything. It was impossible to fight off two such persuasive women. But it paid off handsomely. They shut the shop for three weeks while the carpenters and builder moved in. Sheila even took photographs of the place before the job started. A sort of before and after record. The transformation was incredible.

The old dark wooden counter was removed, along with the wall that separated the back room from the shop. They put in a huge window in the front which brightened up the shop. They put in a beautiful oak wood floor and ceiling. Sheila changed the whole atmosphere of the place. Medicines and tablets were stored in the back and she insisted on a window hatch for dispensing prescriptions. A small couch stood by the window, for anyone who had to wait. Cosmetics and skin care products were beautifully displayed on oak shelves. One full section was devoted to perfumes. There were plants everywhere. The shop took on a new life. It was colourful, airy and cheerful.

Sheila had a great manner with the customers. All the young girls came to her for advice on the various cosmetic ranges. She became an expert on the various skin types and what make-up suited them. She was a great believer in herbal remedies. The clientele now came from all backgrounds and ages. Sheila gave each customer time and care and advised them which moisturiser, which cleanser, which shampoo to use. She was such a beautiful girl herself they took her advice. Kate said she could charm the birds off the trees. She was diligent and conscientious too. She investigated every new range of cosmetics. He left all the buying of these to her. He trusted her judgement implicitly.

They did a huge trade in suntan ranges. It seemed that the whole of Galway was heading to the sun this June. His pharmacy was by far the most popular for miles around. The ones in town, and in the Square, were only in the ha'penny place. Trade was booming and it was all thanks to Sheila. The girl was a miracle worker.

Sheila arrived looking stunning as usual. Her green suit brought out the hazel of her eyes.

"Hi, Liam," she greeted him, "can I have a word?"

"Sure. Here's a cup of tea before we open."

"Thanks, I was wondering if I could have next Saturday off. I know it's short notice, but my friend, Mary, is coming for the weekend."

"No problem. She's the girl who's getting married in August?"

"Yeah. She's taking a break from the wedding preparations. We might go off for a few days, to Clifden maybe."

"Well, we certainly have the weather for it now. Enjoy yourselves. The boss will be in to help out, don't worry."

Liam always referred to his wife, as "the boss". Kate O'Flaherty seemed to like it. She came in on Saturdays when they were busy. In the summer months they did a huge trade.

"Thanks, Liam."

"What about Peadar? Will he go with you?" Liam's eyes twinkled mischievously. "When are you two going to give us a day out?"

Sheila groaned. "Amn't I tired telling you all that we're just good friends."

"Go on with ya, you're not fooling me. The man is cracked about ya."

Sheila gave up. She fixed her hair in front of the mirror and went to open up. What was she going to do about Peadar? She was very fond of him, but only as a friend. There was no physical attraction there at all. At least not for her. She went out with him once a week, for a meal or a drink, but that was it. That's the way she wanted it. He was like a brother. Deep down, she knew he wanted more but

131

she'd always been straight with him. It wasn't as if she were leading him on.

Sheila picked up Mary at the station on Friday. It was a balmy summer's evening. They decided to go for a drink.

"The Southern?" Sheila beamed at her. "We might bump into your old flame."

"Don't fecking remind me. That twit gave me the creeps."

"You're quite safe. He's married," Sheila informed her as they made their way across the Square. "The Skeff OK?"

"Sure. Who's the poor unfortunate?"

"Some girl from Spiddal. I think she was up the pole." There was no criticism in Sheila's voice. "I don't think they're very happy. He drinks a lot, according to Seán."

They'd no chance of a seat in the crowded lounge. They had one drink and left.

The spare room was full of bottles and potions.

"Sorry about this mess," Sheila apologised. "I hope you've enough room. It's just for one night. I was thinking we could take a trip out to Connemara tomorrow and maybe stay over in Clifden tomorrow night."

"Great. What's in these bottles anyhow?" Mary was intrigued.

"Ah, I'm trying to make my own skin creams. I've been at it for ages without much success. I'm trying to work with natural elements, plants, flowers and things. Peadar brought me home some juniper oil from the Canaries. Essential oils, they've some wonderful properties. You'd be amazed."

"God, you're great." Mary was impressed. "It's a hobby, like?"

"For the moment it is. I'd love to go into it seriously though. I'm not having much luck. I tried to make soap a while ago."

"How?"

"You boil fatty oils with alkalis."

This was double Dutch to Mary. "Come on, I didn't do science at school. What are alkalis?"

"Soda or potash," Sheila explained. "I did it with tallow first, then I tried coconut oil. They have glycerine in them. When you boil them, the potash replaces the glycerine and neutralises the fatty acids. Then they form soap."

"Brilliant." Mary was agog.

"In theory it is. I was never very successful. The result was too grainy. The coconut oil one was like a liquid soap, but it was a mess. Anyhow, I'm more into making face creams now."

"The future Elizabeth Arden, what?" Mary slagged her. "I can always say I knew you when you were nothing."

"You'll be in a wheelchair by then." Sheila grinned. "But I'm going to keep trying."

"Bully for you," Mary said. "Now, about this wedding. I've decided on jade green for the bridesmaids, if that's all right with you?"

"Yeah, I love green."

"Well, it certainly suits you. Joanne's dark so it'll

be fine on her too. I thought something flowing might be nice. Joanne isn't as slim as you, so she can't wear anything tight fitting."

"I've put on loads of weight," Sheila protested. "I'm a twelve now."

"Jesus, twelve is tiny. You look fabulous, better than ever."

"I've still put on a stone. Mam never stops stuffing me. How do you think my dad looks?"

Mary thought for a moment. "The truth? I think he's failed a lot."

"Yeah, I know. He has to have a young lad in now to do the garden. It's sad. He's getting terribly forgetful too."

"But your mam's terrific. She's a bundle of energy, just like mine. This wedding has given my mother new life."

"I'd say so. Mam's grand except that she never stops nagging me. Your wedding is making her worse. She thinks I should marry Peadar. They all do. Except Caroline, of course."

Mary could understand Sheila's frustration. "But your mother has a life of her own, hasn't she?"

"She keeps busy with her golf and her bridge. She's thirteen years younger of course."

"Thirteen years younger than your father?" Mary was astonished.

"Yeah, did you not know that? She's only sixty-two. He didn't get married till he was forty. He was fifty-one when I was born."

"The randy git." Mary laughed. "And your mother was thirty-eight?"

"Yeah, I think she thought she was past it when I came along. Seán was ten by then."

"Jesus, men are never past it, are they? They have it every way."

"You can say that again," Sheila agreed. "Come on downstairs for a drink. We'd better have an early night and then we can start off early tomorrow."

"How's the car going?"

"It's a banger. Let's just hope it copes with the drive."

The scenery was breathtaking. Mary was enthralled.

"Oh Sheila, it's fantastic! The colours are magnificent: blue skies, blue sea, golden sands and the green of the lakes. I've never seen anything like it. Aren't the stone walls brilliant? Jesus, you can't beat Ireland for scenery. I never realised there were so many lakes in the West."

"Yeah, it's a fisherman's paradise. The deep-sea fishing is good too, for blue shark and thresher. And there's water sports too: sailing, surfing, water skiing."

"You're a mine of information. It's guided tours you should be thinking of! Myself, I'd prefer dry land," Mary commented. "I can't even swim. God, the views are really spectacular. Look at all the sheep on the mountain. Jesus, watch out! That was a narrow bend." Mary's excitement was contagious.

"Do you want to stop?"

"Yeah, is there anywhere we could go for lunch?" Mary was hungry as usual.

"We're bound to find a pub," Sheila remarked

dryly. "It doesn't matter how remote the area, you're guaranteed to find a pub."

"Where are we now?" Mary consulted the map. "We're a few miles from Cleggan."

Sheila drove on past the lake and, round the next corner, they spotted a village, nestling deep in the valley.

"Will we have a look?" Sheila suggested.

"Yeah, it looks really quaint."

"Quaint? Jesus, you're beginning to sound like an American tourist."

"Do they speak Irish here? I've only *cúpla focal*."

Sheila laughed. "Fear not. This area isn't Gaeltacht at all. In fact North Connemara is very anglified. They look down on the native speakers. They call them the *tá sé* men!"

They drove into the tiny village where a make-shift signpost said Carrigeen. Sheila had to stop to let sheep cross the road. "This is the only traffic jam you'll find out here." She laughed.

The village was one main street with a shop, a few houses and pubs and a church at the other end. They pulled up at O'Malley's pub. Sheila went up to order two glasses of beer and sandwiches.

"You were having a great chat with his nibs." Mary was a bit miffed. "I never realised you'd such a gift for the gab."

"I'm a Galwegian, don't forget. We spent most of our summers here. I went to Carraroe Gaeltacht all through my schooling. He's bringing us ham sandwiches. It was all they had." Sheila apologised.

"That'll do. I'm so hungry I could eat a horse."

Two or three old men sat in the corner, obviously talking about the girls.

"Look at the auld lad in the corner. He's staring at us."

"We're foreigners here," Sheila explained.

"I thought you said the natives were friendly."

"They are. But we're still strangers. Look! He's coming over. He's dead curious."

The old man sat down beside them and started to chat them up. Mary couldn't understand a word he was saying. It might be English, but his accent was very difficult to follow. He was muttering something about the skinny croot.

"What's the skinny croot?" Mary was lost.

"He wants to know if we took the scenic route, you fool." Sheila laughed.

"Jesus, the scenic route! What's he on about now?" The old man was giving Mary lascivious looks.

"He says you're a fine woman," Sheila giggled. "Are you sure you want to settle for Jim?"

"God, he's a horny auld bugger. Who's the girl at the bar? The owner's daughter?"

Sheila asked the old man.

"He says she's yer man's wife."

"Good God! She's years younger."

"Apparently not." Sheila replied. "Ignore his leering, I told him you were engaged." The owner served their lunch. The ham was like plastic and the bread was stale.

Two women came in delivering vegetables. Sheila was struck by their beauty. Like the barmaid, they had magnificent skin. She mentioned this to the old man.

"He said it's the carrageen," Sheila told Mary. "That's why the village women have such good complexions."

"Well, they must be having baths in it," Mary replied tartly. Sheila repeated Mary's comment to Seamus, the old man.

"He says that's exactly what they do. God, they're beautiful women, aren't they?"

"Absolutely. And not just the young ones either. What age would you say the woman behind the bar is?"

Seamus replied "sixty". He winked at Mary.

"Sixty? I don't believe it. She looks about forty, at the most. Carrageen. Is that their secret?" Mary ignored the wink.

"He says if you could bottle it, you'd make a fortune." Sheila was now deep in thought. "Mary, remember I told you I was trying to make creams and stuff from natural oils?"

"Yeah? Are you getting ideas about carrageen moss?"

"You could say that," Sheila replied.

They said their goodbyes to Seamus and left.

"You've made a friend there," Mary said as she strapped on her seat-belt.

"No harm in making contacts," was Sheila's mysterious rejoinder.

They had dinner in the hotel in Clifden on Saturday night and then headed out for a pub crawl. The tourist season hadn't really begun yet, so there were mainly locals in the pubs. There was a session in King's, which drew in a large crowd. *Craic agus ceoil*.

"This will be our last time together like this."

Mary noticed that Sheila was a bit down. "Not a bit of it," she said light-heartedly. "My marriage won't change things between us, Sheila. I can still visit and you can come to Dublin whenever you like. On that very subject, you'll have to come up for a fitting next month."

"That shouldn't be a problem." Sheila sipped her vodka and bitter.

Mary looked at her anxiously. "How long is it since you were up?"

"Not since Karen's birth."

Mary had wondered when this would come up. She was apprehensive. She'd no wish to open old wounds.

"Is it any easier now?"

"I keep busy. I try not to brood, Mary. But she's always on my mind."

"Time isn't the great healer it's meant to be," Mary said wistfully.

"It's just that she's out there somewhere. I wonder if she's still in Dublin. She could be anywhere. Maybe she's not even in Ireland."

"Yeah." Mary fiddled with her hair.

"I'm not as bad as I was. I used to stare into prams. Ridiculous, isn't it? I mean the chances of her ending up in Galway are a million to one, but I still used to stare into prams and wonder. Once, I almost took a baby."

"What?"

"Oh I didn't, of course. I was going into the butcher's one day and there was a pram standing outside. I peered in and there was a gorgeous little baby asleep. It took me all my strength not to push the pram down the street."

"God, Sheila. That's desperate." Mary was appalled.

"I know. Anyhow, I'm over that stage. She must be in school by now. I wonder if she's changed much. I keep her photo hidden in my underwear drawer and I take it out from time to time."

"You're so close to the twins. Does that make it harder?"

"Yeah, definitely. Especially at their birthdays or at Christmas. It's Karen I'd love to be buying presents for. Do you remember when that doctor told me to convince myself the baby was dead?"

"How could I forget it? I couldn't believe it when you told me that. It was so damn insensitive."

"Yeah, it was. But now I think I know why he said it. Sometimes it'd be easier for me if Karen were dead. That's an awful thing to say, I know. It's selfish and despicable. But you can let go when someone you love is dead. Do you know what I mean?"

"Yes, I do." Mary nodded. "Do you still talk to your Dad about her?"

"No, it wouldn't be fair to him. He's the best in the world, Mary, but he's old and infirm. I can't burden him with it. I have Caroline and she's terrific. She always brings me out on Karen's birthday."

"The twenty-fourth of September."

"You remembered." Sheila was grateful to Mary for that.

"Remember that old battle-axe, the matron? And the professional breast-feeder?" Mary grimaced.

"Proper bitches, the pair of them. I often think about the nurse, Laura. I wonder what ever happened to her?"

"She was great. It was a good job she was there. So, at least you've Caroline, that's good. And Seán?"

"Nothing. He hasn't mentioned her in years. Once I came off the medication, it was over as far as Seán was concerned."

"I told Jim. I hope you don't mind."

"No, I don't. Not at this stage. How did he react?"

"He was very upset, actually. He admires you."

"God, what is there to admire? I abandoned my daughter."

"Sheila, will you quit it. You didn't abandon her. You gave her a life. You gave her a good start."

"Let's hope so. I'll never know, will I?"

"You might, some day. You might be able to find out."

"Doubtful. But if there is a way, I will find out. I will. In the meantime, I'm going to do the best I can to make a success of my life. I don't intend to stay in O'Flaherty's forever."

"You're really serious about this skin care business?"

"Absolutely. I'm going to ask Peadar to help."

"Good old reliable Peadar."

Was there criticism in Mary's voice? "He's all into it." Sheila insisted crossly.

Mary offered her a cigarette but Sheila refused. "I'm trying to quit. It's not good for the skin."

Mary went up to the bar. Better to avoid any hassle. Why did she have to open her mouth about Peadar? Would she never learn? She knew that it was another sensitive area. Sheila wasn't using him, that was obvious. But any hint or suggestion that she was drove Sheila mad. Mary tried to pay for the drinks but a local insisted. God, these Connemara men were desperate lechers. Did they never give up?

They took their time on the drive back the next day. The sun was still shining. Three days with no rain . . . a minor miracle. Recess, Maam Cross, Oughterard, Moycullen and back to Galway City.

"Pretend we got Mass. I don't want a lecture," Sheila warned Mary.

"Don't worry."

"When do you want me up for the fitting?"

"The middle of June. I'll give you a ring when the dressmaker's ready. I'm moving home to Drumcondra next week."

"You're giving up the flat?"

"Sure there's no sense in wasting rent."

Sheila wondered what Mary's parents made of that. It seemed to her that Mary knew when to suit herself. She told herself not to be bitchy.

"I hope I don't bump into you-know-who in Dublin. I know it's a big place but you always seem to meet someone you don't want to. I could face anyone but him."

"Don Juan? No worries. I've news. I wasn't going to mention him but now that you have . . ."

"News?" Sheila said nervously. "He's married?"

"Married my ass! He's still messing around. I met Joe Byrne. Remember him?"

"Vaguely. He was in Don's Spanish class, I think."

"That's right. He was teaching with Don in Finglas for the last three years. He told me that Don had gone off to Spain."

"Has he given up teaching?"

"No, just fed up with the scene in Dublin, from what I gather. He's teaching English as a foreign language."

"I'm glad he's gone." Sheila's tone was flat.

"You didn't love him, did you, Sheila?" Mary was beginning to wonder.

"I thought I did at the time. He was so flighty though. I couldn't take him seriously."

"Nobody could. He was a shithead."

Sheila nodded. He was out there in Spain without a care in the world, totally unaware of the damage he'd done. Sheila didn't really care. It wasn't as if he'd abandoned her or the baby. She hadn't given him the chance.

CHAPTER ELEVEN

Sheila spent hours studying the books on aromatherapy which Peadar lent her. She was fascinated by the whole thing. She was working on a cleansing cream. She tried rose absolute as her essential oil. It was supposed to be good for dry skin. She used the enfleurage method of extraction as it yields greater quantities of oil. She read that this method went back to the ancient Egyptians. The petals are steeped in fat which absorbs their fragrance. When Sheila tried lard, her mother thought she'd finally gone around the twist. Their kitchen at night smelt like a rose garden. But the cream became rancid in a few days. Peadar said that plant oils would prevent decomposition. Her father was very interested in what she was doing and followed Sheila around the kitchen in his dressing-gown.

"This is turning into a mad house," Rita remarked dryly.

Sheila then tried it the French way. She laid the rose heads on sheets of glass and covered them with a cloth soaked in olive oil. This perfumed oil was called *huile antique*.

"I don't for the life of me know why you can't use Ponds like everyone else." Rita was scornful. Sheila ignored her.

The doorbell rang. Sheila answered it, knife in hand.

"What are you at? Matricide?" Caroline followed her into the kitchen.

"I'm making cold cream."

"With a knife?"

"It's for shredding the beeswax."

"Jesus, I thought that was for furniture."

"Funny, funny." Sheila laughed. "It acts as a carrier for the essential oil. It thickens and emulsifies."

"Speak the Queen's English, will you?" Caroline laughed.

"Come on, I'll show you. Do you want to help?"

"Sure. Sheila, that cream you made up for me works a treat."

"The carrot seed?"

"Yeah, it's absolutely brilliant. You should sell it in the chemist. My skin feels soft and supple. Even Seán noticed. What's in it?"

"The usual ingredients except this time I used carrot seed instead of the rose."

"Carrots? Ordinary carrots?" Caroline was astonished. "I knew they were meant to improve your eyesight, but I didn't know they were good for the skin."

"I didn't use ordinary carrots," Sheila explained. "These were wild carrot plants that Peadar found in ditches."

"You're kidding?"

"I'm not. Look out for them the next time you're out for a drive. They've long stalks, and white flowers with a purple centre. I used the whole plant to obtain the essential oil. Carotene is very good for the skin as it converts to vitamin A."

"God, this is brilliant. Talk to Liam. I'm sure he'd let you sell it in the shop."

"Yeah, I might. I'm still working on other creams though. I'd like to have more research done before I go public."

"Do you think I could try it on Ciara's eczema?"

"Well, it won't do her any harm. Is the soya milk not working?"

"She hates it. She's gone off milk totally. Seán always said it was some sort of allergy to dairy products. I don't know, though. She can eat chocolate and yoghurt and they don't seem to do her any harm.

"Try it and see. I'd say nothing to Seán though."

They both laughed.

"Here." Sheila handed her the almond oil. "Measure out forty grams."

"What have you got there?"

"Rosewater." Sheila measure out forty grams exactly.

"Now what?"

"Now we have to shred the beeswax. Mind the knife, it's very sharp."

"There. Is that OK?" Caroline was quite proud of her efforts.

"Grand."

Sheila put the almond oil and the beeswax into a stainless steel bowl and the rosewater in another bowl. She put both bowls into a shallow pan of water over a gentle heat. Sheila stirred the oil and wax until they melted. She added the water to the oil mixture a drop at a time while Caroline beat it with a rotary whisk.

"This is like making mayonnaise." Caroline laughed.

"Hey! Stop beating! Stop!" Sheila screamed.

Rita ran out. "What's wrong?" she roared.

"Nothing, nothing," Sheila brushed her mother aside. "It's just that you shouldn't overbeat when the water is absorbed or the cream will separate."

"You and your damn creams. I thought the house was on fire." Rita left the kitchen in a huff.

"My God," said Caroline. "The mood's pretty bad."

"Yeah. Dad's not well at all. He spent the day in bed. She's tired running in and out to him. I can take over tomorrow as it's Sunday."

"On your day off? That's desperate."

"I don't mind. He's very easy to manage really. I think it was a mild stroke he had last week."

"So does Seán. You know he could get your dad into the hospital to give Rita and yourself a break."

"Mam wouldn't hear of it. No, we're fine, honestly."

"Well the offer's there."

"Thanks. Now, we better get on with this."

"What now?"

"This amount will only give us two jars. You hold the jars while I pour."

Caroline was disappointed. "Two bloody jars for all that work?"

Sheila laughed. "You need patience for this."

"Ah, it'll be worth it when you're rich and famous. Is that the carrot seed oil you're adding to the jars?"

"Exactly. I could vary the oils in each jar. Dad's keen for me to try his lavender."

"What's that good for?"

"It's supposed to promote the growth of new cells. It might be helpful for eczema too. We can try it some time. Now we'll put the jars into the fridge to set."

"Speaking of jars, do you want to go for a drink?"

"No, better not. Caroline?"

"Yeah?"

"You wouldn't take Mam out for one, would you?" Sheila gave her a pleading look.

"No problem."

"You're a brick."

"Is your dad awake? I'll slip into him for a minute."

"I think he is. I'll keep your half of the profits in the fridge for you."

"I'm getting a jar?"

"You did half the work," Sheila insisted.

* * *

Sheila joined Peadar for lunch in the UCG canteen on the following Tuesday.

"What have you got on the carrageen?"

"I'm studying its constituency. Mucilaginous fifty-five percent, nitrogenous ten percent, mineral fifteen percent. Useful as a gum or glue."

"Not very helpful. What about the iodine?"

"Yes, it's used in photography, dyes and medicine. It's sometimes used in the treatment of thyroid disease."

"But what about the skin? I've read that it's used in pharmaceutical preparations."

"It is, as a suspension medium. It could act as a kind of gel to bind your other ingredients."

Sheila was disgruntled. "There's got to be more to it than that." She couldn't hide her frustration.

"More coffee?" Peadar tried to placate her.

"No thanks. Look, I'm really grateful for all you've done. But Peadar, you should have seen those women. Honestly, they looked wonderful. I've never seen such perfect skin. They swear it's the carrageen."

Peadar stirred his coffee thoughtfully. "I'll keep at it. I've no doubt it is good for the skin. I mean people eat it so it stands to reason. When you boil it in water, it forms a jelly. You need about twenty to thirty times its weight in water."

"They use it in their baths," said Sheila.

"Well, what about a bath gel?" he asked hopefully.

"Yeah. But there must be some way of incorporating it into my creams."

Sheila was like a dog with a bone. She wasn't going to give in.

"As I said," Peadar continued, "I'm not finished my investigations. It must have properties which are good for the skin, but I'm not sure about its rejuvinating powers."

"I wish you could see the women in that village."

"Why don't you take me out to this Shangri-La next weekend?" he suggested.

"OK. It depends on how Dad is. Sunday maybe?"

"Sunday's fine. We'll bring my car," he added with a grin.

* * *

Carrigeen lay sleepy and deserted in the July sunshine. They walked through the village, and around by the lake.

"It's beautiful here." Peadar sat on a tree stump. "No sound but the birds."

"Isn't it fantastic? So peaceful," Sheila agreed.

"This valley is a wonderful location for the village. It's a pity the cottages and houses are so shabby and run-down."

"It's a poor area," Sheila said. "Most of the young people have emigrated or gone to Dublin or Galway. Jobs are practically non-existent."

"Come on. We didn't come here to sit and stare. How far to the shore?"

"Five minutes. Race you." Sheila took off like a hare. Peadar puffed along behind her. He'd definitely have to lose weight, he told himself.

They clambered over the slippery rocks, gathering up the purple and brown seaweed. Sheila's long auburn hair blew softly in the gentle sea breeze. Peadar thought she'd never looked so beautiful. She seemed to be in her natural element with the dark blue sea and the white foam and the sun beating down on the rocks. She'd pulled her trousers up around her knees. She wore no make up and her skin had a translucent quality. He longed to take her in his arms and kiss her. But he knew that was impossible. Even now in such a happy moment, he could see that faraway look in her eyes. The expression, although smiling, was tinged with sadness. He wished he could make her happy.

"Is this enough?" She shouted gaily at him, her arms full of the sticky Irish moss. "Look at these bits up here, they're greenish yellow. They look totally different."

"Bleached by the sun." He joined her on the upper rock. "Sheila. Look over there." Peadar pointed excitedly to a clump of bushes with silver-green leaves and pale blue flowers.

Sheila bounded over the rocks up to a point further away from the sea. She knelt down to examine a bush and a bee almost landed on her nose. She screamed.

"What's wrong?" He came up behind her.

"Nearly bloody stung." She laughed.

"Bees won't sting you." He knelt down and smelled the flowers. "It's rosemary, I think. It has a lovely smell."

Sheila smelt the perfume of the flowers. "Rosemary, are you sure?"

"Yes. Pick some and we'll bring it back. We could be on to something."

They picked some of the wild flowers and Peadar stuffed them into the bag along with the carrageen.

By the time they got back to the village, the pub was open. Seamus was delighted to see her again. They bought him a Guinness and one for his son, who was back from England on holidays. Conor had been a potter in the area, but lack of work had forced him to go to away.

"I'm working on the roads along with the rest of the Paddies."

"You miss home?" Peadar asked sympathetically.

"Yeah, I do. I'm there ten years, but I never got used to it. I hate the labouring. I miss the pottery too. I still have the kiln. When I've saved enough I want to come home and give it another go."

Seamus nodded gravely. "We'd love to have you home."

"Who owns the barn at the end of town?" Sheila inquired.

"Dad does," Conor replied, nodding over at Seamus. "It hasn't been used in years. There used to be dances there in the old days."

"And the cottage beside it?"

"His too. That's where meself and the wife are staying at the moment. It's quite damp. It needs a lot of work. Why? Are you thinking of buying?" He laughed.

Sheila smiled. "You'd never know."

Seamus sat up and took notice. This could be an opportunity to make a few bob.

The owner's wife came over to say hello.

"Hi Maura. This is a friend of mine, Peadar Joyce."

Maura shook hands. "I believe you're interested in the carrageen? Seamus was telling us."

"We are," Sheila replied. "We found something else today. Peadar, show her."

Peadar took out a sprig of the rosemary and handed it to Maura.

"Aye, the sea dew. Hasn't it the lovely smell though?"

"Sea dew?" Peadar exclaimed. "We thought it was rosemary."

"It is, lad. In these parts we call it the dew of the sea."

"Of course," it struck Peadar, "that'd be the translation from the Latin."

"You know the legend of course?" Maura asked them.

"No, what legend?" Sheila was really interested now.

"You see the blue flowers? Well, they were once white. They say that the Blessed Virgin hung her cloak on a rosemary bush, on the flight into Egypt. And what do you think happened?"

Sheila and Peadar looked at each other. What was she on about?

"The white flowers turned blue. Now, what do ye make of that?"

"Are you saying the plant has miraculous properties?" Peadar asked her.

"Ah, sure I'll leave you to decide on that. We use it a lot to decorate the altar up in the church. Sometimes, we'd burn it for incense. Sure the sea dew is great for preserving things too."

"That's right," Sheila agreed. "My mother always puts it on the meat."

"Do you remember old Rosie O'Gorman?" Maura asked Seamus. "Sure she used to smell it all the time. She said it helped to clear her head."

"Nothing helped to clear her head." Seamus sipped his pint. "She was drunk half the time."

Maura gave him a look. "Some say it's good for a blocked nose too."

"Sinusitis?" Peadar was delighted. "God, I could try that myself so."

"Some of the old folk used it for arthritis," Seamus puffed at his pipe. "Ah, there's a lot of old wives' tales knocking about! Guinness is yer only man."

The others laughed. But Sheila was intrigued. "Do the people here still use it?"

"The women do," Seamus muttered. "Dump it in their baths. That and the seaweed, God bless us."

Sheila looked pointedly at Peadar. She was absolutely thrilled.

* * *

Pat sniffed the blue flowers. "Oh God, Sheila. That brings me back."

"You know it, Dad?"

"Sure I used to grow it out the back, years ago. Until Moses decided to dig it up."

"That was one of the bushes he destroyed?"

"Yeah. That and the jasmine. Bloody pest he was."

"He grew out of it." Sheila tried to pacify him. "Look at the way he sits by your bed now. He's very faithful."

Her father leaned down to pat the cocker. "We're both getting on, old boy." The dog licked his hand. "I think our days are numbered."

Sheila had a huge lump in her throat. It was true, what he said. Moses was fourteen years old, a great age for a dog. Her father was seventy-five. He looked much older. Every day she could see a deterioration in him. But he tried to remain cheerful.

"Mary's big day is coming up soon." He lay back on his pillow.

"Yeah. I was on the phone to her last night. It's in three weeks' time. I think her mother is getting on her wick with all the wedding arrangements."

"Women love fussing. Do you like being bridesmaid?"

"Not particularly. I don't like fuss. Still, I'm proud to do it for Mary."

"He's a good lad?"

"Yeah, he's very good to her. He's doing well too."

"And she still likes the teaching?"

"She loves it. She's a born teacher. She's mad about kids."

"Well, she'll soon be having her own, no doubt."

Sheila nodded. Her father patted her hand gently. He knew she was hurting.

"Do you want a cuppa? I'm off to the kitchen to try the rosemary. Liam gave me this kind of retort flask for the distilling. I don't know if it'll work. I'd love a proper still."

Pat looked at her thoughtfully.

"You're really serious about this, aren't you?"

"I'd love to go into it full time. Fat chance of that. I'd need a premises."

"So, what's stopping you?"

"Money. I might try the bank, but I've only a couple of thousand saved. My car's on the way out too."

Pat gave a little secret smile. "This is the right time."

"Right time for what?" Sheila thought he was getting confused again.

"Go over to my wardrobe. Top shelf."

Sheila did as he asked her. She found a large envelope. "What's this?"

"Open it." Her father looked positively chuffed.

Sheila found a copy of his will. "Dad, I don't want to see this."

"Listen, my girl. We have to face facts. I'm not getting any younger or stronger."

"Dad, I won't have you talking like this. It's depressing."

"Divil a bit of it. Everybody should have a will made. Anyway, the will doesn't concern you."

Sheila was slightly taken aback. Her father smiled at her.

"Look in the small envelope."

Sheila drew out a cheque and handed it to him.

"This is for you." He handed it back to her.

Sheila looked at it in disbelief. The cheque was for twenty thousand pounds and was made payable to her.

"Dad, I can't accept this. It's a fortune." Sheila gasped.

"No, it's not a fortune. But it may be enough to set you up."

"But this is your nest egg. I couldn't take it." She protested.

"It's the money from the farm. The money's been sitting in the bank for nearly twenty years, gathering interest. I don't need it. What could I spend it on from this bed? Last week I wrote this cheque and I want you to have it."

Sheila bit her lip. "What about Seán?"

"Seán'll be getting this house when your mother dies." He spoke softly.

"I can't stand this, all this talk of death." Sheila sighed loudly.

"You're young. Why should you talk about it? At my age though, it's different. These things have to be faced."

She hugged him. "Dad, please don't talk about dying again. I really can't stand it."

The old man patted her head, just like he used to do when she was a child.

"It's all right, Sheila. I've no intention of dying yet. But I want to live to see you enjoy that money. I want to be able to see you start up your business and make a success of it. That'll keep me going better than anything else."

"What if it isn't a success? What if I make a mess of it?"

"You won't. You've great determination. You get that from your mother."

"Mam? What's she going to say?"

"What she doesn't know won't hurt her." He smiled again.

"Oh no, Dad. She'll have to be told, and Seán too."

"Ah, let them think you've borrowed it." He couldn't see the problem. He didn't think it was any of their business.

"I couldn't start with a lie. It would be like a bad omen. Everything has to be above board." Sheila was adamant.

"Whatever you like," he sighed. "If you can face the wrath of that pair, good luck to you."

Sheila kissed him.

* * *

That night she called over to Peadar with her great news. He was astounded.

"You're really going to do it?"

"Yep. I'm going to work out my notice with Liam. Then I'm off to make Seamus an offer on his cottage and his barn."

"You'd set up in Carrigeen?"

"Where better? Isn't that where I'll be getting the raw materials?"

Peadar was torn between delight and disappointment. "Are you going to move over there?"

"No, I wouldn't leave Dad. Sure it's only an hour's run from Galway."

"In a good car, maybe."

"Ah, the mini will be a thing of the past," Sheila sang nasally, in an effort to mimic Dylan. "The times, they are a changin'!"

"What did your mother say?"

"Nothing yet. I haven't told her. You're the first. Peadar, I'm hoping you'll continue to help?"

"Wild horses wouldn't keep me away." He was relieved. "You'll be needing a lab."

"Yeah, and a distilling room." Her enthusiasm was infectious.

"When we expand we could employ some of my students for holiday work."

"Cheap labour? You're catching on fast." She laughed at his puzzled expression. "I'm only kidding. We can get some of the locals to harvest the carrageen."

"Next you'll be employing that Conor to make the jars and pots for you."

"Jesus, Peadar you're brilliant. That's a fantastic idea."

"Hold it, hold it, woman. I think we're getting a bit carried away."

"Think big. That's my motto from now on."

In the five years he'd known her, Peadar had never seen her so excited, so happy.

"Can you bear some bad news?" he asked.

"What?" What was he going to tell her?

"It's about the carrageen."

"Go on." By his expression, Sheila knew she wasn't going to like this.

"It's just as I told you already. The thallus, which is the fruitful part we'd use, is rich in mucilage."

"So?" Sheila interrupted him rudely.

"It has emollient and laxative properties." He tried not to smile.

"Laxative?" Sheila repeated, "laxative properties?"

He wanted to say: "I know you don't give a shit about that," but he didn't think she'd appreciate the joke. So he continued in a serious tone. "In the pharmaceutical industry, the thallus is used to treat chronic diarrhoea for its emollient properties and as a laxative against constipation."

If she kept glaring at him like this, he'd need to rush to the loo himself.

Sheila was fuming. "That's it?" She challenged him.

"No," Peadar continued in the same dead-pan tone. "It's also recommended as an expectorant."

"Are you telling me that carrageen can't be used for cosmetics." Sheila was fit to be tied.

"No, that's not what I'm saying. It's used for relaxing baths and in slenderising products."

"Bloody marvellous." She was not impressed.

"Look Sheila, there's no point in taking this out on me. I told you it could be used as a gel for your other ingredients. It's the essential oils that have the real skin properties. Carrigeen has the emollient which would be good for soothing the skin. You'll have to be happy with that."

Peadar could go and jump. He was suffering from chronic diarrhoea himself. Verbal diarrhoea. She didn't care what he said. The women in Carrigeen swore by it. They had beautiful skin. That was proof enough for her. He said she could use it to bind her other ingredients. She'd be using it for that all right, but she knew in her gut that it was good for the skin too. "If it's good for the insides, it's good for the outside," her mother always said. Didn't everyone know that mothers were always right?

CHAPTER TWELVE

Emily O'Callaghan triumphantly brought in the statue of the Child of Prague from the back garden. Now, let Maurice laugh all he liked. The sun beat down in all its glory. No doubt he'd dryly point out to her that they were having a heat wave anyway, but you couldn't rely on a heat wave in a country where it was possible to have the four seasons in one day. She cleaned off the statue and put it back in its place in the hall. She was getting the breakfast tray ready when she heard her husband roar:

"Em . . . Emily . . . EM-IL-Y."

Jesus, Mary and Holy Saint Joseph, you'd need the patience of Job with that man.

"I'm coming," she roared back as she trundled up the stairs. He was all caught up in his shirt and trousers.

"Here," she scoffed at him. "Let me do it. You're as helpless as a baby."

"Bloody stupid suit," he muttered as she untangled him and fixed his collar. "They named it well, I feel like a right monkey."

"You look gorgeous." She beamed at him. "You'll be the handsomest man there."

He did look great in his tails. "Try on your top hat." She handed it to him.

He examined himself in the mirror. "What am I like?" he asked her despairingly.

"Spencer Tracy," she assured him as she left to wake the girls.

No need. They were already up. Joanne came out of the bathroom. "Mornin', Ma. Isn't she lucky with the day?" She kissed her mother. "How long are you up?"

"Ages. I'll bring some breakfast up to this pair."

"Wouldn't bother. Sheila is giving Mary a massage."

"A massage? Good God!"

"Yeah, far out. Lavender oil, she says it has a calming effect."

"God, I wish she'd try it on your father then. He's like a herring on a grill."

Joanne had a mental picture of the beautiful Sheila, dressed in sexy underwear, giving her poor old dad a massage. The mind boggled.

"What time did Brian go out?" Joanne was annoyed that her husband had left early on Mary's wedding day, leaving her to look after the kids. Still, he was a groomsman so she supposed he had things to do.

"He went with Peter about an hour ago to collect the flowers. They'll call over to Jim's house then. He'll be needing moral support too. I hope they don't call into the pub on the way back. What time is your appointment in Frank Hession's?"

"Ten-thirty. Do you want a hand with the breakfast?"

"No, I'll just give them scrambled eggs. What would you like?"

"Don't worry about me. I'll have some cereal with the kids. Are they out the back?"

"Yeah. Do you want me to call them in?"

"Just Orla. I'll have to get her dressed. I'm sorry now that Mary has her as flower girl. I'll never be able to keep her clean."

"Listen, leave her be for the moment. I'll get her ready when the three of you go to get your hair done."

"You're a star."

Maurice paced up and down his bedroom. He'd never get this speech learned off. He'd start with great gusto, get carried away and then dry up. He wanted to be sincere without being maudlin. He wanted to throw in a few gags, but they shouldn't be corny or in bad taste. He'd welcome the Ryans, the other guests, tell Jim he was delighted to have him as a son-in-law and then tell a story about Mary when she was young. What about the time he took her fishing and she fell out of the boat? Perhaps not. God, he remembered that day well. She was like a drowned rat when he pulled her out, but she just laughed and suggested that they stuck to fish fingers. She was a great kid. He was happy that she'd found such a good man, but he had to admit he was sad too. There was something very final about it all. By four o'clock today she wouldn't even have his name.

"Quick! Give me a fag," Mary begged, eyes closed. Sheila smoothed on her eye-shadow.

"In a minute. Hang on. I think you'd better do the mascara yourself."

"OK. Fag first?" she implored.

Sheila handed her the packet. It was a good job that Mary was still in her slip and bra. Ashes on the wedding dress wouldn't be the thing. Mary took a long drag on the cigarette.

"That's better." She left the cigarette burning in the ash-tray as her shaky hand applied the mascara brush to her long lashes.

"Don't overdo it," Sheila warned. "You don't need much. You've lovely eyes."

"There. That's it. OK?"

"Gorgeous." Sheila said sincerely. "Your gold stud earrings are something old. Your dress is something new. Here. Put on the garter, something borrowed.

"I forgot something blue." Mary panicked.

Sheila handed her a sprig of dried rosemary. "Stick it in the garter."

"Rosemary, that's for remembrance," Mary quoted. "Very apt."

"Now for the dress." Sheila took it from its tissue paper. She helped Mary into it and fastened the pearl buttons at the back. The gown was a soft white crêpe-de-chine. It had a low round collar, short puffed sleeves and it fell in folds from under the bust. Reminiscent of Jane Austen in its simplicity. It had a short train. Her long black hair was swept up into a bunch of curls. The head-dress, a wreath of silk flowers, fitted nicely around the curls. Sheila fixed it in place and draped the long net veil. She stepped back to get a better look.

"Mary," she whispered, "you're so pretty. No, don't hug me. You'll crease everything!"

Mary smiled. "Thanks for everything, Sheila. Some day, I'll do the honours for you.

"You look lovely, Joanne," Emily complimented her elder daughter. "He did a great job with your hair." Joanne's dark straight hair was cut in a fashionable page-boy style. The soft jade crêpe dress suited her. Joanne was thrilled that she didn't have to wear the usual satin. She was too plump for that.

"If you think I look good, wait till you see Sheila. She's stunning."

"Is she still helping Mary to dress?"

"Yeah. Her boyfriend just phoned and said he'd meet us at the church."

"I don't think you should call him her boyfriend, dear. Sheila says they're just good friends." Emily had already made that mistake.

"Thanks for dressing Orla for me. She looks a treat. It was great the way the dressmaker altered her communion dress. The jade sash and trim are just the ticket."

"Here, bring these up to them."

"Vodka? Do you think that's all right before Mass?" Joanne was doubtful.

"One little drink won't do any harm. Mary must be quaking, despite the lavender massage. And your father and Paul are up there, locked into my bedroom, guzzling whiskey. The father of the bride and the best man. God knows what their speeches will be like.

Emily got into her new beige suit. She had a coffee-coloured blouse, with shoes and bag to match. Her hat was beige with a wide coffee ribbon. She checked herself carefully in the wardrobe mirror. Not bad. She'd better organise the men. She knocked on the bedroom door. Paul unlocked it. Her son looked really well in his wedding attire. He had the same dark curls as Mary and was tall and well built. He gave his mother an appreciative whistle. She gave him a dig in the ribs. Maurice swirled her around. "My lady wife will outshine the bride."

"That's the whiskey talking," she said in mock reproof. "The wedding cars will be here in half an hour. Paul, are you all right for driving? It's time you picked up Jim."

"I only had the one, Mother dear." He put on his jacket and was half way down the stairs when Emily called after him, "Your hat. You forgot your top hat."

He bounded back into the room. "No sweat, see you in church."

She raised her eyes to heaven. "Now, Maurice. Are you finally ready?"

"Yes, yes, woman, stop fussing. Joanne, Sheila and yourself go in the first limousine. Mary and I follow a few minutes later. What about the kids?"

"Brian is taking them in their car."

"He won't be able to drink at the wedding?" Maurice was aghast.

"He will. His father's a teetotaller. He'll drive them home tonight."

"Oh God, Mr Gordon Davis, I'd forgotten he was coming. Mean as shite. Remember that lousy present he gave to Joanne and Brian on their wedding day? Waterford glass. For his own son. I didn't mind forking out on the wedding. Wouldn't you think he could have given them some cash? They had to honeymoon in Wexford. Mean old bastard. If he stood on his wallet he could paint the ceiling."

"Will you be charitable on your daughter's wedding day, for God's sake." Emily was in no mood to listen to this.

The neighbours were all gathered outside the terraced house on the Lower Drumcondra Road. The bridesmaids were the first to emerge. Sheila, as Joanne had said, looked stunning. The green of the dress and the tiny wreath set off her luxurious auburn hair. Her slim figure seemed to float down the garden path. Joanne held Orla's hand until they were safely in the car. Traffic was always busy on this road. They were finally joined by Emily, who'd been waylaid by the neighbours who wanted a blow-by-blow account of the morning's proceedings.

Maurice waited impatiently in the hall for his daughter. He was up the walls. He had to do this well today for Mary's sake. God, he hated these fussy affairs. There was a lot to be said for elopement. His new shoes were squeezing the life out of him. His collar was too tight. He was in a sweat.

He'd be OK once he reached the top of the church. He hated the thought of the walk up the aisle. He'd never be able to time his steps to the wedding march. Now, one last check that he'd the speech in his pocket.

Mary appeared on the top of the landing. "Are you right, Dad?"

She stood there, holding her bouquet, serene as royalty. She was beautiful.

Peadar sat in his pew and admired Iona Church. It was an elegant building inside and out. Huge pillars supported the arched roof. The imposing altar with its high dome was very impressive. Masses of white flowers and lighted candles lent their own enchantment. The stained-glass windows were high and narrow, but the sunlight filtered through. The church reminded him of cathedrals he'd seen in England. There was a large party of guests sitting on both sides. He felt out of place. It'd be ages before he could be with Sheila. She'd be busy with the wedding party till after the meal. He was beginning to regret that he'd come. Jim Ryan seemed very nervous. Paul O'Callaghan whispered earnestly to him. The other groomsman ushered the last few guests into their seats. He must be Mary's brother-in-law from England. God, he didn't even know

169

who was who at this damn wedding. He definitely shouldn't have come. It wasn't as if he were Sheila's boyfriend. They might all think he was. Oh God, why did he let Sheila persuade him to come? Suddenly the wedding march sounded.

It was the nicest Mass Sheila had ever been at. A special choir from Mary's school sang. The *Panis Angelicus* always had an effect on her. But when she heard Gounod's *Ave Maria* she couldn't stop the tears. She sat up at the side of the altar with Joanne, facing Paul and Brian on the other side. Everyone was visibly moved. Emily O'Callaghan dabbed her cheeks with her hankie. Sheila gulped hard. It was impossible to remain dry-eyed. Mary radiated happiness as she said, "I do". When the priest pronounced them "man and wife", the congregation burst into spontaneous applause. Sheila didn't know what she felt.

She was delighted for Mary. This was what Mary had always wanted. But Sheila felt a pang of loneliness. Mary was married. Mrs Mary Ryan. She looked positively ecstatic. What must it be like to be that happy? To have your dreams come true? Would she ever find such happiness? Would she ever love a man the way that Mary loved Jim? She noticed Peadar give her a longing look.

After the signing of the register came the inevitable photographs. The bride and groom in front of the church door. The bride and bridesmaids in front of the grotto. The groom and groomsmen in front of the church door. The bride's family beside the shrubbery. The groom's family ditto. The two families together. Poor Jim was short of immediate family. His parents looked a bit pained. The group photo. That took about fifteen minutes to organise. Sheila introduced Peadar to Mary's Uncle Joe who went with him out to the reception in Clontarf Castle. Then the mad dash out to the rose garden in St Anne's for more photos of the wedding group.

Clontarf Castle did them proud. Emily loved its old world style and high ceilings, panelled walls and exquisite furniture and chandeliers. The sherry reception loosened things up as the two families began to mix. Jim's father, Denis, was a dote. His mother, Eileen, was a bit withdrawn, but that was understandable. Her only child had just got married. It was a big deal. Jim's Aunt Phyllis and Uncle Fred were the life and soul of the party. The proverbial Darby and Joan. They still held hands. Mary hoped that she and Jim would be like that after twenty years of marriage. Most of the other guests on Jim's side were business acquaintances. Sheila couldn't help noticing that one of these men was giving her looks. He was a fine thing. Tall, thin, dark hair and moustache. "Who's he?" Sheila pointed him out to Mary.

"John Harris. The solicitor for Jim's firm. He's been staring at you for ages. Bloody cheek. That's his wife in the pink dress."

"He's very handsome," Sheila whispered.

"Yeah," Mary agreed. "Joanne said she could wet her knickers looking at him. Pity he's spoken for. Jim says his marriage is a farce. No kids."

The meal was really good, much better than the

average wedding fare. The beef was tender, the carrots and broccoli crisp, not like the usual mush. The fresh fruit salad was mouth watering. Then came the speeches. Paul spoke well, as did Denis Ryan. Emily's heart was in her mouth when Maurice got to his feet. He was grand, a bit nervous, but he managed to get a polite laugh or two if he didn't exactly make them roll in the aisles. He had a stiff whiskey the minute he sat down. Jim's speech was the best. He thanked his mother and father. Eileen Ryan had a little cry while Denis consoled her. He spoke about how much he loved Mary and how he'd do his best to make her happy. Sheila knew how happy he'd made her already. They toasted the bride and groom. When they toasted the bridesmaids, John Harris gave Sheila a big wink. She was furious that he'd caught her looking in his direction. Peadar saw the wink too and his face was like thunder.

The three-piece band was typical. They had to cater for the oldies and the younger set. Jim and Mary took the floor to the tune of "Michelle" (at Mary's request). Everyone clapped. They were followed by Joanne and Brian and Sheila and Paul. Soon everyone was on their feet and the two sets of parents swapped partners. Sheila danced with Peadar. He was disgruntled. Uncle Joe had bored him stiff throughout the meal. He felt like getting drunk, but he had to stay sober because he was driving. Sheila had booked him into the Skylon. He could pick her up from O'Callaghans' the following morning. Sheila did her best to cheer him up. The band started "Some Enchanted Evening" and Peadar had begun to unwind when he felt a tap on the shoulder.

"Mind if I cut in?" It was John Harris. Sheila's heart skipped a beat. Peadar skulked off as Sheila was swept off. He held her tightly and hummed into her ear. "And somehow you know, you know even then, that somewhere you'll see her again and again."

He was so good looking. Sheila's heart thumped. God, what if he could feel it beating? He pressed up against her so tight she could hardly breathe. The music was slow and smoochy. She could feel every part of him. He was aroused. She was too excited to be offended. He swirled her around and around, holding her close. They were like one body. Fused together. She knew this was ridiculous, but she never wanted the dance to end.

"I want you," he whispered into her ear. On and on, round and round. Sheila felt dizzy. The steady drumbeat of the waltz reverberated in her ears. The dancers beside them floated by in a haze. The music, the lights, his body against her. She might have fainted if he hadn't held her so tightly. She could smell his aftershave. She could feel the wispy touch of his lips on her neck. Suddenly the music stopped.

"I have to see you again," he said urgently. Sheila stared into his eyes. The magic had disappeared with the music.

"Where's your wife?" she said coldly. He bowed

stiffly and went back to his table. Sheila went back to Peadar.

Then came the sing-song. Mary naturally sang a Beatles song with her guitar. "In My Life" was a good choice. Every time she sang the refrain: "In my life I loved you more," she looked at Jim. She had a lovely sweet voice. Denis Ryan sang next. He had a mellow baritone voice and gave a great rendition of "Old Man River". Maurice insisted on getting up. He was a bit tipsy and Emily did her best to drag him back. She was mortified when he started "Phil the Fluter's Ball". The composer hadn't intended five changes of key. But what really took the biscuit was Uncle Fred's version of "This is My Lovely Day." He screeched the top notes and made the rest of it so melodramatic that Aunt Phyllis gave him a good puck when he tottered back to her. Sheila cringed with embarrassment. There was no way she could be prevailed upon to sing. Mercifully, the band started up again.

Mary came down in her going-away outfit. It was a beautiful red suit. Long jacket and straight mini skirt. Time to throw the bouquet. She aimed it right at Sheila who was standing with Peadar at the foot of the stairs. Sheila stepped out of the way. The bouquet was caught by little Orla. Peadar went red. The bride and groom ran out to the taxi, pursued by most of the wedding group. Sheila got caught at the back of the crowd. She tried to make her way to the car, but she couldn't. Amid all the hugging and kissing, Sheila couldn't get through. The taxi pulled out, laden with old boots and a "Just Married" cardboard sign. It sped away. They were gone. Off to a secret destination for the night and the plane tomorrow to Antibes, paid for by the Ryans. Sheila stood there, shivering in the night air. Abandoned for the second time in her life.

Peadar was inside sitting with Jim's uncle and aunt. He had a vodka waiting for her.

"Did you say goodbye?" he asked her.

"Didn't get the chance." Sheila was close to tears.

"Never mind, love," Uncle Fred said kindly. "You'll see them when they get back."

She wouldn't. She'd be back in Galway by then, up to her neck in hassle. She had to start things rolling. She'd one more week in the chemist and then it would be full steam ahead. There was so much to organise. She hadn't told Seán yet or her mother. She could imagine their reactions to her windfall. When would she see Mary and Jim again? Mary and Jim. A couple. They'd set up home together. Mary would go back to school. Winter would soon be upon them. Sheila would be busy, very busy. It would never be the same again. Never.

"Have you two got any children?" Aunt Phyllis asked politely.

Peadar flinched. "We're not married," he answered quickly.

No, Sheila thought wretchedly. No marriage . . . no kids. You can't have one without the other. No children. Plural noun. Children. But she had a child, didn't she? She had a daughter somewhere out there. Perhaps in this very city. Where was she now?

* * *

Two streets away, in the quiet suburb of Clontarf, Liz Shaw looked in on her sleeping daughter. The little auburn curls peeped out of the pink covers. A nightlight flickered on the bedside table. Liz gently blew it out.

"Goodnight, sleep tight and don't let the bugs bite," she whispered to her child as she did every night.

"Is she still awake?" Liz's husband Frank approached the bed.

"No, she's fast asleep. What story did you tell her tonight?"

"Cinderella. That's her favourite." He tucked in the eiderdown round the child's feet. "Don't want her to catch cold."

"Did you check Peter?"

"Yeah. He'd kicked off all his blankets. It's time we put him in a bed too," he sighed. "They grow up so fast."

Liz nodded. These were the precious moments. They wouldn't last forever. They'd been so lucky to get these two. Privileged. She leaned down and kissed her daughter lightly on the cheek.

"Goodnight, my darling Karen. Sweet dreams."

CHAPTER THIRTEEN

"Twenty thousand pounds!" Seán hissed. "Twenty thousand!"

His mother shrank. "Try to keep calm, love."

"It's scandalous. My God, what's he thinking of? It's the stroke. It's addled his brain. Think of it . . . twenty thousand pounds. I could buy three houses for that."

No denying that. Rita felt aggrieved too, but she managed to hide it better. "She's going to start a skin care business." In her naïveté, Rita thought that this would appease him. It had the opposite effect.

"A business. Ha! What the hell does Sheila know about business? It gets better and better. A business, if you don't mind. What next? She's no background in business. You have to have the know-how. You can't just up and start a business. Farcical, that's what it is. Bloody farcical."

"Well, she does seem to know her stuff when it comes to those creams. O'Flaherty's can't get enough of them. She's made batches and batches and they're walking out of the shop. I think there is a market for that type of thing."

"Fine, fine. Let her sell her creams to O'Flaherty

then. That's a different matter. She could have a nice little sideline there. But how the hell can she start up a business on her own? Women don't do that, for God's sake. She needs her head examined." He thumped the table violently.

"She'll have Peadar to help her."

"Peadar? Don't make me laugh. What use is he? He's a bloody academic not a businessman. He's like a child. I suppose he thinks he's on to a good thing."

"He's investing some money in it, as far as I know," Rita replied.

"How much? How much is he going to invest? That's what I'd like to know. And where are they going to set up this cosy little enterprise. In the boudoir?" He was practically foaming at the mouth by now.

"She's bought a place in Carrigeen. She's gone into the solicitor this morning to sign the contract."

"Carraig what? Carrigeen? Jesus, there's a village called after that slimy stuff?"

"It's somewhere on the road to Cleggan, I think." Rita was upset by this onslaught. It wasn't her fault.

"Oh my God, sure that's in the back of beyond. How is she going to set up a business in the back of beyond?"

"She said most of her raw materials are there."

"Raw is the operative word when it comes to Sheila. And Peadar? Christ Almighty, what a combination! Has she a name for this so-called company?"

"I don't know, love. Mary gave her some

suggestions, so did Liam. Maybe Caroline might have some suggestions. Hasn't she great experience in that type of thing? Sure she worked in that advertising agency before you married her."

Seán glared at his mother. "Caroline was a graphic artist not a copywriter. She won't be much help. Where does she think she'll get enough customers to keep a business going?"

"She'll try the other chemists in the area. Liam thinks she'll get customers, no problem."

"Crap. Utter crap. I suppose she intends to move out there?" The thought suddenly struck him that he might have to help his mother to take care of his father.

"No, no. She'll stay here. She'll have to get a new car."

"Ah sure why wouldn't she? Sure a new car'd be grand for her. Grand altogether. Meantime, Caroline and I've to settle for an eight-year-old Cortina which we have to share. I've to use the bike when she picks up the kids from school. Local doctor on bike. Great for the image, isn't it? What's she going to buy? A Mercedes?" Seán's voice reached a pitch of anger Rita had never heard before. "She'll be bankrupt in a year. If she lasts that long."

"I don't know, love. Your father thinks she could make a go of it, anyway. He thinks Sheila's quite shrewd."

He laughed bitterly. "Shrewd. Yeah, she must be quite astute, not to mention downright cute, to wangle that amount of money out of the old man. Poor unfortunate bugger. It's a disgrace!"

"Would you like another cup of tea?" Rita asked meekly.

"Tea? Tea? I haven't time for tea. I've to get back to my practice. I've to earn a crust. Twenty thousand pounds! I could start up a private clinic with that. At least I'm qualified. Jesus, I can't believe this. Dad is very poorly. Does Sheila realise that? This isn't an ideal time for her to get involved in such a scheme. She's really selfish. She always was."

Rita agreed with her son up to a point. Pat should have thought this out a bit more carefully. But you couldn't talk to him. Once Pat Crosby made up his mind, that was that. She too had been upset when she'd first heard. She thought it was unfair to Seán. But Pat never listened to her. He just pretended to, she thought sadly. In all their married years, she'd never known what salary he earned. She certainly hadn't known about this inheritance. She had scrimped and saved for years when Seán was in college and again when Sheila went to UCD. They hadn't been on a decent holiday in years. She was entitled to some of that money as well.

Was Seán right? Was Pat confused? No, he was bedridden now and his speech was bad again, but he was perfectly coherent in his thinking. When Sheila was ill years ago, Pat had wanted to help her. He'd offered her a foreign holiday, but she refused. But she couldn't refuse this chance. It was what she'd always wanted, her own business. Rita decided to accept it. Seán was very unfair to say that Sheila was selfish. Nothing could be further from the truth. Sheila was very good to her father. She sat with him every evening and talked to him for hours. He'd lost most of the vision in his left eye. She read to him, all his favourites, Dickens, Hardy and Scott. She got up early in the morning to tend to him before she went to work. She even came home at lunch-time with the paper for him. Sheila was a great help to her as well. She cleaned the house on her days off. No, when she thought about it like that, she wouldn't begrudge her daughter. Sheila deserved the money.

She fervently hoped that the business would be a success. Times had changed. Sheila wasn't interested in marriage and children. Why shouldn't a woman have a successful career instead? Or indeed both, if that's what she wanted? Caroline was bored being the little housewife, Rita was sure of that. Caroline was at a loose end now that the twins were in school most of the day. Sheila had no wish to settle down. She'd said that often enough. Maybe she had a point? How did any of us know what was right for another? Although Rita still harboured secret desires of her daughter getting married and producing grandchildren for her, she'd have to recognise the fact that this wasn't what Sheila wanted at this moment. She'd dreamt of this business for ages. It wasn't a passing phase. The girl was almost obsessed by the idea. She was very determined. Deep down, Rita admired Sheila's get-up-and-go. Couldn't the husband and children come later, at a more opportune time? She was still only twenty-four after all. She'd her whole life ahead of her. Let her get this business bug out of her system. If she did fail, so what? At least she wouldn't be up to her neck in debt. But Rita didn't think her daughter would fail. Neither did Peadar or Caroline. As for Liam O'Flaherty, he thought Sheila had the Midas touch.

Sheila rearranged the window display for the last time. Her last day on the job. Unbelievable. She was really excited about her new business, but she was frightened too. Liam pulled down the shutters and locked the door.

"What are you doing? It's not six o'clock yet." She'd never seen him close early before. This was their best time of the day. Lots of customers came in on their way home from work.

"We have to mark the occasion," Liam insisted. There was a tap on the window and Kate O'Flaherty bustled in. Before Sheila knew it the champagne was popped and they drank a toast to her success.

"I'm going to miss this place. Honestly."

"Not as much as we're going to miss you. You've made this shop what it is today, Sheila. I'll never forget you for that. Ah, sure won't we be seeing you all the time? You'll be in with your merchandise, what?"

"I hope so. I'm relying on you two to sell lots of it. Murphy's and O'Reilly's have given me an order too."

"You'll be run off your feet, girl. This is only the start. I can foresee a great future for you. You're a natural."

"I hope you're right," Sheila gulped down the rest of her drink. "Natural. That's what Mary wants me to call my skin care range, Natural Woman. What do you think?"

"Great," Kate enthused. "It's a great name. It makes sense. You're using natural ingredients. It's a name that will appeal to women. I can just see it now. You'll need some nicely decorated bottles and containers."

"I'm thinking of pottery. It's just an idea."

"A brilliant one. Pottery jars are so pretty. God, you definitely have the makings of an entrepreneur." Kate toasted her again. "Here's to Natural Woman."

"I'll miss working here though. We had some good laughs."

"I'm sorry to lose you. Who'll protect me from this dragon?" Liam groaned. Kate punched him playfully.

"Leaving a job's never easy, but I know you're doing the right thing." Liam handed her a package. "A token of our esteem, as they say." He laughed nervously. Sheila fumbled with the string. She unwrapped the parcel to discover more wrapping inside. She peeled off layer after layer. "You've spent a fortune on wrapping paper!" Smaller and smaller, more and more paper. Finally she got to the end of it. A tiny box.

"I'm afraid to open it!" she exclaimed.

"Go on, love," Kate egged her on.

Sheila opened the box. Keys. Car keys. She was speechless.

"Come on." Liam grabbed her. "It's round the back."

* * *

"How did your last day go?" Caroline, tea towel in hand, opened the door.

Sheila grinned at her. "Fancy a spin?"

"The car. You bought the car?" Caroline screamed with delight.

"Didn't buy it. Liam and Kate gave it to me as a present. Can you believe it?" Sheila skipped with excitement. "Come on, come on. It's brilliant."

"The kids. I can't leave the kids."

Sheila shouted up the stairs, "Hey you two, coming for a drive in my new car?"

"Shh, Seán has a few in the surgery," Caroline warned her.

"Oops, sorry." Sheila hugged her nephew and niece. The four of them piled out onto the street to behold the new marvel. Caroline gaped in awe.

The brand new Renault 16 TS was parked at the kerb. A dark red saloon.

"Climb aboard everyone," Sheila shouted merrily.

Ciara and Colm clambered into the back. "Deadly!" was Colm's reaction.

"God, Sheila, I love the smell." Caroline ran her hands over the black leather upholstery. "The seats are real comfortable. Is that the gearshift? Up under the steering column? I don't know if I'd like that."

"I'll get used to it. Look, Caroline, there's even a

left arm rest. You can rest your arm when you're changing gear."

Sheila put the key in the ignition and the car spluttered. "Sorry, I'm not used to it yet." Another try and they were off. The car ran smoothly down the street and they headed off to Salthill. "The suspension's terrific. Just what I'll need on my trips to Connemara."

"And around the country," Caroline added. "You'll be delivering far and wide."

"Some day, with any luck. So, what do you think of it?"

"Fabulous. What a present. Still, it's no more than you deserve. You gave that shop your all."

"See where the kids are sitting, that's all storage space. The hatchback's great, like a double boot. I'll need that for lugging my wares around."

"Can we stop for chips, Sheila?" Ciara asked solemnly. She thought she'd no chance.

"Why not? But after that we'll have to get back." She pulled up in front of the chipper. She whispered to Caroline, "I haven't the insurance fixed up yet. Can you imagine me being stopped? Poor Dad would have a seizure. Ex-local sergeant's daughter charged for no insurance. Great story for the local rag."

"Sheila, Seán was talking about your dad last night. He thinks he's quite bad. He'll know more when he gets the test results back."

"He's been bad before and he rallied round." Sheila locked the car door and examined the registration. 488 ZI. "Hope it's a lucky number."

"Yeah." Caroline said no more. Sheila was kidding herself if she thought her father was going to come out of this. But why worry her unduly? She was ecstatic about her car. Let her enjoy the moment.

CHAPTER FOURTEEN

Pat woke early. It was a grey Sunday morning. Seven o'clock. Good, he'd have the priest today. He was thankful to be able to receive Holy Communion. He remembered the days when he was a daily communicant. He never missed. He'd leave the house at seven, walk up to town to the early Mass and go on to work. God, if he could only walk again. His body felt like an old sack. He had no feeling now in his legs. The left side of his face was paralysed and that affected his speech. It was really frustrating when he couldn't make himself understood. He was blind in the left eye and the vision in the other one was dim.

So they were moving him downstairs. That was good. It would be easier on Rita, save her climbing the stairs all day. He missed the telly, especially the sports programmes. At least he had the radio. The morning programmes on Radio Eireann were entertaining. He missed reading most of all. Sheila was his life-saver there. Imagine her reading the news to him on her lunch-break. She was so thoughtful. It wasn't as if he were a vegetable yet. No sir. The old grey cells still worked. Seán thought he was on the way out. Pat hoped his son was right. He didn't want to lie here like a zombie day in and day out. Seán was good, in his way, but he had a very jealous streak. Maybe Seán had inherited it from him? He hoped not. His son had good points. He was a caring husband and father. He was kind to his mother and his patients. Deep down though, he was mean spirited. He was peevish. Pat wasn't sure he liked his son. Was that normal? Not to like your own son? Pat had never really warmed to him. It was quite odd.

Rita, on the other hand, thought Seán was God's gift. She hung on his every word as if she couldn't imagine how they had created such a wonder, a genius. Rita was simple and child-like. That's why he'd fallen for her all those years ago.

Eight o'clock. He heard Sheila move around downstairs. She'd be in soon with his breakfast. Father O'Meara wouldn't be in till midday. Poor Sheila. She was stuck here. She'd had to delay her plans because of him. She said it wasn't that at all. She had to work out her strategies and get the building in Carrigeen organised. Bullshit. He knew he was holding her up. He wished that Rita would agree to a nursing home. That's exactly what he wanted. He'd prefer to be in a nursing home, looked after by professionals who were constantly relieved by their colleagues. Shift duty wasn't possible for poor Sheila or Rita. He didn't want to be a burden any more. He watched his wife age before his eyes and he could do nothing about it. He was the cause of the trouble, but it wasn't his fault. Why wouldn't they put him in a home? He'd prefer it, genuinely. There he'd be one among many invalids and not some freak, as he was now. Rita was loyal to the bitter end, but sometimes loyalty could be misplaced.

Thank God for Liam O'Flaherty, Sheila thought. He'd put her on to Dermot O'Neill, the solicitor who specialised in this sort of thing. She hadn't realised it would be so complicated. Dermot had given her every help and advice. He was expensive, but worth every penny. He had shown her how to register the company. He'd advised her to make it a limited company as that way there'd be no personal liability in, God forbid, damages claims. The company would be a separate legal entity. A separate person, so to speak. So Sheila'd be the owner of a Private Limited Company. Fantastic, but bloody terrifying! Peadar was the other shareholder and production manager. He'd be in charge of their lab. Caroline had agreed to be company secretary and marketing manager. She was thrilled at the prospect. Seán was livid. Sheila, naturally, was managing director and had the full responsibility that that entailed.

Sheila sat at the kitchen table, examining the documents: Memorandum of Association, Dermot had helped her to set out the type of business, i.e. skin care products; Articles of Association, transfer of shares, meetings, etc. They'd only one meeting so far and that was in the pub! But Caroline had insisted on having a Minutes book to record the meeting. She was taking this very seriously! She'd come into her own. Sheila was thrilled to see her so involved. There was the Company Seal to be stamped on all official company documents, and a Certificate of Incorporation, issued by the Registrar of Companies. It all looked very impressive and they hadn't even moved in yet. Dermot had recommended Finian O'Toole as a good accountant. Sheila would employ a receptionist/secretary as soon as the premises were ready.

They weren't ready yet. Not by a long shot. The barn was in a very bad state of repair. Sheila wanted to divide it into a lab and a workshop. She'd also need to build a warehouse for storing the raw materials. The adjacent cottage could be a reception area for meeting clients. A few of the Carrigeen locals could do the building and carpentry work, but Sheila was out of her depth when it came to planning the renovations. A chemist's shop was one thing. This was something else. Still, she'd figure out something. It wasn't going to get her down. She glanced at the clock. God, she'd nearly forgotten to check on her dad. It was after ten o'clock. Her mother was still at her bridge game.

The sitting-room was in darkness. He was in a sound sleep. She didn't like the look of him. His colour was very grey. It was probably just the dim hall light. Sheila didn't like the night time. It was full of shadows and dark thoughts. Everything seemed worse in the dark. She moved closer to the sofa bed. His straggly white hair spread out on the pillow . . . his face was skeletal . . . Sheila shivered. Her dear, dear father was fading before her eyes. The once big-boned brawny man was now an invalid. Sickness had broken him. He was forced to suffer the indignity of dependence on others to wash, feed and change him like a baby. He didn't complain. But he'd lost his spirit. That was the cruellest thing of all. Sheila felt a huge sadness weigh her down. Why did he have to suffer like this? Why did he have to lie in that bed, day after day, hour after hour, staring vacantly out of the window? Nobody deserved an existence like that, least of all her father. The phone rang shrilly in the other room. Sheila crept out to answer it. She didn't want to wake him. He deserved some rest, some respite.

"Sheila? Hi!" Mary's voice on the other end. God, it was great to hear her.

"How's married life?" Sheila asked excitedly. "How was the honeymoon? I'm dying to hear all your news? Did you get my letter? Was the address right?"

"Hold it," Mary burst in. "One question at a time."

"Sorry, I'm just so glad to hear your voice."

"Same here," Mary replied. "OK, here goes. Married life's a laugh a minute. I ruin all Jim's dinners. I burnt his shirt. We'd the two sets of parents to dinner last week and we nearly had to build an extension. The house is tiny, but I love it. When are you coming up?"

"God knows. Dad's very bad, Mary. I don't think he'll last."

Mary could hear the catch in her voice. "I'm so sorry, Sheila. Is there anything we can do?"

"Pray, I suppose. His death would be a terrible blow, but I'd hate to see him linger on when he's suffering so much."

"Is he in pain?"

"No, I don't think so. He never complains. God, if you saw him, Mary. You wouldn't recognise him. He's skin and bone. He's no appetite. He's helpless. He hates using the commode. It's demeaning for him. It'd nearly be better if he were senile, but he knows everything." Sheila didn't want to burden Mary, but it was a relief to be able to talk to someone outside the family.

"This is a rotten time for you all. Especially for you. How are your plans going or have you abandoned them for the moment?"

"No, things are slow though. The building hasn't been properly designed yet. I'm finding it difficult."

"Listen, that's why I rang you. I read between the lines of your letter and I spoke to Jim. I'm going away next week to Stratford-on-Avon with the school. Jim has a few days off and he wants to know if you'd like him to go down and help with the design?"

Sheila didn't answer. She was stunned.

"Sheila, are you still there?"

"Sorry, Mary. Are you serious? Jim wants to come down?"

"Sure. What do you think?"

"Jesus, it's fantastic. My own architect. Why didn't I think of it before?"

"No way is he your architect. He won't take payment. He's your friend and it's a favour."

"I couldn't accept that, Mary. Business is business. Either he's paid or he needn't come."

"You'll never change, do you know that?" Mary laughed. "Have it your own way. He won't fleece you anyhow."

"You haven't told me about the honeymoon. How was Antibes? Expensive, I'd say."

"That's an understatement. But it was fabulous, Sheila. You'd love it. We went to Cannes, Nice, Monte Carlo and Juan les Pins. Monte Carlo was a dream world. The land of the rich and famous. We sat in the harbour and drank beer like the plebs we are, while the beautiful people partied on their yachts. You could smell the money. The bleedin' poodles were dyed the colour of their mistresses' outfits. Sick."

Sheila laughed at Mary's graphic description. "Sounds exotic. Did you get a great tan?"

"Jim did. I went my usual lobster red. And the mosquitoes, Jesus, I was eaten alive."

"Did you not use spray repellents?"

"No bloody use. If there was one mosquito in the country, it'd land on me. Rich blood, that's what they say."

"Well," Sheila giggled, "you'll have to have a complete blood transfusion before you go again."

"Yeah. Now for the good news. We went to Grasse, you know, the perfumeries. An experience of a lifetime. You have to go. Claim business expenses."

"Some day, I'd love to," Sheila said eagerly.

"Listen, I brought you back loads of essential oils. Jim smuggled half of them. There's bergamot, mandarin and jasmine. You know it takes a thousand kilos of flowers to produce one kilo of concentrate? It's an expensive business."

"God, Mary, you're great. How did you know what to buy?" Sheila was amazed.

"We met this guy, Marcel. He was lovely. I wouldn't kick him out of the bed. Anyway, I explained what you were doing, so he gave me what he thought you'd need. I have his name and address. Maybe you could use him? As an agent or something?"

"Yeah, maybe. I'll pay you for the oils. You must have spent a fortune. It's lucky I only use a drop or two in the creams."

"Jesus, would you stop talking about payment? You're so bloody independent. It's a present, right?"

Sheila was amazed by her generosity. "Thanks," she accepted graciously.

"Anyhow, he gave us a reduction. I think he fancied me. Oh yeah, we got some sandalwood and cedarwood extract too. He told us they were male fragrances, if you don't mind. And something called ylang ylang. Have you heard of it? Jim thought it was a howl."

"I have, yeah. It's meant to be like an aphrodisiac." Sheila laughed. "Do you want me to make you up a massage oil for Jim?"

"Later maybe. When I run out of ideas. At the moment our sex life is fine."

"Lucky you. Seriously though, I'll have to investigate the male market. Natural Man."

"Is there any such thing?"

Leave it to Mary for the quick retort. "I wouldn't know," Sheila said emphatically. "Tell Jim I'd love him to come. I'll expect him some day next week."

"It'll probably be Wednesday. He'll phone you, OK? Let me know about your father, won't you?"

"Yeah, I will. Good luck in Stratford."

"I'll need it. Thirty fifth years loose on the B and I crossing. We won't get much sleep. Ah, I'll survive. It's very good for them to see Shakespeare properly performed. I'll enjoy it once I've stopped counting heads."

"Right. I'll see your beloved next week then. I'll look after him well. It'll be good for Mam to have someone else here for a day or two. She fusses over Dad too much."

"Jim'll enjoy being fussed over. I think he misses his mother's cooking. Can't say I blame him. Anyhow, I hope he can fix you up. How's Peadar?"

"My production manager is fine, thanks," Sheila said smugly. "We're on an official business footing now and that's the way I like it."

"You're a hopeless case. Oh Jesus, I nearly forgot. Casanova's left his wife."

"Who?"

"John Harris. Remember? The one who mauled you at the wedding. If you ask me, she's had a lucky escape."

"If you say so." Sheila was non-committal. "I think I hear Dad. I'll have to go. Thanks a million for everything, Mary. How can I ever repay you?"

"There she goes again. Shut up, right? You can remember me when you're rich and famous, sailing around the South of France with your toy-boy in tow."

Sheila was still smiling when she put the phone down.

CHAPTER FIFTEEN

Jim Ryan did a great job. He charged Sheila a pittance. The building and renovation took another two months. The wet weather didn't help. Sheila, true to her word, employed builders and carpenters from Carrigeen and the outlying areas. Meanwhile, she divided her time between looking after her ailing father and making more creams in her kitchen. The chemist in Salthill, the one in Clifden, and O'Flaherty's in Galway City, gave her bigger and bigger orders. Sheila couldn't wait for the premises to be ready. Rita moaned continually. She said she was comatose from the fumes of the lavender.

No such luck!

As Pat was so ill, Caroline offered to go to Dublin to the Patents Office. The experience of a lifetime. The office, in the bowels of the earth, was dark and dismal. The staff looked as if they hadn't seen the light of day for years. Caroline was sure she'd been transported back in time. She wouldn't have been surprised to see Pickwick or Mr Snodgrass emerge. She registered the name of the company and they made three copies. It'd take a full year before the patent was theirs.

Finally the big day arrived. The move to Carrigeen. There was torrential rain. Sheila and Caroline arrived first in the Renault. The car was laden with papers, boxes and bottles. Peadar met them outside the building.

"Let me help you get all this stuff inside." He was wearing a mac and wellington boots. He looked farcical.

"Later." Sheila was too excited to be bothered with hauling everything in. "First we have to give Caroline the grand tour."

"We've an audience." Caroline smiled at the small crowd gathered in the road. Seamus arrived with the key. Sheila opened the door and, to her surprise, they all clapped.

"Thanks, everyone," Sheila acknowledged their support. "We'll see you later."

Her tone was polite but firm. They could see they were in the way, so they moved off.

"Was that a bit rude? They were just excited. We're the blow-ins." Caroline thought that Sheila had been too abrupt. These people had a right to be there. It was their village.

"This is our moment, Caroline. The three of us. They can come and gawk later. Come on, wait'll you see inside." Sheila ran in like a giddy schoolgirl.

"Peadar, look! The lab. I can't believe it! It's fabulous."

Peadar was a bit smug. "Naturally. I was the one who supervised the fitting up of all the equipment. What did you expect?"

Sheila hated it when he was like this. It drove

her nuts. She could see he was ready to wax lyrical on the merits of their distillation method. She escaped into the other room.

"What on earth are all those?" Caroline pointed to the racks and grids.

"For steam distillation," Peadar explained. "We put the plants on the racks over the heated water. The steam passes up and breaks down the walls of the plant cells. That releases the plant essence in the form of vapour."

"What's that pipe for?"

Peadar laughed at Caroline's bewilderment. "The steam passes through that pipe and then through those cooling tanks there."

"Merciful hour, it's like Frankenstein's laboratory." Caroline was sorry now she asked the question because, once Peadar started, there was no stopping him.

"In the cooling tanks," he went on, totally oblivious to the fact that Caroline couldn't care less, "the mixed vapours return to liquid form so they can be collected in those vats."

Caroline dutifully examined the vats. "That's . . ."

What could she say? She wanted to say something appropriate but what? What the hell did she care about cooling tanks and vats, for God's sake?

"Wonderful," she finally managed.

"The essential oil collects in the upper part of the vat and we can separate it easily from the watery part. We could use the watery distillate for flower-water. I must say that to Sheila. Where is she?" He looked around.

Yeah, where the bloody hell is Sheila? Caroline thought. She'd kill Sheila for subjecting her to this. God, he was such a bore. Did he ever lighten up? What would he be like in bed? Probably give you instructions and a running commentary.

"Now we wouldn't be using that method for the carrageen. That can be boiled in water. Direct distillation."

"Riveting." Caroline didn't care if her sarcasm hit home. She was dying to get away. "Sheila? Where are you?"

"Back here." Sheila shouted in from the back room. "Come in and have a look."

Caroline left him to it.

The other room was large and bright. The whitewashed walls were a bit antiseptic looking. Bare except for shelving.

"The storage room," Sheila said proudly. "Loads of space for the raw materials and the stuff I'm going to import."

"Did you write to that guy, Marcel? The agent?"

"Yep. He rang me yesterday. He's a terrible chancer."

"Oh?" Caroline was surprised. "Wasn't he real nice to Mary and Jim?"

"Nice, but he's a cute hoor! Those oils he sold Mary weren't essential oils at all. Not the real thing. They're called nature identical oils. He really pulled the wool over Mary's eyes. She thought she was getting a bargain."

"Jesus, would you be up to some people? It's a good job you know your stuff."

"Well, I certainly put him straight. He got a bit of a fright. Of course he pretended it was a language problem that caused the mix-up."

"So, are you going to use him as an agent?"

"Not on your life. I didn't say that to him of course. I'm going to go to Grasse and suss out another agent. I wouldn't do business with his type."

"Dead right. Seán and I can help your mother when you go. It's not right that it should all be left to you." Caroline was angry with Seán. He resented Sheila and now he resented her for working for Sheila's company. He saw it as a betrayal. Stupid twit. When would he realise that this job offer had saved her sanity?

"Now for your domain." Sheila grabbed her arm. "To the cottage." Sheila led the way. Caroline ran after her and crashed into Peadar who dropped a pile of papers all over the floor. Sheila pulled Caroline on.

"Should we not help him?" Caroline turned to go back.

"Leave him for God's sake. Let him play with his equipment!"

The cottage was quaint with its thatched roof. The door and windows were painted white. A small black and white sign over the door read: Natural Woman. Caroline grabbed Sheila and swung her round in a circle. "This is it! You made it."

"Correction," Sheila hugged her back, "we made it. It was a consolidated effort. Peadar, you and me. The three musketeers."

"The three stooges more like." Caroline giggled.

"And Dad," Sheila said sadly. "It's all thanks to Dad." A grim shadow crossed her face. "It's desperate that he'll never see all this."

Caroline linked her into the cottage. The front room was converted into a small reception area, with desk, two chairs, a filing cabinet and bookshelves. There was a two-seater couch and a coffee table. A small display case as well. The flagstoned floor had cleaned up beautifully.

"Mam made these." Sheila pointed to the yellow and white curtains and cushions. They made the place cosy.

"Rita?" Caroline was amazed. "Rita made them?"

"Yeah, she was so grateful to get all my paraphernalia out of the house, she'd have made a carpet if I asked her!"

"So, this is where I'll be spending my time. It's terrific."

"I hope you feel at home here," Sheila smiled.

"God forgive you, that's the last thing I want," groaned Caroline. "What's in the back?"

"Another office. For me. Anyhow I think we'll need to employ a full-time secretary. I want you to devote your time to the marketing end of things."

"Super. Have you anyone in mind?"

"Yeah," Sheila nodded. "Maura, from the pub, has a daughter who's just finished her course. I'm interviewing her this afternoon."

"It's only sinking in now. This is for real." Caroline hugged her again. "I think you're great, Sheila. I don't care who else helped, it was your idea, the whole thing. You were the one with the guts to take the risk."

"I don't have anything to lose, Caroline. Except my pride, maybe. But I don't intend to lose that because I'm going to make this place a success."

"I know you'll succeed. You've grit and determination."

"There are bound to be some failures along the way. Some set-backs. But I'll handle them as they come along. This time I'm not going to be beaten. This time I'm in control."

Caroline understood exactly what she was saying. Sheila thought of the adoption as a failure. She blamed herself for the way she'd handled it. She thought it was her fault. She felt she had been manipulated and hadn't stood up for herself or the baby. She'd let Karen down. She really believed that. Now was her chance to get back some semblance of self-respect. Caroline had to admire her. This company was now Sheila's baby. She was older and more self-confident. She was persistent. She was willing to listen to advice, but not to be bullied. She had clear goals and objectives. She knew what she wanted. This time she was going to get it. Caroline was in no doubt. Sheila had changed.

A head peeped around the door. It was Seamus.

"Are ye ready for lunch? Maura sent me over. She's put on a big stew. Come on, we're all famished."

* * *

Within the next six months, they had ten skin creams on the market. The local people harvested the carrageen, the wild rosemary and the carrot seed. Sheila went to Grasse to buy the other essential oils. She signed a contract with Yves Dupont, a French supplier. He was young, energetic and professional. Sheila trusted him. She continued to research carefully the properties of each oil. The rosemary was a good mix with the mandarin or the cedarwood. It was particularly good for toning the skin. The carrot seed blended well with the rosemary too. It had worked wonders on Ciara's eczema. The jasmine was great for dry skin. It was vitally important not to use too much of any one oil. Jasmine could be harmful in pregnancy, so that had to be clearly spelt out on the label. The bergamot was very good for oily skin or for acne. But it could increase the skin's sensitivity so could never be used undiluted.

Peadar trained in Bridget Cummins, one of his postgraduate students. She was delighted to accept a full-time job in the lab. Peadar and Caroline worked mornings only. Caroline got home before the twins came in from school, so Seán had no cause for complaint. Peadar had his lectures in the afternoon. He drove Caroline back to Galway at lunch-time every day. She designed the labels and packaging for the products. She also drew designs for each of the ten jars. One big disappointment for Caroline was the day Sheila announced that they had to decide against using Conor for the pottery.

"But why, Sheila? I thought you had your heart set on pottery? You said the jars were so pretty."

"When I costed it, Caroline, I realised it just wasn't feasible. Not for the skin creams. They'd have to be hand moulded, kiln dried and glazed. It'd cost a fortune. We'll have to stick to glass." Sheila was adamant.

"OK, but I'll have to rethink these designs then. Look at the drawings I've done. There's the one for the rosemary. A simple sprig. How can I manage that on a glass jar?" Caroline felt defeated. But Sheila was the boss.

"Leave it with me. I'll have to give it more thought." Sheila put on her jacket. "I'm off to do the deliveries."

"Did you get in touch with the chemist in Castlebar? He seemed genuinely interested."

"I'll drive up there tomorrow. Come on, Caroline. Cheer up. We'll be able to use your designs somehow. But remember cost effective is the name of the game. We're in this to make a profit not to give employment to down-and-out potters."

Jesus, Sheila was getting very tough. She was a different person since she'd started up the business. She even looked different. Sterner. More efficient. Caroline, though she didn't like to admit this, thought she saw a lot of Seán in Sheila. The same dogged determination.

Caroline got back to work. She developed a marketing plan. Sales forecasts were essential for profit plans and budgets. Profits, the name of the game. That's what Sheila wanted. That's what she'd get. She spent hours and hours drawing up her outline. Her plan covered the next three years. She did her projections on their particular market, its characteristics, structure, distribution, etc. Sales volume. Sales value. Market prospects. Branding. Pricing policy. Customer structure. Sales promotion. Advertising plans. Now, she looked at all her paperwork with glee. Let Sheila put that in her pipe and smoke it!

Sheila got back before lunch. She came into the office with a small parcel.

"Now, Caroline. Have a look at this. I called into the glass factory on my way back."

She handed Caroline a tall plain glass bottle. "What do you think?"

Caroline stared at her deprecatingly. "I think it's a glass bottle. What am I supposed to think?"

Sheila smiled slowly. "You wanted a simple design with a sprig of rosemary, right?"

"Yeah. But not on a glass bottle. It'd be ridiculous."

"Why?"

"You wouldn't see it, that's why. Unless you're going to order special coloured glass."

"No, I'm not. Think again."

Jesus, what was she on about? She looked so bloody self-satisfied. She really was getting like Seán.

"Sheila, what's your idea?"

"No, come on. I want you to see it yourself. What are you looking at?"

"A glass bottle. A ruddy glass bottle. That's what I'm looking at."

"Right. How would you describe glass?"

Good God, this was infuriating. "Glass. Well, it's kind of clear, see-through . . ."

"Exactly," Sheila shouted triumphantly. "It's see-through."

"So?"

"So," Sheila continued excitedly, "We want a sprig of rosemary, right?"

"Yeah, right." Caroline was losing patience.

"So we don't draw it on the bottle. We have it in the bottle." Sheila held it up with a flourish.

"What are you talking about?"

"For the massage oils I'm working on. The rosemary essence goes into the carrier oil, OK?"

"Yeah. The oil'd give the colour, is that what you mean?"

"Yes, but the sprig of rosemary can be in the bottle. An actual sprig."

Caroline said nothing for a full minute. Then she smiled slowly.

"Sheila, you're a genius. Why draw it when we can have the real thing?"

"We can do the same with the lavender and the pine. They'll look terrific."

Caroline laughed loudly. "Jesus, you really are a natural."

Seamus got four thousand pounds from Sheila for the property and the two fields. He was able to send for his son. Conor and his family returned from England, moved in with Seamus and he started up his pottery again, to the delight of the whole village. Sheila gave in. She did give him some work. She decided to use his pottery jars for her handcreams, but not for her other products. Word spread. He got orders from all over, especially the tourist shops in the area, but Sheila was the one who gave him his start and Caroline was appeased.

By the summer of '73 Natural Woman had trebled its profits. Caroline mounted a successful promotion all around the west coast. Sheila did her own delivering in the highly reliable Renault. They were now supplying the creams and massage oils to retailers in Westport, Ballina, Castlebar and Ennis as well as the Galway chemists. Business was booming.

Pat Crosby survived the winter, but his strength was failing rapidly. Sheila had hired a retired nurse to come in in the mornings. Rita and Sheila took turns in nursing him the rest of the time. He was an angelic patient. He never moaned and always tried to have a smile on his face. It was pathetic to look at him. He seemed to have shrivelled and had gone down to seven stone. He dozed for most of the day. His eyes lost their brightness. His appetite was completely gone. Sheila prayed that God would release him.

One sunny morning in late July, Pat asked Sheila

if could he see his garden. Sheila had a premonition that this would be the last time. The nurse managed to borrow a wheelchair and Sheila wheeled him out to his beloved sanctuary.

"I've missed this most of all," he whispered feebly to his daughter. He blinked in the glare of the sunshine. Sheila went back into the house and got him an old straw hat to protect his head. She trembled at the sight of the emaciated figure, wrapped in a rug, staring at his flowers.

"The lavender was always my favourite." His voice was suddenly stronger. "I'm so glad you're working with plants and flowers, Sheila. Nature is a great healer."

"Yeah it is, Dad." She tucked in the rug around him.

"I'm so proud of you, Sheila. You're doing so well. I'm glad I was spared to see it."

Sheila couldn't get over it. The colour came back to his cheeks. For a fleeting moment, she caught a glimpse of the old Pat. Then the deathly pallor came back. He beckoned to her.

"Some day you'll meet her, Sheila. I know. I've something for her. For Karen."

His voice got weaker again. "It's a letter I wrote when you told me about her . . . Give it to her . . . with my love."

Sheila was choked up. The familiar lump came back to her throat. The heaviness in her chest. What would she do without this man? Her father. He understood her so well.

He pointed to the yellow roses. She patted his

knee and went to get the secateurs from the shed. She cut the prettiest rose and brought it back to him. She placed the delicate flower on his lap. His head fell forward. He must be dozing again. Sheila nudged him gently. No response. She put her ear up to his mouth. No breath. He was gone. He had died quietly and peacefully just as he had lived. She put her arms around him. A single tear rolled down her cheek and splashed on to the yellow rose.

PART TWO

CHAPTER SIXTEEN

Mary Ryan put down the paint brush in dismay. Another blob smeared the kitchen floor. Jim'd kill her if she made another mess. She scrubbed in the turpentine and miraculously it worked. Four o'clock. Nearly time for Davy's bottle. She peeped into the pram. He was sleeping peacefully. Maybe she'd have time to finish off the kitchen door. Jim wouldn't be home till about six. He had an important meeting in the Shelbourne today and she was keeping her fingers crossed. He was now a senior partner in the firm. He had done really well.

Five years of marriage and they were still blissfully happy. His salary combined with her teaching job had allowed them to buy this dream house in Sandymount. She loved the Strand Road. It was brilliant to have the sea literally at your door. The village was handy for shopping and Blackrock was a short drive away. The neighbours were friendly and obliging, but she missed some of the women she had befriended in Ringsend. They were the salt of the earth, those women. But they'd their hearts set on this house. It was much more spacious and had a long back garden. More suitable for kids.

The only drawback was the heavy traffic, but they didn't have to worry about that yet as Davy was far from walking.

There was a helluva lot to be done to the house and Mary took full advantage of her summer holidays to get on with the decorating. Jim spent ages stripping off the old multicoloured wallpaper the previous elderly owners had favoured. It was a large three-storey house with imposing high ceilings. The ground floor contained a fine dining-room separated by beautiful oak folding doors from the front sitting-room which overlooked the sea. The nicest feature of this front room was the huge white marble fireplace. The narrowish hall had two steps leading down to the kitchen. They'd sanded the floors here and she was painting the doors. The fitted kitchen had cost a bomb so there was nothing left in the kitty to pay for a decorator. Anyway, Mary found that she actually enjoyed choosing and matching colours. She'd time for painting when the baby slept.

They'd done up the basement and converted it into a self-contained flat. Jim joked that it'd come in handy after the divorce. No fear of that in Ireland. However, the flat was there waiting for any of their family or friends who wanted to stay. Joanne and Brian were due to come next month. The top floor had three bedrooms. The master bedroom was huge, the full length of the house front. The view was stupendous across the bay. The Poolbeg lighthouse stood majestically at the end of the pier. It had been designed by Captain Bligh, after the famous "Mutiny on the Bounty". Mary had heard that it was the best place for fishing for conger eel in Ireland. In the distance they could see the Bailey lighthouse in Howth.

The bathroom was her favourite room in the house. They had done it in wood; the floor, the ceiling and the bath surround. The rich peach curtains and wallpaper went perfectly with the ivory bathroom suite. It reminded her of a log cabin in the mountains when she lolled in the bath.

She'd just painted the last stroke when the baby started to mooch. She took the bottle from the sterilising unit and spooned in the formula. This was the only part of motherhood that got on her nerves. The warmer was plugged in. She switched on the radio.

"The taxman's taken all my dough and left me in my stately home, lazing on a sunny afternoon . . ."

My God. The Kinks. The summer of '67. Ten years ago. Mary shuddered as she remembered.

Ten years ago since that awful summer. Imagine, ten years ago. They were so green, so young. Nineteen, naïve and vulnerable. How was Sheila supposed to cope with such a trauma? She was far too young to have had to make such a decision. It was so unfair. If Mary knew then what she knew now, she would never have allowed it to happen. Adoption. Everyone, including Mary herself, thought it was for the best. Best for whom? Certainly not for Sheila.

Mary picked up Davy protectively, cooing softly at him. She loved the feel of him, the milky smell of him. She cuddled him tightly. He looked so cute in his little lemon babygro. The image of his father. She went up to the front room cradling him in one arm, the bottle in the other. Three hands were necessary to manage a baby. She eased herself down on to the couch and gave him his bottle. His little lips clung to the teat, a vice-like grip. His funny sucking sounds made her smile. The sunlight streamed in the window. She was so lucky. Why did she have so much joy and happiness? She was living a charmed life. She knew that. Tomorrow she'd ring Sheila and invite her over. Jim wouldn't mind.

At six on the dot she heard the Volvo drive up. Jim breezed in cheerfully.

"We did it, love! We got the contract with O'Neill's." He picked up his son and whooshed him up in the air. The baby squealed with pleasure. "Your daddy's a genius. What is he? A genius!" Jim was euphoric.

"What do you fancy for your tea? I don't know what's in the fridge. I've been painting all afternoon."

"Is that it? And here's me thinking you were going prematurely grey."

Mary looked in the mirror over the marble fireplace. White streaks speckled her fringe.

"Bloody hell! Not exactly the ideal spouse for a successful businessman, am I?"

"You'll do," Jim smiled. "Go up and have a soak. I'll change Davy. There's no way you're cooking tonight. We're going out to celebrate. I'll ring Angela to see if she's free."

Mary kissed him. She was dying to get out for a few hours. She could hear Jim on the phone to the babysitter as she ran her bath.

She rubbed in the oil tonic that Sheila had given her. It contained 100% pure plant extracts: sage, mint, hazelnut and, of course, rosemary. Sheila still swore by her rosemary to improve the elasticity of the skin and firm the tissues. She massaged in a small amount, and following the instructions, had a cool shower. It certainly felt soothing and relaxing.

Mary's bathroom was a shrine to Natural Woman. There were almost forty products on the market now: cleansers, toners, face masks, day cream, night cream, eye make-up remover, revitalising day creams, firming neck creams. The list was endless and Mary had tried most of them. She had oily skin so she used the products containing bergamot, lavender and geranium. The actual amount of the essential oils Sheila used was minimal. Apparently overuse could be dangerous. Sheila told her on no account to use lavender when she was pregnant in the early months. She loved the face creams too, but she wondered if anything would improve her skin. Maybe Polyfilla!

Clad in black bra and panties, she eyed herself critically in the full-length bedroom mirror. Her figure was nearly back to normal, thanks to hours of strenuous exercise at the fitness clinic. Myra had told her that she still needed to lose an inch or two from her tummy. She also said that Mary had to tighten up her dropped bottom. Honestly, that woman was a scream, but she certainly got results. On one occasion she'd handed nude photos of obscenely obese women around the sauna. She called overeating "oral masturbation". That was enough to put anyone off food for life! No, Mary was quite happy with her body. Her breasts were as firm as ever. She'd avoided stretch marks because Sheila insisted on her trying the jasmine blended with mandarin and lavender. It worked. Not that Jim would have complained. Their sex life wasn't great. Her fault? She remembered vowing after Davy's birth that nothing would ever get in there again. Not even a tampon. She'd been so sore. Nobody tells you the full story about giving birth. Just as well or the population'd drop dramatically. You did, in time, forget the pain. A healthy baby was recompense for anything. They were the lucky ones, she and Jim. What about Sheila? What recompense had Sheila? Nothing. She came out of the hospital with nothing but bad memories. Mary had been as sympathetic as she could be at the time. But it was only now, having her own child, that she fully understood what Sheila had gone through.

Going over and over it like this wasn't doing any good. But she couldn't get it out of her mind. She couldn't forget it. Sheila couldn't forget it. There was a ten-year-old little girl somewhere wondering where her mother was. Mary tried to imagine giving Davy away. She couldn't.

"Mary? What's keeping you?" Jim shouted up the stairs.

"I'll be down in a minute." She'd better get a move on.

She decided on her red top and black skirt. She slipped the blouse over her head. It was a bit low cut. To hell with it! If you've got it . . . that's what Joanne always said. She swept up her dark curls into a chignon. Very chic. She put on her mascara and her lipstick. Her teeth weren't in great shape. She'd need a crown on her front tooth. It was going grey even if her hair wasn't. She'd had a root canal filling the year before and the dentist had warned her it would eventually need a crown. Another few hundred, well it'd have to wait. Grin not and bear it! The doorbell rang. That'd be Angela. The girl was so reliable and she adored Davy. It was difficult to find a good babysitter, but Angela was a brick.

They ate in the Quo Vadis. It was full as usual on a weekend night. Even midweek they did a good trade. They both chose the veal milanaise. The sauce was out of this world. The two bottles of Chardonnay went down a treat. They'd taken a taxi so they could drink with a free conscience. The pianist's excellent repertoire added to the cosy atmosphere. The crowd at the next table were having a ball. It was a fortieth birthday party and they were determined to prove that her life was only beginning. After dessert, Mary had a Tia Maria. She was getting fond of liqueurs.

"Jim, we really have a lot to be thankful for, don't we?"

Jim smiled at the earnest expression on his wife's face. She was such a good person. She was soft and warm-hearted. He marvelled at her sometimes. He was amazed at her lack of guile, her innocence. It was no wonder her pupils idolised her. She'd always seen the goodness in them. She never bitched about them. She understood them, even the brats who drove some other teachers mad. She had endless patience. She was loyal and honest and sincere. She deserved to be happy. He was a lucky man. His career was on the up and up. Contracts were coming in at a fierce rate. Davy had arrived, perfectly planned. They'd found their ideal house after five years of saving. Life was good, very good. He wondered would the bubble ever burst.

"Yeah, we've a lot to be grateful for," he agreed. He raised his glass to hers.

"I've been thinking about Sheila today. I haven't seen her for a while."

"Invite her for dinner some night. She could sleep over."

"Right. She's awfully busy with the shop and everything though. She's totally immersed herself in the business. I thought that when she moved to Dublin I'd be seeing more of her, but it hasn't worked out like that at all."

"How long is she back in Dublin now?"

"Nearly three years. She couldn't wait to get out of Galway after her father's death. Remember? She stuck it out for a year and then she moved up."

"When she got that order from Brown Thomas. Yeah, that was her big break."

"I know. She's very successful. But I still think she devotes body and soul to that business at the expense of her personal life. It's not good."

"What else has Sheila got? That business is her life."

"She'll never have anything if she buries herself in work," Mary insisted.

"Sure she's always out at dinners and functions. She meets more people than you do, when I think about it."

"OK, but that's different. I have you and Davy. I'd like Sheila to have someone too."

"What age is she now?"

"Twenty-nine. She'll be thirty at the end of this month."

"Not exactly over the hill. She's plenty of time to marry and have kids, if she wants." Jim poured out the last of the wine for himself. Mary refused any more. She stirred her coffee vigorously. "There has to be more to life than work."

"That's what success is all about, Mary. Sheila's built that business up from nothing. There's no substitute for hard work. She has to put in the time." Jim lit a cigar. "I'll be working harder too from now on."

Mary gasped. "Harder? You couldn't work any harder than you do now. You're a workaholic, for God's sake. That's why they made you a senior partner. You do more than all the others put together."

Jim grinned at her. "Thanks for the vote of confidence. When I say harder, I mean longer. I'll have to go away more. Two of the contracts are in the North and there's one job in England."

Mary puffed hard on her cigarette. "God, I hate it when you're away."

"I know, but unfortunately it's a necessity. Do you want another drink?"

"Uh huh, I don't want a hangover in the morning. You better ask for the bill."

Angela was watching *The Late Late Show* when they got back. Davy had been no trouble. Angela had a cup of coffee with them. She'd just finished fifth year in school and was undecided yet about a career after her Leaving. She was thinking of going to art college. She was very talented and very bright. Mary encouraged her. It was so important to choose a suitable career since we spend so much of our time at work. Angela was at a good school and had a super careers guidance counsellor. She was one of the lucky ones.

Jim walked Angela home even though she lived a few doors away. These days it wasn't safe anywhere. Davy started to cry. Good. Mary was glad. If she fed him now, he might, he just might, go through the night.

Jim was back in a minute. "Do you want me to do that?" Mary was giving Davy his bottle.

"No, you go on to bed. I'll be there in a minute." She winked at him.

He kissed Davy and pecked her on the lips. "Don't be long."

Davy took ages to drink the bottle. He kept falling asleep. If he didn't finish it he'd wake her in the middle of the night. She changed his nappy and tried again. Now he wanted to play. He gurgled happily up at her. No, sonny boy, this isn't the right time for this. Mary was dying to go to bed. She was feeling randy. Wait'll Jim got a look at her in the sexy underwear. It'd drive him nuts. She'd undress slowly and seductively for him. That always turned him on. She might even suggest a massage. She visualised his long lean body covered in oil as she rubbed him all over. Come on, Davy, come on. She put the teat back in his rosebud mouth. He sucked slowly at first, then furiously. Good boy. Then she'd blow gently in Jim's ear and he'd cup her breasts. Her nipples'd go hard. He'd stroke her slowly. He'd place her gently on the bed and kiss her deeply and passionately on the mouth. His hands'd be all over her. She'd undo her hair and let it cascade down on her shoulders. He loved the feel of her hair on his bare chest. She'd unhook her bra and let her breasts fall free. They'd finger each other lovingly. He'd enter her. They'd make love slowly and build up to . . . God, she couldn't wait.

Davy finished his bottle. She hugged his sleepy little body. "Now it's Daddy's turn," she whispered to him as she carried him upstairs to his cot. She tucked him in and kissed him goodnight. She stripped down to her bra and pants in the bathroom. She'd make a dramatic entrance. She took off her make-up and brushed her teeth. She put a touch of perfume behind her ears. Passion. That should do the trick!

She crept into their bedroom. The bedside lamps were on, giving a soft glow. Jim had his back to her. Ah ha! Playing hard to get, was he? She'd show him. She approached the bed on tiptoe. "Hello, lover," she breathed into his ear. Jim grunted and pulled the bedclothes up around his ears. He started to snore.

Blast him anyway!

CHAPTER SEVENTEEN

Sheila woke with a splitting headache. She reached
for the jug of water which she always kept on the
bedside table. What day was it? Thursday. She
puffed up her pillow and lay back for ten minutes.
She gave herself this time every morning to get her
thoughts together. She did a mental check of what
she had to do today: go over to the shop this
morning and see how the new sales assistant was
working out; ring Mr Allen, the landlord, to find out
when the first floor might be available for renting;
call into BT's this afternoon for a meeting with
Sandra. She wondered how the new range of oils
was selling. Bridget Cummins was very excited
about it. She'd developed three different oil
treatments for dry, dehydrated and combination
skin. Each contained hazelnut which prevented
moisture loss. Sheila found that the one with the
sage and rosemary suited her best. Her skin was
prone to oiliness. Hence the pint of water that she
drank morning and night. Diet was as important as
the skin products.

Bridget was now in charge of the lab in
Carrigeen and she was wonderful. Her enthusiasm

was infectious. She had two assistants working full-time. Peadar, although still a major shareholder, had become a sleeping partner. Not in the way he had envisaged, mind you! Promotion to senior lecturer in UCG left him little time for other pursuits. It suited Caroline fine. Caroline . . . Sheila had never seen anyone blossom like that. Her official title was assistant director and she ran the company like the captain of a ship. Seán never stopped complaining. Caroline's salary had doubled. She'd her own car and he was now the proud owner of a Saab. Although he felt this was much more appropriate for his image, he resented the fact that it was Caroline's money which had made it possible. Silly twit! Men and their fragile egos.

Sheila had to smile as she remembered his initial resistance to Caroline working full-time. Who'd look after the twins? Who'd iron his shirts and cook his meals? He had to have a hot meal waiting when he came in from work. Enter Nora Maguire. A jolly woman in her fifties, who loved housework, minding children, and cooking. Seán had never had it so good. Now he'd two doting women who danced attendance on him: his mother and Nora. Caroline was off the hook.

Sheila stretched and swung her legs out of the bed. Her head was still throbbing. Probably tension. She'd been running around all week trying to catch up with herself. That couple on the floor below didn't help matters. She was sick of their late night drunken revelries. The noise travelled upwards to her top floor apartment. She needed her sleep.

Inconsiderate buffoons. Mr Allen was demented with complaints about them. The doctor on the first floor had complained for ages to no avail. Now he was moving out. Sheila couldn't blame him but she was damned if they were going to drive her out. She wanted the first floor for her new idea. Hopefully Mr Allen would have good news for her this morning.

She opened her wardrobe. What to wear today? She decided on the navy pinstripe suit and her white Chanel blouse. She ran her bath and added carrageen gel. That might relax her a bit. As she waited for the bath to fill up, she went into the kitchen to put the kettle on. The kitchen was very shabby. Mr Allen, despite his promises, had done nothing to do the place up. Sheila had offered to get it done, but he wouldn't hear of it. He was an old man and being the landlord of a four-storey house was too much hassle for him. The apartment didn't quite suit her, but she adored this house. It had so much potential.

Fitzwilliam Square, the smallest and last built of Dublin's Georgian squares . . . an ideal place to live. The red brick houses were stylish and beautifully appointed. There was an elegance and grace about the place that Sheila loved. The address was a bit of a status symbol too. Good for business. The central garden was the private domain of the residents. That was another bonus. Sheila lived on the north side of the square, beyond Pembroke Street. She had the best of both worlds, the peace and tranquillity of the square, unusual in the heart of a city, and the magical excitement of Grafton Street a few minutes away.

Sheila dried herself briskly with a hard towel. Lately she thought she saw signs of the dreaded cellulite. No way was she going to let that develop. She cut out coffee completely and cut down on alcohol, which was difficult as she attended so many functions and dinners. Stress seemed to aggravate the condition too. Sheila used her geranium and rosemary blend in the bath. They had a detoxifying effect. She sat down to a breakfast of fresh fruit and water. For lunch she'd have a salad. She'd call into that new health food store to buy more fennel tea.

The phone rang just as she was about to leave.

"Hello, dear." Rita sounded chirpy this morning. She always rang when Sheila was rushing somewhere.

"Hi, Mam, how's everything?"

"Great, great. Just ringing to know if you're coming down this weekend."

"No, did Caroline not tell you? I'll be down next Tuesday for a few days. Molly wants me to interview a new secretary."

"Molly?"

"You know, Maura's daughter. She's running the office in Carrigeen." Sheila was tired explaining things to her mother. Rita never listened. Then she moaned that she wasn't told anything. There was no pleasing her.

"Right, oh now I remember," her mother said dismissively. "Sheila, I hope you're looking after yourself in that apartment. Are you eating properly?"

Typical. "Yeah, I am. Don't worry. Are you keeping well?"

Why did she feel so uncomfortable talking to her own mother? It was weird.

"Fine, dear. I'm fine. So you'll be home next Tuesday? See you then."

Sheila replaced the receiver. Home. She'd be back in Galway next Tuesday, but she no longer looked on it as home. Not since her father's death. Without him, it was just a house. A house with too many memories. She felt down. Guilty. Why did she feel guilty every time she spoke to her mother? There was no need. Rita was acting the merry widow to perfection. She played bridge and golf three or four times a week. Caroline said she was never at home. When she was in the house, she had visitors. She certainly wasn't lonely. In fact, a couple of months after Pat's death, Rita came into her own. She rearranged the furniture in the house, got rid of Pat's bed and gave his writing desk to Seán.

Sheila took her father's death very badly. Despite the changes her mother made, Sheila could see him everywhere: in his garden, sitting by the fire in his old rocking chair: dozing by the kitchen range. No changes could wipe out her father's presence from the house. Sheila and her mother drifted further and further apart. They lived together, but were estranged.

Sheila felt like an intruder. She wanted to get out

of there. When the buyer from Brown Thomas signed for her products, Sheila knew she'd have to settle in Dublin. She had to be more accessible. Once Caroline agreed to run the show in Carrigeen, there was no reason for Sheila to stay. Even Seán put up no objections. Rita was relieved when Sheila broke the news to her. Of course, she pretended to be upset, but Sheila knew she wasn't a bit sorry to see her daughter go. Two adult women alone in the one house was a recipe for disaster.

She shut the main hall door of the house, ran down the front steps and almost collided with Mr Allen who was on his way in. He doffed his hat in salute.

"Good morning, Miss Crosby. I was hoping for a quick word with you."

He was such a dapper little man with his bowler hat, long overcoat and umbrella. A Joycean figure. He always carried his umbrella, even on a fine summer's morning like this one.

Sheila didn't want to be rude, but time was moving on. "Mr Allen, I'm dreadfully sorry. I was going to ring you later today. I can't stop to chat now. I have an appointment in twenty minutes."

Mr Allen nodded politely. "Don't worry, my pet. You young people are so busy these days. Hustle and bustle, rushing to and fro. I understand. Will you be in tonight?"

"After nine, if that's not too late for you?"

"That's perfect. My son will drive me over tonight." With a stiff bow, he went on into the house. Sheila ran down the road, hurried up

Merrion Row, past Stephen's Green, and arrived at her shop in Duke Street by nine-thirty. It wasn't the ideal location for trade, but it was all she could afford at the moment. She'd decorated it tastefully in pine. Sheila loved wood. It was natural. She had the same sign over the door as the one in Carrigeen. She took charge of the window displays herself every week. It reminded her of her time in O'Flahertys. Some day she'd get a better premises.

Lily was serving two customers when she went in. Sheila greeted them pleasantly. These were two of her regulars. They bought their purchases and left.

"Where's Valerie? In the back?"

Lily went red. "She's not in yet."

"That's the second time this week," Sheila said coldly. But Lily knew she was far from calm. "Have you done the stocktaking yet, Lily?"

The girl looked flustered. "I . . . I'm sorry, Miss Crosby. I meant to start it this morning but . . . there were a lot of customers . . . I'll do it now."

Sheila hated to see her discomfort. Lily was trying to cover up for that lazy little madam. How could she do the stocktaking when she was left alone to serve in the shop?

"Never mind, Lily. I'll do it. I wanted to sort a few things out anyhow. I'll be calling in to Brown Thomas this afternoon and I have to see what they need too. When I've finished making up the order, you can ring Paddy. OK? The van comes to Dublin on Fridays."

"Right. Would you like a coffee?"

"No thanks."

Sheila went into the storeroom. She left the door open to let in more air. The back room was small, dark and stuffy. Sheila was halfway through the order when she heard the door chime announce the arrival of Valerie. Nine-fifty. This just wasn't good enough. She'd have a strong word with her after she'd written up the factory order.

"Hi Lily! Missed the bleedin' bus again. All quiet? No sign of Frosty?"

Lily nearly died. She tried to signal Sheila's presence in the back room, but Valerie was too busy putting on her lipstick to notice. Another customer came in. Sheila peeped out. It was Mrs Reidy, a retired nurse. She'd been widowed the year before. She'd told Sheila that her shop had given her a new interest in her looks. She came in once a fortnight to buy face cream and handcream. She was a gentle old lady. Sheila was very fond of her.

"May I help you, madam?" Valerie asked in a condescending tone.

Lily came over with the two creams. "The usual, Mrs Reidy?" she suggested politely.

"Thank you, my dear. I wanted to get some advice. I was going to ask Miss Crosby, but eh, maybe you could help."

Sheila stayed where she was. She wanted to see how the girls would handle this.

"What is it you want?" Lily encouraged her.

"Well, I know this must sound very silly, in a woman of my advanced years, but . . . eh," Mrs Reidy started to stammer. "Could . . . could you

recommend s-s-something for sagging skin? It's my
. . . chin, you see." The old lady looked
embarrassed.

"Certainly," Lily smiled at her. "Try this cream
here. It's the first one ever made by Natural Woman.
Rosemary and carrot seed."

Good girl, Sheila thought. Exactly right. The old
lady was just about to pay for it, when Valerie
drawled sarcastically, "Mrs Reidy, have you tried the
Californian solution?"

Lily stared at Valerie. What was she talking
about?

"No, my dear. What is it?"

"Well, it's quite expensive of course. But some
people of your age swear by it." Valerie gave her a
smug look.

"Oh?" Mrs Reidy was annoyed by the reference
to her age. Sheila held herself back. If she went in
there now, she'd kill Valerie.

"Oh yes, it's a minor miracle for sagging skin."

"What is, dear?" Mrs Reidy arched an eyebrow.

"A face lift." Valerie smirked at her.

The old lady's face turned white. She put her
creams back on the counter. "I've changed my
mind," she muttered as she hurried out of the shop.

Sheila saw red. She stormed out from behind the
door. Lily was in shock, but the culprit was grinning
from ear to ear. "Stupid old cow. Sagging chin.
That's not all she had sagging."

"Valerie, you're fired. I want you out of this shop
now." Sheila clenched her teeth.

The girl looked back at her defiantly. "Suits me.

This place is a hell-hole anyway. Who'd want to work here? Not exactly Yves St Laurent, is it?"

Sheila spoke icily, "You are an obnoxious young woman. There was no call whatever to insult a customer like that. I'll give you a week's pay, but you're going now. I couldn't tolerate your presence here one moment longer."

"Mutual," pouted Valerie. "I can get a job anywhere I want. Who do you think you are? Natural Woman. Ha! You're nothing but a dried-up old spinster."

Sheila gave her a scathing look. "You may crawl back to whatever gutter you slithered out of. I find your language and behaviour offensive. My customers don't deserve such treatment."

"Jaysus. D'ya hear her? Queen o' bloody Sheeba."

Sheila opened the door. "Out."

"I'm goin'. You and your hoity-toity airs an' graces. I'm headin' straight back to the employment agency. I'll be in a new job by lunch-time."

"You may find it hard to get similar or any employment without a reference."

Valerie cursed as she slammed the door behind her.

Lily was quaking. Sheila put her arm around her. "Don't mind her, Lily. You're doing very well. You know how to treat the customers with respect. I'm very pleased with you. I'll have a proper replacement for that bitch before the day is out. I'll ring the agency this minute. Can you manage on your own this afternoon?"

"Of course, Miss Crosby."

"How long have you been with me now?"

"Six months."

"Well, I think it's time you dropped the 'Miss'. Call me Sheila." Sheila returned to the store room. She put her head around the door. "Or even Frosty!"

* * *

Sheila met Sandra in BT's at three. The natural oil ranges were selling really well. They were running out of the handcreams and bath gels too. Sandra had written out a huge order. Sheila was pleased, but she was still upset about the morning's episode. She left Brown Thomas at three-thirty and went home to get her car. Luckily she had Mrs Reidy's address. She had enough time to drive out to Santry with an apology and a present before she had to meet Finian O'Toole, the accountant. He made a monthly trip to Dublin to see his sister and he took the opportunity to fit Sheila in too. A year's supply of creams for Mrs Reidy might help to soften Valerie's insult and cheer her up. Valerie had big problems. Such a chip on her shoulder. Good business depended so much on having a good staff. Sheila counted her blessings when she thought of the gang in Carrigeen.

Sheila pulled up at the end house in the close. Mrs Reidy opened the door.

"Come in, my dear. How nice to see you."

Sheila followed her into the cluttered sitting-room. A man sat on the chesterfield suite.

"This is Alfred Moore. Alf, this is Miss Crosby from the store."

Sheila shook the old man's hand. She accepted a glass of sherry from Mrs Reidy.

"To what do we owe this unexpected pleasure, my dear?"

Sheila didn't know quite how to put it. "It's about this morning. I'm here to apologise for the behaviour of my sales assistant. I realise what she said was inexcusable but I hope you'll be able to put the whole incident out of your mind. You don't know how much I value your custom. The girl, of course, has been sacked."

"Oh dear, I thought that might happen. I said that to you, Alfred. Didn't I?"

The old man nodded. "In a way, it's my fault Miss Crosby," he mumbled.

"Your fault? I don't understand."

"Well you see, I sent Agnes in to get something else, but her courage failed her when you weren't there. She was too embarrassed to ask for what she really wanted."

"I'm afraid I don't follow you." Sheila bit her lip. "You wanted something else, Mrs Reidy?"

Agnes Reidy burst out laughing. "A massage oil."

"Pardon?" Sheila didn't catch what she said because of the laughter. Alfred was chuckling too.

"Some of your ylang ylang oil. Alfred read somewhere that's it's very good for . . . you know. . ."

236

"Spicing up our . . . our . . . relationship," Alfred spluttered.

Sheila couldn't believe her ears. Everything suddenly took on a new perspective. Alfred was the boyfriend. Mrs Reidy had come in to get a massage oil for Alfred. Incredible.

"You see, Miss Crosby," Agnes explained, "I didn't want that other cream at all. What do I care about sagging chins? At my age?"

"Yeah," agreed Alfred. "It's not sagging chins that concern us." His shoulders shook with laughter.

"So you didn't feel insulted then?" Sheila was relieved and amused at the same time. Here she was feeling sorry for the old lady who had been so rudely treated by a member of her staff. Sheila had thought of Mrs Reidy as a fragile, lonely person. The truth was that the old dear was living it up with Alfred. It was hilarious. That was the last time Sheila'd jump to a conclusion.

"You're very sweet about it." Sheila took out the present. "This is a gift voucher for a year's supply of your favourites."

Mrs Reidy shook her head. "There's no need for that, dear. The girl was right in a way. I would need a face lift to do something about those wrinkles. It wasn't what she said. It was the way that she said it. A bit rude. She'll have to learn to be more tactful."

"Yes," agreed Sheila. "But she can learn it somewhere else. I've done with her."

"You're so kind to come all this way." Agnes Reidy appreciated it. It wasn't everyone who would go to such bother.

"Not at all. Please accept the present. It'd make me feel better."

"No, no." Alfred was insistent. "But you could slip us the odd bottle of the ylang ylang if you've a mind to." He winked at her.

"Deal." Sheila smiled.

She met Finian O'Toole in Davy Byrne's at seven. She liked this swish watering hole even if she was only drinking mineral water. The Carrigeen accounts were all in order, Finian told her. He was thrilled with the way Caroline was managing things.

"Great. Could you have a look at the Dublin accounts?" Sheila asked him. "I'll leave them with you."

"No problem. Is the shop doing well?" He sipped his pint.

"Not bad. I'd like to move eventually. Look, I need your advice about something else."

"Shoot."

"I need to borrow money. How's my credit rating?"

"Very good as it happens. Are you going to tell me more? How much will you need and for what?"

"I'm thinking about opening a beauty salon."

"What!" Finian shouted. He ignored the supercilious stares from the people around him. "Another business? Sheila, are you mad?"

"Well, I'm giving it serious thought. I'm meeting my landlord this evening. There's a chance I can get the first floor."

"In Fitzwilliam Square? You'd have the business in the house?"

"Yeah, why not? The rooms are in good order. A doctor had them as a private clinic. They'd be ideal for what I want."

"You're talking about more staff though. More responsibilities."

"So? I haven't shirked my responsibilities up to now, have I?"

"No, no you haven't," he was forced to admit. "But would all the extra hassle be worth it?"

"Definitely. There are a lot of wealthy women out there who want advice and personal attention about their appearance. There's a big market for it. I know from the success of the creams. As it is, I'm dispensing free advice all the time. Might as well make a profit out of it."

Finian agreed. This woman had innate good business sense. There was no doubt about that. Some would even consider her ruthless, but certainly not the people of Carrigeen. According to them, Sheila was a saint. She'd brought jobs, money and new life to the village. "Put Carrigeen on the map," as Seamus kept saying.

"So after I talk to Mr Allen this evening, I'll call you. OK?" Sheila stood up to go.

Finian shook her hand. "Right. Let me look at the figures before you decide for definite, will you?"

"Of course." Sheila took her handbag and said goodbye. Naturally she'd let him look at the figures. That was what she paid him for. But he wouldn't be able to influence her one way or the other. Sheila would make up her own mind.

CHAPTER EIGHTEEN

Saturday morning. Caroline's favourite part of the week. Seán had his morning surgery. Colm was at his football practice. She and Ciara had the morning to themselves. She'd bring her into town to get her new school uniform. Imagine. The twins were starting secondary school in a month's time. Where had the time flown?

Ciara was ages in the bathroom.

"What are you doing, love? Your breakfast's ready."

Ciara shouted back through the closed door. "Shaving my legs. I don't want any breakfast."

My God, shaving her legs at twelve years of age. Ever since she got her periods, three months before, Ciara thought she was a woman. She was so different from Colm. He was still childlike although he was tall for his age. He was mad about soccer and hurling. He couldn't care less about homework, pop stars or girls. Ciara was the opposite. She was meticulous about her schoolwork. She mooned about Abba. She had a huge crush on Stephen Byrne, a fifteen-year-old pimply faced schoolboy who lived in the next street. Girls grew up much faster. In some ways. Caroline turned off the grill as Ciara sauntered into the kitchen in her bathrobe. Her face was coated in a thick white paste.

"I dorrowed yer ace mask. My bores eed closing uh." She talked through her teeth as the mask had hardened on her face. Caroline tried to make it out. Her pores needed closing up. God, how did she even know what pores were at her age?

Ciara sipped her orange juice through a straw. "Dell Vridget the beach snells nice."

"Beach? Oh, you mean peach? Bridget'll be chuffed." Caroline laughed.

"Can dalk." Ciara barely moved her lips. Vital not to crack the mask. She refused the grilled rashers and sausages.

Caroline sat down to eat them herself. Useless trying to convince her that breakfast was the most important meal of the day. Ciara was back on one of her diets. That'd last about two days, then she'd be moaning when there were no crisps in the cupboard. Ciara went back to the bathroom to take off the mask. Caroline would ring Rita. She'd ask her for supper tonight. That's if her mother-in-law had no other plans.

Nice of Caroline to invite her over. Very thoughtful. But there was a do in the golf club so she'd had to refuse. It was a wonder Seán wasn't going to the dinner. He didn't usually miss them. Seán was in very bad form lately. Of course Caroline worked all week. Rita suspected all wasn't well in that house. Funny how things had changed between those two since Caroline had started work. They seemed to be going their separate ways. Seán never consulted Caroline before he made any decisions. Rita had to admit that Seán had turned out like his father. Secretive about his money, his career. Her independence had definitely moved the goalposts. Seán treated his wife like a rival. Rita wondered did the twins suffer because their mother worked. They loved Nora Maguire. She was another granny figure. But they didn't need another granny. They needed their mother. Caroline'd need to watch out. The phone rang again.

"Hi, Gran?"

"Ciara? How are you, darling?"

"Great. Listen, Mam asked me to call you back. We're going in to buy my uniform now. Do you want to meet us for a coffee in Lydon's since you're not coming over tonight?"

"Lovely. I've some shopping to do myself. Tell your mother I'll meet you both at twelve. I'll treat you to a spot of lunch."

"OK, thanks, Gran. See you later."

"Gross, it's gross. I hate navy." Ciara looked at herself in the shop mirror. "It's too long. It makes me look frumpy."

Caroline took a deep breath. "It's not too long, Ciara. It's fine. You'll get used to it. Wait till you see it with your blouse and your knee socks."

"Knee socks! Oh my God." The thought of that nearly finished her.

"They're not as bad as the bulletproofs we had to wear." Caroline was losing patience with her.

"Bulletproofs?"

"Yeah, big thick ribbed tights." Caroline shuddered.

"I'd prefer that. Black tights'd be all right."

"They weren't black. They were a sickly shade of beige." Caroline walked her back to the fitting-room. "How would you like to let Stephen see you in bulletproofs?"

"He's never going to see me in this uniform. I'd rather die first."

"Get dressed." Caroline sighed. "I'll pay for these and then we'll go to meet your granny."

The sales girl smiled sympathetically at Caroline. "They're all the same." She parcelled up the uniform and Caroline wrote a cheque.

"Hello, Mrs Crosby." Caroline felt a pat on her shoulder.

"Oh, Mrs Cummins. How are you?"

"Marvellous, thank you. I just wanted to tell you how happy our Bridget is working for you out in Carrigeen. She loves the job."

"Glad to hear that. She's a brilliant worker. She has some great ideas. Sheila's very pleased with her."

"She has Sheila to thank for that job."

"And Peadar too. He was the one to suggest her in the first place. Funny to think she replaced him."

Mrs Cummins nodded. "They still see a lot of each other, though."

"Bridget and Peadar?" Caroline was surprised.

243

"Oh yes, Bridget consults him when she's not sure about the plants and all that."

"Oh, right. Sheila always did that too. The man's an expert when it comes to plants." He's a bloody bore when it comes to anything else, Caroline thought.

"Bridget swears they're just good friends, but between you and me, I think there's something going on." Mrs Cummins's voice had dropped to a whisper.

"Going on where?" Ciara had come back. She wanted to know what this woman was saying. She hated it when adults whispered.

"Nowhere." Caroline pulled her away. "Nice to see you, Mrs Cummins."

Seán stirred the tomato soup in the pot. He clattered the spoon in anger. Left to make his own lunch again. He was pissed off. He had enough on his plate without being expected to cook for himself. He was worried about one of his patients. Hilda Nolan. Why hadn't she told him about that lump before? God, it was maddening. If women would only trust their doctors. She was afraid, she'd said. She didn't want to think about it. Was she hoping it'd just go away? Seán was very upset. He'd fixed her up with a hospital appointment for next week. The biopsy would be done immediately. He hoped it wouldn't be too late. There was terrible ignorance around. He'd get in touch with the Department of Health. There needed to be more public awareness when it came to cancer. He didn't want to create a scare, but sometimes a little healthy fear is a good thing. There should be a health awareness programme in schools. He'd bring it up at the Dublin conference next month.

"Mam? Dad?" Colm roared upstairs as he slammed the front door shut.

"I'm not deaf," Seán called down to him. "Your mother and Ciara have gone into town."

Colm thudded up the stairs and plopped down on the kitchen chair. "I'm knackered."

"Do you want lunch?" Seán filled a bowl with steaming soup and set about carving the brown bread. It smelt delicious when it came out of the oven. He had Nora Maguire to thank for that. No bloody fear his wife'd be bothered to make brown bread for him. Too busy running up and down to Carrigeen. It's a wonder she didn't move over to the poxy village.

"Naw. Hate tomato soup. Not hungry anyway. Went to the chipper with Eddy and the gang."

What ever happened to pronouns, Seán wondered. "How did the game go?"

"Shite. We lost ten-eight." Colm dumped his football gear down on the kitchen floor. "That fecker Gibbo shouldn't be in goal. He's bloody useless."

"Colm, pick that stuff up and put it in the washing-machine," Seán snapped. "And watch your language. You're turning into a corner boy."

Colm stared at his father. Talk about the pot calling the kettle black. "Sorry. I'm going over to

Eddy's. His da's bringing us fishing. Tell Mam I'll be back for dinner."

He was gone before Seán could tell him to have a wash. Kids.

"That was too dried up." Seán stood up from the table. "You used to make lovely chicken casserole. Of course that was when you'd the time." He went into the sitting-room and left Caroline to wash up. He brought the wine with him. She wasn't in the mood for this. Why should she have to humour him all the time? She left the dishes to soak and went in to see if the twins were asleep.

They'd divided the bigger bedroom in two with a wooden partition. It wasn't ideal. Colm had the far side. He was sleeping soundly, no doubt knocked out by all the fresh air he'd got today. Ciara was reading a Mills and Boon bodice-ripper.

"Don't read too late, love." Caroline kissed her on the forehead.

"I won't. Just a bit longer. I'm getting to the good bit now."

Caroline smiled. What was the good bit? The long-awaited kiss? The grope in the forest? The damsel in distress rescued by her dream lover? These romances always ended with marriage. Happy-ever-after land. They should start chapter one with the return from the honeymoon. Knights on white horses or doctors on ego trips. It was all the same . . . the realities of marriage and compromise. That's what Ciara should be reading about. Ah, let her enjoy the fairytale. Time enough later to understand the rest. By the time Ciara got married, hopefully things would have changed.

Seán sat sullenly on the couch. "You look worn out. You've bags under your eye. You're not able to cope. Admit it."

"No, I'm fine. I'll have a lie-in tomorrow. You don't look so hot yourself. You were very quiet during dinner."

Seán scratched his nose. He always did that when he didn't want to discuss something.

"It's one of my patients. I can't say anything else."

Caroline understood. Seán had great integrity. He saw the privacy of his patients as sacrosanct. Proper order.

"There's something else I want to discuss with you." She poured more wine for him. "It's about Dr O'Hanlon in the Square. Bridget Cummins was telling me he was thinking of retiring."

"He is. He called me this morning. Wanted to know if I'd be interested in taking over his surgery."

"Oh?" Caroline didn't want to appear too eager. "What did you say?"

"Told him it was out of the question."

Caroline bit her lip. She wasn't sure how to put this. She risked him flying off the handle again. "Well, I'm not sure if that's true. We could manage it."

Seán glared at her. He banged his glass down on the coffee table. "What does that mean? More expense?"

"More space, that's what it means. You've always hated living over the surgery, right?"

"I have not. It suits me in fact. It's handy. You're the one who wanted to move." He pointed his finger accusingly at her.

"That's true. I wanted to move out of here. Not any more, though. I like this house. I like the area. The kids have all their friends around. It's just that we haven't enough room. Particularly now when they're getting older."

"We're fine the way we are." Seán hated change or disruption.

"We'd have four more rooms," Caroline argued.

"Yeah, but that kitchen downstairs is very pokey. We'd need to extend it. It's too much hassle, not to mention the expense. No."

"I can pay for it." Caroline jumped up with excitement. "I've loads of ideas. The upstairs kitchen will have to be practically demolished. That'd make a fine bedroom for Colm. Ciara can have our room. We'll go back to the big bedroom. That partition will come down easily. The bathroom's OK."

Seán looked at her scornfully. "What about downstairs? I suppose you've great ideas about that too."

"I have, as a matter of fact."

"No way." He picked up the newspaper. "I'm not going to discuss it. It's out of the question."

Caroline knew exactly what to do. She pulled the paper out of his hands. She snuggled down beside him and kissed him full on the lips. He tried to pull away at first, but the familiar stirrings licked at his belly. He couldn't resist her. His anger turned to passion.

"Let's make love," he whispered as he fondled her breast.

Caroline knew she'd won. This was the one way she could win an argument. It took time, but eventually Seán gave in. Women's wiles. "Ciara's still awake." She opened his top shirt button.

"What's wrong with right here?" Seán laid her gently back on the cushions.

* * *

Sheila arrived on Tuesday afternoon. Carrigeen was a hive of activity. The new hotel was nearly built. There were three new shops: a newsagent's, a bakery and a fishmonger's. Many of the younger set had come home to settle. If this kept up, there'd be need of a school. Conor was run off his feet with orders for his pottery. His wife, Claire, had converted their front room into a shop for his goods. The tourist trade was great in the summer. Sheila smiled as she drove down the main street. It was a different village to the one she and Mary had come across that beautiful June morning five years before.

Molly and Caroline were going through the job applications in the office. There were at least ten suitable applicants.

"Hi, Sheila." Molly stood up and shook hands. "Glad to see you. You've a busy day ahead."

Sheila sat down on the couch. "I'm not going to

sit in on the interviews. You and Caroline can do them."

Caroline guffawed. Molly looked terrified.

"I'm serious. The girl will be working for you two, not me."

"But you always do the hiring," Caroline protested.

Sheila shook her head. "You've got that arsewise. I haven't been running this office for the past three years. You have and, according to Finian O'Toole, you're making a damn good fist of it."

Molly blushed with pleasure. "Thanks. But I've never interviewed anyone before. I wouldn't know what to ask."

"I would," Caroline assured her. "I know exactly what we're looking for."

"Tell me," Sheila encouraged her.

"Obviously someone with the right secretarial qualifications, but much more than that. We need someone we can trust. She has to have initiative, be able to make decisions for herself if we're not around. She has to be reliable and punctual."

"Yeah," Molly agreed. "And she has to be willing to work overtime when there's a rush on. She has to be a quick learner. Honest too."

Sheila laughed. "Superwoman, that's what you two expect. But you have the right ideas. I made a desperate *faux pas* lately hiring an assistant for the shop. I should have got you two slave-drivers to do the interviews for me. Any interesting applications?"

"Yeah." Molly was more confident now. "There's

one girl from Cleggan who seems to be suitable. Her father's the chemist there."

"Ben Raftery?"

"Yes. She knows a bit about our business it seems. She's been helping in the shop for years."

"That's how I started," Sheila reminded them. "Anyone else?"

"There's a girl from the village. She's coming in at eleven for her interview."

"Do I know her?" Sheila asked.

"She's the carpenter's daughter," Caroline said. "Very bright girl."

"God, the last time I saw her she was a child. Pretty little blonde slip of a thing. Was she the one you told me about? The one with the brilliant Leaving Cert?"

"Yeah." Caroline handed Sheila her letter. "They couldn't afford to send her to college. She paid her own way through secretarial school by working part-time in a pub."

Sheila read through the girl's letter. "She may be the right one for the job. Enterprising and clever. Her father's a widower, isn't he?"

"Mm. Sally's the eldest. She practically reared the younger kids herself."

Sheila bit the top of her biro thoughtfully. "I'll leave it to you to decide. Wait till you've seen all the girls before you make up your minds. But if this Sally is as good as she sounds, I can't see any reason not to give her a try. Why bring someone in from outside if we've got what we want right under our noses?"

Molly and Caroline thought Sheila was right. They knew it was her policy to employ the people of Carrigeen where possible. It made sense.

"Right. I'll call in on Bridget in the lab. See what she's up to."

Bridget was on the phone when Sheila came in.

"Right. That's settled then. See you tonight."

Sheila cocked an ear. "What's this? A hot date?"

Bridget blushed crimson to the roots of her brown hair.

"No, no, not at all. That was Peadar."

Why did she look so flustered, Sheila wondered.

"Oh Peadar. How's he then?" Sheila strolled around nonchalantly.

"Grand. He's grand. I was just asking him about the cedarwood blend."

"What are you using it for?"

"Our new astringent for oily skin. I was wondering about a shampoo range. Apparently cedarwood's a good hair tonic. It's supposed to be effective against seborrhoea of the scalp."

"Shampoos?" Sheila thought for a moment. "Yeah, why not?"

"Of course, I'll have to research the other ingredients."

"No problem to you, Bridget." Sheila smiled sweetly.

Bridget felt decidedly uncomfortable. Was Sheila being sarcastic? Had she done something wrong? She wasn't sure she liked Sheila very much. She wondered if she'd put Sheila's nose out of joint when she took over the lab. Ridiculous. Sure Sheila was the one who wanted to move to Dublin. She was the one who gave her the promotion. Still, Bridget felt uncomfortable. As if Sheila was waiting for her to make a mistake. She must be getting paranoid.

"Carry on." Sheila patted her on the arm. "I wouldn't want to disturb the good work. If you need me, you know where to find me. I'm just at the other end of the phone."

"Thanks, Sheila," Bridget muttered. God, she wished her boss would go back to Dublin. She hated these fortnightly visits.

Sheila had lunch with Caroline in O'Malley's. To her surprise, Maura brought out a beautiful platter of smoked salmon and mouth-watering hot brown bread.

"Very up-market," Sheila said approvingly.

"Oh God, girl, sure we have to be on our toes now with the new hotel nearly finished. Vying for custom, what?" Maura laughed her deep throaty laugh.

"Competition, there's nothing like it," Sheila agreed. "Where's Seamus?"

"Next door in the pottery with his daughter-in-law, God help her." Maura raised her eyes to heaven.

"Is he helping?" Sheila buttered the hot bread.

"I wouldn't put it quite like that. He thinks he is. But sure he's so big and awkward, he keeps knocking things over. The proverbial bull in the china shop."

"Don't mind her, Sheila." Caroline grinned. "Seamus chats up everyone who goes in. They all buy something. That fella could sell sand to the Arabs."

"Oh they all buy something all right," Maura said begrudgingly. "They'd write a blank cheque to get away from his auld talk." Off she went behind the bar again.

"There's some narking going on around here these days," Sheila whispered to Caroline.

"I know. Isn't it great craic altogether? They're all fighting and squabbling. There's great life back in the place. All we need now is a few affairs to spice it up some more."

"Oh?" Sheila asked innocently. "Are you thinking of making a play for Seamus?"

"No thanks." Caroline smiled at the idea. "Your brother is all I can handle at the moment."

"God help you! Did you get anywhere with the suggestion for the new surgery?"

"Let's just say I'm still working at it." Caroline winked at her. "Sheila, there's a bit of gossip you might be interested in."

"Yeah?" Sheila was all ears.

"Bridget Cummins. I think she's seeing Peadar."

"Jesus, you're joking." Sheila screwed up her face. "Peadar? She wouldn't be interested in Peadar."

Caroline finished her salmon. Typical of Sheila to dismiss it out of hand. She wasn't interested in Peadar herself so she couldn't imagine anyone else falling for him. But, bore or no bore, Peadar was a catch. He was steady and reliable. He was a good person. He was safe. A lot of women would settle for that.

"Time will tell." Caroline was convinced she was right. "How's your own love life?"

"Non-existent. I haven't the time."

"You have to make time, Sheila. All work and no play . . . you know the rest."

"Well, I prefer all work. I like to keep busy."

Caroline knew why. Sheila was driven by ambition. The business was becoming an obsession. "What are you trying to prove?"

Sheila folded her arms defensively. "I'm not trying to prove anything. I love my work. That isn't a crime, is it?"

Caroline could feel the aggression. "No, I guess not. It's just not very healthy, in my opinion. Remember when you used to lecture me? You warned me about putting all my eggs in one basket. You pointed out that the kids'd grow up and be gone before I knew it. You were right. They still need me, of course, but not the way they used to. I adore my job. I've you to thank for that. But I've my home life as well. It's important to have both."

Sheila looked at her sharply. "Well, lucky old you!"

Caroline knew she'd gone too far. Sheila was as touchy as hell.

"Look Caroline, I don't have to justify my lifestyle to you or anyone else. OK?"

"OK, I'm sorry. I'd no intention of offending you. I'm simply concerned about you. We all need to be needed, Sheila. What you've achieved with this company is fantastic. Fair dues to you. You obviously get a great buzz from that."

"Yeah, I do," Sheila said emphatically. "People do need me. What about all the people I employ?"

"Agreed. They've practically canonised you around here. Job fulfilment. But what about your personal life? What about your feelings?"

Sheila was angry. "I try not to impose my feelings on everyone else. People don't want to be bored by self-indulgent whinging."

"Sheila, why are you attacking me? I'm only trying to help."

Silence. Caroline sipped her tea. Why on earth had she started this? She should have left well enough alone.

"Caroline, I appreciate your concern, but it's not necessary. Sometimes talking helps, but sometimes it doesn't. I thought you understood. Obviously you don't."

Caroline wasn't going to let her away with that. No way. She did understand. She understood everything. It was Sheila who couldn't see the wood for the trees.

"What good is burying yourself away going to do for Karen?"

There, she'd said it. It needed to be said.

Sheila stood up. "I don't think there's much point in continuing this, do you? May I see the new brochures you've been working on?"

"Aye, aye, Captain." Caroline stood to attention and saluted.

Sheila had to laugh. She sat down again. "Why don't I get us a drink?"

"That's better. We can look at the designs later. I'll have a glass of beer. I'm parched. It's hard work talking to you!"

Caroline went to the loo. She splashed cold water on her face and told herself off. She'd have to be more careful with Sheila. It might be ten years ago, but the sores were still open and festering. When she came back to the table, Sheila had calmed down.

"I'm sorry, Caroline. I overreacted. You hit a nerve."

"No, no, you were right. Your life is none of my damn business."

"It is. You've always been there for me. You and Mary."

"God, Mary. How is she? Do you see much of her?"

"No, not really. I've been burying myself in my work, as you so succinctly put it. And she's . . . she's busy with the baby."

Oh no. Mary's baby. Another touchy subject. How was Sheila coping with that? It was bound to make a huge difference to their relationship. Mary would be engrossed in the joys of mothering.

"I'm going back to Dublin on Friday. Mary asked me to spend Saturday night with them. You know they bought a beautiful three-storey house in Sandymount."

"Yeah. I'm glad they're doing so well." Caroline

didn't tell her that she'd rung Mary because she was concerned about Sheila.

"Mary's as bad as yourself. She won't be happy till I march up the aisle with somebody. Anybody."

Caroline laughed. "I'm sure that's not true."

"It bloody well is. Now I don't know how to tell you my news without you having a fit."

"What news?"

"I'm starting a new business. Well, not exactly a new business. It'll all be part of Natural Woman."

"Tell me. I won't bite, I promise."

Sheila took a deep breath. "A beauty salon."

"Brilliant. How did you come up with the idea?" Caroline was genuinely impressed.

"From working in the shop. A lot of people come in for advice. So I said to myself, there's money to be made from this."

"Get away, Sheila. Money isn't your objective. It never was."

"No, seriously, I'm really into the idea. When I got the idea for Carrigeen that totally absorbed me. Then, when that was up and running, I got . . ."

"Bored." Caroline finished it for her.

"Not exactly bored but . . . then came the shop. That's working out well too, apart from the fact that I'm not happy with the location. You're running things here. Lily will be ready to run the shop when I get a suitable assistant. So I need to do something else."

"Right. I'm sure it'll work. You'll see that it does. But I still think you're running away from

something. You're like a dog chasing its tail."
Caroline waited for her to explode. She didn't.

"Running away from something? You mean myself?"

"I think that's what I mean."

Sheila thought for a minute. "It's true. I am. I run around like a blue-arsed fly all day. But when I come back to the apartment, I face myself. I have to. Every night when I crawl into that bed on my own, I face it. The loneliness."

Caroline handed Sheila her drink. Loneliness. Emptiness. Christ, what a legacy.

"There, I warned you," Sheila half laughed, half cried. "Self-indulgent whinging. So, what's my solution? Keep busy, that's what."

"Loneliness isn't a crime either. God knows how many people out there are lonely. And it's not necessarily people who live alone. I was desperately lonely when the kids were small. Do you know who realised that?"

"Not Seán?"

"No. Your father. He often used to call on me, unexpectedly. He was lovely, your dad."

"I know. He understood everything . . . except Mam, perhaps. He never really understood her. It's a funny thing about loneliness. It sort of creeps up on you. Nobody wants to admit they're lonely. You'd swear it was a disease. Contagious."

Caroline agreed. Many would tell you they were sick, even depressed. But who'd come up and say "I'm lonely"? It was an admission of some sort of failure, at least that's what people thought.

"Come on, Sheila. Things won't always be this way. I'm glad we've had this talk though. Go back to Dublin. Organise your salon. It's a marvellous idea. Are you going to employ a beautician?"

"Absolutely. You don't think I'm mad then? Starting something new?"

"No, definitely not. Keep busy. You're right. Who the hell am I to be pontificating? You'll be the owner of an empire, laughing at us all."

"What'll Mam say? And Seán?"

"There's only one answer to that and you know what it is!"

Sheila got her handbag. "Let's go. What time's the next interview?"

"Two-thirty. Though I think we've decided on Sally. Hey, wait a minute. Does this mean I have to design brochures and ads for the salon?"

"Afraid so."

"More work. Seán'll have a fit." They both giggled.

Maura watched them leave. Now what was all that about? One minute they're fighting. The next they're practically crying. Then they're bosom buddies again. These business types. Weirdos, one and all.

CHAPTER NINETEEN

Mary hoovered and polished the basement thoroughly. She was expecting Sheila this afternoon. She changed the sheets and the duvet cover. She was thrilled with the colour scheme down here. The silvery grey of the carpet and walls set off the bright yellow of the curtains and bedspread. She had leafed through piles of Home and Garden before she arrived at this choice. She realised she was becoming obsessed by what some people would consider trivia, but she had waited so long for this house. She wanted everything to be right. She scrubbed down the shower unit and kitchenette. The whole basement was compact, like a miniature house. It even had its own hall door. That would give Joanne and Brian the chance to do their own thing when they arrived for their holiday next week. She was pleased with her morning's work. The only thing left to do now was to water the plants.

Sheila was touched by her friend's efforts to make her welcome.

"The house is really super, Mary. It's full of

character. The changes you've made already are incredible."

"There's still a lot to be done upstairs, but I must admit that I'm delighted with the way things have worked out down here. It's exactly the way I wanted it. I hope you'll be comfortable tonight. There are more blankets in the wardrobe if you're cold."

"I'm sure I won't be."

"Now enough of this chit-chat. Tell me all the gossip. How are things in Galway?" She brought Sheila up the back stairs to the big kitchen. "How's your mam?"

"Thriving. You'd have to make an appointment to see her."

"That's great. At least you don't have to worry about her. And Seán?"

"More painful than ever. Caroline's cheesed off with him."

Mary brought her a cup of coffee over to the table. Sheila had no intention of drinking it, but she didn't want to make an issue of it either. "Where's Davy?"

"Angela, our babysitter, has taken him for a walk. She loves wheeling him down to the village. She's at that age. Adores babies. They should be back soon. Let's enjoy our chin-wag while we can. Master Davy tends to take over when he's around."

"How are you going to manage when you go back to school in September?"

Mary lit a cigarette. "I'm steeped. Angela's mother has agreed to be our baby-minder. She's still a young woman. I like her a lot. Davy knows her well and he's used to being in their house. They live down the road. Angela says she'll pick him up in the mornings before she goes to school."

"There's a lot to be organised when you're working."

Was Sheila wondering how she'd have coped? Mary was sure that's what was going through her mind. Better bring the conversation back.

"So, Seán and Caroline are in the wars? Wouldn't you think he'd appreciate her salary? Hey, you're not drinking your coffee."

Sheila excused herself and explained why. Mary thought she was cracked. "Oh God, I'd go mad without my nicotine and caffeine fixes. Don't mention cellulite. I've lumps on top of the lumps."

Sheila laughed. "I've been off the fags for nearly four years now. I don't miss them anymore. I found it harder to give up coffee. At first I got desperate headaches, but when your system clears out they disappear."

Mary made a face. "I'll take your word for it."

"Is Jim working today?"

"No, for once he's not. He's gone to play golf, thank goodness. To tell you the truth, I'm worried about him. He works all the hours God sends. He's away a lot too. Sometimes I resent him. It's not much fun being left alone for days at a time. I adore Davy, but it's hard looking after him on my own when Jim's away. At least when he's in Dublin Jim takes over for a while in the evening. Even to let me have a bath. Babies are gorgeous, but they demand all your time."

Sheila stiffened. Was that a broad hint? Was Mary implying that she couldn't have managed on her own with Karen? Perhaps not. Mary was simply stating a fact. She found it difficult when Jim was away. Why read anything else into it?

"So, will Jim be back for dinner?" Sheila asked.

"No, he's dining out with the lads."

"Very civilised."

"Yeah, although steak and chips wouldn't be your idea of healthy eating," Mary slagged her. "We're having a vegetarian lasagne."

"Great. With garlic bread?"

"Yep and a side salad. I didn't forget. You can make the French dressing. I've some good olive oil."

"Lovely."

"You still drink wine, don't you?" Mary grinned cheekily.

"Don't be so smart, young one! I haven't given everything up."

Mary plonked Davy on Sheila's lap. The chubby little fellow gurgled up at her. He was a dote. Sheila's heart melted as his fat little fingers closed around hers.

"He's a darling, Mary. I could eat him."

"Funny you should say that. I often get this irresistible urge to bite him. Don't worry, I'm not going cannibalistic or anything. It's this incredible feeling that I'd like to smother him with love."

"I can understand that." Sheila nuzzled the baby's neck. He chortled.

"Blow on his tummy, he loves that." Mary went off to turn on the oven. When she came back, Sheila had Davy on the floor, blowing softly on his stomach.

"No, you have to make a noise. You're too gentle."

Mary got down on the floor, pulled up Davy's T-shirt and blew loudly on his soft skin.

"It sounds like a fart, it's disgusting," Sheila said in mock horror.

The baby howled with laughter and kicked up his legs. Mary got a knee in her nose. "Ya little monster." She laughed and scooped him up in her arms. She carried him down to the kitchen and put him in the high-chair. He went mad when he saw his dinner bowl coming.

"He's hungry, isn't he?" Sheila was amused at the child's flailing limbs. He nearly dived out of the chair. "May I feed him?"

"Are you sure?"

"Yeah, I'd love to."

Mary went to the draining board to wash the lettuce. She watched Sheila out of the corner of her eye. She was great with Davy. She was making funny faces and tickling his toes. The baby was besotted with her. You'd swear he was flirting the way he gave her sidelong glances. Then he held up his puckered lips for a kiss. The mashed carrot and potato on his face wasn't exactly enticing, but Sheila overcame any qualms she might have and kissed him smack on the mouth.

"Brave woman," Mary applauded her. "Is this very hard for you, Sheila?"

"I'd be lying if I said it was easy," Sheila admitted. "But he's such a sweet little fellow. Who could begrudge you or Jim your happiness? You both deserve it. You deserve Davy. He's a lucky child to have such a loving home."

"You had the same love for Karen. I didn't realise that then." Mary felt her words were so inadequate. But it was true that it was only now that she fully understood Sheila's loss. "You must still regret the adoption."

Sheila didn't reply at first. She took away Davy's bowl and gave him his bottle. Mary thought she wasn't going to answer. That she was too choked up. She looked over at Sheila but she could see no sign of tears.

Finally Sheila replied. "I don't think I regret it anymore. Maybe I did the right thing. I've had ten years to consider it from every angle. Giving her away broke my heart. There's no doubt about that. But keeping her would've been selfish."

Mary cut up tomatoes and cucumber. Her heart went out to Sheila. It was pitiful.

"I don't know. There's no easy answer." Mary came over and put her arms around Sheila. "All I know is you were very brave."

Sheila smiled. "No, I wasn't brave. I was naïve. I honestly thought I could keep her and look after her by myself. I only gave her up because everyone else said it was for the best."

"And you think they were wrong?" Mary thought she'd been wrong herself.

"No, they weren't wrong. They weren't right either. Who knows? We'll never know. But I did give her up because I loved her so much. I wanted what was best for her. Or what they all said was best for her."

"Jesus, it's all so complicated. I can tell you one thing. I've stopped dishing out advice. We're all different. Every situation is unique. You should have been allowed to make up your own mind without all that pressure."

"I was young. I was vulnerable. Everyone did what they thought was best. Remember Philip and Susan?"

"God, whatever happened to them? Is Seán still in touch with him?"

"I don't know. Seán never mentions it, but I spotted Philip in Baggot Street the other day. My heart skipped a beat. He must still have his rooms in Merrion Square."

"Did you talk to him?"

"No, I couldn't. I couldn't face him. It brought it all back. I ran into a shop. He never saw me."

"I wonder where Karen is, Sheila. I often wonder that."

"Me too." Sheila wiped Davy's mouth. "Wherever she is, let's hope she's happy."

When Davy was asleep, Mary and Sheila had their meal. They polished off two bottles of wine between them. They were relaxed and easy in each other's company.

"This is like the old days." Mary sighed with satisfaction. "I'm stuffed." She opened the top button of her jeans.

The front door opened. Voices. Laughter.

"That's Jim. He must have brought someone back with him. I hate it when he does that." Mary stood up and closed the button again.

"Mary? Where are you?" Jim shouted from the hall door.

"We're in the kitchen," she called back. Her tone wasn't too friendly. She was in no mood for company. Neither was Sheila. They were enjoying their little chat and had no wish to be disturbed. Now they'd have to make small talk to one of Jim's business friends.

Jim came into the kitchen. "Why're you in here? Wouldn't you be more comfortable in the sitting-room?"

"No, we wouldn't," Mary snapped at him. "You go up there."

"Shh, for God's sake," he begged her. "He'll hear you. Hi, Sheila. You're looking well."

Sheila kissed him on the cheek. "Where's your friend?"

"Where are you, John boy?" Jim opened the kitchen door. "Come in, come in. I thought you were behind me."

A man followed him in. A tall dark handsome man. A man with a moustache and the bluest eyes Sheila had ever seen. A man Sheila had once described as a fine thing. She blushed.

"You know John, Mary." Mary stood up and

268

shook his hand. "And this is Sheila Crosby, alias Natural Woman." Jim laughed. "John Harris, my solicitor."

Sheila had to get a grip. Why was her stomach doing somersaults? "Pleased to meet you." She tried a sophisticated smile, but it came out as a silly grin.

He held her outstretched hand for a little too long. The blue eyes twinkled mischievously. "We've met before."

"Oh?" she answered offhandedly. Silly twit. He knew she was bluffing. He knew she remembered him. Why couldn't she be normal? Natural woman, my ass. She was a bag of nerves. Her knees turned to jelly. Insane at her age.

Jim came to the rescue. "Oh, that's right. You met at our wedding. Sheila was our bridesmaid, remember, John?"

"How could I forget? We had a dance." He winked.

Mary was fuming. He actually had the gall to wink at Sheila. That was no dance. It was nothing short of a mating ritual. The nerve of him. Smarmy gobshite.

"Mary." Jim beckoned to her, "I need you upstairs for a minute."

She'd swing for Jim. What was he at? His John B Keane impersonation?

Jim went under the stairs for another bottle of wine and handed it to John Harris. "Pour another drink for Sheila and have one yourself."

He dragged the protesting Mary from the room. Sheila made a huge effort to look composed. Why

was this man having such an effect on her?
Ridiculous. She was a capable businesswoman not
an adolescent groupie. But her hands trembled as
he poured the wine into her glass. "I think I've had
enough already."

"You're not driving, are you?" He sat down
beside her. She shuffled up a bit on the kitchen
bench. He was too close for comfort. Why couldn't
Mary have four kitchen chairs like everyone else?

Jim pulled Mary into the bathroom. "Are you mad?"
She thumped him. "Do you not think you're being a
bit obvious throwing him at Sheila like that?"

"Calm down. It was his idea."

"His idea?" Her voice reached a higher pitch of
anger. "Who the hell does he think he is?"

"What's the harm? He gave me a lift home. He
didn't have a drink all night because he had the car
with him. I asked him in for a night-cap, right? At
first he refused, but when he heard Sheila was here,
he asked me to introduce him. He's interested,
Mary. What's wrong with that?"

"He's a smoothie, that's what's wrong." She sat
on the side of the bath, tapping her foot. "I credited
you with more sense. He's separated too. Sheila's
had enough complications in her life."

"He only wants a date. He's not going to
compromise her virtue."

"Jesus, he's probably seducing her this minute.
I'm going back." She ran out of the bathroom and
down the stairs.

Jim couldn't understand her. He was tired

listening to how Sheila hadn't a normal life. No social outlet. Then, when he tried to introduce her to a highly eligible friend, what did Mary do? Had a go at him. Sheila was no shrinking violet. She could take care of herself. If she wasn't interested in John Harris, she'd be perfectly capable of letting him know. Mary was far too protective.

"So you reckon Brown Thomas was your big break?" John was genuinely interested in this woman. She wasn't like anyone he had met before. She was stunning, even in her jeans and denim shirt. Her thick auburn hair fell in waves to her shoulders. Her skin had a healthy glow. Her green eyes sparkled and her expression was animated when she spoke about her business. But there was something else about her. He couldn't quite put his finger on it. There was an aloofness about her that intrigued him.

"Well, we were doing very well all over the West at that point. Caroline, my sister-in-law, was the one who had the promotion ideas. She was my advertising manager then. One weekend she came up to Dublin with my brother. He's a doctor."

"In Galway?"

"Yes. While he was at a medical conference, Caroline went on a shopping spree around Grafton Street. She loved Brown Thomas. It was so classy. She had a good look at their cosmetic department and was convinced that Natural Woman would be perfect for the shop."

"Was it easy to get in there?" He poured her

another glass of wine. The drink seemed to loosen her tongue.

"On the contrary, it was very difficult." Sheila wondered why she found it so easy to talk to this man. He was different to what she'd imagined. He wasn't just making polite conversation. He wanted to know all about her business. All about her, she suspected.

"So, how did you convince them?"

"We did our homework very well. Caroline literally launched a campaign. She photographed all our products. Big glossy prints. She updated our brochures and leaflets. We changed our printers. It was expensive, but worth it. We had A4 showcards for the display. She has a great feel for what they call customer awareness. We had our documents in a company folder. It was all very impressive."

"Documents? Like the price list?"

"Mm," Sheila's voice rose as she thought back to the excitement of that time. "The official price list, the advertising plan, details of our packaging, a history of the factory in Carrigeen and its employees, the whole concept behind our products."

"Stressing the natural ingredients," he joined in.

"Exactly. There's a huge swing back to natural ingredients and materials. We also had a detailed sales plan and forecast. We had figures to back us up because the products were selling well in the West."

"Highly professional." John was impressed.

"Well, Caroline had experience in advertising. She knew what she was doing."

"So BT's welcomed you with open arms?"

"Not at first." She laughed. "I rang the buyer and had to use all my powers of persuasion to get an appointment."

Mary bustled back in. Why did she cough before she opened the kitchen door, Sheila wondered. What on earth did she think was going on?

"Sorry about that, Jim wanted to talk to me about . . . his mother." She knew the excuse was feeble. "We're planning a surprise birthday party for her next week." Mary sat down and took out a cigarette. John leaned over to light it for her. Oozing charm, Mary thought cynically.

"Sheila was filling me in on how she got into Brown Thomas," John explained.

Mary took a long drag on the cigarette. "God, I remember the day you came up to meet the buyer. I met you for lunch in Bewley's after it. You were in bits."

"I know. It was a desperate ordeal."

"What was?" Jim loped into the kitchen and headed straight for the kettle. "Anyone for coffee?"

No takers. "What was the big ordeal?" Jim asked again as he joined them at the table.

"Sheila meeting the buyer in BT's," John said. "Go on, Sheila. What happened?"

"It was nerveracking. I was brought into this big boardroom. I was very nervous, as Mary said, but I had to project this cool sophisticated image."

"No bother to you." Jim hiccuped.

"Maybe you should have a coffee yourself." Mary nudged him. She'd only just realised he was quite merry. "Oh, I nearly forgot. There's cheese and crackers in the fridge. Jim, will you bring them over?"

Jim laid them on the table with a flourish. Brie, Camembert and Gorgonzola. He plonked a packet of cream crackers in the middle of the table.

"We do have plates," Mary protested. "Where are the water biscuits?"

"Jesus, you're as fussy." Jim sat down grumpily.

Mary sighed and got up to get the Carrs. "You're hopeless." She glared at him.

Sheila was embarrassed by this tiff, but John Harris stayed as cool as a cucumber. "Carry on, Sheila."

"Ah, you don't want to listen to this. It's boring."

"It is not," John insisted. "You can't leave us hanging there. Go on. You were sitting in the boardroom and . . . ?"

"I was talking nine to the dozen, the way you do when you're nervous. The buyer, Sandra Murphy, listened politely and nodded from time to time. But she said very little and I was there floundering around like a fool."

"I'm sure you weren't." John Harris smiled at her. "You were well prepared, like you said."

"Anyhow, to cut a long story short, she said she liked the products but they were too expensive. She also said they had no space."

"A typical ploy." Jim hiccuped again.

"That floored me for a minute," Sheila continued. "I had to think fast. I told her we could reproduce all the products in trial sizes. You know, miniatures.

Then I suggested an introductory offer, a kit bag of the products at a special price."

"Brilliant." John spread some Brie on a cracker. "Did she go for that?"

"She began to waver. She agreed to see me again in a month when I had the trial sizes ready."

"And what about the space problem?" Mary interjected. "Tell John how you got around that."

"I was grabbing at straws by then. I told her we'd our own stand, a small display case."

"And did you?" John munched on the cracker.

"We did in the office in Carrigeen. But that was too bulky to move. I knew I'd have to design another wood cabinet that'd be easier to move around. But she wasn't to know that, was she? Then, when I saw that she was going off the idea, I told her I had my own salesgirl who I'd pay myself to do the promotion. Another big spoof, but I'd a month to train someone in so I thought, what the hell."

"I have to hand it to you, you're very persuasive." John winked at her again. "I wouldn't dream of fighting you off."

Mary stubbed out her cigarette in the ash-tray. He was still coming on to her. Sheila seemed to like it. Well, it was up to her.

"Why had you only got a month?" Jim asked.

"This was February '74. Skin products do well at certain times of the year, summer and Christmas mostly. I wanted to cash in on the summer market as we'd just started our new range of suntan creams. March is the best month to launch new products."

"So you obviously got what you wanted." John squeezed her knee. "Fair play to you."

Sheila didn't remove his hand. It felt quite comfortable there. Reassuring.

"Yeah, in the end I did. I trained in a girl from Carrigeen. Aoife. Her father worked for us, harvesting the carrageen. She knew what we were about. She's a beautiful girl and quick to learn. She took to it like a duck to water. She loved Dublin. She stayed with her aunt at first. Now she has her own flat. She was brilliant in Brown Thomas. She loved the glamour of it all. She stood there in her specially designed Natural Woman sash and sold the products very successfully. We were on a six-month trial on a strictly SOR basis."

"SOR?" John didn't understand.

"Sale or return," Sheila explained. "That way there was no risk for Brown Thomas. We'd taken out a big glossy ad in *Woman's Choice* too. Then *Woman's Way* gave us a good write-up. We were lucky."

"It's more business acumen than luck." Mary was vehement in her praise. "There's no stopping this woman when she's her mind made up."

"I can see that." John looked admiringly at her. "Jim was telling me you've your own shop now."

Sheila nodded. She was embarrassed by all these questions. They were too pointed. She didn't like talking about herself to strangers. Although he didn't seem like a stranger. It was weird. Mercifully, Jim changed the conversation. They started to discuss John's law practice. He had a hilarious story from a barrister friend of his. This character, a true Dublin codger, was hauled into court for selling pornography on a stand in O'Connell Street.

"He got off scot-free too." John laughed. He had a lovely laugh, Sheila thought. Deep and hearty.

"How did he manage that?" Mary wanted to know. "Aren't the censorship laws very rigid?"

"He told the judge he couldn't read."

They all laughed.

"It seems selling magazines is a highly lucrative profession," John continued. "His wife was overheard saying that they didn't know where to go on holidays this year. Apparently they were 'sick o' the bloody aul Alps.' Hilarious!"

"Unbelievable." Mary gasped.

"Yeah," John agreed. "And to add insult to injury their children are on the free book list in school."

Mary had experience of this kind of thing herself. "These people'd live in your ear."

It was two o'clock when John Harris got up to leave.

"Nice meeting you," he murmured to Sheila. "I hope we can meet again soon. Would you like to go to the theatre some night?"

Sheila stalled. Mary and Jim were clearing the table. She didn't want them to overhear.

"Maybe. I'm going to France next week. To Grasse. I'm quite busy, actually."

"Fine. I'll leave you this." He placed his business card on the table. "Give me a call."

He said goodnight to Mary and Jim left him to the door.

"Well," Mary said triumphantly. "I knew he was a sleazebag. He's so cocksure of himself. I'm glad you gave him a put-down."

Sheila took up the card. "It wasn't a put-down. I liked him. He's good company. I think I will phone him when I get back from France."

You could have knocked Mary down with a feather.

By the time Mary crawled into bed, Jim was snoring softly. She wanted to talk to him, but this wouldn't be the right time. Not when he'd had a few jars. A good few jars. He got silly with drink. Don't we all? What was Sheila playing at? Was she really going to ring John Harris? That'd be a big mistake. She yanked back the sheet from Jim. He'd rolled himself into a ball and wrapped the sheet around him. Typical. No, Sheila'd never do it. It was the wine talking. She'd think differently in the morning. What had John Harris to offer? He was separated, for God's sake. Why bother having a relationship that could go nowhere? Or would that suit Sheila? Was that just what she wanted? She'd never have to commit herself to him. Yeah, Mary thought. That's what attracted Sheila. He wasn't really up for grabs at all, was he? Separated meant free, but not completely free. Not legally. She'd ask Jim in the morning if John had a legal separation. She'd bet he didn't. Where was his wife now? That was another thing she'd try to find out. The last thing Mary

wanted was for Sheila to be messed up by another
Don Juan type. Honestly, Sheila was like a sitting
duck when it came to men. Talk about masochistic.

What was all that earlier on? Sheila said she
didn't regret the adoption any more. Crap. Mary
could see through that little charade. Who was
Sheila trying to kid? Herself, maybe. Mary knew her
better. It was blatantly obvious that Sheila still
regretted it bitterly. Caroline had even said so. She'd
rung Mary a few weeks ago to say she was worried
about Sheila. It was the middle of August now.
Karen's tenth birthday was coming up next month.
Sheila said she'd given Karen up because she loved
her. That was true all right. But that didn't mean she
didn't regret it. Mary would take an oath that not a
day passed when Sheila didn't regret it. She was
great today with Davy. That couldn't have been
easy. None of this was easy. Ah, let her have a fling
with John Harris if she wanted. What harm could it
do? So long as she didn't take him too seriously. No
point in getting hurt again. As for marriage, Mary
knew that Sheila genuinely didn't want that. Or
children either. It was a terrible pity.

Sheila couldn't sleep. She was too excited. John was
lovely. She really liked him. Usually she found men
boring. He was different. He was entertaining. He
was interested in what she had to say. God, he was
so handsome. She tried to imagine what it would be
like to kiss him. She imagined herself on his arm
walking on the beach. They'd eat in fancy
restaurants. He'd mentioned something about a

play. She'd like that. She wanted to see him again, that was definite. It was time she gave a man a chance. The single life of a career woman wasn't all it was cracked up to be. What was it that Valerie bitch had said? That she was a dried-up old spinster? Sheila smiled at the thought of it. Maybe it was time to thaw out a little.

She turned off the bedside lamp and lay back on the pillow. She thought about Mary and Jim upstairs. They had it all. Did they realise that? She sensed a certain tension between them tonight, but she knew she was the cause of it. Mary didn't approve of John Harris. That was very clear. But it was all very fine for Mary to make judgements. She was living in a cocoon of comfort and security. What did she know about loneliness? Or frustration? No, Mary could criticise all she liked. But she'd have to accept Sheila's decision. She was going to phone John Harris as soon as she got back from her trip to Grasse. She was going to go for it.

She turned on her side and stretched her left leg down the bed. She bent her right leg up. This was her most comfortable position for sleep. Before she drifted off she said a prayer for Karen. She did this every night. The ritual brought her some solace.

CHAPTER TWENTY

The shop was busy on Monday morning. Their August profits would be up. That'd keep Finian O'Toole happy. Amanda Donoghue was the new girl. Sheila knew she'd made a better choice this time, but she'd check with Lily anyway.

"Amanda, would you drop over to Bewley's and get some cream cakes for the coffee break?" Sheila got her purse.

"Thought you said she never ate muck," Amanda whispered to Lily.

"Normally she doesn't." Lily knew that Sheila wanted a few minutes alone with her. She finished sticking the price tags on the new shampoo range. She'd try the one with the rosemary extract herself tonight. Sheila swore it encouraged hair growth and Lily hated her thin wispy mane. Amanda went off to get the cakes.

"Well?" Sheila turned to Lily. "Your verdict?"

"She's perfect. She really is," Lily enthused.

"Go on." Sheila wanted to know more. A lot depended on what Lily was going to say.

"She's good with the customers. She's friendly and helpful."

Sheila nodded approvingly. "Not too pushy, I hope. People like to browse without being followed around the shop."

"No, not pushy at all," Lily assured her.

"Good. What about her time-keeping?"

Lily smiled. There was no way Sheila was going to forget the Valerie débâcle. Lily knew her boss believed in learning by her mistakes. "She hasn't been late once."

"Fine."

"She's very easy to get along with."

"What about when I'm not here? Does she take instructions from you?"

This really was the third degree, Lily thought. Where was it leading? "She always does what I ask her, and willingly too. Not that I boss her around, of course, but she seems to think I'm in charge when you're not here."

Sheila was pleased. This was what she'd been hoping for. "Do you fancy a rise, Lily?"

"Pardon?" Lily was taken aback. "A rise, did you say?"

Sheila put her arm around the younger woman. "How would you feel about managing the shop?"

Lily stepped back. "Are you serious?"

"Deadly serious."

Lily looked doubtful. "I don't think I'd be capable enough. I mean I'm OK when I know you'll be around."

"You coped fine on your own when I fired Valerie. All the customers like you. Even Mrs Reidy has rejoined the fold. You know how to do the stocktaking and the accounts. I've the utmost confidence in you."

Lily beamed with pleasure. Sheila didn't hand out compliments easily. This was praise indeed, coming from her. "Thanks."

"You won't be on your own. I'll continue to drop in and you can ring me if there's a problem. It's just that I'm going to be tied up with the new salon for a while. The decorators are in at the moment, but it'll be ready in a fortnight. I've got to get everything organised and I'll have to hire new staff. So, if you could run the shop, that'd be a huge weight off my mind."

Lily took a deep breath. "I'd love to give it a go." To Sheila's surprise, Lily gave her a big hug. "I'll work very hard. I won't let you down."

Sheila squeezed her hand. "I know you won't. You'll be starting this Thursday when I go to Grasse."

Lily looked dismayed. "Thursday? Oh God, I didn't think it'd be that fast. How long will you be away?"

Sheila chuckled. "You should see your face! It's not the guillotine you're facing. Don't worry, Lily. You'll be fine. I'll only be away for five days. It'll be a good test for you."

The phone rang. Lily was startled out of her trance. She picked it up and then beckoned to Sheila. "Someone looking for the owner."

"Probably Caroline or Maura." Sheila went to pick up the receiver.

"No," Lily whispered, "it's a man."

"Hello," Sheila assumed her business voice. "Sheila Crosby here."

Lily couldn't help noticing the deep flush spreading over Sheila's cheeks. Tactfully she went into the back room.

Lily re-emerged when Amanda arrived back with the goodies. Sheila put down the phone. Amanda arranged the coffee slices and the éclairs on a paper plate and went to put on the kettle. Lily thought that Sheila looked flustered.

"Amanda, you'll be working for Lily from now on. She's the new manager, all right?"

Amanda nodded politely. "Yes, Miss Crosby."

"If you prove yourself you'll be entitled to a rise after six months."

"Thank you, Miss Crosby." Amanda was stiff and formal. Truth to tell, she was terribly in awe of this glamorous woman. She'd be far more relaxed with Lily as her boss, Sheila thought somewhat sadly. She must be getting very school-marmish to have this effect on her staff. She put on her navy blazer and tied her silk scarf loosely around her neck. "I'm off, ladies. I'll see you tomorrow."

Amanda's mouth opened wide. "What about your éclair?"

Sheila shook her head. "Not for me, thank you. A minute on the lips, a lifetime on the hips." She laughed as she clicked the door shut behind her.

"Far gone," Amanda sighed. "She's acting really funny today. You'd swear she was on something."

Lily tucked into her coffee slice and muttered,

"Maybe she's in love." Before Amanda could reply, three customers came in.

Sheila was lucky that Louis managed to fit her in. Usually you had to make an appointment days in advance. She had her hair washed and sat draped in a clean towel, waiting for Louis to begin his ministrations.

"Special occasion, Miss Crosby? You don't normally come in on a Monday?" He ran his fingers through her wet tresses.

"Yes, Louis. I thought I'd have it cut."

"Cut? Oh no," Louis clicked his tongue disapprovingly. "A little trim, perhaps. The fringe needs reshaping. No point in having marvellous eyes if you cover them up." He brandished his scissors and started to snip. Louis was temperamental, but a wonderful hairdresser. Hair designer, he called himself.

"I'll cut an inch from the side layers, I think. Give you a fuller style."

Sheila agreed. There was no way she'd interfere with Louis's judgement.

"So, where are we off to tonight?" Louis always used the royal we. It was an affectation, but it was endearing too.

"I'm not sure," Sheila replied dreamily. "It's a surprise."

"Oh lovely, darling. I love surprises, don't you?"

Sheila didn't respond. She was lost in thought. She had butterflies in her tummy ever since John had phoned an hour ago. Imagine, it had only taken him two days to phone her. She'd never dreamed he'd be that eager. It saved her from making the first move which she'd fully intended to do. She would have rung him when she got back from Grasse. His phone call was a bit sudden. He'd been mysterious on the phone, refused to tell her where they were going tonight. He said he was sure she'd enjoy it. Was it a play? Or a concert? Maybe a film? She hoped not. She'd prefer to go somewhere they could talk. She didn't know him well enough to be comfortable in a theatre. In fact, she'd prefer to have their first date in a pub. It'd be more relaxing.

"Well? Does the lady like her new image?" Louis handed her a mirror so she could get a back view of her hair-do.

Although he'd only trimmed her layers and her fringe, her hair had more body and bounce. The shorter fringe made her look younger. "It's lovely, Louis. Thank you."

Louis nodded gravely. Did he ever smile? "It's easy when one has a beautiful subject like yourself."

Sheila blushed. She was uneasy with compliments. She paid by cheque and left the salon. She'd skip lunch. She had no appetite. Next stop Brown Thomas. She had spotted a lovely black dress there on her last visit. Jean Muir was one of her favourite designers. Who cared if many ridiculed her style as being too simplistic? Miss Muir, as she liked to be called, was credited with "the little black dress". but Sheila knew it was Coco Chanel who had launched it in 1924, over fifty years ago. Even now, in the late seventies, a girl couldn't go wrong with a little black dress. Classic designs conquered time and trends. She'd invest in a new bag and shoes too, go for the total look. Accessories were just as important as the dress. Her gold necklace and earrings would be perfect.

Ten past seven. He'd be here in less than an hour. She was up to ninety. God, she hadn't felt like this in ten years. Not since Donald Fagan. Look what that had led to. She'd better watch out. She sipped her fennel tea slowly. It helped to calm her down a bit. The phone rang. Oh God. Was he going to call it off? Why not let it ring? She listened to the shrill sound for a half a minute. Each ring made her more jumpy. She couldn't bear it. She dashed over and picked up the phone.

"Hi."

Caroline. Sheila stifled a sigh of relief.

"Trying to get you all day. You're like the Elusive Pimpernel. Were you down in the salon?"

"No," Sheila answered hurriedly.

"Are you OK? You sound out of breath."

"I ran out of the bathroom," Sheila lied. "I'm getting ready to go out."

"Oh? A business meeting?"

Sheila paused. "No, as a matter of fact. I've a date."

Caroline whooped with glee. "Great. You didn't lose much time."

"Since your lecture," Sheila reminded her.

"Who is he? Where did you meet?"

"He's Jim Ryan's solicitor. John Harris."

"Not the fine thing from Mary's wedding?" Caroline gasped.

"The same." Sheila couldn't keep the triumphant tone from her voice.

"Well fair bloody play to you!"

"Listen Caroline, I'll have to go. I'm standing here in my knickers. If he arrives early I'm in trouble."

"Right. Get yourself dolled up. Knock him dead, kiddo."

"I nearly forgot. What did you want me for? Is anything wrong?" Sheila still didn't know why Caroline had rung.

"No, nothing's wrong. Bridget's sent you up an order for Grasse. She said you should get it by Wednesday at the latest."

"No problem. I'm flying out on Thursday morning."

"Right. Have a great time tonight and don't do anything I wouldn't do."

"That gives me lots of scope." Sheila laughed. "I'll ring you tomorrow to tell you all."

Caroline put down the phone. She hadn't told her. There was no way she was going to spoil her date. Anyway, maybe Sheila wouldn't care. Still, they'd been friends for so long. It was bound to be a bit of a shock. Peadar engaged. Rita would be raging when the news got out. A possible future son-in-law bites the dust. Bridget would suit Peadar down to the ground. They were two of a kind. Sheila was in a different category altogether. This solicitor guy might be the right one for Sheila. He sounded like a cross between Cary Grant and Clark Gable.

John linked her down the front steps. He'd left his BMW parked at the kerb.

"We'll walk. It's a lovely evening." He slipped his arm around her waist. "You look gorgeous this evening."

"Thanks." She wasn't embarrassed at all. How come he could flatter her and she didn't feel ridiculous? She glided down the street with him at her side. It felt right to have his arm around her. The August evening was balmy. It was great too see people out walking the Dublin streets in their short sleeves.

They turned into Leeson Street. Where was he bringing her? It was hours too early to be here on The Strip with its glitzy night clubs. He stopped outside the Tandoori Rooms. "Here we are."

Sheila was impressed. This was one of the poshest restaurants in Dublin. John led the way. A waiter showed them to their table. The place was the epitome of elegance: pristine white Irish linen tablecloths, subtle lighting and a tasteful bronze sculptured candlestick holder on each table. Sheila looked around admiringly as she took her seat. She examined the candlestick holder. "This is an Eddy Delaney, isn't it?"

"Indeed," John glanced up from the wine list. "Mike believes in having the best."

"Mike? Oh, I almost forgot, Mike Butt is the owner, isn't he?"

"Do you know him?" John beckoned to their waiter.

"Only by name. He's well know, in the West. Does his fishing in the Screbe river in Connemara."

"That's right. He's probably there right now. It must be coming to the end of the salmon fishing season. He comes in here and proudly shows off his catch to the diners. He's a lovely man."

Sheila nodded. "So I've heard. Impeccable manners, they say."

John ordered a bottle of St. Emilion with Sheila's approval.

"The Golden Orient is upstairs," John told her. "Have you eaten there?"

"No. It's not quite as up-market, is it?" She smiled at him.

What was she implying? That he was a snob? He wasn't going to fall into that trap.

"Ludicrous, isn't it?" He smiled back at her. "It's the same place, basically. Same kitchen, same chefs. Just not as exclusive! It's probably packed this minute."

Sheila arched an eyebrow. "So, why are we here downstairs?"

He took her hand in his and stared into her eyes. "Only the best for you, my love."

God, he was such a charmer.

They took their time over the meal. Normally Sheila didn't enjoy Indian food, but their chicken tikka masala was delicious. The rich creamy sauce was subtle, not too spicy. John was easy company. He entertained her with more stories of his law practice. She told him all about her plans for the salon.

He could see that this woman was intelligent and ambitious. He'd have to tread warily. From what he gathered from Jim, she hadn't had a relationship for ages. He knew why. He was going to play it cool. No sense in frightening her off.

"Have a look." John gave a slight nod in the direction of the corner table. "We're in good company."

Sheila let her eyes wander over. Mike Smurfit was sitting with some business colleagues.

"I'm all agog," Sheila said in mock delight. "When will Tony O'Reilly appear?"

"You never know your luck!" He poured her another glass of wine. "Seriously, do you like it here?"

"How could I not? The food is scrumptious. Our waiter is attentive. Everything's perfect."

"We could come back again some night when it's not so quiet. The weekend is best. I'd like you to meet Mike. He'd be very interested in you, what with the Carrigeen factory and all. You have a lot in common."

Was this his way of making another date? Sheila didn't refuse the coffee he handed to her. She wasn't going to be prissy tonight. Her diet plans could take a turn on the back burner. She surprised herself by accepting a cigarette. She nearly choked on the first puff, but quickly got the hang of it again. She smirked to herself as she took a long drag. She felt quite debauched. It was a good feeling.

It was twelve when they arrived back in Fitzwilliam Square. He walked her to her door. This was it. She was going to ask him in. She had the seduction scene all planned. She'd put her black satin sheets on the double bed. She had wine cooling in the fridge. She'd even invested in a skimpy négligé.

He bent down and kissed her lightly on the lips. "Thanks for a terrific evening."

She faltered. What now?

He kissed her again. This time a little harder. His lips were warm and dry.

"I know you're very busy so I won't keep you up any later." He walked back to the pavement. "May I ring you when you get back from France?"

Sheila was dumbfounded. He was actually going. God, this wasn't what she'd had in mind at all.

"Of course. I look forward to it." Why was her voice shaky? She wanted to seem nonchalant. What if he could read her mind?

He blew her a kiss and went back to his car. Sheila waved back, opened her door and went in.

She went up to her flat. She was boiling mad. What had gone wrong? Did he not fancy her? She hung up her dress. So much for the little black number! Had she been too formal with him? Had she talked too much about the salon? She must have bored

him stiff, that was it. God, why had she been so
bloody stand-offish? She'd given out all the wrong
vibes. He got the wrong impression of her. He
thought she was only interested in business. She
was useless at making small talk, she knew that.
Damn and blast. He'd said he'd ring her. Jesus, they
all said that. It was the classic brush-off line. Sheila
took up the silk night-dress, screwed it into a ball
and threw it, in disgust, into the bottom of the
wardrobe. She went into the bathroom and took off
her make-up. To hell with the moisturiser. She
wasn't going to bother. She couldn't understand
why she was feeling so annoyed. After all, what was
John Harris to her?

What did she know about him? Sweet damn all.
Sure he talked about his job. He'd told her about his
mews flat in Waterloo Road. He'd talked about his
décor, even asked her advice on house plants. But
she knew nothing else about him. He hadn't
mentioned his wife. Not once. Where was she now?
He'd no children. Not that he'd said anything. Mary
had told that. Why had he got no kids? Was it by
choice? Did he not like children? Even if he didn't?
Why was that important to her? For God's sake,
she'd better cop on. They'd had one date. That's all.
She'd probably never see him again. He knew
nothing about her either, come to think of it.
Nothing. She hadn't blurted out her life story to
him, had she? He had an image of a successful
career woman. He knew nothing about her inner
thoughts, her feelings. He knew nothing about
Karen. Why should he? One date, that's all it was. If

he rang her, well and good. If he didn't, that was OK too. She wasn't going to lose sleep over it. She'd enough on her mind without worrying about him.

She slipped into bed and leaned over to the bedside locker. She took out the framed photo of Karen. The usual lump came to her throat. In four more weeks Karen would be ten. She'd be going back to school next week. Fourth class. Was she clever? Was she pretty? What was her school uniform like? Did she like reading? What TV programmes were her favourites? She knew nothing about her daughter. Karen knew nothing about her. Yet. But some day she'd know everything. Sheila kept a diary. Every year, on Karen's birthday she cut out the newspaper headlines. She wrote a few pages about how her life was going. She talked about Colm and Ciara, Karen's cousins. She wrote about Rita and Galway and Carrigeen. Sheila had got the idea from her father. She'd no notion of what was in the letter he'd written to Karen, but she thought it was a wonderful idea. If Karen couldn't share her life now, she could some day. She could read this diary and get some sense of her real mother. She had a right to that, hadn't she? The worst thing for an adopted child must be to have no sense of identity, no knowledge of blood relationships, of roots. Karen had a right to know about herself. Everyone had. Sheila put the photo back and switched out the light. What would her dreams be like tonight?

John Harris sipped his cognac and thought about the evening. It had been a great success. Jim had warned him not to come on too strongly. Sheila was vulnerable. Well, he was in no rush. Sex was a cheap commodity he could get any evening in one of the clubs. Sheila Crosby was no push-over. That's why he was interested. He'd take things nice and slowly. She was a classy lady and he'd have to handle her properly. He'd seen the stares of admiration in the restaurant. She was a real stunner. It felt good to be with her. A bit of an ego trip, he admitted. Yeah, she could do wonderful things for his image. He congratulated himself on his restraint. It hadn't been easy. She was very attractive. There was a definite physical thing between them. Electric. He hadn't felt such an urgent desire in years. He wondered about her kid. She hadn't mentioned the child. Still, it wasn't something she'd just mention casually, was it? He'd play it cool until she trusted him enough to tell him herself. He'd wondered about her aloofness until Jim had filled him in on the story. What was she looking for in a relationship? Not marriage, Jim had said. What then? A fling? No, she was too serious minded to enter into what she'd consider a sleazy little affair. He guessed that she was lonely. He could understand that. So was he, in a way. But it was different for women. Single women were more cut off. She probably wanted a long-term relationship without the complications of marriage. Suited him fine. That's precisely what he wanted. Tomorrow morning, he'd send her a single red rose. No message. Keep her guessing. Subtlety was the name of the game.

CHAPTER TWENTY-ONE

Sheila came out of the small arrivals building in Nice airport. A blast of hot air hit her immediately. She signalled to a waiting taxi.

"Avenue du Pylone, Antibes," she told the driver. "C'est loin?"

"Vingt ou trente minutes, Madame. Ça dépend de la circulation."

He put her single suitcase in the boot. She felt something nip her toe. A damned mosquito. She'd sprayed herself from head to foot, but she'd forgotten about her open-toed sandals. She detested those vampirish bloodsuckers. If there was only one in the entire country, it would land on her. The driver was not very talkative. Not like the Dublin taxi drivers who were great conversationalists. She hung onto her back seat belt for dear life as this maniac sped through the streets. He must have been practising for the Grand Prix. They whizzed down the flower-edged Promenade des Anglais and were soon out of Nice and on the road to Antibes. She loved the Côte d'Azur. The white cliffs, the rugged coastline, the clear blue sky and sea, the tall white buildings, the boats and yachts in the harbour

. . . there was truly nothing to compare with the South of France. This time, she'd get to Monaco, she told herself. Mary had made her promise. On her visit last year, she just hadn't had the time.

The taxi pulled up outside Yves's villa. He'd insisted on her staying with him. The driver carried her suitcase to the gate.

"Merci, Monsieur." She gave him a handsome tip.

"De rien, Madame!" He went off delighted with himself.

Yves Dupont came bounding down the steps. "Bonsoir, ma petite." He kissed her warmly, the compulsory left cheek, right cheek, left cheek. Sheila kissed him back. It had taken practice to get this custom right. She was genuinely glad to see this man again. His big brown eyes lit up with pleasure. He ushered her into the spacious sitting-room with its whitewashed walls, tiled floors and scattered rugs. She had a glass of champagne in her hand before she even sat down on the long couch.

"Et Sophie, comment va-t-elle?" Sheila liked Yves's wife. She was a petite brunette who bristled with energy and enthusiasm.

"Chez sa mère. Malheureusement, la vielle dame est malade en ce moment. Les enfants sont avec elle."

"Je suis desolée d'entendre cela," Sheila replied politely. So, Sophie wasn't here. Nor the children. That put a different complexion on it. How long would they be spending with Sophie's mother? Was Sheila expected to stay five days with Yves alone in this house? Yves was a polished gentleman, but she didn't know him that well. Things could be awkward. His English wasn't great either. It was a good job she'd kept up her French lessons in the Alliance.

He brought her out to his back garden. She stepped into another world. Purple lilac, pink carnations and bright yellow mimosa . . . a wonderful splash of colour and a mixture of the sweetest fragrances. Her father would have loved it here. Yves had the barbecue on.

"Ce soir, on va manger des steaks, hein?" He coated the meat in olive oil.

"Je préfère le steak bien cuit." Sheila reminded him

"Brûlé, vous voulez dire." Yves would never understand how these foreigners loved to overcook their meat. It was sacrilege.

Sheila felt hot and sticky after the flight. "C'est possible d'avoir une douche?" she asked.

"Quoi, mon petit chou?" He hadn't heard her.

The first time he'd called her that, she thought it was an insult. She didn't fancy being called a little cabbage! The French had some weird terms of endearment.

"Une douche?" she repeated.

Yves slapped his forehead in exasperation with himself. "Mon Dieu," he exclaimed. "J'ai totalement oublié. Bien sûr! Suivez-moi."

He lead her down a tiled corridor to a big blue bathroom. A wet towel was thrown on the floor. "Zut!" He picked it up quickly. It was obvious his wife was away. Sophie was extremely house-proud and would have died if she'd seen anything out of place.

Sheila wanted to unpack. "Où est ma chambre?" She was amused by his rattled expression.

"Oh là là, que je suis bête!" Again he asked her to follow him. He was all in a dither by now. Her room was at the end of the hall, overlooking the garden. He'd had the presence of mind to have it aired, at least. He left her to unpack and hurried back to his barbecue. The tiled floor was cool under her feet. Soothing. She plugged in the special mosquito repellent tablets. They weren't going to have another go at her tonight. She took out her carrigeen gel and stripped down to her underwear. It was a good thing she'd remembered her silk dressing-gown. Yves was liable to pop up anywhere.

When she came back to the garden, the smell of the barbecued steaks wafted on the air. She realised she was famished. She'd refused the plastic food on the plane. She'd changed into a loose white cheesecloth dress and flip flops. Her hair was still wet from the shower.

"Magnifique." He hugged her warmly. A little too warmly. She shrugged him off and sat at the resin patio table. It was just beginning to get dark. The noise of the crickets was the only sound that disturbed the silent peace of the evening. Yves lit two large candles. The scene was romantic. Where was John Harris when she needed him? Yves served up the steaks with a beautiful niçoise salad and a tray of freshly sliced baguette. He left the French window of the sitting-room open and the tones of Charles Aznavour filled the garden. Sheila hated Charles Aznavour but who wanted to complain when everything else was perfect? They discussed their plans for the next few days. Tomorrow was the trip to Grasse. She needed more essential oils, bergamot, jasmine and geranium. They were running out of lavender too. And she was going to invest in some fennel. It had a great reputation for keeping wrinkles at bay. He was delighted when he heard she wanted to go to Monaco. He told her he'd be delighted to drive her there on the Saturday.

"Je ne veux pas vous déranger," Sheila said apologetically. She didn't want to impose upon his hospitality.

But he insisted. "Quand le chat n'est pas là, les souris dansent!" He stroked her knee.

My God, Sheila thought, he's flirting with me. She brushed his hand away and tut-tutted. But she wasn't annoyed. She was secretly pleased. He fancied her. Good. Let John Harris put that in his pipe and smoke it. She hadn't lost her sex-appeal after all. She was still desirable. Still attractive. Now, how was she going to keep Yves at bay without being rude? Would the fennel work on him? Ah, she'd have another glass of wine and worry about that later. She'd go with the flow, as Mary would say. If Mary could see her now, she'd be green with envy. The first of September. Mary'd be back in school today. Her first separation from Davy. That'd be hard.

"Tout va bien?" Yves asked her.

"Très bien." She lifted her glass to his.

Later that evening, Sheila began to get chilly so Yves suggested they go inside for their cognac. He went to get her a shawl. One of Sophie's. Had he no shame? He joined her on the couch. The combination of the plane journey, the wine and the cognac made her sleepy. She let her head rest on his shoulder as Sacha Distel sang love songs. Big mistake. She must have dropped off for a minute because she woke with a start. Yves had slipped his hand under her right arm and was touching her breast. When the cat's away the bloody mice dance all right!

"Non!" She jumped up, spilling the brandy in the process.

Yves grabbed her and kissed her hard on the mouth. His tongue brutally forced her lips apart. "Faisons l'amour." He bit her neck.

Jesus, what kind of a madman was he? She struggled. He was stronger. He pushed her back on the couch and literally dived on her. She raised her knee and gave him an almighty dig where it hurt most. He crumpled in pain and landed on the floor.

"Vous êtes saoul!" she shouted at him and staggered off.

Sheila tottered down the corridor, into her room and locked the door. Tears rolled down her cheeks. She was in convulsions. "Eat your heart out, John Harris," she hiccuped as she collapsed on the bed in another fit of laughter. Five hours in France and she'd been bitten twice! What way would her skin be after five days? What cream would possibly remove a love bite? This time Natural Woman had no solution!

Yves was suitably subdued at breakfast the following morning. He was too embarrassed to even mention the incident of the previous night. Sheila wisely made no reference to it, but her manner was much cooler.

The drive to Grasse was very enjoyable. Sheila wore her white shorts and her blue top. She'd intended to tuck it under her bust, but last night's grapple was still fresh in her mind. No point in inviting more unwelcome advances. She took her big straw hat too. Her skin was fair and she'd no intention of getting burnt in the scorching sun. Yves had the sun-roof down and Sheila relished the soft breeze as they sped along the country roads, past the terraced walls of the farms. Soon they were up in the hills, the woody country of pines, fir trees and narrow valleys. It seemed as if they were driving through the clouds.

"Il y a des brumes matinales souvent ici," Yves explained to her.

But there was no mist now, only clear blue skies. As they approached the town of Grasse, Sheila saw nothing but flower gardens: roses, violets, carnations and jasmine . . . a veritable Eden. She was in her element.

Visitez la Parfumerie, invited the coloured poster at the edge of the town.

"D'abord, allons voir les vues qu'on a de ces collines," Yves suggested.

Sheila agreed. They drove east by the Boulevard, past the juncture with the Route Napoléon.

"Napoléon a pris cette route après s'être échappé d'Elba," Yves informed her.

They came to a terrace edged by a balustrade. Beyond this was a narrow cactus garden. From this height they had a magnificent view over the roofs of the lower town, down, down over miles of gardens and farms to the cornflower blue sea by Cannes, twelve miles away.

"J'ai oublié mon appareil," Sheila said in dismay.

"Pas de problème," Yves went to the boot and took out his camera. He took a photo of Sheila standing at the edge of the balustrade with the panoramic view behind her. Then back to the town for the business in hand.

Grasse was a busy town packed with shops, houses and the usual manic traffic. French drivers loved to hoot their horns! Sheila loved the outdoor cafés with their red tables and chairs, and the gaily striped sun-awnings over the shop windows. The main industries here were the perfume factories and fruit-preserving factories. The streets were filled with sweet scents. Yves parked the Renault.

They went by the main shopping centre and round by the casino to the Fragonard Parfumerie. Yves lead her across a little courtyard, under an arched doorway, to the reception desk. There was a bus-load of American tourists in the waiting-room for their guided tour.

"Par ici, s'il vous plaît," said the guide. He had black hair and a moustache. Who did that remind her of? He wore a blue and white striped T-shirt. Typically French. All he was missing was the beret and the string of onions! Sheila decided to join them for the crack.

"Vous n'êtes pas touriste," Yves said in disgust.

Sheila laughed. "Je vais faire semblant."

Yves gave in. If Sheila wanted to join this tour group, that was up to her. This Irish woman was a little crazy, he thought. He went off to get a coffee and arranged to meet her later at the reception. They could fix up her order then.

Sheila was amused by the reaction of the Americans to the facts and figures. Every year these factories used ten billion jasmine flowers, three million pounds of rose petals, four million pounds of orange blossom. It took five tonnes of rose petals for one kilo of concentrated rose essence. Nearly seventy thousand acres of the land of Grasse was devoted entirely to flower-growing. They harvested different flowers in different months; violets in February and March, hyacinths in March and April, orange blossom in May and June, jasmine and tuberose in August. Sheila followed the group into the frame room where they pointed out racks of shallow trays with fat on the sheets of glass. Sheila remembered explaining all that to Bridget. The fat absorbed the smell of the roses, or whatever flowers they were using. One American woman said it was a good thing that none of them had eaten garlic that day. Their distillation room was huge. Carrigeen was definitely in the ha'penny place by comparison. Nevertheless, Sheila wondered about the possibility of guided tours of her factory in the summer months. She'd mention it to Caroline. In the showroom, the Americans invested in perfumes, soaps and cosmetics. This was another possible market.

When her order was finalised, Yves drove Sheila up to the old town. This was the real Grasse with its crooked gables and flat red roofs. The Cathedral with its square tower dominated the town. They stopped at a little bistro for a lunch of barbecued sardines and salad. These were truly delicious, a far cry from the tins of sardines her father and Sheila used to have for lunch.

It had been a wonderful day. That evening, back in Antibes, Sheila insisted on taking Yves out to dinner. No way was she going to risk another groping session, although she knew that Yves had learned his lesson. He'd been the perfect gentleman all day. Maybe he'd thought she'd expected to be seduced? Frenchmen, unlike their Irish counterparts, didn't need to be sloshed to make a move! Love, or rather lust, was part of the national psyche.

They ate in a smart little restaurant in Juan les Pins. Candles flickered on the tables. Sheila adored eating out of doors. You could sit and watch the beautiful people go by. So different from rain-sodden Ireland. Sheila started with crudités. The raw vegetables were crisp and succulent. For their main course they both had lobster with sautéd potatoes. To Sheila's consternation, a fiddler serenaded them. She was quite chuffed with herself. This was the second time in the one week that she'd had dinner with a handsome man. Not bad for a dried-up old spinster.

Sheila spent Saturday afternoon shopping in the fashionable boutiques of Juan les Pins. She bought a leather handbag for Caroline, a gold necklace for Mary and a silk scarf for her mother. She sat sipping *citron pressé* on the terrace of a café and wrote a postcard for Karen. Another moment captured for her daughter. She was glad of these hours to herself. Yves was grand but, when you were used to living on your own, any company could get tedious.

On Saturday night, as promised, Yves brought her to Monaco. They took the coast road and crossed the neck of blunt cape which forms the eastern guard of the Nice sea-front. The blue waters of Villefranche were soon visible, this quaint fishing port on its sheltered inlet.

"On pêche des homards et des sardines," Yves told her.

They travelled across the base of a club-shaped and thickly wooded cape. Lovely villages nestled on the hillside. They drove on by Beaulieu with its splendid villas and tropical vegetation. They left France and drove into the independent Principality of Monaco.

Dusk was falling. Sheila was mesmerised by the spectacle unfolding before her eyes. Below the

luxuriant gardens, the hotels, the offices of La
Condamine. Stretching out to sea, dark blue waves
creamed against the steep cliffs. In the rock was set
the old town of Monaco and the Prince's palace
with its huge battlements.

"Les Grimaldis sont ici depuis 1297." Yves could
see she was enthralled. "Pendant les siècles,
Monaco a été protegée par l'Espagne, la Sardaigne
et la France."

"Quelle est la population?" Sheila asked.

"Environ 28,000."

It was much tinier than Sheila had thought. The
whole area measured about one square kilometre,
Yves said.

Yves and Sheila headed towards the
underground lifts which took them up to the Café
de Paris, the exclusive casino. Sheila couldn't help
being impressed with the glamour, wealth and
opulence. She followed Yves around the tables, but
she didn't place any bets. She wasn't the gambling
type. He introduced her to several people and she
made polite noises. She liked a few of the men she
met, but she thought the women were very
superficial. Maybe that was unfair? How did she
know what lives these painted, dyed-blonde ladies
led? Who was she to judge? But she couldn't
imagine any of them out on the rocks in Carrigeen
in their wellies, gathering sea moss.

Yves had a lucky night. They left the tables at
about ten and went for a stroll in the evening air.
Beautiful landscaped gardens surrounded the
casino, which itself was a magnificent edifice, more

impressive than the palace. A couple from a tour bus were taking photos of the fountain. They turned out to be Irish so Sheila stopped for a chat. They were disgusted because they hadn't been allowed into the casino with their young son. The child ambled on, bored by the conversation of adults. To his great glee he discovered two statues, huge marble figures of a naked man and woman. The male statue was endowed with a golden penis. The boy insisted on having his photo taken with his new-found treasure. His mother reluctantly obliged.

The harbour was fairyland. Lights from the boats and yachts cast an enchanted shimmering glow on the water. Sheila strolled arm-in-arm with Yves along the quay, reading the names of the boats. Suddenly he stopped. "Nous sommes ici."

"Qu'est-ce-que vous voulez dire?" Sheila was astonished as Yves pulled her up the gangway to a large yacht. Sounds of laughter and chatter meant there was a party in progress.

"C'est privé." She pulled back.

Yves laughed at her confusion. "Nous sommes invités. Voici mon frère!"

Yves's double helped Sheila on board. He kissed her warmly. Sheila had never been so amazed in her life. Wait till Mary heard this!

The party was something else. Gaston turned out to be a diplomat. He and his wife, Claudette, spoke fluent English. Sheila was relieved. It was difficult to speak French for long periods of time. She was introduced to bankers, businessmen and politicians.

Some of them flirted with her. She was surprised at how many were divorced.

"You should move over here," Claudette advised her. "There's no shortage of rich eligible men."

Sheila laughed that off.

"No, I'm serious," Claudette argued. "With your lovely Irish eyes and your wonderful red hair, you'd be a real hit."

Sheila thanked her but assured her she was far too busy at home. They drank champagne, ate oysters, crab and shrimps, canapés of all kinds. They chatted and danced till the early hours. Gaston took photos and promised to send them to her. Sheila would remember this night in the Dublin winter evenings, huddled up to her cosy fire. This was a fleeting glimpse into another world.

"Regardez la lune!" Yves whispered to her.

Sheila gasped in awe. It was a divine sight . . . a luminous orb dropping gently, slowly, gracefully into the tranquil waiting water. No special effects in any film could have managed anything so spectacular.

* * *

Sheila got off the Aer Lingus Boeing late on Monday night. Mist and drizzle. Bloody typical. No delay in customs at least. She walked through the glass doors of the arrivals building and was about to go outside for a taxi when she heard someone call her name. She turned quickly. John Harris.

"Welcome back." He kissed her cheek.

Sheila smiled, trying to hide her embarrassment. Never in a million years had she expected this.

"How did you know?"

"No flight from Nice, so I guessed you'd be on the Paris flight." He took her suitcase. Sheila followed him out to the BMW.

"How did it go?" he asked as they drove through Santry.

"Wonderful. I'd a fantastic time."

"You look happy and relaxed." He patted her knee.

When he pulled up outside her door, she leaned over and kissed him. "Fancy a glass of champagne?"

"Are you sure you're not too tired?" He kissed her neck. Sheila giggled. That was the exact spot that Yves had bitten. But this was different. Totally different.

"Of course I'm not." Sheila kissed him again, got out of the car and led him up the steps. This time she wouldn't let him get away. This time she'd be in control. All those Frenchmen had given her confidence. John Harris didn't stand a chance tonight. The black satin sheets were ready and waiting. So was she!

CHAPTER TWENTY-TWO

Two weeks back in school and Mary was exhausted. She had a very early start every morning. She had to have Davy dressed and breakfasted by eight so that he'd be ready when Angela called for him. Then the drive to Drumcondra to school. She felt she had a day's work done before she even started teaching.

Her time-table this year was dire. She had three Leaving Cert English classes, two Inter Cert, and a first and second year. The corrections for exam classes in English were mind-boggling. The sixth year essays were usually about four foolscap pages long and, with thirty students in a class, you'd be talking about three hours correction per class. Those who gave out about teachers' holidays didn't realise how much work had to be done outside the classroom. Mary reckoned she spent about twenty hours a week correcting. Then there were the preparations and class plans. What about all the voluntary time teachers spent taking sport, drama and other extra-curricular activities? Forty hours a week how are ya! She wouldn't be able to produce the school play this year. She'd have to be home by five to pick up Davy. She'd have to hand the production over to Brian Darcy. Men were definitely freer because they weren't so tied by child-minding. This was a sore point with Mary. She'd miss the fun of the rehearsals. Instead, she'd devote her lunch-times to starting up a debating society. Public speaking was an important skill for the students to acquire. Debating was a social outlet too. Wasn't that how she'd met Jim?

Thank God, it was Friday. She came out of her first year class in stitches. One of the girls had written a paragraph on Donkey Otay! Maybe the kid was right. Only an ass tilted at windmills! Another student had insisted that she was always on time when Mary commented on her punctuation. The second years had a mock trial of Friar Laurence. It was brilliant. They questioned his culpability in the deaths of Romeo and Juliet. They had lawyers for the prosecution and the defence. They had witnesses from the Capulet and the Montague camps. They were armed to the teeth with relevant quotations. The class was highly excited and eager for the verdict. In the end, the judge, a compassionate fourteen-year-old, dismissed the case! By break-time, Mary was worn out and she had two sixth year classes and a third year before lunch. These activity-based classes were definitely good for the girls' but they demanded great energy of the teacher. Her third years would have to make do with chalk and talk. She'd have to reserve some energy for the rest of the day. On Friday mornings she'd barely time to go to the loo.

Her honours sixth years in the afternoon were a delight. Talk about a pleasure to teach. They were her form class too. This meant Mary was their mentor. She listened to their problems, sorted out misunderstandings, dealt with the other teachers' complaints. She was in charge of their term reports. In *loco parentis* took on a new dimension when it came to form tutors. She also monitored their attendance and kept a check on their homework. She met their parents when necessary.

They were studying Shelley at the moment. Mary took three students up to the front of the class each day to read out their answers. At first they hated this, but they soon adapted. Mary remembered how mousy she'd been in school herself. She wanted to encourage these girls to be able to express their ideas confidently. Anyhow, it'd be extremely boring for them to have to sit in rows, listening to a teacher all day long. Mary believed in self-directed learning and student interaction. They did a lot of group work. The students learned from each other. Anne, one of her brightest students, was into Shelley.

"His imagery is beautiful, Miss. Look at his description of the leaves in stanza one."

Mary asked her to quote her favourite phrases.

"Breath of autumn's being, Like ghosts from an enchanter fleeing, Pestilent-stricken multitudes." Anne read the words in a reverent tone.

"Yeah, those lines are lovely. So is his description of the waves in the third verse. But what about that awful line in the second last verse?" Joan argued.

"What line?" Anne was ready for a dispute. She was well prepared to defend her hero.

"I fall upon the thorns of life, I bleed!" Joan moaned the lines. "Over the top, far too melodramatic."

"Rubbish!" Anne retorted. "He's overcome by emotion. What's wrong with that?"

"It's too much. It wrecks the poem. It alienates the reader." Joan was adamant.

At this stage Anne was nearly apoplectic. "You just don't understand. You haven't experienced that kind of heartbreak."

"And you have?" Joan asked scornfully.

It was time for Mary to intervene. "Why not write out your views? Writing things down clarifies our thoughts, I find."

"I'm not going to change my mind, Miss." Joan wasn't going to give an inch.

"You're perfectly entitled to your own views," Mary stressed, "providing . . ."

"You base your argument on the text." The class shouted out in chorus.

Mary laughed. They had her well taped.

Finally the last bell rang at four. Mary went back to the staffroom to collect her copies and books.

"Can you come for a drink?" Frances Whelan asked her.

"Uh huh, I'm dashing as usual." Mary stuffed the essay copies into her bag.

"How's Davy?"

"He's great. He's the two bottom front teeth now and he's real cute when he smiles."

Frances grinned. "You're still dewy-eyed about him."

"I know. We're desperate suckers, we mothers, aren't we?"

"Do you get any free time to yourself? You need it, you know."

"Well, by a major miracle, Jim is actually at home this weekend. He's letting me out tonight."

"Going somewhere special?" Frances finished her second year attendance rolls.

"No, just for a drink with Sheila. But it'll be a break to get out."

"She's the girl with the skin care business, isn't she?"

"Yeah." Mary nodded. "She's flying high at the moment. More luck to her."

"I'd never be brave enough to run my own company," Frances said ruefully.

"Me neither." Mary got out her car keys. "We're safe in our secure pensionable jobs, what?"

"Safe, what a lousy job description," Frances groaned as Mary dashed out.

Davy was thrilled with the little brown bear Mary had picked up for him in Sandymount village. She managed to get her shopping done on the way home. It was a mad rush, but it was better than leaving it to the following morning. Saturday was the only day she had time to do the cleaning. On Sundays they visited her parents, or Jim's. Her parents were mad about Davy, of course, but Jim's parents took the biscuit. This was their first grandchild and Denis and Eileen Ryan spoilt him rotten. He'd more clothes than Little Lord Fauntleroy.

Mary made a casserole as it was the handiest thing to heat up if Jim came home late. It was easy to chop into small pieces for Davy. Mary couldn't believe that some babies had to be coaxed to eat. Davy went crazy when he saw his bowl. She had to shovel it into him to keep him happy. His little cheeks were very red tonight, must be another tooth coming. She'd leave out the Calpol for Jim, just in case. When she'd fed Davy, she put him into his play-pen. It was called a lobster pot, because of the soft strings which criss-crossed around the sides. It was much better than the old-fashioned wooden play-pens kids used to bash their heads against. He loved being in his lobster pot. He had his little blocks and his soft toys to play with. She spent her time picking up the toys he'd fling out at regular intervals. This was a huge joke to him. Six o'clock. She'd have time to make a start on the corrections.

Jim was home by seven. He found her at the kitchen table, surrounded by copies.

"Still at it?" He pecked her on the cheek.

"Yeah. I'd like to get some of them done tonight before I go out. Your dinner's in the oven."

"Have to see this little guy first." He picked up Davy, who howled in protest at being taken away from his toys. "Give Daddy a kiss." Jim tickled him. Davy screeched.

"Leave him be, Jim. He just wants to play on his own."

Jim reluctantly put the baby back in his play-pen. He took his casserole out of the oven and moved some of her copies. "Could you not leave those till tomorrow?"

"No, I've to prepare notes for the sixth years on the prose. Bacon is quite difficult."

"God, why do they have to study that crap?"

"It's not crap." Mary was annoyed. "It's important for them to study different styles of writing. It helps them with their essays."

"Theoretically maybe," Jim shook a lavish helping of salt over his dinner. Mary hated him doing that. He'd have high blood pressure soon. "We have a school leaver in at the moment as a filing assistant. Honestly, she can barely spell. They'd be better off learning basic English at school instead of this high-falutin' nonsense."

Mary didn't answer. She was in no mood for a debate about the educational system. Everyone had views on school and the curriculum and most people were talking through their hats.

"What time are you meeting Sheila?"

"Nine. I'm calling to her flat. We'll go for a drink locally." She started to chuckle.

"What's so funny?"

"This essay. I was trying to get this class to widen their vocabulary. Experiment with language, you know."

"And?"

"Well, we've just finished studying *Pride and Prejudice*. I was talking about life in Jane Austen's time and how the people behaved and were expected to behave. I mentioned the word decorum."

"Did they understand that?" Jim asked. He couldn't imagine how they'd know such a word. It'd be archaic for this generation.

"No, so after a lengthy discussion I summed up by telling them not to worry about it, that basically it meant manners."

"Yeah, it does in its broadest sense," Jim agreed.

"Exactly. But this student here has written a gem. She's talking about her neighbours and how they're such lovely people. Listen to her next sentence. 'My parents like the Murphys too because they have lovely decorums'."

Jim laughed. "Sounds obscene. Well, at least she's trying."

"Most of them are," Mary agreed, but the irony was lost on Jim. Great. She'd half the copies done. She'd finish them tomorrow night. That would leave Sunday night for Bacon.

"Are you taking your car tonight?" Jim poured himself a glass of milk.

"Better not. I intend to have a hassle-free night."

"I'll drop you over to Sheila's. It'll only take ten minutes at that hour. No traffic."

"What about Davy?"

"We'll bring him. A spin before bedtime might make him sleepy. He loves going out in the car."

"He's usually in bed by eight."

"So? This is the weekend. He can sleep later tomorrow."

Mary knew this was wishful thinking. No matter

what time Davy went to sleep, he'd be awake, bright-eyed and bushy-tailed and ready for action by seven o'clock.

Mary and Sheila went for one drink in O'Donoghue's for old times' sake. The traditional session had drawn in a huge crowd and the heat was overpowering. Bodies shuffled together, squeezed in like the proverbial sardines. Mary had her white jacket on. It'd be a miracle if she escaped a dark creamy pint spilling over her. They decided to leave when Mary spotted her brother, Paul, with his latest girlfriend in tow. They waved and Paul and the girl inched their way over.

"Hi. This is Margaret. Mags, this is my sister, Mary, and Sheila Crosby, her friend."

They shook hands. Margaret, it turned out, worked with Paul in the Department of Finance.

"Great session, isn't it?" Margaret said. "Yer man on the fiddle is brill."

Sheila agreed. The music brought her back to her early days in Dublin, her first year in UCD, when she'd the whole world at her feet, or so she thought.

"Remember that guy from the history class? He was a great box player." Sheila reminisced.

"Who?" Mary hadn't the foggiest.

"Ah, you remember him. He had a beard and he always drank here in O'D's."

Mary looked around. Nine out of ten men in this pub had a beard. Sheila's description wasn't exactly graphic.

"Anyhow, it's nice to be back," Sheila continued. "The barmen here are real friendly."

Mary wasn't enthused. She was performing a balancing act with her drink and she'd no room to even light a fag. Besides, any attempt at conversation was doomed to failure. She'd loads to find out from Sheila, but it was impossible to talk here.

"What are you drinking, ladies?" Paul was on his way to the bar again.

"No, we'll just finish these," Mary said quickly. "I want to go somewhere else. I hate being crushed to death. OK, Sheila?"

"Fine by me." Sheila didn't mind either way. She was beginning to feel as if she were in a rugby scrum.

Paul sympathised with his sister. It took practice and training to be fit for O'D's. The body contact mightn't be everyone's cup of tea. "If I stand here long enough, I could end up with a paternity suit." He laughed. "Where are you heading?"

"Doheny and Nesbitt's?" Sheila suggested.

"Much more your scene," Paul slagged them. "How's my favourite nephew?" he asked his sister.

"Terrific. Why don't you and Margaret come over some night next week? Jim'll be away again. I could do with some company."

"Great. How's Wednesday?" He consulted with Margaret.

Wednesday was fine. They said their goodbyes and squeezed their way out the front door. More of the crowd squashed into the doorway.

There was a more civilised crush in Nesbitt's. Sheila thought it hadn't changed over the years. The atmosphere was friendly.

"Do you want to go into the snug?" Sheila asked Mary.

"No way." Mary walked up to the bar. "I'm out at last and I want to see everything that's going on."

You'd never know who'd you'd bump into here. Mary loved the buzz. You could have a jar in peace without being hassled, or you could be chatted up, if you felt so inclined. Just as Sheila was ordering, a couple got up to leave. Two seats at the bar, this was manna from the gods.

"How's school?" Sheila sipped her vodka and bitter.

"A laugh a minute." Mary smiled. "Ah, the kids are great. I get great mileage out of them. Now, give me all the gory details."

Sheila ordered ten Benson and Hedges.

"Jesus," Mary gasped. "The dead arose and appeared to many. When did you go back on the fags?"

Sheila handed her one. "I'm not really back on them. I like the occasional one when I'm out."

"Stone the crows! Next you'll be telling me you're drinking coffee again." Mary was delighted. She loved human weakness, especially in others. Fags or no fags, Sheila looked better than Mary had seen her look in yonks. There was a twinkle in her eye and she had a glow about her.

"Go on, tell me all about his nibs. Jim is useless. I get no info from him at all."

Sheila flicked her ash. "What do you want to know?"

"Sheila Crosby, don't be so bloody infuriating! I want to know everything."

"He's gorgeous, but you already know that. He's sophisticated, well read, mannerly, witty, generous and thoughtful. Now, are you satisfied?"

"Huh, you are anyway. That's obvious." Mary took a long drag. "How often do you see him?"

"Two or three times a week. We go for a meal or to the theatre or the flicks. Sometimes we stay in and watch TV."

"In your place?"

"Usually. My flat's no great shakes, but I prefer it to his pad, as he calls it."

"Why? What's it like?" Mary was all ears.

"It's got great potential, but his taste is lousy. He has a mews at the back of Waterloo Road. It's in a lovely garden. It's whitewashed. In fact it's lovely on the outside. But John's mucked up the interior. The bedroom's OK and the bathroom, but the kitchen-cum-dining-room is like a brothel."

"A brothel?" Mary echoed. "What do you mean?"

"He has this striped wallpaper and cushions to match, strewn around the pine floor."

"Jesus, cushions matching the wallpaper! Gross! And a low couch I bet and a bean bag?"

Sheila laughed. "Yeah, he thinks it's seductive with the low lamps. Anyhow, he's agreed to redecorate and I'm choosing the colours."

"Sounds like a cosy scene of domesticity," Mary teased her. "So, the bedroom's OK, you said. I gather then that you're . . . you're . . ."

"Well," Sheila grinned at her, "we're not playing tiddlywinks!"

Mary ordered the next round. She didn't know what to say. She was embarrassed. So, they were at it. Well, it wasn't her business, was it? Sheila wasn't a schoolgirl. She was a thirty-year-old woman who could do as she pleased. It wasn't as if she'd broken up his marriage. They were both mature consenting adults. So long as they weren't hurting anyone, what was the problem? Who was she to pass judgement? She just hoped that Sheila wouldn't get hurt again. An intimate relationship always made a woman vulnerable, in Mary's opinion.

"Look!" Sheila poked her in the ribs. "There's that one, Anne Nolan, going into the snug."

Mary remembered her impassioned speeches in the L and H. She was a reporter in RTE now. The press frequented Nesbitt's, so did a lot of others with literary ambitions.

"Let's drink to romance." Mary raised her glass to Sheila's.

Sheila clinked her glass. "I'd much rather drink to friendship. It's more reliable."

"True." Mary nodded. "Now, tell me all about the salon."

"A delay, I'm afraid. The decorators are still in. They found some damp, so it has to be treated."

"There's always something."

"It doesn't matter, really. It gives me longer to find good staff."

"How many do you think you'll be employing?"

"I'm not sure yet. I'll need a receptionist, of course, and a beautician. I was thinking about a masseuse."

"Very exotic!" Mary drawled.

"We'll have to wait and see. I want someone who's trained in aromatherapy, but that hasn't caught on in Ireland yet. It's meant to be the in thing in London."

"I'll have a word with Joanne. Maybe she could find out for you. I thought there were a lot of masseurs here." Mary smirked.

"Besides the seedy places you're referring to," Sheila smiled, "the others do Swedish massage mainly. But I want to use my essential oils."

"Of course." Mary could see that. "Remember the massage you gave me on my wedding day? That was really relaxing."

"Yeah, but I'm an amateur. I need someone who's been trained. So, ask Joanne where I might be able to find one, will you?"

"No sweat," Mary agreed. "You'll be offering the usual facials and all that, I suppose?"

"Ah ha, and eyelash and eyebrow tinting, manicure, pedicure, a complete make-up and skin advice service too."

"What about waxing?"

"I'll have to. It's quite disgusting you know."

"Oh?"

"The wax has the most offensive smell. It comes

off in big wads, it's like cracking cement and then they melt it down again for re-use."

Mary grimaced. "You're not serious? Jesus, what about all the hairs stuck to it? They'd be floating around when it melted down."

"They're filtered out."

"Oh God, I'll stick to my razor, thank you."

Sheila agreed with her. There had to be a better way. "Oh, I nearly forgot to tell you the latest from Carrigeen. Peadar's engaged."

"Peadar? I don't believe it." Mary gaped at her. "Peadar? I was convinced he'd never marry. It must be on the rebound. It has to be. Sure he was nuts about you."

Sheila shook her head. "I'm glad for him. Bridget'll make him a good wife."

"Your mother must be hopping."

"That's the understatement of the year. But she'll get over it. Caroline told me that Mam nearly pukes every time she bumps into Mrs Cummins in Lydon's. You can imagine the way Bridget's mother gloats around the town. Poor Mam."

"Poor Bridget, you mean." Mary got off her stool and went to the toilets at the back of the pub. A tall grey-haired man Sheila vaguely recognised made a move towards her.

"May I get you a drink?"

Sheila politely refused. He sat down on Mary's stool.

"I'm sorry. The seat's taken. My friend'll be back in a minute," Sheila said firmly.

He took the hint and shuffled off. Mary came

back with more drinks. "Was he trying to chat you up?"

"I think so. Do you know him?"

Mary laughed. "I do indeed, so do you."

"He did look kind of familiar. Who is he?"

"He, my dear, was one of your lecturers at the old Alma Mater. You definitely attract these chemistry types. He's a desperate boyo. Did he pinch your bum?"

"No, thank God." Sheila shuddered at the thought of it.

"I dunno." Mary lit another cigarette. "I thought you'd be used to that after your French trip."

"No." Sheila smiled. "In France, I was only bitten and jumped on. Nobody pinched my derrière!"

"Jumped on by a Frenchman. Some people have all the luck!"

"Actually it was extremely funny. I'll tell you all about it back at the flat. No, no more drinks, Mary. You'll be sorry in the morning."

The thought of Davy in the morning was enough to sober Mary up. "God, I better head for home. I have to get a taxi."

"Come back to the flat for coffee. I'll ring for a taxi. It'll be much easier than standing at a rank. You'd be waiting ages."

"OK. Can I have brandy in my coffee?"

"You're incorrigible, do you know that? Still, you may as well enjoy yourself when you do get out. I know you're stuck in a lot."

"It's being on my own I hate, when Jim's away."

"Well, he's not away tonight, is he?" Sheila reminded her.

"He'll probably be snoring by the time I get in." Mary put on her jacket.

"I'll give you some ylang ylang. I know someone who swears by it." Sheila wondered how Mrs Reidy and Alfred were.

"Jim'd need more than that. He's getting very middle-aged in his ways and he's only thirty-two."

"I'm telling you, this man says it works and he's seventy-five if he's a day!"

CHAPTER TWENTY-THREE

"Well, I'm not getting any younger. It's time I sorted out my life." Peadar looked at Sheila. Was that a hint? It was like old times to be sitting here in her mother's kitchen with him.

"I know you and Bridget'll be very happy. You've a lot in common," Sheila said in all sincerity.

Peadar puffed his pipe. Sheila could guess what he was thinking. She used to have a lot of interests in common with Peadar too. But that wasn't even enough basis for a relationship, never mind a marriage. Sheila poured him another cup of tea. The key turned in the front door. God, her mother was back. Sheila had hoped he'd be gone before her mother arrived back from her golf. Rita breezed into the kitchen and stopped dead.

"Peadar! What a nice surprise!" She shoved her clubs into the broom cupboard.

Peadar stood up to shake her hand. "Hello, Mrs Crosby. How are you?"

"Oh, pulling the divil by the tail, you know. You look very well, I must say. How is Bridget?" The words nearly stuck in her throat. Sheila was on tenterhooks. Her mother was liable to say something smart or cutting.

"Fine, thank you." Poor Peadar looked most disconcerted.

"So, when's the big day?" Rita sat down with them at the kitchen table and poured herself a cup from the pot. Sheila groaned inwardly.

"Not till next summer. June, we think."

Rita tried to smile. "There's no rush, so?"

Jesus, Sheila felt like thumping her. If that nasty insinuation was meant to offend Peadar, it hadn't worked.

"Ah no, there's no rush. Mrs Cummins wants time to organise it all properly." He managed a smile.

"Very nice, we'll look forward to that, won't we Sheila?"

Sheila nodded reassuringly at Peadar. "Yes, we will."

Rita was in one of her moods, sugary sweet on the outside and acid underneath. "We never see you these days. Too busy, I expect. Remember when you and Sheila were locked into this kitchen every night with your creams and potions."

That's right, mother dear. Go for the jugular, Sheila thought. Try to make him feel guilty and embarrassed.

"Ah, that was a long time ago." Peadar laughed nervously. "Before Sheila headed off for Dublin and turned into the great success she is."

Rita smirked. "Oh sure our Sheila is a regular business tycoon, isn't she?"

Sheila glared at her mother but Rita carried on regardless. "There's a lot to be said for a good job, of course. But family is more important, wouldn't you think?"

Peadar didn't know how to answer. He was uncomfortable. He didn't know who she was getting at, him or Sheila. There was no need for him to reply anyway as Rita was now in full flight. "Let's hope you're blessed with children. Sure you'd make a great father, Peadar."

Peadar flushed. Sheila lit a cigarette. Her mother'd have her back on forty a day.

"My grandchildren are such a joy. Of course I thought I'd have more than the twins. This one here is a dead loss." She glanced over at Sheila. "Work, work, work. That's all Sheila cares about. Now Caroline is as bad. Poor Seán hardly ever sees her."

Peadar felt obliged to say something. "It's important to feel fulfilled though, whether you're a man or a woman. Where would Carrigeen be without Sheila? It's great to see her doing so well. Three of my former students have work now, thanks to Sheila."

"Does that include Bridget?" Rita asked snidely.

Peadar decided two could play this game. "Oh indeed it does, Mrs Crosby. Sure it's thanks to Bridget's salary that we can buy the house." He knew his words hurt her mother, but he was aware of Sheila's grateful glance.

"Very gratifying." Rita stirred her tea with venom. "Fulfilment. That's it, you see. In my day women were fulfilled by looking after their husbands and families."

"Rubbish!" Sheila lost the cool. "They were not. Women were unpaid dogsbodies. Doormats."

Rita stood up. "You'll excuse me, Peadar. I must go and have a bath. Will you stay for dinner?"

Stay for dinner? Peadar couldn't wait to get out of there. He'd visited Sheila because he wanted to see her. They went back a long way and he felt he owed her some sort of respect. Not that she'd take his engagement badly, he knew Sheila had never harboured any secret desires for him. God knows, he'd tried to get her interested in him for years. But they did have a good friendship. That mattered too. His marriage next year would put them on a new footing. Things just wouldn't be the same. Sheila and Bridget would never be friends, he thought sadly. They'd be able to meet socially, but that would be it.

"Thanks, Mrs Crosby. I'm afraid I'll have to decline the invitation. We're going over to Mrs Cummins for tea."

"Lovely," Rita smirked again. "Tell her I was asking for her. Call again soon. Don't be such a stranger." Rita made a dramatic exit out of the kitchen leaving Sheila furious.

"God, she's getting worse," Sheila said by way of apology. "Don't mind her. To be perfectly frank, my mother had you singled out as her future son-in-law."

This was the first time Sheila had mentioned the unmentionable. She studied Peadar's face.

He smiled at her and took her hand. "May I be perfectly frank?"

Sheila pulled her hand away. "Better not, Peadar. Some things are better left unsaid."

He nodded and stood up to go. "I'd better be off. For what it's worth, I admire you. You've done a terrific job with the company, better than most men could have done."

Sheila gave him a hug. He really was a decent man.

"Where's your mother?" Seán stormed out of the bathroom in a rage and into Ciara's bedroom. Ciara had her Abba records blaring all over the house.

"Turn that down," he bellowed at his daughter. "Where's your mother?"

Ciara turned down the music. "Gone to the factory with Sheila."

"On Saturday morning? Ridiculous. I can't find a clean shirt."

Ciara laughed at her father who stood there in his vest and underpants. "Try the hot press. Nora did a pile of ironing yesterday."

"Thank God for Nora," Seán muttered through his teeth. "I'm going to the surgery. Will you make lunch since your mother has better things to do."

"Sorry. Can't." Ciara sat at her dressing-table and put on some cold cream. "I promised Stephen I'd go to the park with him. We're taking his dog for a walk."

"What about your lunch? And why are you putting that muck on your face?" Seán growled at her.

"Tch, it's not muck. It's the new bergamot blend. Terrific for oily skin." Ciara spread more on her face, just for spite. "Don't worry about my lunch, Mum gave me money for burgers. I'm treating Stephen."

Seán stomped off to the hot press. His shirts were stacked in two neat piles. He had to admit Nora Maguire was a wizard. But he hadn't married Nora Maguire. It didn't feel right to have an outsider doing his laundry. That, by right, was Caroline's job. Honestly, his wife was really pushing it. She worked all week and now she was there on Saturday morning. It was all Sheila's fault. She was footloose and fancy-free and had no obligations to anyone but herself. His sister had no conception or idea of how she was disturbing his family life. It just wasn't good enough. When did he see his wife? When did they eat together as a family? When did they go out together? The weekends should be theirs to spend together. Then Sheila swooped down for the weekend and Caroline went off like a shot, dancing attendance on her. Bloody sickening. It really was. Tomorrow night, Caroline had informed him, she was going for a meal with Sheila. Just the two of them. Fine. He'd go for a drink with Liam O'Flaherty. What was sauce for the goose was sauce for the gander. He felt redundant in his own home. Even the twins seemed to live lives of their own, totally independent of him. Their mother had them ruined with pocket money. They'd have no respect for hard work when they grew up. You spoiled children when they got things too easy. Try telling that to Caroline.

"See ya Dad," Ciara called up the stairs. The door slammed behind her. Seán went into his son's room. Colm was buried beneath a pile of bedclothes.

"Get up, Colm. Look at the time. You've to mow the grass today."

Colm opened one bleary eye. "Later," he mumbled and turned over on his side.

Straight back to sleep. Seán would have shook him awake but the phone rang. He hurried down to the hall to answer it.

"Seán dear?" His mother. "What time will you be finished in the surgery?"

"About one, one-thirty, Mam."

"I was wondering if you'd like to drop in for lunch."

Thank God somebody still thought about his needs. "Great, I'd love to."

"I bought some nice ham, thinking Sheila would like it. But she went out early this morning. I feel a bit abandoned."

"I know how you feel."

"She's only home every second weekend. Wouldn't you think she'd spend more time with her mother?"

"I've given up thinking," Seán moaned. "That bloomin' business of Sheila's has turned my world upside down."

"Shocking," his mother tutted down the line. "I'm going to have a word with her. I'll see you at about one-thirty so. Looking forward to it."

"So am I." Seán meant it. He could do with a bit

of company. Last night Caroline had gone to bed early. This morning she was up and gone before he woke. They were like ships that passed in the night. Some marriage. Now, on Saturday morning, he'd have at least two hours in the surgery and God knew how many house calls. The work was no problem. That was his vocation and his duty. But it would be nice if his wife could be home when he finished work. No, not a bit of it, gallivanting off with his sister. If it weren't for his mother, he didn't know what he'd do.

Rita made a nice roast for Sunday lunch. She was determined to fatten Sheila up. This was her first chance to cook for Sheila since she came down on Friday night. She'd a nice piece of lamb with mint sauce. Sheila only pecked at the dinner.

"You'll be skin and bone if you carry on like that," Rita admonished her. "Peadar looked well on Friday, put on a bit of weight, I thought. It suits him. When I think of it, Sheila, it makes me mad. It could be you getting married next June."

Sheila cut her meat and tried to hold her tongue.

"What's wrong with the meat? You're fiddling with it for the last five minutes. I got it in Riordan's and he said it was very tender."

"It's very nice." Sheila forced herself to eat. "I don't want a huge lunch. I'm eating out with Caroline tonight."

"I want to talk to you about that, Sheila. Seán's very upset, I can tell you. You tend to monopolise Caroline when you're down. It's not really fair."

Sheila sighed. "Look Mam, Seán's only happy when he's moaning. Anyhow he's going out for a drink with Liam tonight."

"But sure why would he stay at home when his wife's always out? He needs some enjoyment too. He'd rather be going out with Caroline than with Liam O'Flaherty anyway. I'm going over to sit with the twins. Not that I mind that, God knows. I love those kids and they're very good, no trouble at all. But Seán has to get out too. He works hard for a living. He's at everybody's beck and call."

Sheila agreed that her brother worked hard. There was no doubt about that. He took great care of his patients. He was trusted and liked by all of them. But that wasn't the bone of contention.

"Caroline works hard too. She runs Carrigeen very efficiently and that has its own pressures. I don't know what I'd do without her." Sheila cleared away the plates.

"She might be better suited to running her own home. You don't understand, Sheila. Being a mother and wife is a whole-time job. Seán needs some back-up."

That was it! Sheila couldn't stand another minute of this. "Mam, Caroline's never been so happy. She told me that only yesterday. She's earning good money and she feels useful and needed. The twins don't resent their mother for working. They look up to her, especially Ciara. She's very proud of Caroline. You can see it when she talks about her. And Seán is not neglected. Far from it. He has Nora Maguire to look after him. He's spoiled rotten in fact."

"Nora's a housekeeper not a wife." Rita raised her voice in anger.

"Well it's time Seán got a new definition of the word wife. Caroline's not a bond slave, is she? And Seán has forgotten what the extra cash means. He couldn't have got the surgery in the Square without Caroline's money. Financially, they've never been better off. Maybe that's what's really bothering him."

"We managed fine on one salary," Rita said defiantly. "We weren't rich, but we were comfortable."

"Were we? I remember you having to watch every penny. Dad's salary didn't go that far."

"You didn't suffer anyway, did you? Your father used his inheritance to set you up." Rita was red in the face with annoyance.

"Do you think I don't know that?" Sheila bellowed back. "That's another reason I like employing Caroline. At least some of the money's going back into the family. I refuse to feel guilty about the money Dad gave me. I put it to good use. The business is thriving. I've given employment to a lot of people. Neither you nor Seán can argue with that." She lit a cigarette and puffed furiously. She was close to tears.

Rita knew she'd overstepped the mark. "I know, I'm sorry. I shouldn't have said that. Pat was so proud of you, Sheila. So am I, honestly. I just don't understand you, that's all. When are you going to settle down with a family of your own? Do you not want a husband? Do you not want your own children? I just don't understand, I really don't."

Sheila could feel her cheeks burning. She needed some air. She was suffocating. "I'll go out for the Sunday paper. Which one do you want?"

"*The Press*," Rita stacked the dishes on the draining board. "Thanks, love, we won't argue any more. What date is today? I've an eye appointment for the twenty-ninth."

"It's the twenty-fourth." Sheila replied in a choked voice.

"The twenty-fourth? Are you sure?"

"Positive." Sheila grabbed her jacket and ran out of the kitchen. She was afraid of bursting into tears. She couldn't let her mother see that. She badly needed to get out in the air.

Rita made herself a cup of tea. What had got into Sheila? She'd been so crabby since she got up today. What started the row, Rita wondered. Was it her fault? Had she said too much? Sheila fought back tooth and nail. She had a temper too. They shouldn't be fighting like this on her weekends home. Pat wouldn't approve at all, Rita told herself. She'd have to learn when to keep her mouth shut. She should have noticed that Sheila wasn't herself at all this morning. What was wrong? Was it the new salon? Sheila had taken on far too much work. She wasn't eating properly either. If she went on like this for much longer, she'd end up with an ulcer. Maybe it was Peadar's engagement? Oh, they all said that Sheila wasn't interested in Peadar, but all the same they were friends for a long time. Maybe the thought of his marriage to Bridget did rankle. Everyone knew there was no love lost between the two women. Sheila was bound to be feeling something. Regrets? Who knew the answer to that? On the other hand, hadn't Seán said something about a new boyfriend? Not that Sheila had mentioned him. Rita wasn't going to ask any questions either. Sheila could tell her all about him when she felt ready. Maybe it was all off? Yeah, that was it. Why couldn't Sheila meet a nice man and hold onto him?

No, there was something else. Sheila always got annoyed when her mother sprang to Seán's defence. That must be it, the whole cause of her bad humour. But why had she been in bad form since she got up? Something about this date had sparked her off. Rita went over to the wall calendar. The twenty-fourth of September. What was the significance of that? It couldn't have anything to do with her thirtieth birthday, that was three weeks ago. But maybe being thirty and not settled and then the news of Peadar, maybe those were the straws that broke the camel's back. Ah, Rita gave up. She couldn't figure it out. She stacked the dishes in the press and went into the front room to put her legs up. No point in getting varicose veins if she could help it. She might have a little snooze for herself too. Sheila would have calmed down by the time she got back with the papers. Things were said in the heat of the moment, but didn't that happen in all families?

"God, that was delicious." Caroline licked her lips. "I love the peppered steak here."

"Me too," Sheila said, but she hadn't eaten much tonight either although McSwiggins was one of her favourite restaurants in Galway. The food was good and the atmosphere was very friendly and relaxed. There was nothing pretentious about the place. They'd had an aperitif in the bar before they got their table in the restaurant.

"Is the wine OK?" Caroline asked. "I know it's not up to your usual standard!"

"Get lost." Sheila stuck out her tongue. "The house red here is always good. I'm no connoisseur. I hate people who are snobbish about wines. It's usually those who haven't a clue anyway.

"Yeah," Caroline sniggered. "Your brother for example."

"Oh God, don't mention the war. Seán's name is anathema to me at this moment. I had a bellyful with Mam today. It was desperate. I lost the rag."

"I'm not surprised. She's always making digs at me too."

"How do you put up with it?" Sheila asked in exasperation. She didn't envy Caroline having to live with this type of aggravation.

"Ah, I refuse to rise to their bait. My own mother's very supportive of me. She's delighted I've found my own niche, as she says. My mother's a lovely lady, do you know that? She devoted her whole life to my sisters and me when my father died. It wasn't easy. She was a great dressmaker. She used to make all the children's dresses for the families for miles around. That kept us going, but it was a constant struggle."

"What's she doing with herself now? Is she living alone?"

"Yeah, she is. Molly, my eldest sister, lives near her. Their kids are in and out all the time, so she's not lonely. For years her only outlet was bingo. That really depressed me. I thought there was something pathetic about it. But since I went back to work, she decided to broaden her own horizons. She started up a widow and widower's social group."

"You're not serious. Fair dues to her. What sort of things do they do?"

"They go on tours, they have card nights, and one of the group has started a ballroom dancing class in her house. It's hilarious."

"You have to hand it to her. She must be getting on a bit now?"

"Late seventies, but there's plenty of life in the old girl yet. Sure your mother's the same. She might moan and groan, but I'm telling you she has a great social life. More power to her for that, but I wish she'd stop interfering in other people's lives. Mine, especially."

"Amen to that." Sheila sighed. "Once she gets a bee in her bonnet she never stops. I know it's concern for Seán and myself that makes her the way she is, but it's very hard to take. No matter what you say, she thinks that her poor son is deprived and ignored. Its makes me want to throw up."

Caroline laughed. "He is ignored a lot of the time, even by the twins. They're at that age when parents become irrelevant. All Colm wants is his food and his football and Ciara's totally occupied with school, her friends and Stephen. By God, am I glad I have the job to keep me occupied. And Seán conveniently forgets that he's at work day and night and doesn't have that much time for us, either. In the early days of our marriage, I was the one stuck at home on my own practically the whole time."

"Yeah, now he hates being on his own for a few hours." Sheila thought of how he reacted to their day in Carrigeen yesterday. A forty-year-old man acting like a peevish four-year-old. "Then when Mam's finished on the subject of Seán she starts on me. Honestly, I'm sorely tempted to stay in Dublin and not bother with these weekend trips home."

"Don't you dare abandon me!" Caroline warned her with a smile. "You'll just have to put up with your mother. You said she started on you this morning. What was she on about?"

"Marriage and kids, the usual stuff. Peadar's engagement too. She even got at him when he called around to see me. I was mortified. She insinuated that they had to get married. I could have throttled her."

"She'll never forgive Bridget Cummins for stealing him away from you."

Sheila groaned. "The field was clear when Bridget met Peadar. You know I was never very fond of her, but I genuinely think she'll be good for Peadar. She has a spark. You couldn't fault her on her work either. I was very impressed with the new range yesterday. I'll have four massage oils now for the salon. She's going to do some more work on the eye make-up lotions too."

"The eye make-up remover with the witch-hazel? Yeah, I heard her discussing it with Jean, one of the new lab assistants. They're a good team in the lab. They work well together and Bridget is nice with the staff. She manages to tell them what to do without throwing her weight around."

"OK, I know. Bridget's lovely." Sheila laughed. "It's just that I never feel comfortable with her."

"It's the other way around, I think. She always feels you're checking up on her."

"That's my job, Caroline. I can't pussyfoot around my own factory because Bridget is supersensitive."

"And there's Peadar. She must know how he felt about you."

"Do you think so?"

"I know so. Have you forgotten what good old gossip is like?"

"No, we've plenty of it in Dublin too."

"So Rita got on your goat? This weekend hasn't been a bundle of laughs for you, has it?"

""I hate it when she goes on about me. You'd think she'd be more sensitive. I can take the bit about a husband, but when she nags me about not having children, I nearly lose my reason. This morning I thought I'd hit her."

"Jesus, today above all days." Caroline sympathised.

"Well, she wasn't to know. She knew I was upset about something though because she more or less apologised after. Look at me, thirty years old and I still let my mother get to me. Wouldn't you think I'd have more sense?"

"Mothers can get to you at any age." Caroline puckered up her lips. "There's something about mother and daughter relationships that can needle the sanest of people. Ciara accuses me of emotional blackmail. I find myself saying things to her I swore I'd never say to a child of mine. That's the most frightening part of parenting. You begin to sound like your own parents."

"Jesus, that is frightening." Sheila blew a smoke ring in the air. "Are we having dessert?"

"Yeah, I'm going to have their largest gâteau." Caroline cheered up at the thought of it. "I know how you can shut your mother up, once and for all."

"How?"

"Tell her the truth. Tell her you're having an affair."

"God, can you imagine it? She'd have a fit. She'd think I was a scarlet woman."

"You never know. She mightn't. You should bring John down for the weekend some time. Sure he'd charm the pants off her."

"Do you really think so?" Sheila couldn't imagine it.

"Absolutely. A solicitor. God, she'd be on high doh."

"Not when she heard he was married. Mam doesn't agree with separation. She thinks once people make their bed, they should lie on it."

"That's the way all that generation think. But I bet if she met him, she'd be highly impressed. At least it'd give her something different to worry about. That's all she needs."

"Could you stomach more of her moans? You'd be the one who had to listen to her saying that she'd love me to meet some eligible man. I can just hear her going on about him being on the rebound. Ah no, Caroline. It's not a good idea. It'd be disastrous."

"Ah Sheila, go on, do it for the crack."

"Someday maybe. Not yet. I don't want to frighten him off."

"Maybe you're right, on second thoughts." Caroline gave a wry grin. "Your family would put anyone off."

"It didn't put you off!"

"No, because I was mad about your father. I was mad about Seán too. I was young and foolish as they say."

"You were mad, in other words." Sheila laughed. "I know you're still in love with Seán."

"Of course I am. Deep down, he's one of the best. He adores the twins and me. But he can't accept the changing roles in the family. He expects the kids to stay the way they were when they depended on him for all the answers. Now, they do their own thing. Perfectly normal of course, but he can't accept it. He finds it hard to let go. With me it's exactly the same. He was happy when I was literally tied to the kitchen sink. He wanted me to be the contented little housewife. But I wasn't happy, I was bloody miserable. He's extremely clever in some ways, but in others he has no cop-on at all."

"Loads of academics are like that. When I was a young child he used to make me learn heaps of Latin off by heart. To be honest, I looked up to him. I was ten years younger and I thought he was so clever and sophisticated. He got a brilliant degree and Mam was so proud of him. But I think he's lost some of his spunk over the years. He's kind of stuck in a rut, I think. I don't think Seán ever saw himself as the local GP. He had great ambitions. He wanted to specialise."

"You're right. But there's nothing to stop him now. His excuse was always that he had to look after his family, that his financial commitments were too heavy. I shouldn't say this or you might dock my wages, but I'm actually earning more than Seán is now. That's what really galls him."

"Probably." Sheila called over the waitress. She ordered black forest gâteau for Caroline and a Cointreau for herself. "I didn't even finish my degree and that really bugs him too. He never thought I'd make it in the business world."

"No, he didn't. I feel a bit sorry for him." Caroline bit into her dessert. "God, this is mouthwatering. Mmh, I love moist cakes. The rum flavour is gorgeous. Anyway, what was I saying?"

"That you felt sorry for Seán."

"Yeah, that must sound very supercilious, but I don't mean it like that. Seán was never one for change. He likes his parameters clearly defined.

He's sort of lost his sense of identity. He's not sure of this new me. I'm not the girl he married."

"No, you're wrong there," Sheila said. "You're back to the girl he married. You're capable and highly organised. When the twins were small, you had a different role. I think you lost some of your confidence then."

"I did, definitely. I thought I'd never be able to go back to work. I thought there'd never be an end to the nappies, the bottles, the housework. I think I was really depressed. I nearly forgot how to make conversation. I was a cook, a cleaner, a laundress, a nurse. Then Seán expected me to attend to his needs."

"Yeah, hang out the other boob."

"What did you say?" Caroline spluttered. "Hang out the other boob?"

"It's one of Mary's expressions. Good, isn't it? So, Seán got used to that safe little housewife and he liked it. You replaced Mam for him."

Caroline squirmed. "Jesus, that thought sends shivers down my spine. Thank God you set up the business. It's a life-saver for me. Plus, I think it's good for the kids. They don't take me for granted. I'm not saying anything about women who choose to work in the home. I think they're terrific. I really do. That's what they want. Nobody works harder than a woman who stays at home. Rearing children is the most important job of all. But it's not for me. Having said that, I couldn't do what I do without great help. Nora Maguire's a brick."

"Yeah, you were lucky to get her. But you've

combined both, Caroline. You did your stint at home when the twins were small and needed you. I often think about Karen's mother. Does she stay at home? I wonder what I'd have done myself if I'd got married and had kids. It's a tough decision." Sheila was deep in thought.

"Let's drink a toast to Karen. Her tenth birthday. I wonder did she have a party?"

Sheila sipped her drink. "I'd say she did. A gang of ten-year-olds from school. You can picture it."

"Yeah, fairy cakes, rice crispie buns and crisps and coke. Gunge, that's what they all love. Karen'll be just the same. Ten years old, God." Caroline saw the wistful look in her sister-in-law's eye. "Are you OK, Sheila?"

"Yeah, fine. I hope she got loads of presents. I hope she had a really great day. I'd give anything to see her." Sheila said longingly. "Anything."

* * *

Liz Shaw finally got to the end of the washing-up. More food had ended up in the bin and on the floor than anywhere else. Fifteen ten-year-olds had been a bit of a handful today, but they were nice children. She didn't mind. It was worth all the hassle to see the smile on Karen's face.

Frank looked over the newspaper. "She's delighted with her bike, isn't she?"

"Thrilled. I hope she'll be careful. I warned her to cycle on the path." Liz wiped her hands on the towel on the back of the kitchen door. "Anything new in the paper? I never got a chance all day to even glance at it."

"There's a piece here about Steve Biko's funeral in South Africa. A crowd of 15,000 attended."

"Oh my God, it's terrible. What's going on over there at all? I think he was murdered."

"Of course he was. Died in police custody. That's a euphemism for beaten to death for speaking out."

"That apartheid's a disgrace. Is there nothing that can be done?"

"There'll be international protest about this, anyway. Here, read it. I'll go in to Karen to say goodnight."

Karen was sitting up reading one of her new books. She put down the book and hugged her father.

"Thanks a million for the bike, Dad. It's cool."

Frank kissed the top of her head. "I'm glad you like it, love. You're such a good little girl that Mum and I wanted to give you something very special. But you must be careful on it. You know how Mum worries about you."

"Can I join the tennis club next summer?" She hugged him tighter. "Please?"

Frank took the book and put it on her bedside table. "We'll see. I'm sure you can. Now it's time to put out the light. You've school tomorrow. You don't want to fall asleep at your desk, do you?"

Karen pouted. "I'd never do that. I'm the best in the class. Mrs O'Shea always says that. It's probably because I read such a lot."

Frank tried to hide his smile. She was so earnest about everything. It was true that she was excellent at school. She tried so hard to please.

"Can I say goodnight to Mum? Just for a minute. I want to ask her something."

"All right, but then it's sleep, young lady." He kissed her again and went to call Liz.

Liz took Karen's uniform out of the wardrobe and hung it neatly over her chair for the morning.

"Goodnight, sweetheart." She leaned over and kissed Karen's cheek.

"Mum, what time was I born at?"

"What love?" Liz couldn't believe she was hearing this.

"You know, what time of the day was I born at?"

Liz hesitated. How was she going to answer this? "I'm not sure, why?"

"A girl in school told me you couldn't have a proper horoscope done unless you knew the time you were born at."

"I don't know, Karen. Remember I told you about your other mother?" How could Karen have forgotten that? Mind you, it was a while ago.

A smile spread over Karen's face. "Oh yeah, you weren't there when I was born. That's weird, isn't it? Was Dad there? He might know."

Liz gulped. This was very difficult. It was important to handle it carefully. "Dad and I got you when you were six weeks old, honey. We brought you home and had a big party to celebrate your homecoming. Granny Whelan was there and Grandad and all your cousins. Everyone made a big fuss of you. You were such a gorgeous little baby. We all fell in love with you."

Karen smiled. "Did you know the other lady? My other mother?"

"No pet, we didn't." Liz wanted this conversation to end, but she had to reassure the little girl.

"Maybe I had another daddy too?" The thought suddenly struck Karen. "You have to have a daddy and a mammy to make a baby."

"That's right. But you have a mammy and daddy here who love you very dearly. You're a lucky little girl. And you have your brother too." Liz hoped she wouldn't ask about Peter's natural parents. She couldn't face it tonight. She'd have to have a chat with Frank. They obviously hadn't dealt with the whole issue in enough detail. It was time for another visit to the counsellor. Karen lay back on her pillows and put her arms up for a final bedtime hug. "I love you, Mum. You're the best mammy in the world."

Liz turned out the lamp. She said a silent prayer of thanks. It was over for the moment. But how would it be in the future?

CHAPTER TWENTY-FOUR

John Harris was terribly disappointed. Sheila had just rung to cancel their date for tonight. He wanted to see her. He missed her. This was getting ridiculous. He was lucky if he saw her once a week now. She was so damn busy. If it wasn't the shop, it was the salon or a business dinner or an interview for one of the glossies. He was sick of it. Natural Woman was a household word. Ever since she appeared on *The Late Late Show* she'd become a celebrity. She was recognised wherever they went. He didn't like it. People actually came up to talk to her in pubs and restaurants. Talk about invasion of privacy. But Sheila seemed to lap up all the attention. He was more like her escort than her lover. He admired her, of course. Anyone would. It was great to see her enjoying so much success. But her life was taken over by the business. It was all-consuming. She had no time for anything else. No time for him. He was beginning to feel superfluous to requirements.

He took his coffee into his bedroom and turned on the radio.

"I've been waiting such a long time, reaching out for you but you're not here. What's another year?"

Jesus, he could have written the words for Johnny Logan. At least the singer got something for his trouble. Ireland's Eurovision winner. Love and pain and the whole damn thing. What's another year was right. 1980. Three years with Sheila and what did he have to show for it? Nothing. The odd night of passion when she was available. He hadn't meant to get involved to this extent. He hadn't bargained on it at all. He was crazy about her. He wanted more from their relationship than she was able or willing to give. Every time he suggested that they live together, she ignored him. Yeah, like Johnny, he was getting used to being alone.

He turned off the radio and rang his office. His secretary reminded him he had a briefing session with Niall McGonagle, the barrister, at ten. It was a straightforward car accident case. His client was hit from behind at high speed. The car was a write-off and there was a medical claim for whiplash. The other driver's insurance company offered a pittance in compensation. The case was due in court the following week. When it came to the crunch they'd be persuaded to settle out of court. Niall McGonagle was very persuasive. John's big bogey at the moment was another case. Unfair dismissal. It was a tricky one. This sleazebag, Tom Murphy, deserved to be fired. He was extremely aggressive and John guessed he'd be impossible to work with. He was a barman and apparently had a stand-up row with his employer in front of the customers. He was threatening all sorts of revenge including getting in the heavies to "do" the publican. John hoped to mediate between them. He wanted to avoid going to court with this lunatic. He'd meet him at twelve but he wasn't looking forward to it. He could do without this.

John wore his Louis Copeland blue suit. In the mirror he noticed the grey hairs at his temples. Not bad. Gave him a distinguished look. Had to look the part for Sheila. He hated the taunts of his colleagues at work. They now referred to him as natural man. Funny. If only he could laugh at it. He took his briefcase and left the mews. Nine-thirty. The worst of the traffic would be gone.

No such luck! Every traffic light was red around the Green. Pedestrians ran out on suicide missions. Going around by Trinity was a nightmare. Nobody was in the right lane. He finally got to O'Connell Bridge at nine-fifty. Another red light. He turned on his car radio: Gay Byrne chatting up the housewives. Well for some. He hoped he'd get parking in Parnell Square near his office, but it was doubtful. As he drove around by the Rotunda he spotted a driver pulling out. He was in luck.

"Good morning, Mr Harris." Rebecca Morley, petite, blonde and thirty-something greeted her boss.

"Hi, Rebecca. Any calls?"

"Mr Murphy rang to cancel his appointment. His wife's been taken into hospital."

"Oh?"

Rebecca hesitated. "I shouldn't say this. But I thought he sounded drunk on the phone."

John nodded. "Did you fix up another appointment for him?"

"No, he said he'd phone again."

"Right." John went into his inner office. It was small but comfortable. Plain green carpet and curtains, mahogany desk, a filing cabinet, two high-backed chairs and two black leather armchairs. The bookshelves were packed with his private law library. The desk was strewn with papers, files and documents. He'd just got out the file on the car accident when Rebecca buzzed him.

"It's Jim Ryan. Will you talk to him?"

"Yep. Put him through. Jim? How's it going? Grand, grand. Tonight? Yeah, I'm free as a matter of fact. Where? O'Neill's? Perfect. See you at nine. Cheers."

Good. At least he wouldn't be stuck in tonight after all. He could hear Niall McGonagle chatting up Rebecca at her desk. Niall was a notorious lecher. Reminded him of what he used to be like himself. Never missed an opportunity. But that was in the past. All John wanted now was to settle down.

"So, how's life treating you then?" Jim stood at the bar in O'Neill's, pint in hand.

John grabbed a vacant stool. "Not bad." He ordered a whiskey for himself and another pint for Jim.

"How are the kids?" John asked.

"A handful. Maeve's into everything now. Mary

355

had to get those special fixtures to put over the plugs, you know? She's a desperate climber too. Up on the tables and presses. You can't take your eyes off her for a minute. She's a terrible bully. Terrifies the wits out of Davy and he's a year older. Mary kills her, but I'm no use. Once she smiles at me, I melt. She's a minx."

John laughed. "How's Davy?"

"Just started playschool, would you believe? He loves it. They need kids of their own age. He can read a few words already. Brilliant, isn't it? At three and a half. Mary's thrilled with him."

John could see that Jim was thrilled with him too. He envied Jim. Two lovely little kids and a devoted wife. "You're a lucky man, Jim."

Jim had a look around. The crowd were really young. Mostly students. "God, I used to love this pub. We came here in gangs in our Uni days. Then a bag of greasy chips and the walk home. The pub hasn't changed but I have. Take a look around. I'm beginning to feel ancient."

"Do you want to go somewhere else? The Old Stand, maybe?"

"Good idea. Have you eaten?" Jim asked.

"No, I'd lunch out today, but I didn't bother cooking after work." John didn't see the point in cooking for one. "Do you want to go for a meal?"

Jim thought about it. "Why not? Mary's out on a staff social night. They've gone bowling in Stillorgan, so, Angela's babysitting. I'll give her a ring and tell her I'll be a bit late."

"She mightn't like that." John lit a cheroot.

356

"Angela? Not at all. She won't mind. She has her books with her. She's in her second year in the College of Art. She needs the extra cash," Jim said. "Remember when we were impoverished students?"

"Light years ago," John replied. "I didn't mean Angela. I meant Mary. Won't she be expecting you back early?"

"Ah, Mary'll probably go to The Orchard for a drink after bowling. She'll go straight to bed when she comes in. There's no sweat. I'm not on a leash yet. If we're going to The Old Stand for a drink we could pop over to the Trocadero after."

"Terrific." John finished his whiskey as Jim went off to find a phone.

The Old Stand on Exchequer Street was an old pub furnished in Victorian style. The huge semi-circular bar covered half the floor space. Most people preferred to stand or sit at the bar instead of taking a seat by the sides. There was always lots of chat. It was usually packed with sporting types, particularly the racing crowd.

"This is where Sheila loves to come after the Curragh," John said. "We know a lot of the punters." He waved over at a couple on the far side of the bar. "That's Sheila's manageress in the shop, Lily O'Brien. She's just got engaged to yer man, George Burke. Big money. His family has a stud farm. Sheila introduced them. His sister is a regular in the salon."

"Do you and Sheila go racing much?" asked Jim.

"When she has the time. I went to the Galway

Races with her last year. Great craic. We stayed in the Great Southern. Race week in Galway is bloody mad. You'd need a holiday after it to recover."

"You both stayed in the hotel? Her mother must have been impressed."

"She didn't seem to mind. Sheila had made her out as some sort of ogress but I quite liked her. We took her out for a meal. But that was last year. Now I'm lucky if I see Sheila for a couple of hours."

Jim could see he was agitated. He knew there was something up. John wasn't his usual gregarious self.

"She's a lot on her plate," Jim said. "Jesus, it's amazing how that business has taken off. She told Mary ever since *The Late Late Show* she can't keep up with the orders in the shop. The salon's doing a bomb too. Then there's the trouble at home. Sheila's caught in the middle." Jim swished his pint. "Look at the head on this pint. Bloody perfect."

"This pub's always served a good pint. What did you mean by trouble at home? Her mother?" John looked surprised. "Sheila said nothing to me."

"Didn't she?" It was Jim's turn to look surprised. "Ah, she probably didn't want to bother you with it. Families can be a right pain in the butt."

John wasn't having that. If Sheila had a problem, she should have told him. He had a right to know. Christ, it was getting worse. He was beginning to wonder if he knew Sheila at all. She was definitely shutting him out. "Well, what is it? It can't be too private or you wouldn't know about it."

Jim regretted ever bringing this up. John was

very edgy. "The only reason I know about it is because Mary was talking to Sheila last night on the phone. Sheila said she had to go home because there was a fierce row between her brother and his wife."

"Seán and Caroline?"

"Apparently Caroline walked out."

John was shocked. "Jesus, I can't believe it. Seán and the son, what do you call him?

"Colm."

"Yeah. Seán and Colm were up in Dublin two weeks ago. They stayed with Sheila."

"I know. For the All Ireland Hurling Final. Galway's first win in fifty-seven years. Beat the shite out of Limerick. It was mighty, did you see it?"

John had no interest whatever in hurling. He didn't give a fiddler's who won the blasted thing. What he wanted to know was what was going on in Sheila's family, and more importantly, why she hadn't told him the truth. She'd lied to him this morning. Said she was meeting Finian O'Toole, her accountant. Said she was tied up with meetings for the rest of the week. "Has she gone home?" he asked Jim.

"Drove down this morning. I don't know what good she can do. But Caroline might listen to Sheila. They get on very well according to Mary. Right, will we go over to the Troc?"

John was still lost on thought. She'd actually lied to him. Why? Could she not trust him? Did she not think he'd be interested? Had she so little faith in him?

"John, are we right? We'd want to go now if we want to get a table."

"I've lost my appetite. I feel like getting drunk. Would you mind if we didn't eat?"

Jim was a bit annoyed, but he wasn't going to push it when John was in this mood. "No problem. I'll get us another drink so."

John stared at his drink. He was still brooding. Jim had never seen him like this before. Maudlin. He was turning into a right pain. Mary had worried that John would hurt Sheila. Bloody ironic. It was the other way around.

"Come on, John. Snap out of it. Let's forget the women for one night. Drink up."

John took a large swig and then shuddered. "I can't forget, that's the point. Why didn't she tell me she was going to Galway? Why?"

"She didn't want you to worry. Who knows? Who can figure out women, for God's sake? Let it go. Enjoy your drink and forget about it." Jim's patience was running out.

"It's all right for you. You have Mary. You have the kids." There were tears in John's eyes.

Ah Jaysus, Jim thought, if he's going to start blubbering, I'm out of here.

"What have I got? Nothing." John's voice shook. "Thirty-eight years old and what have I got to show for it?"

"Would you cop on, for fuck's sake." Jim snapped at him. "You've a good job, money in your pocket, a nice little pad and one of the best-looking women in town. You drive a BMW. Jesus, you're laughing, mate."

"Doesn't mean a thing. If I lose her I've got nothing." John sniffed. "I want it all, Jim. Marriage. Kids. The whole scene."

Jim was very angry now. "Wasn't that what Anne wanted?"

John's expression took on a wounded look. "That's below the belt."

"Maybe. But it's true. You had the marriage bit. You had the chance of kids. You blew it, John."

"I was too young then," John said sadly. "Anne and I were too young when we got married. I didn't want the responsibility of kids. I wasn't ready."

Jim sighed into his pint. He'd heard all this before and he was pissed off with it. "So you think you're ready now, do you?"

"Yeah. I want to get a foreign divorce. I want to marry Sheila and have kids. She's only thirty-three. She could have children if she wanted to."

Jim couldn't believe his ears. "If she wanted to? Are you fucking crazy? That's the whole shagging point. That's why she chose you in the first place. Sheila will never have another kid. She made that quite clear to you from the beginning." What kind of a moron was John? He must know the way Sheila felt. That's the way John himself had felt. The relationship suited him. Did he honestly expect Sheila to change her mind now for him?

"You're a selfish bastard, do you know that?" Jim handed him another whiskey. "I wouldn't mention kids to Sheila, if I were you. That'd be one sure way of losing her."

"That's great coming from you. You've two already and for all I know you could be expecting a third. What's that you said to me on your wedding day? That you'd have seven or eight?" John sneered. "Maybe you could hire one out to me."

"Too late, mate. Had the snip last year. There'll be no more kids for Mary and me."

But John wasn't listening. He was too wrapped up in his own misery.

* * *

"How did the bowling go?" Jim crawled into bed beside Mary. "Mmh, you smell good."

Mary put her arms around him. "Two spares and a strike. I'm getting better. Something gas happened. Do you know Frances?"

"Mmh." He nibbled her ear. She squirmed with pleasure.

"Wait a sec, I want to tell you this." She pushed him away. "Frances was watching this guy bowling in the next lane. He was a real pro, had all his own gear. A bit of a show-off. But Frances was really impressed with him. The next thing she shouts to me, 'Look Mary, that fella's brought his own balls!' Jesus, we cracked up laughing."

Jim went back to kissing her neck. "God, you smell really sexy. What is it?"

"One of Sheila's moisturisers. Rose oil."

"God, don't mention that woman to me." Jim sat

up and lit a cigarette. "What a night I've had. John's a walking disaster."

"John Harris? What's wrong with him?"

"What's right? He moaned all evening. He's really cut up about her. He's afraid she's going to ditch him, I think."

"She wouldn't do that. She's very fond of him."

"Fond? He'd have a stroke if he heard you saying that. He's more than fond. He's bloody obsessed," insisted Jim.

"John Harris? Are we talking about the same man?" Mary couldn't believe what she was hearing.

"No, I don't think we are. He's not the same man at all. He wants to marry Sheila and, wait for it, have children."

Mary took the fag from him and puffed hard. "Jesus, are you serious?"

"Afraid so."

"What a turn up for the books. He's mad if he thinks he'll talk Sheila into that." Mary handed back the cigarette.

"That's what I told him. You better not say anything to her either. Let them sort out their own problems."

"Don't worry," Mary said emphatically. "It's weird though. That's what Sheila's gone to Galway for . . . to sort out Seán. He's acting up because he feels neglected by Caroline. He says her job is wrecking their marriage. She couldn't take any more."

"This Natural Woman has a lot to answer for. Two men being made miserable." John stubbed out the cigarette and put the ash-tray on the floor.

"Aren't you glad you married a teacher? Regular hours and plenty of homework to keep me in at night."

"And long holidays." He switched off the light and turned to her.

"Don't you start on that." She bit his shoulder.

"No, I know how hard you work. Oh, I have to go up North again next week." He slipped his hand under her nightie.

"Not again, Jim! I'll be calling Sheila in here to sort out our marriage. You're never here."

His hand travelled down her stomach and met elastic. "Take off your knickers and make the most of me when I am here."

His lips crushed hers and prevented her from further discussion. Mary wasn't complaining. Her tongue probed his mouth as he climbed on top of her . . .

CHAPTER TWENTY-FIVE

Caroline's mother lived in a quiet cul-de-sac ten minutes drive from the centre of Galway. Sheila'd phoned the house last night and Caroline had agreed to see her. Caroline's mother, a tiny woman with her steel-grey hair caught up in a bun, was standing on the doorstep, a walking-stick in her hand.

"Thank God you're here, pet." The old lady kissed Sheila warmly. "We're in an uproar. Come in. She's in the dining-room. I'm worried about her, Sheila. I never thought she'd do anything this drastic. You have to convince her to go back to Seán." Mrs Cunningham brought Sheila down the narrow hall into the back room. The room was small, dusty and cluttered with furniture. Patterned wallpaper, carpets and curtains made the room seem smaller. Caroline was sitting at the huge dining-table, examining large glossy prints. She came over and hugged Sheila. "Glad you're here. I want you to vet these. They're for the new brochures."

Sheila put the photos back on the table. "Later, Caroline. That's not why I'm here."

"I know that. But I've a lot of stuff I want you to see. Now's as good a time as any."

"Is it?" Sheila raised an eyebrow.

"I haven't left work, Sheila, just because I've left your brother. Nothing's changed between you and me. The work comes first."

This wasn't normal, was it? Caroline had walked out on her husband and here she was discussing work. "Maybe it shouldn't come first," Sheila replied a bit abruptly.

"I'll leave you to it," Mrs Cunningham said quietly. She knew Sheila needed to be alone with her daughter. "The kettle's on, Caroline. Make tea for Sheila. I'm waiting for Gladys to pick me up. I'll go into the sitting-room. I'll be able to see her car from the window. We've our ballroom dancing over in Helen's."

Sheila was fascinated. The old dear walked with the help of a stick. How was she going to trip the light fantastic? "You're still dancing?" Sheila hoped she'd managed to disguise her astonishment.

The old lady roared laughing. "Dancing is it? Not at all, girl. Sure these old pins barely keep me up these days. No, no, I gave up the dancing ages ago. But the young ones have to have music, you see. I'm the official pianist. The female Liberace!"

"Mam still has a lovely touch," Caroline said to Sheila.

"Good to see you again, Sheila." Mrs Cunningham took sheets of music from the sideboard. "How's your mother keeping?"

"She's grand thanks."

"Do your best," Mrs Cunningham whispered to Sheila. She left, shutting the door gently behind her.

"Your mother's amazing, Caroline."

"I know. She's easy to get on with. Eighty last month. The young ones she was talking about are in their seventies." Caroline looked tired. Her eyelids were puffy and red as if she'd been crying.

"She's very concerned about you," Sheila said. "Wants you to go back."

"I know. Look what she gave me last night." Caroline handed over a photocopied page.

"The Fascinating Womanhood Way To Welcome A Man When He Comes Home From Work." Sheila read the title out loud. "What the hell is this?"

"It's something Mam kept. Her niece in Canada sent it to her years ago. Mam thinks it'd be of use to me. Read it. Go on. It's unbelievable.

Sheila continued to read aloud. *"'One. Get your work done. Plan your tasks with an eye on the clock. Finish an hour before he is expected. Your anguished cry, "Are you home already?" is not exactly a warm welcome.'"* Sheila threw the page on the table in disgust. "What is this bull?"

Caroline picked it up again. "You have to read on. It gets better. *'Two. Have dinner ready. Plan ahead to have a delicious meal on time. Most men are hungry when they come home and the prospects of a good meal are part of the warm welcome needed.'* Good advice, what?" Caroline raised her eyes to heaven.

"Does your mother honestly believe in this crap?

Jesus!" Sheila lit a fag. "Go on, I'm dying to hear number three."

"Number three's the best one." Caroline put on a dreamy voice for added emphasis. "*Three. Prepare yourself. Take fifteen minutes to rest so you will be refreshed when he arrives. This will also make you happy to see him instead of too tired to care. Turn off the worry and be glad to be alive and grateful for this man who is going to walk in. While you are resting you can be thinking of your FW assignment and all you can do to make him happy and give his spirits a lift.'*"

"What's FW?"

"Fascinating Womanhood, how could you forget?" Caroline uttered in mock horror.

"Fecking weird, more like it!" Sheila squirmed in her seat. "It's sickening!"

Caroline wouldn't be put off. "You haven't heard the best bit yet. I'm still on number three, right? *'When you arise, take care of your appearance. Touch up your make-up, put a ribbon in your hair and be fresh-looking. He has just been with a lot of work-weary people. Be a little gay and a little more interesting. His boring day may need a lift.'* Now I know where I went wrong, Sheila. I forgot the ribbon in my hair."

Sheila laughed loudly. "Can I have a copy of this? I'll put it up in the salon for the women to read."

"You could sell copies of this. It'd make a fortune. Can you imagine girls learning this tripe in school? This was in the fifties in Canada. Christ, our nuns were more enlightened than that. At least they encouraged us to improve ourselves."

Sheila was still glancing at the page. She read out more of the headings. *"'Clear away the clutter. Prepare the children. Minimise all noise. Be happy to see him. Don't complain. Make him comfortable. Listen to him. Make the evening his.'* This is really crazy stuff. Mind you, I remember the no noise bit at home. Mam never even turned on the washing-machine when Dad came home. We had to be quiet. In fact, most evenings she had me in bed before he came home."

Caroline nodded. "It was different for us because Dad died when we were young. Mam has this idealised memory of him. She thinks the world of Seán too. Doesn't understand what I'm talking about. She thinks that if Seán is not beating me up, having affairs or getting drunk all the time, I should consider myself lucky."

"Yeah. Different expectations. They accepted everything as their lot. Sad, but luckily not our fate."

"Have you seen Seán?" Caroline asked defensively. "No doubt he's been ballyragging me all over the place."

"Not yet. I wanted to talk to you first," Sheila replied gently. "Come on, tell me. What happened?"

"Tch, you know it all already. There's no point going over it again."

"Your job?"

Caroline sighed deeply. "What else? On and on, over and over again. The same old story. He's wearing me out. He never stops picking on me. I couldn't take it anymore. I packed a bag and walked out."

"I don't blame you. It's mental cruelty."

"Honestly, he's impossible. Tried to drag the twins into it too." Caroline sniffed.

Sheila took a tissue from her bag and handed it to her. "Here, have a good blow. What did the kids say?"

"Ciara sided with me. Told him he was a cranky old bugger." Caroline half laughed.

Sheila could picture the scene. Ciara was well able for her father. She didn't suffer fools gladly. She'd been outspoken since she was a little girl.

"How did Seán take that?"

"He started on her then. Went on about Stephen. How she was spending too much time with him. She gave him short shrift, I can tell you. He hadn't a leg to stand on. She got eight good honours in her Inter Cert, as you know, and she threw that back in his face."

"Good for her," Sheila said approvingly. "And Colm?"

"He kept out of it. Colm hates rows."

"Yeah, he's like Dad. But what made you leave? Why not throw him out?"

"Good question. He could go back to your mother. That'd be just up his alley. She's to blame for half of this. Interfering old bitch. Sorry Sheila, I know she's your mother, but she's been a thorn in my side for years."

There was no need for Caroline to apologise.

Sheila fully agreed with her. "I don't think you need worry about Mam anymore."

"Oh yeah?"

"I had strong words with her last night. I didn't pull any punches."

"Doubt if that'll do any good. Sure you spoke to her before." Caroline screwed the hankie into a ball. She was really tense. "She doesn't listen. Neither does he."

"She listened last night. She got an awful fright when she heard you'd left. She was the one who rang me."

"I thought it was Seán."

"No. I'd be the last person Seán would phone. He wouldn't want me poking my nose in."

"Well, I want you to, Sheila. You're the only one in that family I can speak to. The only sane one. Since your dad died, the pair of them have been ganging up on me."

Sheila nodded. It was true. Rita and Seán Crosby. Doting mother and puling son. A lethal combination.

"Mam will definitely be off your back from now on. I guarantee it."

"Why? What did you say to her?"

"Told her there was a place for you in the Dublin office, if you wanted it."

"You did not!" Caroline gaped.

"I did. 'Course she said you'd never leave the twins," Sheila said cheerfully.

"She's right. I wouldn't. Not for the world."

"I know that, silly. But I told her I'd plenty of

371

room now that I owned the whole house in Fitzwilliam Square. Told her you and the twins could have the second floor to yourselves."

"Jesus, Sheila, you're a ticket. But sure Seán knows your plans for the second floor. He told me all about it when he came back from Dublin after the hurling final. Are you really going ahead with the gym?"

"I'm not sure yet. John doesn't think it's a good idea. Afraid I'd be more tied up. Why don't you come back to Dublin with me for a few days? You haven't been up since last year. You wouldn't recognise the place now. Come up, I'd love you to."

"What about Carrigeen?" Caroline was doubtful.

"Molly's more than capable of taking over for a few days. You need a break."

Caroline considered it. Sheila was right. She did need a break. She was exhausted. "I might go up with you. To tell you the truth I haven't been feeling all that well lately. It's more than the ongoing battle with Seán. I think I'm starting the menopause."

"At forty-three? You're too young, surely."

"Apparently not. My periods are very irregular. They're much heavier and more frequent. I'm tired all the time. Of course Seán blames the work for that."

"We could take a trip to the Well Woman when you're in Dublin. Maybe you need a thorough check-up."

"You could be right. Come into the kitchen and I'll make that tea." Caroline was noticeably cheered up.

The kitchen was in an awful state. Dank and dirty. The scullery had damp patches on the walls and the paper was peeling off. "Excuse the mess. This house is getting too much for my mother, but she hates having decorators in. Hates the fuss."

"Sounds like Mr Allen. He got beyond it too. When I bought it, I had the whole place done up from top to bottom. It cost an arm and a leg. But I was dying to have it the way I wanted it. Mr Allen's in a nursing home in Blackrock now. The sale of the house is probably paying for the home."

Caroline poured out the tea. "I don't think Mam could afford to redecorate anyway. She's going to Lourdes with the parish pilgrimage next month, so I've organised the painters to come in then. It'll be a surprise for her. Buck her up for the winter."

Caroline was a good daughter. She was a good mother and wife too. Pity Seán didn't see that. Sheila took her cup of tea. "You're not really going to leave him, are you, Caroline?"

"I don't know. At this moment I don't care if I never see him again."

"You don't mean that."

"I do," Caroline insisted.

"What the two of you need is a break from one another. How long have you been married?"

"1964. Sixteen years. A life sentence." Caroline groaned. "No, I'm joking. We were happy at times. The trouble is we weren't happy at the same time. For the first few years Seán was delighted with life, even though we were poor. I was miserable. Now, it's the other way around. We're not really synchronised are we?"

"No." Sheila laughed. "The main question is, do you still love him?"

"Of course I do," Caroline answered without hesitation.

"Why? No, don't look at me like that. Why do you love him?"

"He's . . . he's a good person. He's thoughtful . . . at least he used to be. He's a hard worker. He's kind in his own way. He's reliable. He's intelligent. He's . . . I still fancy him like mad."

"Good. Now what do you dislike about him?" Sheila prayed this list wouldn't be longer.

"He's too obstinate. Never wrong about anything. Bloody infallible, like the Pope. He's unreasonable."

"About everything, or about your work?"

"About everything that has to do with my work. The money, mainly. He sees it as mine, not ours. But he wants to be the sole provider. He's my other half, but he refuses to accept that."

It was just as Sheila had anticipated. "He didn't learn much about the equality of the sexes in our home. That's one sure thing. He could have written that shagging article. Fascinating Womanhood. I still can't get over it. Anyhow, I'm going over to Seán now."

"Is that wise?" Caroline poured more tea.

"Probably not. But I'll try to talk to him. I'll even listen. See what he has to say for himself. OK? I'll collect more clothes for you. We'll head off in the morning at eleven. I'll pick you up."

"Right. I can get the train back next weekend. That's if I decide to come back at all."

"You'll do no such thing. Let Seán drive up and collect you. It's time he had to crawl."

"Yeah." Caroline's eyes lit up. "This time he can do the running."

* * *

Nora Maguire served up Seán's dinner. Pork chops with apple sauce, boiled potatoes and fried onions. Just what the doctor ordered, she giggled to herself.

"There we go, Doctor. I made some trifle for your dessert. The twins had their dinner earlier. Your clean shirts are airing in the hot press. If that's everything, I'll go on home now."

"Yes, you head on. Thank you, Nora. See you tomorrow."

Nora shouted goodbye to the twins and shut the door behind her. The poor doctor! Her heart went out to him. Imagine her nibs just up and leaving him like that. Ah, it was desperate. And him such a lovely man. Never complained. Worked all the hours God sends. Terrible. Nora wouldn't have a word said against him. He was the best employer she'd ever had. He was such a good doctor too. Worked a miracle on her bunions. The young wives today expected far too much. When Nora got to the gate, she spotted Sheila's car drive up. Oh ho! Trouble brewing. There'd be blue murder now.

Thank God, she was on her way out. "Evening, Sheila."

"Hello, Mrs Maguire. Is my brother in?"

"Ah he is, God help him. Just got in from his surgery. He's having a bite to eat now."

Sheila smiled and waved her off. By rights she should have a word with her too. Nora wasn't helping matters. Fawning over Seán like that. But you can't teach an old dog new tricks, as her father used to say. Sheila rang the bell.

"Sheila! Hi!" Ciara threw her arms around her aunt. "I'm so glad to see you. Grumpy boots is having his dinner. Come in. Your jacket's cool. I adore suede."

Sheila followed her into the hall and took off the jacket. "Here, you have it."

"No, no I couldn't."

"I insist. I hardly ever wear it. Have you anything to go with it?"

Ciara hesitated. "Well, it'd be lovely with my brown cords."

"There you are then. Wear it with my compliments."

"Mam'll kill me. Did you see her today?"

"I did. She's fine. She's going to come to Dublin with me for a few days. Do you mind?"

"'Course not. We're fine. Nora Maguire's feeding us up to the gills. I presume you want to see Dad. Tread warily," she warned Sheila. "The humour is lousy."

Ciara went back upstairs to finish her homework. Sheila tapped on the kitchen door and walked in.

"What are you doing here?" Seán growled at Sheila. "Here to gloat, I suppose."

Sheila sat down at the table. "I'm here to talk to you, Seán. Let's start as we mean to go on. No rows, right?"

"If you're here to plead Caroline's case, you can forget it. She walked out of her own free will. Didn't give a hoot how her family were going to get on without her. Totally irresponsible."

Sheila eyed his dinner plate. "She knew you wouldn't starve."

"Did she? Well, she's right. We're getting on OK without her. When did I ever see her anyway? You'd hardly know she'd left in fact. I don't miss her. What is there to miss?"

Sheila said nothing. Let him get it all out of his system.

"She leaves here at seven in the morning before the rest of us are awake. When she gets home at seven I'm in the evening surgery. By the time I arrive back at nine, she's in bed. Some life. Isn't it? It's largely your fault. You and that damn business. That's all she eats, sleeps, breathes. Even the weekends aren't our own. Once you appear, off she goes. I've put up with eight years of this shit, and I'm not putting up with it a day longer."

Sheila stayed calm. "Are you quite finished?"

"No," he roared. "I am not finished. She insisted I move into the Square and now my practice has doubled. I'm run off my feet."

"I'd have thought that'd please you. You wanted to make more money. You were always complaining about lack of funds." Sheila watched him turn redder and redder.

"Money? What do I care about the money? We've no bloody time to spend it, thanks to her. She's done up this place like the Taj Mahal but she's never satisfied. Always wanting something else. She usedn't to be like this. But you've given her all sort of notions. Nothing's good enough for her anymore."

"Don't be ridiculous. You're talking like an idiot."

"Oh am I? Am I?" Seán got up and stuck his plate in the dishwasher. He brought in a huge bowl of trifle.

"That looks good. May I help myself?" Sheila went to get a dessert bowl.

"Feel free. Help yourself. Whatever's mine is yours. But you know that. You've taken over my family already." His eyes flashed in anger. He was like someone demented.

Sheila got up to go. "Seán, you're a dead loss. Nobody could talk sense to you." She moved to the door, but he sprang up and barred her way.

"And you can tell my dear wife not to bother coming back here tomorrow, all tears and apologies. I don't want her."

Sheila brushed him aside. "She's no intention of coming back. She's coming to Dublin with me tomorrow morning."

"Good. She can stay there for all I care."

Sheila was afraid for a minute that he'd actually strike her. "I'm going upstairs to get some of her clothes. All right?" She tried to keep her voice steady.

"Take the whole bloody lot."

"You're pathetic!"

"And you," he roared after her as she went upstairs, "you're one of life's tragedies!"

Rita dragged herself out of bed early the following morning. She felt all of her seventy years. She looked up at the photo of Pat on the bedroom wall. It had been taken in the garden in the summer. He sat in his old armchair, pipe in his mouth, staring down at her. Seven years dead. What a lot had happened in that time. She missed him. She hid it well, but she did miss him. Sheila didn't know that. Rita missed his good humour, his smile, even his sarcasm. She missed their little chats. Most of all, she missed him in her bed at night. She missed the feel of him, the smell of him. She didn't like living alone.

Oh, she put on a brave face. She kept active, but that was because she was terrified of ending up a lonely old widow, a burden to her children. Her children. God, what had happened to them? Sheila was all right, or was she? She had it all . . . a big Georgian house, a thriving business, a posh car and a charming successful boyfriend. But Rita often noticed that sad look in her eyes. It was fleeting, but unmistakable. Sheila was sad.

And Seán. What had happened to Seán? He was so disconted. Why? He had a nice home, a good career, a lovely wife and two gorgeous children.

Sheila said he was jealous of Caroline. Was she right? Sheila had said a lot yesterday. Most of it was hurtful. But maybe it was true, Rita was forced to admit. She had always mollycoddled Seán. He was her first-born. Maybe she'd overdone it. She shouldn't have meddled in his marriage. She saw that now. Caroline was a good daughter-in-law. Pat always said so. She mightn't be a good wife in the traditional sense. But times had changed. Caroline was a career woman now. She couldn't be expected to do what she did when they were first married. Seán would have to accept that. Every time he moaned, Rita had taken his part. That'd have to change. He'd have to grow up. Rita would interfere just one more time. She'd have a heart-to-heart with her son.

"Mam? You up?" Sheila called from the bathroom.

"Yes, love." Rita came out on the landing.

Sheila kissed her. "You look tired. Didn't you sleep?"

"Not much," Rita admitted. "I had a lot to think about."

"My fault," Sheila apologised. "I'll cook us some breakfast."

Rita followed her daughter downstairs. Soon the smell of grilled rashers and sausages filled the kitchen.

"So, you'd no luck with Seán?" Rita set the table.

Sheila cracked two eggs onto the pan. "Uh huh. Couldn't get through to him at all. He's very annoyed with her. He never thought she'd do it. Leave, I mean."

"Men never do." Rita buttered some bread. "I can understand why she did though."

Sheila nearly dropped the pan with shock. What was her mother saying? That she understood Caroline's position? "Can you, Mam?"

"Yes," Rita said slowly. "I've changed my ideas a lot since yesterday."

"Since my tirade, you mean?"

"No, you were right about everything. I did make matters worse between them. There's no fool like an old fool. What time are you collecting Caroline?"

"In an hour." Sheila served up the breakfast as her mother made the tea. "And you're no fool, Mam."

Rita smiled. "Your poor Dad. He loved a cooked breakfast. Then he had to give them up."

Sheila saw the tears in her eyes. Her mother was much softer than she'd thought.

Rita hesitated. "I'd like to ring Caroline before she goes."

Oh no, Sheila thought. Not a good idea. Caroline might go for her.

Rita saw the look of alarm on Sheila's face. "Just to say hello. To tell her to enjoy her trip to Dublin."

"I don't know, Mam." Sheila avoided her eyes.

Rita didn't argue, but she was disappointed. She looked old and forlorn and Sheila felt like a heel. "I'll tell you what. Why not let Caroline settle in with me for a few days. Then I'll get her to phone you. How's that?"

Rita's face broke into a wide beam. "Would you, Sheila?"

"Definitely. Now, eat up your food. It's getting cold."

"You're beginning to sound like me," Rita said with mock pride.

"Perish the thought! Just joking!" Sheila grinned. But she wasn't joking.

* * *

They arrived in Fitzwilliam Square at four. Sheila parked the Merc in front of the house

"Is it safe?" Caroline wondered. She'd heard a lot about burglaries in Dublin. Young unemployed kids stole cars for the fun of it. Joyriders.

"Probably not. Last week some bastard slashed the tyres. Did all the cars."

"God, it's a beauty, Sheila. Never felt a single pothole all the way up. My Fiesta's desperate on long runs."

Sheila took the cases from the boot. "It's a great car all right, but do you know what? I miss the Renault. That was my pride and joy."

"Yeah, that had sentimental value too. Liam and Kate."

"Oh God, I meant to drop over to see them. It completely slipped my mind."

"Not surprising. The last two days weren't exactly a party." Caroline looked at the house. It was transformed on the outside. "Terrific. It's amazing what a coat of paint does. I love white. Ah, you've lovely window boxes on the second floor." Caroline was delighted. "They make a huge difference."

"Wait'll you see inside." Sheila carried the cases up the steps.

"What's down in the basement?"

"My office and a storeroom. I'll bring you down there later." She opened the door and Caroline stepped into the spacious hall. "Jesus!" she gasped.

The hall was magnificent. The white tiled floor gleamed in the afternoon sun. The huge marble staircase was restored to its pristine condition. The banisters were stripped back to the original wood. A dark green chaise longue stood against the far wall. The dado was brilliant white in contrast to the upper part of the walls which were painted a jade green. An array of charcoal prints showed up the jade beautifully.

Sheila was thrilled with Caroline's reaction. She loved showing off this house.

"What do you think of the green? John thinks it's a bit much."

"No, no, it's perfect. The hall's so big and you've loads of white to balance it. I love it. I really do."

"Dump the bags there. Now for the salon. This way, madam."

Caroline followed her into the rooms on the right. The first was the reception area. Lemon walls, grey carpet and curtains and couches in a grey and yellow chintzy material. "I stole this colour scheme from Mary," Sheila confessed.

A young gorgeous-looking brunette sat behind the grey desk. "This is Patti, our receptionist. Patti, this is Caroline, my sister-in-law."

Patti shook Caroline's hand. "Nice to meet you. I've heard a lot about you."

"Don't believe a word of it." Caroline smiled.

"Anything strange or startling since I've been away?" Sheila asked the girl.

"No, everything's ticking over nicely. There are a few letters for you to sign. A bill came from Grasse. We're booked up for the next few weeks. Some guy from *Image* called. I told him you'd phone back. Oh yeah, Mr Harris has been on a few times. You've to ring him. It sounded urgent."

Sheila gave Caroline a look. Another neglected male to worry about. "Fine. I'll do it now. Who's inside? I was hoping to show Caroline around."

"Mrs Donnelly. In for a complete facial. She should be out in a few minutes though and the next appointment is for five."

"OK. We can slip in before that. I'll go down to my office to make that call. I'll be back in a sec, Caroline, and we can finish the guided tour."

Caroline flicked through their brochure. "Might treat myself to an overhaul. I could do with it."

A tall blonde middle-aged woman came out of the salon. Her skin was gleaming and she looked very pleased with herself.

"Put me down for the same time next week,

Patti. Bye-bye, dear." She nodded at Caroline and swept out of the room.

Caroline looked at Patti in amazement. "She comes in every week?"

"Most of them do. Well for them."

Caroline didn't agree. She thought it was ludicrous. Too much money and too much time on their hands. Was that what Seán wanted for her? On the other hand, if women didn't care about their skin, she'd be out of a job. That was definitely what Seán wanted.

Sheila came back looking frazzled. "Salon free?" she asked Patti. "Right, come on, Caroline. I'll introduce you to Nuala, our beautician."

"Did you speak to John?" Caroline asked.

"No, he spoke at me. Gave me a lecture on commitment and responsibility."

"Jesus, they're all tarred with the one brush!"

The salon was separated from the reception by a tall oak door, again stripped back to the wood. This bigger room was decorated in the same muted yellow and grey and was divided into four cubicles, each with its own door. They were entirely separate and private. Nuala, a pretty redhead, showed Caroline into the first cubicle. There was a high couch bed with a bolster pillow. Caroline sat up on it and lay back. "This is really comfortable. Is this for the massages?"

"Yes," Nuala told her. "The women who are having facials sit there." She pointed to the grey-upholstered armchair-type seat which tilted backwards.

A long mirror covered one wall and there were

more prints on the others. A tall fern stood in a pottery holder in the corner.

Caroline pointed to the plant-holder. "Is that one of Conor's?"

"Yes. Nice, isn't it?" Sheila answered. "There's one in each cubicle. I've his stuff all over the house."

"God, Nuala. How do you manage four cubicles at the one time?" Caroline asked the beautician.

"I don't. We have two at a time at the most. Ms Crosby is looking for another girl at the moment. She mucks in herself too."

Sheila nodded. "Yeah, I can do the cleansing and moisturising. I leave the hard jobs, like the eyebrow and eyelash tinting and shaping, to the professional here."

Nuala laughed. "Yeah, she leaves the waxing to me too. It's a lovely job, I don't think!"

"Messy but effective. The resin waxing's great. Gets right down the follicle, not like with a razor. It lasts six weeks." Sheila said.

"When have you a free slot?" Caroline asked Nuala.

"What are you having done?"

"The works!" Caroline laughed as Nuala checked the appointment book.

The rooms on the left off the hall had three sunbeds, again in separate cubicles. Sheila wasn't at all in favour of tanning, but it was in great demand. They advised the women with fair skin or moles to avoid the beds. They insisted that the clients used a special spray to minimise possible skin damage and to wear the goggles provided. The time was strictly monitored. They started with ten-minute sessions and worked up to twenty minutes maximum. The beds had to be cleaned thoroughly to avoid fungal infection. Sheila thought there should be a sign saying, Instant Ageing Beds. She regretted now that Nuala had persuaded her to invest in them. They were a money-spinner but Sheila's conscience still niggled.

Caroline thought she'd give that a go too. Sheila thought she was mad, but at least Caroline had olive skin and was used to sunbathing. Seán wouldn't approve of course. Melanoma was one of the chief causes of skin cancer in Ireland. But Caroline was an adult and must make up her own mind.

The second floor rooms were unfurnished at the moment and were painted magnolia. The colour was bright and less dramatic than on the first floor. The dividing wall between the two rooms on the right had been knocked down to make one huge area. The floorboards had been sanded and polished.

"This, I presume, will be the gym?" Caroline walked around. "The back windows are huge. There's loads of light. This'd be ideal. What about equipment? It'll cost a fortune."

"I know. The initial outlay will be enormous, but I think it'll be an investment. Most of my customers go to a fitness centre somewhere else first and then make their way over here. Why not have everything under the one roof?"

"That makes sense," Caroline agreed. "You'll need showers and toilets."

Sheila walked her over to the two rooms on the other side. "Here. The front room, I'm going to convert into a sauna and the back room, which is much bigger, can be converted into shower units. I've spoken to a plumber. He said it could be done. There's a huge bathroom at the end of this landing which we can make into two or three toilets."

Caroline thought it all sounded terrific. "What about staff?"

"I'll need two instructors on a shift basis and someone to supervise the sauna and the showers."

"What about a receptionist?"

"No, Patti can book them in on the first floor. She'll be paid extra of course. There's a doctor next door if we've any accidents.

"God forbid. Mind you, the insurance will be enormous."

"Don't I know it! Now, come up to my little palace on the next two floors."

Sheila had her private sitting-room and dining-room on the third floor. They were beautiful rooms. The dining-room was painted burnt orange and cream. A gigantic dark mahogany table sat twelve comfortably. She had furnished this room with antiques she'd bought at auction rooms. There was a magnificent sideboard with a display of crystal glass and bone china. A Persian rug covered half the floor. The place smelt of beeswax. Huge vases, Conor's creations, filled with geraniums, adorned the table and the corners of the room.

"We'll have a dinner party before you go back," Sheila promised Caroline. "I'll invite Mary and Jim. You haven't seen them for ages. And Lily and her fiancé."

"And John," Caroline reminded her.

"Naturally. Friday night, maybe?"

"Great. I'll give you a hand."

The room behind was Sheila's state-of-the-art kitchen. It was completely tiled in white. It would have been antiseptic, Caroline thought, if it hadn't been for the bottle-green presses. Sheila had always loved green. Naturally it was all built-in. The startling white of the sink, the washing-machine, the dishwasher, the fridge/freezer and the cooker contrasted with the dark green presses. On the window-sill stood a selection of green plants, mostly ivies and spider plants. The kitchen table and chairs were white. Sheila opened a press. All the pots and pans were in the same dark green. Caroline complimented her on the kitchen but, in fact, she didn't like it. She thought it was too cold looking. Different strokes for different folks.

The sitting-room was very pretty. White walls with the slightest tinge of peach. The suite was white leather and comprised a three-seater, a two-seater and two single armchairs. The carpet was pale peach. A long sheepskin rug ran along the white marble fireplace.

"It's beautiful," Caroline exclaimed. The colours were so restful. Totally impractical for a family room, but Sheila didn't have to worry about sticky fingers or footballs. This room was like something out of a show house. There was a stereo in the far alcove and a beautiful white bookcase built into the other one. A Jack Yeats painting graced the main wall. Very impressive.

"No TV?" Caroline asked.

"In the bedrooms," Sheila replied. "I hate television in the living areas. It's so intrusive."

Caroline had to agree. When someone called to their house, the kids put up an argument when the TV was turned off. But then the art of conversation was long gone in her house. Pity.

Sheila finished the tour on the top floor. Sheila's bedroom was pink and white. Pink walls and a fluffy white carpet. White curtains with a tiny pink flower matched the duvet and pillows on the king-sized bed. Her dressing table and built-in wardrobes were white. A white cane chair with a pink cushion. On the bedside locker was the photo of Karen, newly framed. There was something very sad about it. Kind of like a shrine.

Caroline thought she was daft to have a white carpet. John must have to leave his shoes at the door! The room was like something Barbie would have. Caroline thought it was gross, but she made all the right comments to Sheila. Naturally Sheila had the room en suite. A bigger-than-usual bathroom with bath, toilet, shower and bidet. White tiles. A huge mirror covered one wall. Pink towels and mats.

Sheila put Caroline in one of the two guest-rooms. It was much more to her taste. Lavender walls and duvet. Grey carpet and curtains. A built-in wardrobe took up one wall. There was an armchair, a table and a portable TV in a wall unit. Caroline was delighted with it. The bathroom was next door.

"You go ahead and have a bath if you like," Sheila told her. "I've to go down to my office for an hour. Things to catch up on and phone calls to make. Would you like to see the basement?"

"Later." Caroline was exhausted. The tour had lasted an hour and she was worn out. She was running out of adjectives too. Sheila's house was remarkable and she'd done a great job, even if a lot of it wasn't to Caroline's taste. But enough was enough! It was turning into a bore. People loved to show off their houses, of course. This house was definitely one to be proud of. But you can have too much of a good thing. It was like when someone came back from holidays and insisted you admired the photos and enthused about places you'd no intention of ever visiting. Excruciating.

"Right," Sheila said good humouredly. She obviously hadn't noticed Caroline's pained expression. "You unpack and have your bath and relax for a while. Watch some television. Do you want to stay in or go out for dinner."

"Would you mind if we stayed in?"

"Not at all. I've some steaks in the freezer. I'll defrost them now. See you later."

Caroline felt physically relaxed after her long soak. But not mentally. She lay on the bed and used the remote control to flick on the TV. Some soap opera. She watched, but her mind wasn't on it. What was she doing here? Was she mad? God, she'd really done it. Left Seán. It hadn't seemed real when she was in her mother's. But it was real now. He'd never forgive her for this. He'd never let her forget.

His pride would have suffered another shattering blow. He'd feel he had lost face in front of the kids. Should she phone him at the surgery? No, what was the point of that? She wasn't going back. Not till he apologised. And that wouldn't be till hell froze over. No, they were deadlocked. Total impasse. She'd like to speak to the twins though. She'd risk phoning home. He wouldn't be in at this hour.

She used the phone in Sheila's room. Nora Maguire answered. The voice was cool. Cheek of her! Let her mind her own bloody business. Nora told her Ciara was over in Stephen's house. Colm came on.

"Mum? When are you coming home?"

Oh God, he was missing her. Caroline's heart thumped in her chest. She felt like Judas. "I don't know, Colm. That depends on your father. Are you OK?"

Silence. Oh, he wasn't going to cry. Was he? She couldn't bear that.

"Are you OK, Colm?"

He hesitated. "Yeah, I'm fine but . . . I need some money. My football burst. I have to get a new one. You know what Dad's like! I can't ask him."

Jesus, he missed her all right. He missed the handouts.

"Go into the sitting-room. There's some money in the teapot on the top shelf of the china cabinet. There should be a twenty pound note."

"Cool! You're deadly, Mum. Thanks."

"Don't mention it." Caroline sighed. "Everything else all right?"

"Great. See ya, Mum. I have to go over to Eddy's."

"Bye love" . . . the phone went dead. Caroline felt as if she'd been slapped in the face.

CHAPTER TWENTY-SIX

On Wednesday Caroline got an appointment in the Well Woman centre. She refused Sheila's offer to go with her. So Sheila went over to the shop in Duke Street. While she was there, Mary rang.

"Did you tell me you were looking for another beautician for the salon?"

"Yeah, I'm interviewing at the moment." Sheila handed back the order book to Amanda. She'd have to have a word with Lily.

"I know someone who might suit." Mary sounded eager.

"Yeah? Who?" Sheila was only half listening.

"Her name's Eileen Brophy. She's a past pupil of mine."

"Is she qualified?"

"Oh yeah, did her training with Jill Fisher. She's a lovely girl, Sheila. I'm sure she'd be just right for you. She's very personable. She's quick and obliging."

"Is that your reference, Mary?" Sheila loved the way Mary stuck up for her pupils, past and present. "Tell her to give me a ring and I'll fix up an interview. I can't make any promises, though."

"I understand that."

"Where is she working at the moment? She'll need bona fide references!"

Silence on the other end. Then Mary spoke. "She hasn't been working for a few months. The thing is, she was abroad. She . . . she had a baby. She's a single parent."

"Oh?"

"That won't make any difference, will it? I thought you'd be sympathetic."

"I am. But that wouldn't sway my decision. I'll set up an interview. We'll take it from there."

"Thanks, Sheila. I owe you one. See you Friday night."

"Mary, I'm still not promising . . ." Too late. Mary had already hung up.

Sheila talked to Lily about the stock. Some of the products, especially the bath oils, weren't selling that well. Sheila suggested a reshuffle of the articles on the shelves. She told Lily to put some of the creams and oils on special offer. Amanda offered to do a complete inventory. She'd give Sheila a breakdown on what was selling and what was not. Sheila thought it might be time for new packaging. But she didn't want to burden Caroline at the moment.

She rang John. "Free for lunch?"

"No, I'm tied up. Sheila, I can't talk now. I'm with a client. I'll phone you later."

God, he was in lousy form. Very offhand. What was he at? Trying to pay her back? Very childish.

"Here are the letters you wanted signed, Patti. Is my sister-in-law back yet?"

"Yes, Ms Crosby. She's upstairs. Oh, there was a phone call from an Eileen Brophy about the beautician's job. I checked the diary and you're free for an hour in the morning so I set up an interview for her at eleven."

"Fine."

Hmm, this Eileen Brophy certainly didn't waste time. Sheila gave her credit for that. She'd keep an open mind. Sheila wasn't in the charity business. She wasn't going to offer her a job out of some misguided sense of pity. But if this girl's training and experience were up to scratch, she'd give her a try.

"I'm going upstairs, Patti. I don't want to be disturbed." She walked to the door of the office. A thought struck her. "Unless Mr Harris rings."

Patti smiled to herself. Lover boy hardly ever rang the office. He'd ring their love nest upstairs. Patti envied her boss. John was dreamy.

Caroline was sketching at the kitchen table.

"Hi, I rang you at the shop but I missed you. Lily told me you were considering new packaging. What do you think of something like this?"

"Jesus, would you stop." Sheila didn't even glance at the drawing. "You're supposed to be here for a rest. How did you get on at the clinic?"

"OK. They gave me a thorough check-up. Everything's in working order. I had a smear test too. It's very important, Sheila."

"I know. I'm a bit lazy about going myself. I'll do it soon, I promise. Did you tell them about the tiredness and the bad sleeping?"

"Yeah, par for the course, the doctor said. It's the start all right. They call it the perimenopause."

"I'm dying for it!" Sheila hoped Caroline wasn't going to give her all the gory details. She'd find them out for herself some day.

"The doctor was lovely, very understanding. She recommended vitamin E and evening primrose oil. I might have to consider HRT later. But I don't really fancy the idea."

Sheila didn't blame her. The side-effects could be awful.

"She told me to rest more. I nearly laughed in her face. When do I get the time to rest?"

Sheila sat down beside her. "Caroline, I've been thinking about all this for the last two days. Seán might be right."

"What? You're not going to side with him now?" Caroline pouted.

"It's not a matter of taking sides. Most of what Seán says is rot, but I think he has a point when it comes to your hours."

"What do you mean?"

"There's no reason for you to be in work so early every morning. Molly lives in Carrigeen. She's on the spot. You could start at about ten and finish at four."

"No way. I'm not ill, just a bit tired."

"Exactly. And you've a long drive every day too. The shorter hours would ease the pressure."

Caroline shook her head. "It'd create a different pressure. I'd be rushing everything. It wouldn't work."

Sheila persisted. "You don't delegate enough work to Molly." She tried to read Caroline's face.

Caroline looked as if she were considering it. "That might be true. Molly's always asking me for more to do."

"There you are. Will you think about it?"

"All right. I'm not accepting any cut in salary though!"

Sheila gave her a sardonic grin. "Not even to please Seán?"

Caroline threw a dish-cloth at her.

That night Rita phoned. Delighted with herself. She'd had a long chat with Seán and the upshot was that he'd agreed to take on a partner in his practice.

"Brilliant, Mam! I think I've persuaded Caroline to work fewer hours. Now, if we could just make them go away together on a holiday."

"Sheila, girl, if we could just make them talk to one another, we'd be doing well."

"True. How's his form now?"

"A bit better. These things take time though. He misses her. You can see it. But he's still hurt, still on the defensive. They're an awful pair. When I think about your poor father . . . never a cross word between us."

Sheila let that go. But it wasn't the way she remembered things. Selective memory again. "Do you think he'll phone her?"

Rita paused. "I think he might. Ciara's working on him too. Will you both be in tonight?"

"We've no plans to go out."

"Good. How's John?"

Even when Rita was being nice, she had an uncanny way of hitting a sore point. Had she second sight, or what? "He's fine. Busy, you know."

"That'll keep him out of trouble." Rita laughed. "I'll let you go. Ring me if you've any more news. Bye, love."

* * *

Seán's phone call came at ten. Caroline was in a flurry of excitement when she got off the phone. "Oh God, Sheila. I can't believe it! He was . . . he was really nice . . . kind of shy. It was lovely."

Sheila laughed at her moonstruck expression. "You're some fruitcake. What did he say?"

Caroline giggled. "He said he loved me. I know it sounds daft but I went over all funny like. He hasn't said that in years. Then I told him I loved him too. It was very emotional."

"Jesus, Brady Bunch eat your heart out!"

"Ah, stop it. You're too cynical. No, he told me he's thinking of getting a partner and I told him about your idea of working less hours. He said to thank you, by the way. So thanks!" Caroline ran over and hugged her.

"So you think your problems are solved?" Sheila was a bit sceptical. Seán wasn't going to change overnight. At least not without a lobotomy. Still,

398

Sheila'd give him the benefit of the doubt. Maybe the last few days without Caroline had finally woken him up.

"We both need to change," Caroline said thoughtfully. "We've a lot of talking to do yet."

That was good. At least she realised that this wasn't going to be plain sailing. "Is he coming to Dublin to pick you up?"

"On Friday. I can't wait! I asked him to join us for the dinner party. I hope you don't mind."

"No, I'm glad he's coming. What'll he do about evening surgery?"

"He's getting a locum to cover for him."

Jesus, that was unheard of for Seán. Only an emergency would stop him from attending his surgery. He was going to drop everything for Caroline. The signs were good so far.

"He'll have to stay the night, if that's all right." Caroline wasn't sure how Sheila would take that.

"No problem. You've a double bed in the lavender room. Oh God," Sheila groaned, "I have to ring John. I haven't even told him about the dinner yet. He'll be furious."

Caroline wasn't paying a blind bit of attention. She was lost in her own thoughts. She was planning what she'd wear on Friday night.

"Caroline, I've a favour to ask you. Would you ring Mam? She's anxious to talk to you. I know you're annoyed with her but I do think she was instrumental in Seán's change of heart."

"Yeah, he told me." Caroline was not one to bear grudges. "I'll do it now. I've to thank her, anyway. She's staying at our house on Friday night to be with the twins. Better to make my peace with her before I go back. I'd rather have your mother as an ally than an enemy."

Sheila thought that was fair comment. But she didn't foresee any further problems with Rita. Her mother had learned her lesson.

Sheila kept ringing and ringing John's flat. No answer. Was he out or was he not answering? Sheila was agitated. He was obviously playing games to punish her. Ludicrous. She hadn't realised he could be so stupid. She'd ring him in the office tomorrow. Men! They accused women of being unreasonable. God, she was sick of humouring the blighters. First Seán. Now John.

Caroline had offered to do the shopping for the meal tomorrow. Sheila had that interview in the morning and she'd have to go over to BT's after that. Also she had to make a start on planning the gym. She'd an appointment with a friend of Lily's, who was working in a fitness centre in Rathmines. She'd find out what she needed to know. She wanted to get a reputable company to fit out the gym. The machines would have to be top quality. Then she'd have to organise the builders and the plumbers for the saunas and the showers. This was another huge undertaking. But she'd cope. She always did.

* * *

Eileen Brophy was older than Sheila had expected. Late twenties. She was tall and had beautiful long blonde hair. Immaculately groomed.

"I see you were trained by Jill Fisher," Sheila said.

"Yes. Ms Fisher was extremely thorough. We learned a lot."

Sheila nodded. She had heard stories. Personal hygiene was high on Ms Fisher's list of priorities. The girls were subjected to all sorts of tests, including checking their feet to see if they'd dried between the toes. The lady certainly had a great reputation for training her girls well.

"Where did you work when you left the beauty school?"

"I was in London for four years. Then I went to California. These are my references." She handed them to Sheila. "I learned a lot about aromatherapy in California. I believe you favour this type of massage."

The girl had done her homework. Another good sign. Sheila scanned the references. They were glowing.

"When did you come back to Ireland?"

"Last year. I got pregnant in America and I came back to have the baby here. I wanted to be with my family."

Unusual. Most Irish single mothers would try to leave the country. The child's father must be an American. None of her business. Sheila admired the way she spoke so openly about the baby. No hang-ups.

"I see by your address you're living in Sutton."

"Yes, Ms Crosby. I stayed at home with my mother till Kevin, that's my son's name, was six months. Then I moved to Sutton. A friend of mine and her husband own the house. They moved to Brussels for his work. I'm their new tenant. They don't intend to come back for years. It was a lucky break for me. Now that Kevin and I are settled, I'm really anxious to get back to work."

Sheila didn't want to probe too much, but the girl seemed eager to talk. "Renting a house can be very expensive."

"Normally yes, but I'm paying very little rent. They could get four times the amount I'm paying them. I owe them a lot. I'd never have coped without them. They're a terrific couple."

"You're very lucky to have such friends." Sheila remembered when Karen was born. She had no lucky breaks.

"I know I am. My mother's very supportive too."

Sheila nodded again. She liked this girl. She was bright. She was attractive. She was friendly. That was important in this job. Clients came in to get treatment but they also liked someone they could talk to. Nuala swore she was like a psychiatrist, listening to women's stories all day. If Nuala liked this girl, Sheila thought she'd give her a six-month trial.

"How will you manage Kevin when you're at work? Your mother?"

"No, a neighbour has agreed to mind him. That is, if I get the job of course."

"Well, it's time you had a look around the salon." Sheila smiled at her. "Follow me and I'll introduce you to Nuala, our beautician. I've other applicants to see of course. I'll let you know by early next week."

"Well, Nuala? What did you think?"

"I liked her. She knows her stuff. She was delighted with our set-up here. She's all into the essential oils too. She'd be an asset, I think. And she's not bashful by any means. I can see her getting on with all the clients, especially Mrs Mooney."

"Mrs Mooney won't leave you. You're like a daughter to her," Sheila said.

"I know. But she loves meeting new people to tell her traumas to. She's very nice, but she'd wear you out. Eileen'd be more than welcome to her. Plus a few others I could mention. Anyhow, I liked Eileen. I think she'd fit in here."

"Great. I liked her too. How many more have I to see?"

"Two, tomorrow morning. She's certainly the best so far as regards training and experience."

"And chat," Sheila added.

"Definitely the chat," Nuala agreed. "I'm finished for today. See you tomorrow. Oh, when does Caroline want her overhaul, as she calls it?"

"Friday morning." Sheila checked the appointments book. "Yeah, she's down for ten o'clock. Give her the works. She's a heavy date tomorrow night."

"Date? I thought she was married to your brother. Or do they have one of these modern marriages?"

Sheila moaned. "Believe me, they don't. No, this date is with her husband. She wants to look especially good tomorrow night."

"Isn't that sweet?" Nuala smiled at the thought of it. "It's great when married couples make an effort for one another."

Oh, spare me, Sheila thought. If Nuala only knew the half of it.

Sheila rang John's office. She hoped he wasn't in court. Rebecca Morley answered the phone. "Oh hello, Ms Crosby. No, he isn't here."

Was this another evasion? Was his secretary following instructions? She'd play along. "Maybe you could give him a message?"

Rebecca hesitated. "I could, but not until Monday morning."

"Monday morning?" Sheila's voice came out like a squeal.

"Yes, I'm afraid he had to go out of town for the weekend. Something came up."

Sheila was aghast. Out of town for the weekend. On business? She couldn't ask Rebecca that. She couldn't put the girl on the spot.

"I see. Thanks, Rebecca. Will you tell him I phoned?"

"Certainly. Bye, Ms Crosby."

Sheila hung up. Out of town for the weekend. She couldn't believe it. Why hadn't he said anything? Something came up? What? What, in the name of God, came up? Why hadn't he told her? He could have let her know. No, he was up to something. She guessed this was another of his schoolboy tactics. She'd drive over to Waterloo Road and see if his car was there. Ah, she couldn't do that. No point in being infantile. He was annoyed with her and he was playing it cool. So, she could play it cool as well. He certainly timed his tantrum well. What was she going to do for a partner tomorrow night? Lily and George, Mary and Jim, now Caroline had Seán. She was damned if she was going to play gooseberry. Then, she remembered. Finian O'Toole was in town. She'd give him a ring. He'd be perfect. He knew Caroline, Seán and Lily. He'd be an ideal guest. When he wasn't talking money, he was a good laugh too. John could go and . . . she didn't finish the sentence in her head. She was beginning to get a migraine.

CHAPTER TWENTY-SEVEN

Sheila was very happy with the way the meal was going. They'd had salmon mousse for a starter. Light and appetising. She decided on an easy main course, chicken chasseur. The sauce was made with tomato, herbs and mushrooms. Caroline had teased her about using a recipe with rosemary. She served it with rice and individual side salads.

"This is delicious, Sheila," Finian said appreciatively.

"Indeed." George Burke was a man of few words. He only had eyes for Lily. He had recently sold two racehorses for a fortune. Dermot Weld, the famous trainer, was visiting the stud farm the following week. This was the big time for George.

Sheila chatted to Mary, beside her, but she kept an eye on Seán and Caroline. They were like two lovebirds. Sheila was mesmerised. Seán actually looked younger. Maybe this blow-up was the best thing that ever happened. The air would be cleared and they could make a fresh start.

"So, how did your trip to the fitness centre go?" Lily was dying to know.

"Great. Excuse me for a moment." Sheila went

into the kitchen and brought back the dessert. Poached pears with caramel sauce served in separate serving glasses. They all oohed and aahed.

"How did you get the pears to stand upright in each glass?" Mary asked. This'd be a gorgeous dessert to make when Jim's parents came to dinner this weekend.

"It's dead easy," Sheila explained. "You just cut a thin slice from the base of the pear."

"Riveting," Finian remarked drily. "You still haven't told us about the gym."

"Don't mind him," Sheila said offhandedly. "He's just worrying about me getting into debt."

"Somebody has to." Finian was adamant.

Sheila winked at him. Tried to make him smile. This wasn't the time or place for one of Finian's lectures. The man was a great accountant but he was terribly cautious. Worse than her banker. "The gym will be a gold mine, mark my words."

"Did you get any ideas yesterday?" Lily still hadn't heard the answer.

Sheila nodded and went to the sideboard to get ash-trays. "It's all about weights, basically. I went twice around the gym and I was in bits after it. But the sauna and shower were very reviving."

"Did the owner know you were spying?" Lily loved intrigue. She had a funny habit of nudging George every time she spoke. The poor guy's arm would be black and blue by the time he got home.

"Of course not. She wasn't there. Your friend,

Joan, showed me around and then insisted I try everything out. She's a sadist!"

"What did you have to do?" Jim asked. Looking at Mary, he added, "you could do with losing a few pounds. Remember you went to a gym after Davy was born? Myra. The one who told you you'd a dropped bottom."

Mary belted him one. "When you go to the bathroom have a look in the mirror, Fatso." It was true Jim was developing a little paunch.

"I'll try to ignore all these rude interruptions and continue." Sheila passed the red wine over to George. "You start with a few limbering-up exercises. Then you put these weights on your feet. They're like lead and they're strapped over your runners. Then it's thirty high swings of each leg. You keep your legs straight."

"You'd topple over," Seán insisted.

"Oh, I forgot. You hang onto a bar."

"Like a ballerina." Lily said to the others.

"More like an elephant," Sheila answered her with a grin. "Next you use the dumb-bells. They're for the upper arms and the bustline."

"You don't need to lose weight on your bust," Jim said admiringly.

"Jesus, how would you know?" Mary gave him another puck.

Sheila laughed. "John probably told him." For some reason, Mary and Jim looked uncomfortable. Sheila noticed the look that passed between them. "Then you do these squats with a weight on your shoulders. Of course the weights are light when you start. You build up to heavier ones as the weeks go by."

"I'd be afraid of muscles." Caroline was going off the idea of keeping fit.

"No way," Sheila scoffed. "After the squats, you do side-bends with another kind of dumb-bell. Then it's sit-ups. You lie on this thing, it's leather and it's like a narrow surf board and you put your feet under this strap. It's brilliant for the stomach. Then you sit up on this high thing, like the horse we had in the school gym, but this one has a bar at the end and you put weights on each side. It's for the legs."

"You sit up and raise your legs up with the weights on?" Mary didn't understand.

"Yeah, the bar rests just above your ankles. Then you roll over onto your tummy, you tuck your feet under the bar and raise your legs from the knees. That's great for the front of the thighs."

"Jesus, sounds like hard work." Jim opened another bottle of wine.

"It is, but you feel good. Then you have a turn on the exercise bike. You start at a low speed and work it up over the sessions. Then the belts. That's the relaxing part. You stick the belt around your waist first and turn on the machine. It shakes at a rapid rate. Then you lower it around your hips."

"Not a pretty sight." Seán pictured the scene. "Obese women shaking the hell out of their blubber."

"None of the women I saw were obese," Sheila said tartly. "They're there to prevent that."

"The whole thing sounds gruelling." Caroline made a face.

"Gruesome, you mean," Seán piped in.

"When you're finished that, you do it all again." Sheila smiled at them. "I got the name of the company that supplies the machines. I reckon my fitness centre will be up and running by January. Anybody signing up?"

Everyone groaned.

They adjourned to the sitting-room for their brandies. Caroline put on a Tchaikovsky tape. Romeo and Juliet. The love theme was mellow and flowing, the tragic overtones floating through. At least she and Seán were no longer star-crossed lovers. It was good to see them getting on well. Some stories have happy endings, Sheila was glad to see.

"Where's John tonight, Sheila?" Seán asked his sister. Like mother, like son. To be fair, he didn't know anything was up. Not that Sheila knew for sure what was wrong.

"He's away on business." She hoped her expression was suitably serene. Once again she saw the look Jim gave Mary. She wondered what the hell was really going on. They obviously knew something.

"What did you think of Eileen Brophy?" Mary spoke quietly to Sheila. Jim was examining the record collection.

Sheila swirled the brandy in her glass. "I was

surprised at her age. I couldn't believe you had a past pupil of that age."

"She's twenty-eight. She was in sixth year in my first year of teaching. The girls were seventeen and I was twenty-two."

"No wonder you'd a good rapport with them," Finian remarked.

"Mmh," Mary agreed. "The trouble is the kids stay the same age and the teachers don't. Anyhow, Sheila, did you like her?"

"Just what we were looking for. She's well trained and experienced. Very outgoing. I meant to ask you, how come you were still in touch with her."

"We met again by accident. I thought she was still in the States. Jim and I went for a walk one night down by the front, and there she was wheeling her son. We stopped for a chat."

"She was out walking in Sandymount?"

"Yep. Lots of people come out in the summer evenings. She was with her mother. They'd parked in the car-park right opposite our house so I asked them in for a cuppa."

"Well, it was a lucky thing for her that you did. I've decided to take her on a six-month trial. I'll ring her on Monday."

"Oh thanks, Sheila. I'm absolutely thrilled. She won't let you down. I'd stake my life on it."

"No need to thank me. As I said, she's what we were looking for. What's her son like?"

Mary's face lit up. "A little darling. All smiles."

Sheila felt quite emotional. This girl's story had a

strange effect on her. She'd had a baby out of wedlock, but she'd managed to get her act together. She had good friends and a supportive mother on her side. But there was more to it than that. She had spunk. She kept her child. Times had changed, but not that much. There was still a stigma attached to illegitimacy. People still loved to judge. Scandal kept some people going. Sheila admired the girl. She was like a breath of fresh air. The child was bound to be smiling. He had a happy mother.

"Here, what are you two nattering about?" Jim sat down between them on the couch. "I've put on Neil Diamond, hope you don't mind, Caroline. Not quite as highbrow as your choice."

"Tchaikovsky's hardly highbrow," Mary retorted. "My husband's a pleb, you'll have to excuse him."

Mary stood up. "Jesus, I can't stand that record. What a beautiful noise, my foot."

"Leave it on," Seán begged. "I want to hear 'Sweet Caroline'."

"Oh my God," Mary groaned. "Sheila, I'll go and make the coffee before I puke. This is too soppy for me. Married couples holding hands! Shouldn't be allowed."

Caroline didn't think it was soppy. She was thrilled with this public display of affection. Sheila thought it was like the change before death.

"I've a new patient, by the way." Seán helped himself to another brandy. "There's a bit of news some of you may be interested in."

"You never discuss your patients." Caroline looked at him in amazement.

"This isn't top secret. It'll be common knowledge soon. Bridget is three months pregnant."

Sheila was stunned. A crazy reaction, she knew. Why wouldn't Bridget be expecting? They'd been married for two years now. But she felt a definite stab of jealousy. Peadar with a family. More cosy domesticity.

"That's good," she heard herself say. "I'll go in and give Mary a hand with the coffee."

Mary had the cups and saucers ready on a tray. "I made instant. Hope that's all right. Will I stack the dirty plates in the dishwasher?"

"No, leave them. Mrs Flanagan will be here in the morning." Sheila got the milk out of the fridge.

Mary had forgotten that Sheila had a housekeeper. She was so busy she'd never have time for mundane things like cleaning up. Mary could do with somebody herself. Even once a week. She'd talk to Jim about it.

"Mary, I want to ask you something." Sheila saw a faint expression of alarm on her friend's face. "Do you know where John is? He didn't phone me back. Is there something I should know?"

Mary swallowed hard. "It's probably nothing to worry about. He went down to Waterford for the weekend." She didn't sound convincing.

Sheila stuck a sugar bowl on the tray. "To see Anne?" She wanted to know and, at the same time, she didn't want to know.

"Yeah. Apparently she rang him while you were in Galway." Mary saw the betrayal in Sheila's eyes.

"It's most likely some sort of business thing, Sheila. She's always at him for more money."

"I know. But I thought since he fixed her up with that flower shop she'd leave him alone." Sheila was angry.

"They're not legally separated. I think she wants him back. Look, that won't happen if you play your cards right."

"What's that supposed to mean?" Sheila looked at her accusingly.

"Sit down for a minute."

"What about the coffee? It'll be stone cold." Sheila took up the tray.

"Here, give it to me. I'll bring it in. Stay there and light me a cigarette. Back in a second."

Sheila did what she was told. What was Mary going to tell her now? The night had started well, but things were taking a turn for the worse. She kept seeing Peadar pushing a pram. She saw John back with his wife. She felt as if someone had kicked her in the stomach.

Mary came back. "Right, here we go. Drink your coffee."

"Go on, Mary. Tell me the worst."

"It's nothing that bad really. Jim went out for a drink with John last week, the day you went to Galway. Jim said he was very upset with you."

"With me?"

"Mmh, now listen. John felt you had lied to him. He was annoyed that you hadn't told him about the trouble at home."

Sheila butted in. "I was trying to spare him. Why

414

should he have to concern himself with my family's squabbles?"

"Yeah, well he didn't see it like that. He feels left out. He said you'd no time for him anymore."

Sheila thought about it. Lately, she had been a bit distant. But when she tried to involve him in her business plans, he didn't like it. He didn't approve of the fitness centre. He thought she spent too much time in the salon and the shop. He didn't like eating out with her anymore because she was recognised everywhere they went. What did he expect? To sit in every night watching the box? Did he want her to wear a dark wig and sunglasses? He was too demanding.

"If he wants to go back to his wife, that's his prerogative."

Mary stirred her coffee. "I don't think that's what he wants at all. I think he wants to settle down with you."

Sheila looked horrified. "Settle down? Impossible. He's still legally married, as you said."

Mary knew she was going to drop a bombshell. "He wants to get a foreign divorce. He wants to marry you, he told Jim. He wants . . . children."

"Shit. I don't believe it. Why didn't he say all this to me?"

"He said he never gets the chance to talk to you properly anymore. He's really fallen for you, Sheila. Jim said he was turning into a manic depressive."

Sheila laughed. She couldn't help herself. She knew it wasn't the appropriate reaction, but she'd a mental picture of John strapped into a strait-jacket in a padded cell.

Mary was furious with her. "Jesus, will you cop on. This isn't funny. Do you want John or don't you?"

Sheila apologised. "I do want him, but I want him the way I have him."

"No strings attached?"

"I don't mind the strings, it's the ropes that terrify me."

Mary stood up suddenly. "Jim and I will have to go. It's getting late. We'll bring Finian home. He's in no state to drive. Sheila, you'd want to think carefully about what it is you do want. John's not going to stick around for the crumbs of affection you choose to throw his way."

"I know. I'm sorry I was flippant. How was I to know he was going to get so serious."

"Jim was right. He told me you could look after yourself. I never guessed that John'd be the one to get hurt." Mary went upstairs to get the coats.

Sheila went back to the sitting-room and put on a smile.

It was two o'clock by the time Sheila got to bed. She was worn out. She sat up and lit a cigarette. Seán and Caroline were in the next room. Judging by the signs tonight, they'd be making love by now. Sheila felt alone. Peadar, Bridget and a baby on the way; John with his wife; Karen with her parents. Damn. Had she screwed up again?

The phone beside her bed rang shrilly. She hated late night calls. They usually meant trouble. What now?

"Hello?"

Silence.

"Hello? Who is this?"

"It's me." John's voice was a whisper. "Sorry to ring you at this hour. I had to speak to you. I was lonely."

He wasn't the only one. "Where are you?"

"In the flat."

"Mary told me you were in Waterford for the weekend."

"Couldn't stick it. I drove home tonight. I wanted to see you. I missed you."

"I missed you too."

Silence. Sheila hated talking on the phone. It was too difficult when you couldn't see the other person's expressions. "Can you come over tomorrow?"

"Thought you'd be working," he said in a hurt tone.

"I can take the day off."

"Would you?" He was clearly shocked.

Sheila didn't blame him. "We need to talk."

"I agree. Is Caroline still with you?"

"She's going back tomorrow with Seán. The row's over. Peace and reconciliation."

"Good. We could do with some of that."

"Mmh. Do you want to stay tomorrow night?"

"Yes. There's a lot more I want, Sheila."

"We'll discuss it tomorrow. Come over at about three. The coast'll be clear then."

"All right. Have a good sleep. Sheila . . . I love you."

"I love you too. Goodnight."

She hung up. God, she'd said it. It had taken her three years to say it. I love you. She was vulnerable

417

again. That wasn't what she had intended. She wanted to be free. She didn't want to be tied to this man or any man. She didn't want to be in love. It always got too bloody complicated. Sheila was happy the way things were. Why couldn't they have gone on like that? Why mess up a perfectly good relationship with ties, restrictions, commitment? Why?

He'd said he couldn't stick being in Waterford with his wife. He came home early. What had Anne said to him? What did she want? Sheila remembered her from Mary's wedding. She'd looked old then but she was only in her twenties. She must be pushing forty now; the biological clock ticking away. Mary was right. His wife wanted him back. She must think that Sheila was just another insignificant affair.

Wasn't that what Sheila herself had thought at first? John had been with her now for three years. He'd been with Anne for four. Who had the greater claim? God, Sheila admonished herself. This wasn't about rights and claims. He wasn't a piece of property. John loved her. He'd told her that just now. Mary had told her earlier tonight. How much convincing did she need?

What was she truly afraid of? She knew. She was afraid of loving because she was afraid of losing. When you didn't love, you couldn't be hurt. Her father . . . Karen . . . she'd loved them and lost them. Was that what love was all about?

Sheila stubbed out the cigarette and switched off the bedside lamp. She didn't forget her prayer for Karen. She slipped in another one for herself. She was going to ask John to move in with her. That was all she could offer him. Marriage and children were out.

PART THREE

CHAPTER TWENTY-EIGHT

An Roinn Oideachais
Leaving Certificate Examination, 1984
English – Higher Level Paper 1

The sunlight was intense, shining relentlessly through the gym window. Karen put down her pen, fingers aching. She was pleased with her first English paper. It was a lucky thing that Bacon had come up. She was an expert on simulation. She spent her life pretending to be what she was not. Bacon, of course, considered this a vice. Bully for him! For her it was a life-line, a means of survival. Like Prufrock, she had learned to put on a face, a mask. Half of the English course was on the theme of appearance versus reality. Karen understood it only too well. She shuffled out of the hall with the rest of her classmates. Gormley, the English teacher, was pacing the corridor. Some of the students gathered around her. Karen was in no humour for a post-mortem on the exam. She avoided Gormley and met Paula in the cloakroom.

"Well, what did you think?" Paula groaned.

"It was OK. I liked the prose."

"It's all right for you, Karen. You're brilliant at English. What essay did you do?"

"The first one. Silence."

"Jesus, how could you write four pages on that?" Paula gasped. "I did the one about the cosmetics industry. Halfway through I got a blank and I messed up the last paragraph. Gormley'd kill me if she knew. She's always rabbiting on about structure in essay writing."

Karen pulled on her blazer. "Never mind, it's over. Are you going home for lunch?"

"Yeah, I'll walk up with you. I have to learn the quotations from Hamlet for this afternoon. If we get anything on Claudius I'll freak out. Some of the others are saying there'll be something on deception."

"Ignore rumours, that's my advice." Karen refused to listen to the idle speculation of the other students. These "dead cert" suggestions were always floating around before exams. They served no useful purpose.

"What do you think'll come up on Anglo-Irish poetry?" Paula stuffed her *Soundings* into her bag.

"I'm hoping Kavanagh will, but I'd say it could be Yeats."

"Oh Christ, that's me finished then. I can't make head or tail of his later poems. I hate Hamlet too, with his psychological problems! I should have stuck to the pass. You'd need to be a feckin' shrink to do honours English."

"Come on, I'm starving." Karen linked her out of the school.

Four-fifty. Good, she'd just enough time for a quick reread of her answers. Karen was exhausted but relieved. The questions had suited her. Her answer on Hamlet was good, she knew. Loyalty and betrayal . . . God, she could write a book about betrayal. Couldn't she? She was a victim of betrayal herself. At least Hamlet got the chance to confront his mother, to show her the error of her ways.

The Yeats question was fairly easy too. Personal failures and frustrations she dealt with in the first half of her answer and the universality of his themes in the second half. She also managed to time her answers properly, not like in the mock. For fiction she decided on the modern novel. *Lord of the Flies* was her favourite book. She'd intended to answer on Synge for the fourth question but, in the end, she opted for Dryden in the poetry section. She detested Emily Dickinson. Too depressing. Too remote.

Right, she was ready to hand up her booklet. She felt she'd a good chance of a B. An A in English was virtually impossible to come by. She'd better look for Paula. She'd seen her leave the hall earlier so it didn't look good. Paula should really have done pass. She wasn't the academic type at all.

* * *

The lovely Liz had the dinner ready when she got in. Ugh! Soggy stew again. She'd have killed for a burger and chips but her mother insisted she ate "proper food". Carrots were her pet hate.

"Where's Peter?" she muttered between mouthfuls.

"Down in the tennis club as usual. He thinks he might be able to get a summer job there, in the bar." Her mother cut her a large slice of apple tart. "Would you like custard, love?"

Jesus, it was getting worse. "No thanks."

"So, you've finished your first exam. I'm glad you liked it. I'm sure you did very well. You deserve to with all the work you've done."

Karen stood up from the table abruptly. "Thanks for dinner. I'm off to my room to study. If Paula or any of the others ring, tell them I don't want to be disturbed, OK?"

Her mother nodded and cleared away the dishes. She felt rebuffed in some odd way.

Karen had changed so much in the last few years. Not the sunny little girl Liz remembered. Frank told her not to worry, that it was typical teenage angst, but Liz thought it was more than that. Peter was so different. He was a fantastic kid, funny and kind, always in good humour. Karen was withdrawn and sullen most of the time. Was it a typical female adolescent thing? Liz didn't think so.

Karen was an excellent student. Ambition spurred her on. Her teachers were proud of her. She was top of her class and her reports were consistently good. But Liz thought that her daughter was too driven. She swotted for hours every night. She wasn't interested in boys or discos or sports. There was more to education than homework, tests and marks. It was important to take part in the social life of the school too. Karen wasn't interested. She kept to the books. This wasn't healthy.

It was difficult to discuss anything with Karen. She was quiet and polite. They never had rows. She never raised her voice or banged a door. There were no tantrums. She was cool and formal. It was unnatural. Everyone thought that Karen was a model daughter. She kept her room tidy. She was organised and meticulous about everything she did. She wore nice clothes. She had good manners. But her coolness unnerved Liz. Underneath that calm exterior, there was a volcano of emotion waiting to explode. Liz was convinced of it.

Liz and Frank had always been truthful and honest with Karen and Peter. They had explained the adoptions to them from an early age. They assured them they were loved and cherished. There was no problem then. Both of them seemed to be happy, well-adjusted children. But now Karen was . . . Liz couldn't find the right word to describe it. Karen had built up a wall between them. There was no way of getting through to her. The adoption agency had warned them this could happen, but Liz wasn't prepared for it at all.

The key turned in the front door. That'd be Peter.

425

Her son trampled through the hall, leaving a trail of mud and grass in his wake.

"We won the tournament, Mum. It was deadly! Oh, I got the job. Naturally!" He gave her a bear hug. "Is dinner ready? I'm starving."

Liz put down a huge plate of stew before him.

"Cool!" He tucked into it with gusto. "How did Karen get on?"

"She was pleased, I think. She's up studying so don't play your records too loudly, tonight."

"I won't be here. I promised Gran I'd call over to her to cut her grass, remember? Then I'm going to call over to Harry."

Frank's mother lived on Oulton Road, a few streets away. Frank had grown up there. His sister, Lucy, lived around the corner. People born and bred in Clontarf loved to settle in the area. It was a nice community. They had lots of amenities: Dollymount Strand, the North Bull Wall running out into Dublin Bay, with its wildlife sanctuary and St Anne's golf club. Both Karen and Peter were members of the local tennis club. Liz loved living by the sea. Frank had taught her to drive on the causeway twenty years ago. Liz had grown up in Sutton. It was her dream that she and Frank would retire to Howth some day. She remembered going on the Howth tram as a child in the fifties. They used to take the boat from the pier in Howth Harbour out to Ireland's Eye. Still, she'd never be able to move Frank. He always said he'd be carried out of this house feet first.

"Mum, are you in a daze or what?"

Peter's voice brought her back to the present. "Oh, bring this to your Gran. I made two today." Liz put an apple tart on top of the fridge.

"Will do. Are you and Dad going out tonight?" Peter took a slice of bread to soak up the gravy. There was no waste with Peter. He cleaned his plate every time.

"We'll see. He'll be in from work soon. We might pop down to The Sheds for a drink. I'm not pushed one way or the other. It's boring to be sipping an orange when everyone else is guzzling booze."

"How come you don't drink, Mum?" Peter helped himself to a large piece of apple tart.

"Never liked it," she said. Memories of a drunken father were enough to put anyone off. She blotted out that thought. Far better to recall the good times.

"Right. I'm off. Will you remind Dad he promised me an advance on my pocket money?"

Liz laughed. "After I get my housekeeping money, I will. If he gave advances to his customers where would the bank be?"

"He does with his term loans. How do you think they make such a huge profit every year?"

"Your advances are different, though. No question of interest. Your poor father."

"Come off it, Mum. Who ever heard of a poor bank manager?"

Liz made a swipe at him, but he ducked. "Don't be late. What's going on in Harry's, anyhow?"

"Sex, drugs and rock 'n' roll. See ya, Mum!" He was gone.

The house suddenly seemed empty. It always did when Peter went out.

Karen heard them laughing downstairs in the hall. Real chummy, weren't they? The blue-eyed boy, Peter, her brother . . . but he wasn't her brother in fact, was he? They were two waifs brought up together by chance. They were part of this ready-made family. She put down her history notes and lit a fag. She opened the bedroom window to let out tell-tale fumes. Mother dearest would be horrified if she knew her little darling smoked. Liz was so fucking perfect. She didn't smoke, didn't drink, didn't curse. She was a real lady. A happy homemaker; good cook, if you liked plain wholesome food, and Karen didn't. She was a good neighbour, understanding and helpful. She was a dutiful wife and a great mother . . . the catalogue of virtues was endless. The paragon of motherhood!

What about Frank? The successful bank manager. Worked his way up through the ranks. His job said it all. Steady, decisive and reliable. He was refined and softly spoken. Karen couldn't remember him ever losing the rag. He was generous too. A great family man.

And this house? A beautiful bay-windowed residence on the exclusive Mount Prospect Avenue. Just over the road, ladies and gentlemen, we have the famous St Anne's Rose Garden. Yeah, the house was lovely. Downstairs, apart from the usual reception rooms, we have Frank's pride and joy . . .

the conservatory. Bloody typical. The neighbours all mowed their lawns on Saturdays. They were avid church-goers living in Christian fellowship. Ugh! Little minds in little localities.

The adoption agency had chosen well. The ideal home. The ideal parents . . . only they weren't her real parents at all. They were substitutes. Very good, mind you, but substitutes none the less. She'd tried to discuss this with Peter. He didn't feel like she did. He accepted things at face value. She asked him once would he ever try to find his birth mother and he'd looked at her as if she had two heads. No, Peter was happy the way he was. But she wasn't . . . not by a long shot.

What about her so-called natural mother? Bloody unnatural more like it. She gave away her own flesh and blood. Wagon! Probably single . . . a quickie in the back of a car. Found herself up the pole. Had to get rid of it. What would people say? She'd probably be disowned. In order to protect her family she'd forfeited Karen's chance of having a real family. What about her real father? Probably a married man having his bit on the side. What did that make her?

Karen stood up and looked in the dressing-table mirror. Whom did she resemble? The slut or the oversexed boyfriend? Her hair was a deep auburn. Liz's hair was red too, but a much lighter shade. Karen was glad hers was dark. She'd avoided freckles. She liked her green eyes. Paula was always saying how beautiful she was. But Paula was obsessed by looks. Very superficial. To get on in this world you needed more than looks. She'd inherited these looks from one of the randy couple. Not that they were a couple or they could have kept her. Why didn't they keep her? Why did her mother discard her like a bit of unwanted rubbish?

What was she? An unwanted pregnancy. A mistake. Illegitimate. What a cruel word. Maybe the bitch was happily married now with a load of legitimate brats hanging out of her. Karen vowed that she'd find her . . . find her and confront her: "Why did you give me up, Mummy?" But she wasn't ready yet. Oh no. She'd bide her time. It'd have to be when she was fully prepared. She'd be a successful journalist and her mother would be a down-trodden housewife. She pictured the scene . . .

"Would you like a cup of tea, Karen?" The perfect one's voice called gently up the stairs.

"No thanks. I'm fine."

Yeah, she was fine. She'd survive. She'd show them.

She went back to her books. She had to do well in the Leaving Cert. Her future depended on it. She'd applied to Rathmines for the journalism course and there were only about thirty places. She had to single herself out from the hundreds of other applicants. She had to get a place, she had to. She'd always wanted to be a reporter. She loved research, probing for information. She adored writing, especially the discursory essays they did in school. She enjoyed reading decent fiction, but her own talents lay in factual composition. Once she established herself in a job, she'd move out of here.

She had to get away from Clontarf with its pretentious middle-class values. She had to get away from Liz, from this house . . . it was claustrophobic.

When she'd finished in Rathmines she could go for it. She'd take a job anywhere she could. She'd be willing to start on a rural paper. She'd keep her options open. Then she'd try for one of biggie newspapers . . . *The Times* or the *Independent*. After that, who knew? RTE?

She knew it'd be difficult, but she was determined. She was well informed. She read two daily newspapers every day and avidly watched the current affairs programmes on RTE and BBC. She planned out her future like a general plotting a campaign. Once she'd a full-time job she could move out.

When she was set up, she'd find her. She'd find the woman who abandoned her. She'd make her feel guilty. She was guilty, after all. She was a traitor. "Frailty, thy name is woman!" She nearly puked in the exam today when she quoted that. What kind of a woman would give away a baby? Jesus, she must be a hard bitch. Did she even remember? Probably not. She'd want to forget the misery and shame, wouldn't she? She'd swept her little mistake under the carpet and got on with her life. Ha! Karen wouldn't let her away with that. She was sick of pretence.

She'd find her all right, if it took the rest of her life. She'd open up the can of worms. Watch what would come out then! Karen would gloat at her mother's distress. She'd offer her no pity or compassion. The slut had shown her no pity, had given her nothing . . . not even a name. Karen would show her how she had coped without her maternal aid or affection. The thought of the showdown kept her going, fuelled her energies. She'd show them all. She grimly picked up her history book.

Liz plugged in the iron. She looked in dismay at the huge pile of clothes in front of her. Frank's shirts were the worst. She picked up Karen's school blouse. This'd be the last time she'd iron this. In another ten days the exams would be over and Karen would leave school forever. Liz worried about her future. Karen was adamant about this journalism thing. Liz didn't think it would be an easy career. You had to have a hard neck. Maybe Karen did.

"Hello, love. Sorry I'm late." Frank kissed her on the cheek. "Another hectic day."

"Are you hungry? I kept some stew. I could reheat it."

"No, you carry on. I'll make myself a sandwich. Had a big lunch with Gerry."

"How's he?"

"Great altogether. Ready to step into my shoes."

Gerry was the assistant manager. Very efficient. Liz wondered was Frank joking. "He couldn't do that."

"I'm kidding. Still, if they move me on, he'll be the one to take over. Knows all the ropes."

"Are they thinking of moving you?" Liz prayed

they weren't. He was happy in the Dame Street branch.

"Not to my knowledge. But I'm there four years now. One of these days they're bound to shift me. Wouldn't it be grand now if they moved me out here, to Clontarf?" He spread mayonnaise on his salad sandwich. He loved Hellman's. "How did Karen get on?"

"Fine, I think. She didn't say much. God, Frank, you could do with a few new shirts. Some of these are frayed at the collar."

"You get me some next week, will you? You know how I hate shopping."

Liz certainly did. He was a disaster. He'd go into a shop and buy the first thing he saw. He hated crowds. His taste was peculiar, to put it mildly. No sense of colour co-ordination. In fact, Frank was not interested in clothes full stop. He'd leave for work in the morning with odd socks on if she didn't check him. Imagine the reactions of his staff.

He finished his sandwich and made them both a cup of tea. "Karen's in her room I suppose? Better go up to see her."

"No, don't. She gave me strict instructions. No interruptions."

"Rubbish." Frank ignored the warning and went upstairs.

"How's my favourite scholar?" Frank leaned over Karen's desk and mussed her hair.

Karen shook her head. "Don't Dad. I hate that."

"Oh? Uptight, aren't you?" He started to massage her neck.

"Cut it out, Dad. I don't want to be rude, but I've loads to do for tomorrow."

Frank sat down on her bed. "Last minute cramming isn't a good idea, love. You should leave that now. Don't want to overdo it. You want to be fresh in the morning."

Karen didn't answer. How the hell would he know what she needed? He'd done his Leaving in the Dark Ages. She smiled at him. "Just a little longer."

"So, the English went fine, your mother tells me."

"Hard to say with English. But I think so. I liked the two papers."

"Ms Gormley's a good teacher by all accounts."

"She's OK. At least she covers the course. In the end of the day it depends on me, though."

"Of course." Frank could see the mood she was in. "I'll leave you to it, so." He could smell the stale smoke in the room. "Are you OK for fags?" His blue eyes twinkled mischievously.

Karen blushed. What was the point in denying it? She looked him straight in the eye. "If you've any spares, I wouldn't say no!"

He took three cigarettes from his packet and laid them on the desk. "I'll bring you up an ash-tray."

Liz finished the ironing in time for *Coronation Street*. This was the only soap she liked. The characters were so lifelike. It was as though you

actually knew them. She heard Frank running his
bath. He'd suggested going for a walk in St Anne's
Park. It was a nice evening for a stroll. They were to
meet Lucy in Connolly's, better known as The
Sheds, at ten. Lucy was Frank's youngest sister. She
was married to an insurance broker. Frank had an
endowment policy which meant he was worth more
dead than alive. Insurance was a funny business.

He came down dressed in his jeans, navy
sweater and sneakers. He loved getting into his
casual gear at the weekends. His grey hair was still
wet. "Ready?"

"In a minute. I have to change."

Frank looked at her. She was wearing a black
skirt and a white blouse. She looked nice. "You're
fine. You don't have to change."

"Oh Frank, I've been wearing this all day. I want
to freshen up."

Women! How would anyone know what she'd
been wearing all day? They were only going to the
local. No need to dress up. He picked up the paper.
Might as well have a read while he waited for her.

He went to answer the knock at the door.

"Hi, Mr Shaw. Is Karen in?"

"Come in, Paula. She's up in her room. Go on
up."

He smiled to himself as Paula glided up the
stairs, her long black skirt flowing behind her. She
had a loose flowing black top and her finger and
toenails were painted black too. Bangles jingled on
her arm and these two huge dangly earrings nearly
knocked the sight out of his eye. She was a scream,

435

that girl. The make-up was thick on her face. She obviously hadn't spent her night studying. No sign of exam stress there. Pity Karen wouldn't lighten up a bit.

"Ah Jesus, Karen. Are you still at it?" Paula flopped on the bed.

Karen was raging. "Did Mum let you up? I told her I didn't want to be disturbed."

"Your dad got the door. Chill out, will ya? I've news."

Her broad beam irritated Karen. "What?"

"I got the job in Peter Marks. They're taking me on as a trainee as soon as I've finished these bloody exams. So now I don't give a hoot about results or anything else. I'll probably be able to get you cheap hair-dos. Brilliant, isn't it? The auld fella gave me a tenner. Do you want to come for a jar?"

Karen pointed to the pile of books on her desk. "Can't. Too much to do. That's great about the job. I'm glad you got what you wanted. But I've got to study, Paula, or I won't get what I want."

"Tch, you're a desperate swot. Come out for an hour."

"No," Karen said stiffly. "I've got to finish these notes."

"What are you at?" Paula peered over her shoulder. "Keywords, eh?"

"They help me to focus on the main points. Will you get the hell out of here, Paula. I'll see you tomorrow."

Paula got up reluctantly. "You're no fun. I'm

going down to the tennis club. Dreamboat might be there."

"Who?" Karen wasn't remotely interested.

"Steve Clarke. You know him. He lives near your Aunt Lucy on Vernon Avenue. God, he's a bit of all right. Jean's mad about him too."

"Well, ask Jean to go with you. You can fight it out together." Karen was fed up with this interruption. She'd more important things on her mind than drooling over the local talent.

"I'm not asking her! What if he fancies her instead of me?"

Karen had to smile at the unintentional insult. It never struck Paula that this Steve might fancy Karen. Paula obviously felt she'd nothing to worry about with her.

"Look, when the exams are over, I'll go wherever you want. Until then will you please leave me ALONE."

"Don't get your knickers in a twist. I'm going." Paula left the room in a huff.

Frank and Liz walked around by the pond in St Anne's. There were a lot of families out with young children. Others walked their dogs.

"Remember you used to chase the kids under that archway?" Liz linked Frank as they strolled along.

"Mmh, they called it their 'castle'. Further on they had their 'forest'. Oh, the innocence of it all. It only seems like yesterday."

Liz sat on a bench. "God, you were a great one for the stories, Frank. Those magical tales of monsters, dragons and fairy princesses. The kids were enthralled."

"Mmh, and they say that bank managers have no imagination. Young children are wonderful. No sense of guile." Frank had a wistful expression on his face. "They look up to you. They see their parents as the most fantastic people in the world, the solvers of all problems, the cure-all."

Liz knew he was talking about Karen. She'd idolised him. He could do no wrong when she was younger. Now, even he had to admit, there was a drastic change.

"I'm worried about Karen. It's more than the exams. It's not just one of those adolescent things, Frank. I think she's hurt and confused."

"Mmh. Leaving school is a huge upheaval. Full of uncertainties. School is very protective. They're in a cushioned environment in many ways."

"You think I'm too protective too, don't you?"

Frank took her hand. "No, I don't. You're her mother. It's natural that you want the best for her. You don't want to see her suffer. But I don't think there's any way we can stop her fears, Liz. She's a normal kid who wants to know her background. Remember all that questioning? Who am I? Why am I here? What's the point of it all? Every teenager goes through that. But it goes deeper with Karen. She literally doesn't know who she is."

"Did she tell you this?" Liz was wounded. Why couldn't Karen have confided in her?

"No, love. She didn't tell me anything. A few weeks ago, I was coming out of the bathroom and I overheard her talking to Peter. She asked him how he felt about being adopted."

"Oh God, what did he say?" Liz panicked.

"You know Peter. Said he didn't feel anything. When she asked him was he ever going to trace his natural mother, do you know what he said?"

"What?" Liz was afraid to hear the answer.

"He said that, as far as he was concerned, one set of parents was more than enough to cope with!" Frank laughed. "He's bloody right."

Liz didn't appreciate the joke. She was too upset. "How can we help her? We've told her everything we know."

"Exactly. And we know sweet damn all. She wants to know who her birth mother and father were. It's normal. I think we've got to be prepared for the inevitable."

Liz looked down at the ground. "You mean Karen will look for them."

"I think she might. She has every right to. It doesn't mean she's rejecting us. She needs space at the moment. She's a lot of questions that need answers and we can't give them to her. But we can give her our support."

"It's going to be hard." Liz sighed. "Did she say anything to you tonight?"

"No. She wasn't in a talking mood. You know she's smoking?"

Liz nodded. "I pretended it wasn't happening. I thought if I ignored it . . ."

"I gave her some cigs tonight." He laughed at Liz's shocked expression. "I know you don't approve, but if she's going to smoke I'd rather it was in front of us."

"OK." Liz didn't make a fuss. The fact that Karen was smoking annoyed her, but she had much more serious matters on her mind at the moment. Somewhere . . . God knows where . . . a strange woman was lurking in the background . . . a woman who'd take away her daughter. A woman Liz didn't know. A woman she didn't want to know. She'd enter their lives and nothing would ever be the same again. Liz felt terribly insecure. Threatened.

"Look at the time." Frank pulled her up off the bench. "Lucy and Mick'll be waiting." He looked at his wife. She'd turned pale. She looked scared.

"Liz, all this won't happen overnight. It could take Karen years to find her mother. She mightn't ever be able to. There could be worse complications. Supposing she finds her mother and then is rejected? We have to be strong. We have to be there for her. As I said, all this could take years. It might never happen. Karen could change her mind." He put his arm around her as they crossed the road at the bottom of their road. "One step at a time. We'll deal with it, don't worry."

But Liz was worried. Who was this woman who had given birth to Karen? What was she like? How did she feel about giving her child up? Liz had asked herself these question before. But that was years ago, when Karen was a baby. The intervening years had put all those thoughts out of her head. Now they were back with a vengeance.

Liz was sure of one thing. The woman hadn't wanted to give her baby away. They had Karen for five months before she signed the final papers. They were the worst five months of Liz's life. She'd lived in dread. She was terrified of losing Karen then. She was terrified again. "Frank, I don't know how I'll cope. I couldn't bear to lose her."

Frank hugged her in the middle of the Clontarf Road. "You can't lose her, love. She'll always be our daughter. We were there with her the whole of her life. We watched her grow up. We gave her all the love we had. Karen can't turn her back on that. This other woman is the one to be pitied. She lost her child. She'll never have all those precious memories of Karen's childhood that we have. She can't recover the past. She'll never replace you. You are Karen's mother in the true sense of the word." He kissed her forehead. "Now, chin up."

"Thanks. Thanks for being so understanding. I must sound like a complete neurotic."

"No, my sweet, you sound like anyone else in your circumstances would. I'm concerned about Karen too. I hope she won't be hurt and disappointed if she goes ahead with the search. But we'll have to let nature take its course."

They reached The Sheds. Frank pushed the door open. Liz took a deep breath, fixed a smile on her face and walked in.

441

CHAPTER TWENTY-NINE

Sheila poured more water over the coals. She loved the sauna. Every morning before she began work, she did her work-out and then had her sauna followed by a cool shower. She'd never been in better shape. Thirty-seven next birthday and she felt better than she had in her twenties. Her skin was still smooth and wrinkle-free. Let them say what they liked, she still swore it was the rosemary.

After her shower she went down to reception. Patti had just come in.

"Hi, Sheila. Busy day ahead. Nuala's completely booked out this morning and Eileen has two massages and a manicure. She was right about the men's salon. I can't believe that it's caught on so well. I never thought Irishmen would be interested."

"There are lots of Irishmen who aren't, Patti!" Sheila went down to her basement office. She'd a few phone calls to make.

Eileen had certainly been right. Crosby's, as Sheila called the gym, had opened three years ago. They had certain mornings and evenings for the women and other times for the men. Some of the male clients had remarked jokingly that Sheila was sexist with her Natural Woman salon downstairs. What about them? They wanted their own salon. Eileen agreed with them. So Sheila decided to get rid of the sunbeds and start a male salon instead, Natural Man. They did manicures, pedicures, massages and skin care. After all men had skin problems too. John was annoyed when Sheila started up the second salon, but he had to accept it. He'd learned from experience that he'd never be able to stop Sheila from doing what she wanted.

They now had a whole new range of skin and hair products exclusively for men. They employed another chemist and lab assistant in Carrigeen, and a new beautician for the women's salon. Eileen was in charge of the male salon. She was a great hit with the men.

Sheila had sent Eileen off to Grasse last year to investigate essential oils which would be more masculine. She booked her into a hotel. Eileen would be too much of a temptation for Yves! Although by all accounts Sophie kept a good eye on him these days. Eileen had enjoyed her few days away. She'd needed the break. Looking after a child on her own was not easy. Her mother helped out as best she could, but she was getting on. Eileen had great friends who babysat for her when she went away. She came back from her French trip with loads of information and ideas for male fragrances and aftershave lotions.

Sandalwood was particularly good for controlling barber's rash. Cedarwood had astringent and antiseptic properties of benefit to oily skins. It helped seborrhoea of the scalp, dandruff and alopecia. Bridget created a hair tonic, which was very popular with the men, using a blend of cedarwood and rosemary. She manufactured creams using birch for the treatment of eczema and acne. She and Peadar had two children now, a son and a daughter. They were the perfect couple. Sheila felt the odd twinge of jealousy when she saw Peadar proudly pushing the pram.

Amanda was excited by the new range. It meant a new shop exclusively for male customers to be run by her. Sheila changed the name of the shop in Duke Street to Natural Man. She employed another shop assistant to help Amanda.

Meanwhile she was lucky to find a premises in the Powerscourt Townhouse Shopping Centre for her Natural Woman shop. The Powerscourt centre was on South William Street, just back from Grafton Street. This old city mansion belonged to the Powerscourt family who had their principal residence in Powerscourt House in County Wicklow. It was built between 1771 and 1774 and was converted into the shopping centre just three years before in 1981. Sheila and Lily adored it. It had a balconied courtyard and three levels of modern shops and restaurants. Despite modernisation, the building still kept its old world atmosphere. The original magnificent plasterwork had been retained.

Sheila phoned Amanda in Natural Man. Everything was fine. Then she phoned Lily to tell her not to worry about the orders. She'd ring Bridget herself. Lily and Carol, her assistant, were run off their feet. The new premises had doubled their custom. Sheila spent her mornings in the office in Fitzwilliam Square and her afternoons in the new shop. She was thrilled with herself. She now had twenty staff on the Dublin payroll and fifteen in Carrigeen. Caroline's remark years ago that Sheila would be running an empire was turning out to be true.

Mary phoned. "Hi Sheila, I got you a copy of the English Leaving Cert papers. They were hard enough."

"Thanks, Mary. I wonder how she did. What exams have they today?"

"History, I think. That's if Karen does history. Listen, I'm going out tonight so if you want to drop over tomorrow night for a chat, that'd be great."

"Right, I will. Where are you off to tonight? Out with Jim?"

"You must be joking. He's away again. I'm more like a widow than a wife. The kids barely know who he is. No, I'm going out with a few from school. We're off to Leeson Street."

"I don't believe you."

"I am. I need to see a bit of the outside world before I go stir crazy. It'll be a laugh."

Sheila twiddled with her pen. "Well, rather you than me. Have a good night. See you tomorrow night. I'll be over at about nine. Oh, I got a lovely dress for Maeve. It's red with white spots. It'll be gorgeous with her dark curls. Wait'll you see it. I couldn't pass it in the shop."

"You're desperate. You've them ruined."

"I couldn't leave Davy out so I got him goggles and flippers. I know he'd hit me if I bought him clothes. He's still into swimming isn't he?"

"Oh God, yeah. He adores it. He goes twice a week. Every time he bellyflops into the pool I nearly have a heart attack. He'll be thrilled with the goggles. You're right about the clothes. You know the communion blazer he forced me to get him? It hasn't come out of his wardrobe since. Honestly, I knew when I bought it that he'd never wear it again. I should have got him denims. Anyway, the whole thing is cracked. They make their communion far too early. All he remembers about the day is how much dosh he got."

Sheila laughed. "Typical."

"Right, I won't keep you. I know you're up to your neck. See you tomorrow night. Oh, how's John?"

"Mmh, a bit moody. His fortieth's coming up soon. I think he's quite restless."

"Are you throwing a party for him?" Mary wanted to know.

"No, he doesn't want a fuss. I thought a few of us could go for a meal."

"Great. Count me in, and Jim if he's not away."

"OK. We'll talk about it tomorrow night. Bye."

Mary was clearly pissed off with Jim. Sheila would have swapped places willingly. If only John went away more often. Pity he wasn't a sailor. A few ports of call a year would suit her fine. She wanted to see him, but not every blinking day.

Living with him wasn't getting any easier. It was just that she'd been so long on her own, doing her own thing. She'd never get used to sharing. She knew she was set in her ways and a bit selfish, but she felt that was her right. She hadn't wanted this total commitment. He wasn't too happy either. He still wanted them to make it legal with a marriage certificate, as if a piece of paper was going to make any difference. His tenant in the mews was moving out soon. She'd make sure he got another one fast. He was half thinking of selling the flat. No way, baby! She'd insist he kept his own place.

* * *

"Mr Harris. Una Mallin's here to see you. I couldn't put her off. She's no appointment but she said she's really desperate." Rebecca looked worried stiff.

Una Mallin was married to an obnoxious bastard. A wife-beater. A drunkard. But the last John heard was that he'd gone to Wales with his brother.

John had ten minutes before his next appointment. "Ask her to come in tomorrow."

Rebecca hesitated. "Would you not see her, even for a minute? She's in bad shape. He came back."

John thought about it. "Show her in, Rebecca."

Una Mallin came in. She stood there, shaking. Her face was covered in bruises, her lip was cut and she'd a black eye. John was horrified. That bastard had gone too far this time.

"Mrs Mallin, please . . . take a seat. Rebecca, bring Mrs Mallin a cup of tea. Has Mr Kiely arrived?"

"Not yet."

"Could you tell him I'll be delayed for a while. If he doesn't want to wait, make another appointment for him. Give him my apologies." John didn't like cancelling an appointment but this was an emergency. Rebecca was back in a second with the tea. The woman accepted it gratefully and took a large gulp. She was badly shaken and on the verge of tears.

"Can you talk about it?" John asked gently.

She put her cup on the desk, her hands trembling. "I hadn't seen him for six months. I honestly thought he was going to stay away, like the police told him. The kids and myself were watching the TV and all of a sudden there was a loud crash. My heart was in my mouth. I knew it was him. He smashed the glass in the back door and got into the kitchen. Oh God, Mr Harris, I was petrified. I rushed the kids upstairs and locked them in their room. He came charging up the stairs, roaring and screaming like a maniac. He grabbed me and . . . " She burst into uncontrollable sobbing.

John was torn between rage and pity. Four years of this abuse was appalling. The woman was on the verge of a nervous breakdown. He handed her a tissue.

"Mrs Mallin, I know you want to avoid court but I honestly don't think you've any other choice left."

The woman continued to sniff. It was pathetic. She was a well-spoken, well-educated woman of about thirty. She lived in a nice house in Malahide. She worked in Dublin Corporation and had a good salary. She was the one who paid the mortgage. She was the one who brought up the two children. She needed Tom Mallin like she needed a hole in the head. He was no good. He was a layabout and a drunk.

"I know you're right, Mr Harris. You've been right all along. But I have to think of the children. He is their father." She dabbed at her swollen eye.

"He's a funny way of showing that," John couldn't help remarking. "He's lost any right he has to your children. The man is a danger to you and to them."

Her eyes brimmed up with tears. "I know. Tommy, the eldest, has witnessed some horrific scenes. The thing is, Tom only does this when he's drunk."

"I realise that. But he refuses to go back for treatment. He's a chronic alcoholic. The Rutland Centre did all they could. You've done all you could." He looked at her. Was she taking any of this in?

"I thought he'd change. He promises me he will. Even after the beating last night, he apologised." She looked imploringly at John. "I just can't do anything that will bring more misery to the kids."

"You won't be doing that. You'll be giving them some hope of safety. I can't be of any further help to you unless you agree to apply for a protection order."

John knew he sounded severe but he had to be. This woman was a victim. She'd become so used to being a victim that she couldn't make rational

449

decisions any more. She kicked her husband out and then took him back every time he promised he'd reform. The police could only issue warnings. They had very little power when it came to domestic quarrels. But once she had a protection order, if he laid a finger on her, he could be arrested. He had to be stopped before he killed her.

"Where is he now?" John asked.

"I don't know. He might have gone to his sister's place. He'd left when I got up this morning. I'm terrified he'll come back."

"Where are the children?"

"With my parents. They're safe. But I can't impose on my parents forever. We need to be able to live in our own house. I can't go on night after night, terrorised. No child should have to go through that sort of fear." As she spoke her voice became stronger and more confident.

"That's precisely why you need the protection order."

Mrs Mallin took a deep breath. "OK. We'll do whatever you think is best."

John was relieved. At last some definite action. "Right, I'll set the whole thing in motion. We apply for a barring order and then we go to court. It could take up to two months unfortunately. In the meantime, you've notified the police?"

"Yes. My father insisted. Oh God, I hate going to court. It must be nerve-racking."

John could empathise with that. "I'll be with you and I promise I'll make the whole thing as painless as possible."

She stuffed the tissue in her bag. "Thanks, Mr Harris. I hope I'm doing the right thing."

"You are." He stood up and walked her to the door. "Are you going back to your parents' house?"

"Yes, for a few days. I don't want the neighbours to see me like this. Thanks again, Mr Harris.

"Don't mention it. I'll be in touch."

John felt drained after she'd left. Rebecca buzzed to say that Mr Kiely would be back the next afternoon. John rang Sheila at the office but he'd missed her by a few minutes. He tried Amanda and then Lily, but he'd no luck. She was difficult to get a hold of, she moved around so much. He'd settle for a quick lunch by himself and then get back early to prepare for his afternoon appointments. He couldn't shake the image of Mrs Mallin from his mind. What kind of animals were there out there?

* * *

"Sheila? Hi. I'm ringing from the flat. This creep of a tenant of mine has disappeared. No notice. Just packed his bags and left."

Sheila wasn't surprised. She'd been expecting something like this. "What way did he leave the place?"

"In a right mess. I won't be able to re-let it until it's done up." John sounded really angry.

"Look. I'll get on to Noel, my decorator, tell him it's an emergency," Sheila offered.

"I think this bugger's gone off with the key. I

don't like leaving the place unattended." John sounded pissed off.

Sheila tried to calm him down. "No, you shouldn't. Get the locks changed. Is anything missing?"

"I don't know. I'd better check around." He was getting grumpier.

Sheila had to placate him. "Come to me for dinner and then you can pick up whatever clothes you need. I think you should sleep there for a while."

"Would you mind?" John sounded relieved.

Mind! She was absolutely delighted. A few days on her own. It'd be like a holiday.

"Of course I don't mind. These things happen."

John finished off the spaghetti bolognese. "That was great, thank you. So, Noel can start in the morning?"

Sheila put down her fork. "Yeah, he'll be with you before you go to work. Did you get new locks fitted?"

"No, they're coming to do it in the morning. I could sue that bastard only it wouldn't be worth the hassle. At least he's paid up to the end of the week. But you should see the state of the place. He marked the kitchen table with an iron. The lino is torn all around the sink. The walls are covered in grease and grime. It's disgusting. He didn't take anything as far as I can see." John took their plates over to the sink.

"Never mind, Noel will do a good job with the painting. Couldn't you invest in tiles for the floor?" Sheila had never liked the lino anyway.

"I think I might. They'd be more hard-wearing. Permanent. Sheila, I only need to stay there tonight. Once I get the new locks I can give a key to Noel. I don't have to be there when he's doing the job."

Oh ho. Sheila was afraid of that.

"Mmh, still it might be an idea to stay till you get another tenant. There are a lot of burglaries. Head-the-ball might even come back." Sheila tried to sound convincing.

"Sure I have the alarm." John thought Sheila was fussing.

"All the same, there's nothing like an unoccupied residence to attract thieves." Sheila was insistent.

"I don't like leaving you." John put his arm around her and kissed her cheek.

"Don't worry about me. A few days away from one another could spice up things considerably." Sheila's eyes twinkled. "Anyhow I'm due in Carrigeen the day after tomorrow."

"Not again?"

"I haven't been down for a month, John," Sheila said firmly. "I used to go every fortnight. Mam isn't getting any younger either."

"I know. I'm sorry. I do try not to be so possessive but I can't help it. I hate being separated from you." John looked at her pleadingly.

"You're like a kid in some ways."

"That's what you always say."

"Because it's true." She kissed the top of his head and poured out the coffee.

He came down with a packed suitcase. He looked forlorn. Sheila went down with him to the hall door.

"Will you come over tomorrow night?" John held her around the waist.

"Can't. I'm going over to Mary's." Sheila said offhandedly.

"I'll come with you." Mary and Jim were his friends too. He had every right to come.

"No, girls' night only. Jim's away." Sheila was firm.

That was different, John thought. "OK. Meet you for lunch the day after?"

"I told you, I'm going to Galway." Sheila pecked his cheek.

He kissed her tenderly on the lips. "You're very elusive."

"Part of my charm." She opened the door. "Go on, I hate these long goodbyes. I'll ring you when I get back."

He went down the steps. "Hopefully I'll have a new tenant by then."

Hopefully he wouldn't! Sheila waved him off and closed the door.

Yes! She was on her own. Freedom. Peace. She'd have the whole place to herself for two glorious days. Pity she had to go down to the factory. Still, her mother was dying to see her. She owed it to Caroline and Seán too. Rita was her mother and she had to do her bit. She went upstairs for a long soak. She'd have the double bed to herself tonight. Bliss.

John felt weird. He hadn't slept in this place for four years. He'd love to get shot of it. What was the point in keeping it on? Nothing but worry and hassle. Who knew what troubles the next tenant would bring? He had his home now with Sheila, but she didn't want him to sell. He knew why. Still wanted him to have his own patch. He got into bed and took up his PD James novel, *Cover Her Face*. John liked Detective Chief Inspector Adam Dalgliesh. Adam couldn't help getting involved personally in some of his cases, but his professionalism never allowed him to let his feelings get in the way of his investigations. John read for a while, but his mind was not on it. He couldn't help worrying about Mrs Mallin.

John hoped he had dealt with her in the right way. Normally he was distant with his clients, but it was different with her. It wasn't that he felt sorry for her. He admired her in many ways. She'd have a lot going for her if, once and for all, she'd make up her mind not to have anything more to do with that blackguard. When Mallin was away, she coped brilliantly. She was the breadwinner. She had the kids organised and happy. Then when he came back on the scene, chaos returned. Even though she was the strong one, that bum had reduced her to a helpless neurotic. He undermined her confidence. He used the children as a weapon. He was despicable. The barring order was the only solution. That way, if he stepped across the threshold, the police could handle it. John dreaded what could happen if she changed her mind.

The locksmith arrived at eight the next morning. The job was done in a half an hour. John let Noel, the decorator, in and gave him a spare key. He gave him cash to get the paints and told him to stick with the same colours. John really had no interest in the place any more. He had a quick shower and a cup of coffee. He'd made up his mind. He didn't care what Sheila had said. He was moving back today. He shoved his stuff in the boot and drove over to Fitzwilliam Square.

Sheila was having a late breakfast when he arrived. She gaped at him. "What's up?"

He saw the expression in her eyes. Dread. It struck him like a thunderbolt. He felt crushed.

"There was no need for me to stay. The locks are done. I gave Noel a key." He sat down and poured himself a glass of orange juice. Silence. Why didn't she say something, goddammit? He felt ridiculous. Unwanted.

"I thought the few days' break would do us good. I thought we agreed to it." Sheila spoke quietly, but he could hear the annoyance.

That was it. He'd had it. Enough pussyfooting around. "You don't want me here, Sheila, do you?"

She took her breakfast dishes to the sink. Her back was turned. He didn't need to see her face. He knew what she was feeling.

"Do you ?" His voice was louder, more defiant.

He was forcing her into a corner. Sheila bit her lip. She didn't know what to say. She had got up this morning in rare form. She thought she had a peaceful day ahead of her. Now this. Who'd want a showdown at this hour of the day?

She finally spoke. "It's not that I don't want you here, John."

"Oh, isn't it?" He gave her no time to finish. "That's the distinct impression I got when I walked in here."

"I need space. I think we're seeing too much of one another. It's getting very . . . claustrophobic."

"You want me out?" It was more of an accusation than a statement.

Sheila came back and sat down. "I don't want you out exactly . . ."

"Exactly, what the hell's that supposed to mean? I don't want you out exactly. Jesus, would you clarify that, please? I'm living with you or I'm not. It's as simple as that."

"Nothing is that simple, John. Look we've tried it your way for four years now. I don't think it's working out."

"Of course it's not working out," he roared back at her. "Because you've never tried it my way. I wanted us to get married. I wanted you to commit yourself to this relationship."

"I did. You can't accuse me of that." She glared at him.

"You did not. Your heart was never in it."

Sheila was hurt. How could he say that? She'd been with him now for seven years. Four of those he'd lived in her house with her. Her house. She still thought of it as hers and not theirs. Did that mean something? Could he possibly be right?

"Look at it from my point of view, for a minute. I'm more like your lodger than your partner. This is your house. Downstairs is your business. Our social life is mainly with your friends and colleagues. I'm practically irrelevant."

"John, you feel like that because you've wrapped yourself up in my life at the expense of your own. That's what I'm trying to say here. You need your own life too. You need your own space. We're all individuals. You're a major part of my life but you're not the only part. That's the way it is in every healthy relationship."

"You call this healthy? Half the time I'm afraid to say how I feel in case you blow up. I can't be myself anymore. I never really got a look in, Sheila. You gave a part of yourself to me, that's all. I'm beginning to wonder if you ever really loved me."

"I did. I still do, John. You know that."

"No, I don't," he said sadly. "You love me on your terms. You want me in my appointed place. Appointed by you. You have a role mapped out for me in your life. I'm not going to play that role any longer. I can't."

Sheila didn't answer. What he said was true. She couldn't deny it.

"I want it all, Sheila. All or nothing."

She nodded. "I don't blame you. It's just that I can't give what I haven't got. I do love you, John, more than I've ever loved any man."

"I think that's true. But it isn't enough. You're not in love with me the way I'm in love with you. I can't see enough of you. I'm miserable when we're apart. You say we need space. To me, that space is a vacuum."

She lit a cigarette. Another long silence followed. She became aware of the ticking of the kitchen clock.

"What are we going to do?" she asked him.

"Only one thing to do. I'm going to move out." John grimaced.

"No." She hadn't meant to sound so alarmed. "No, you don't have to do that. I'll try to be more loving . . . more giving. I'll try, honestly I will."

John stroked her neck. "I know you'd try. But it wouldn't work, Sheila. We'd be at cross-purposes all the time. You've got to make a choice. I've wanted a divorce now for years. I was hoping you'd suggest marriage. You didn't. I don't think you ever will."

"You know I don't want to get married. I never did. It frightens me," Sheila murmured.

John pulled her closer. "What frightens you?"

"I don't know." She honestly didn't know.

He gently kissed her cheek. "It's the finality of it, isn't it?"

"Maybe." Her voice was a whisper.

"Doesn't have to be final." He laughed, but it was a bitter laugh. "Ask Anne."

"You're giving me an ultimatum, aren't you?" Sheila stared into his eyes. He was so handsome. He was mad about her. Why not say yes?

"I don't like that word, but yes, I am asking you to marry me. I'm asking for the last time. There's no point in dragging it out any longer." He moved away from her.

"Why can't we stay the way we are?" she implored him.

"Because neither of us is happy the way things are, that's why." John was determined. This had to be sorted out now. He refused to stay in limbo.

"Marriage or nothing? Is that my choice?" Sheila looked up at him. He stood there, hands on his hips.

"Afraid so." He shrugged.

Sheila got angry. "What's marriage? People marry when they love each other, want to live together and have children. We love each other and we live together. I don't want children. I have a seventeen-year-old daughter whom I couldn't keep because I wasn't married. I wasn't allowed to love my child without that scrappy bit of paper. How do you think I feel about marriage, John?" Sheila was fuming now. "I'm thirty-six years old. I don't believe in fairytales any more. All I want is your love and friendship, my business, which is my life and, and some day to find my daughter."

John sighed. "You have my love, Sheila. You have your business which you so rightly said is your life. I genuinely hope you will find your daughter. Marrying me won't interfere with that. I'd welcome your daughter with open arms. But we could have a child of our own too."

"I'm sorry, John. I could never have another child. Never. I was too scarred the first time."

"Sheila, that was seventeen years ago. You have to get over that."

"I can't." He'd never fully understood how shattered she was by giving up Karen.

He nodded. "I'm going to ring the office. I'm dead late as it is. We're only torturing ourselves here. We both know the end has come. I'll move out my stuff when you're in Carrigeen."

"John, I'm so sorry. I never meant it to end this way."

"Yeah," he muttered. "I never meant it to end at all."

Neither had she. She'd fooled herself into thinking things could go on as she wanted them to. She stood up awkwardly. They stared at one another. Suddenly she ran to him and hugged him close. "I'll miss you, John."

He kissed her forehead. "I won't demean this moment by telling you that we'll stay friends. I couldn't bear that. It's better that we don't meet each other after."

Sheila pulled away from him and walked out of the kitchen. She didn't look back. She hurried downstairs, not stopping till she got to the door of the salon. Her head started to pound and her mouth had dried up. She couldn't face Patti. She went down to the privacy of her office. She unlocked the door, walked over to her desk, sat down and burst into tears.

CHAPTER THIRTY

Mary Ryan felt decidedly guilty and it was a new sensation for her. Never before in her life could she remember having done anything so stupid and so selfish. What had come over her? She must have been insane. It was now eleven o'clock and she couldn't get out of bed. She was listless. Lethargic.

She could hear the kids below, the television blaring all over the house. She'd have to get up. God only knew what state the kitchen'd be in if Davy had poured out their cereal. She stretched her legs down the cool sheet and yawned. What had she to do today? Maeve had a music lesson this afternoon and it was her turn to bring Davy and his pals to the swimming-pool. She'd have to get the lunch early. Jesus, if she could only get her act together. No earthly use lounging in bed, but her head throbbed and her limbs were aching.

Blast Jim, anyway. It was his fault. If it wasn't one business deal, it was another. This project management thing was a pain. His company was working in association with a large practice in London. He spent more time in England than he did at home with her. She was thoroughly sick of it.

They were expanding, he explained, and he had to travel. What did he expect? Did he think she was going to stay rooted to the spot, while he went here, there and everywhere, meeting new people and having fun? Did it never occur to him that she might be lonely?

OK, she had the kids and they were terrific, but she needed adult company too. He never even asked her to go on these trips with him. She wondered was there a woman in England. No, probably not. He wouldn't have the energy. He'd lost interest in sex lately, at least he had with her. If she wore nothing but her high heels and a garter, he wouldn't even notice. She was beginning to feel invisible. They'd be married twelve years in August. You had to give a marriage time and effort if you wanted to make it work. He gave precious little time and practically no effort. Yeah, last night was his fault.

In any case, what had she done that was so unpardonable? A quick roll in the hay . . . in the back seat to be more precise. So what? What Jim didn't know wouldn't hurt him. Other women were unfaithful and didn't drive themselves nuts with anxiety and guilt. Why should she be any different? He'd never find out. How could he? She gave the guy a false name and phone number. She didn't want an affair. She didn't need any complications in her life. But she was only human. She needed warmth and affection. She needed human touch.

God, last night was good. That guy had been incredibly passionate. She almost blushed in remembrance. She'd never tried it in a car before. Imagine, all the time she was dating Jim, they'd never messed around in his car. Then, she'd have thought it was disgusting. Just went to show how much she'd changed. It'd been really exciting last night. Dollymount took on a whole new meaning!

"Mum, I can't find my togs." Davy's voice bellowed up the stairs. No peace for the wicked.

"I'll be down in a minute," she called back.

Yeah, she'd been wicked. Deliciously wicked. Thirty-six going on seventeen. To hell with it, she'd enjoyed herself. It was nice to be noticed and fancied. It was nice to have someone stroking you and fondling you. When Jim did make his rare advances to her, it was a case of wham, bang, thank-you-ma'am. She was tired of his premature climaxes and his snoring.

She'd put last night's escapade down to a sensational experience and then forget it. She'd no intention of seeing him again. That'd be playing with fire. One night of unbridled passion was no reason to panic, no reason to lose sight of reality. What was reality for her?

She'd a lovely home, two gorgeous kids and a good husband. Good but neglectful. That's why she'd done it. Boredom could drive you to anything. She was terrified she was becoming staid and boring herself. No, she'd put it out of her mind and get on with her life with Jim. She didn't regret it at all now. It'd been good for her, she was sure. She was glad that she could still attract a man . . . an extremely exciting man at that. She could still feel his hands all over her.

She got up and went to the bathroom. God, she looked a mess. Last night's mascara streaked her face and her eyes were totally bloodshot. Definitely time to get her act together. She removed her make-up. Her face was blotchy. She'd get a lecture tonight from Sheila. Not that she'd confide in Sheila this time. Sheila would think she was out of her mind. Maybe she was. She turned on the shower.

"What time is Sheila coming over?" Maeve slurped her soup off the spoon.

"About nine, I think." Mary's head was still throbbing. Too much cheap wine.

"Can I stay up, please?" Maeve begged.

"May I . . . Of course you may, sweetie. Sheila will be dying to see you both."

"Oh Mum," Davy groaned. "Larry's mother said I could sleep over in his place tonight. They've got a new pup."

"Are you sure she said that?" Davy was always trying it on.

"Ring her if you don't believe me." His angry pout made Mary smile.

"I do believe you. I'll drop you there after swimming."

"You'll miss your prezzy, you'll miss your prezzy," Maeve chanted gaily. When was she going to stop trying to stir things?

"Big wow." Davy stuck his tongue out at her.

"Don't start, you two," Mary warned them. Her hangover was bad enough without a squabble.

"I'll get my present tomorrow and then you'll have nothing," Davy said spitefully.

"Put your pyjamas in your carrier bag, Davy, and don't put your wet togs on top of them after your swim."

"Pyjamas?" Davy howled. "Are you nuts, Mum? Nobody wears pyjamas these days."

"Your father does."

"Exactly."

She gave him a clip on the ear but she was laughing. She couldn't imagine her lover of last night wearing pyjamas either.

"What are you laughing at, Mum?" Maeve's innocent expression unnerved her.

"Nothing, darling. It's just that your brother has an answer for everything. Now, you get your music books and I'll drop you off at Ms O'Herlihy's. I hope you practised your scales."

At six, Maeve was young to be doing a music exam but the Prelim exam was easy. Maeve adored the piano and never objected to practising. Davy had given it up after a year, protesting that he wanted a life! He was a tonic, that child.

Mary arrived back at the house with Maeve just after four. She'd felt a bit dizzy at the pool and her stomach was churning. She was never going to drink again. Maeve's little friend, Orla, came in to play. Great, that'd give Mary some time to herself.

She went up to the bathroom and found the

Alka Seltzer. She still looked far from human. She put her Eye Dew drops in and her blue eyes actually shone. She washed her hair and had another shower. There, she certainly looked better than she had appeared in the mirror this morning.

She thought she looked different. Ridiculous. She must be imagining it. Infidelity didn't show on the face, did it? She smirked at her reflection. Forget it. It was over. She had to maintain a cool, calm exterior.

Nobody knew . . . she had to remember that. She'd left the others in the night-club. They presumed she'd gone for a taxi. How were they to know she'd arranged to meet his nibs outside? Why couldn't she say his name, even to herself? She guessed that it was because if she pronounced his name once, even in her own mind, it would make the episode more real. Concrete. No, she'd avoid that. She'd treat it like a dream. She'd convince herself it never really happened. Or she'd store it at the back of her mind and feed on the lingering memory when she needed to. It was all in her head now. Nobody would ever know.

Maeve pulled the curtains back. She was eagerly awaiting Sheila's visit. She danced up and down with excitement when Sheila's car pulled into their driveway.

"Here she is, Mum. Here she is." Maeve dashed to the front door to let Sheila in.

She flung herself into Sheila's arms and wrapped her legs around Sheila's waist.

467

"Hang on, love. Don't strangle poor Sheila!"

Mary's warning fell on deaf ears. The little girl clung on and planted kisses all over Sheila's face. Mary extricated her to give Sheila space to breathe. "Don't complain that you get a lukewarm welcome here."

Sheila smiled and handed Maeve her present.

"Can I try it on?" Her little face lit up when she unwrapped the dress.

"May I?"

"Get off the rostrum, Mary Ryan." Sheila slagged her. "You English teachers, always correcting the rest of us mere mortals. We don't worry about grammar, do we honeybunch?" Sheila helped Maeve to undo the buttons on the dress. "Don't mind your Mum, she likes everything to be right and proper."

Mary blushed. If Sheila only knew.

Mary sent out for a pizza. She hadn't eaten all day and suddenly she was starving. She poured wine for Sheila and nearly got sick. "You're very quiet this evening."

"John and I are finished."

"Oh Sheila, you're not serious."

"Yeah, I couldn't hack it, Mary. When it came down to it, I didn't want to be involved. I blame myself for letting it go on so long. It wasn't fair to him."

"I'm very disappointed. Oh, I know I was dead against him at the beginning, but I think you two were good together. You're going to find it strange being on your own again."

"Yeah. In a way I've always felt alone. It's different for you. You and Jim are like two peas in a pod. You're a real family. That's what John wanted, but I couldn't go for it. It's just not me."

Mary nearly puked. She felt two-faced. Sheila had her singled out as the perfect wife. Last night finished that, didn't it? Mary Ryan, adulteress. The scarlet woman. She should have the letter A branded on her breast.

"So, how did your night out with the girls go?" Sheila sucked on an olive.

Mary got up to get an ash-tray. She couldn't let Sheila see her face. She was burning up. "OK. I enjoyed it."

"What were the men like? Not that you'd have noticed anyway. I haven't been to one of those haunts in years. I presume they haven't changed."

"The usual mix. A lot of married men." It suddenly dawned on Mary that her lover was most likely married. Funny that hadn't occurred to her last night. She'd lied. He probably had too.

"Did Gloria meet anyone?" Sheila asked. Gloria frequented these night-clubs a lot. She'd be still on the look-out when she was fifty.

"I don't know," Mary answered quickly. "I left before them."

"I knew it wouldn't be your scene." Sheila finished her pizza, refusing another slice.

"Put on a record, I have to go to the loo." Mary left the room in a hurry. She took the stairs two at a time. She just made it to the bathroom in time. She retched violently into the toilet. God, this was awful.

Never again. She opened the bathroom window. She needed air. She thought she heard a car drive up. Suddenly Maeve ran out of her room, squealing with delight. "Daddy's home. Daddy's home."

Oh, no. It couldn't be Jim. He wasn't due home for two more days.

"How's my best girl?" Jim bounced his daughter on his knee. "I thought you'd be fast asleep at this hour."

Maeve ignored the remark about bedtime. No way was she going to be sent off again and miss all the fun. "Your best girl? Do you mean me or Mum?" Her quizzical expression was priceless.

"I'm not sure. Mum, I suppose, if she was a good girl when I was away."

Mary felt herself redden. For God's sake, get control. He was only joking.

"Mum's always good," Maeve said seriously.

"I know, honey. I was only kidding." Jim kissed the top of her head.

"How come you're home so early?" Sheila asked.

Mary was wondering the exact same thing.

"The hotel was finished before time. I checked it all out. The owners were very pleased. There was no sense in sticking around so I managed to get a seat on the plane tonight. I have to mind my little brood here, Sheila." He smiled at Mary. "I missed you."

"I missed you too." The words stuck in her throat.

Sheila looked on in envy. They were still so close. It was touching.

"Daddy, did you bring back presents?"

"Oh, Maeve pet. I didn't have time. I was rushing for the plane."

The child's face fell. Jim couldn't bear it. "Of course I brought you something back. You don't think I'd forget my best daughter?"

"I'm your only daughter." Maeve got off his lap. She wanted to punish him for teasing her.

"All the more reason I brought you something very special. Look in the bag in the hall." Maeve skipped off gaily, forgetting her annoyance of a moment before.

"Where's my son and heir then? Asleep?"

"He's in Larry's for the night." Mary went down to the kitchen to make coffee. She couldn't wait to get out of the room. Maeve was in the hall playing with her new doll. It cried when you turned it upside down. She was thrilled with it. She ran back to the sitting-room and hugged her father. "Thanks, Dad. She's lovely. I'm going to call her Sheila 'cos she's red hair."

Sheila smiled indulgently at the child. "Thanks, pet. But I think you should call her something more interesting."

"Flopsy?" Maeve suggested immediately.

"Exactly. She's a real Flopsy if I ever saw one." Sheila stood up. "I'd better go, Jim. I'll tell Mary not to bother with coffee for me. I've an early start tomorrow."

"Off to Carrigeen?"

"Yep."

"John OK?" Jim lit a cigar.

471

Sheila took a deep breath. "It's over."

"Oh my God, he'll be devastated." Jim blew out the match.

"He'll get over it, Jim. It's better this way. We didn't want the same things. He always resented my business. It came between us."

Jim empathised. "I know what you mean. To be honest, that's why I came home early. Mary gets addled when I'm away."

Sheila nodded. Jim loved his family. He had his priorities right. They came first with him. That's how it should be. Did Mary realise how lucky she was? She complained that Jim neglected them. It simply wasn't true. He was a very hard worker but his family meant more to him than anything else. Mary was steeped in luck.

Mary took her time clearing the supper dishes . . . delaying tactics. Sheila had left early. Desperate about the break-up. There was something lacking in Sheila. She was too bloody independent. There was no hope now of her ever having a lasting relationship. It wasn't what she wanted. Mary would have to give up on that. Sheila would never marry. Anyhow, who was she to judge? She'd want to get her own house in order.

Jim was taking his shower. God, he was singing. If he woke Maeve again, she'd go mad. Singing in the shower meant only one thing. He wanted to make love. No way could she go through with that. Not after what had happened. What the hell was wrong with her?

Last night, she'd fallen happily into the arms of a total stranger with no compunction at all. She'd let him do things to her that would make a brothel owner blush. She'd let herself go completely. Was she abnormal? Was she a potential nymphomaniac? Now, when her husband wanted to make love, and that's what it was . . . love, she found herself repulsed by the idea. That couldn't be normal, could it? She was utterly confused. She wanted to discuss it with someone . . . she couldn't disclose her feelings to the girls at work. They weren't that close. She couldn't discuss it with Sheila. Sheila would never understand.

If only Joanne were here. She could say anything to her sister and not be judged or criticised. But Joanne was in London.

"Mary, when are you coming up?" Jim was on the landing. She could hear the anticipation in his voice.

"In a few minutes, Jim." She tried to sound as natural as possible.

Could he hear the strain in her voice? Did he suspect anything? Her stomach was still churning. Jesus, this was the pits. She'd pour herself a brandy. So much for never drinking again. Still brandy was medicinal. That might calm her down. What was she going to do?

She simply could not make love to Jim tonight. It was out of the question. She'd made up her mind. But how could she put him off? What could she possibly say? "Sorry love, I've got a headache." No way could she try that one. "I'm not in the mood tonight, darling." Charming. The poor sod came back early and his wife was not in the mood. What about the truth? "You see, Jim. I'm worn out after a night of mad passionate love." That'd do the trick all right. That'd put him off for life. Or how about, "I don't fancy you anymore, Jim. I met a fantastic hunk last night and he taught me what sex should be like. You just don't match up."

Oh God, this was a nightmare. She loved Jim. She did love him. She didn't want to hurt him. This mood was bound to pass in time. She'd get back to normality soon. But tonight was her immediate problem. She couldn't face it tonight. She couldn't look into his eyes and tell him she loved him. She couldn't kiss him after having betrayed him. She didn't want his wet kisses on her mouth. She didn't want his hands exploring her. She'd feel defiled.

Marriage is a sacrament . . . the words went around in her head. Married love is sacramental . . . whom God has joined together let no man put assunder . . . This was what she was taught. This was what she believed.

So, how come she felt like this now? It must be a reaction to last night. She was guilty. Yeah, it was remorse. She'd sort out her head later on. She'd blot it all out of her mind and everything would be OK between them again.

Suddenly she had a brainwave. That was the answer. Why hadn't she thought of it before? She'd tell Jim it was the wrong time of the month. How was he to know that she was not due for another two weeks? The curse would get her off the hook. Relief flooded over Mary as she made her way upstairs.

CHAPTER THIRTY-ONE

"Is she mad or what, Caroline?" Rita stirred her tea. "I mean she'll never get a chance like that again. He was lovely. He was so good to her."

Caroline thought it was better to listen and say as little as possible. Rita didn't want answers anyhow. She wanted a listener.

"First there was Peadar Joyce. Now, why couldn't she have married him? Sure didn't we all know that he was crazy about her. It still galls me when I see that Bridget hanging on his arm. He married her on the rebound, definitely. And the two children. Rather plain, aren't they? Of course she's no oil painting. Sheila would have had beautiful children don't you think?"

"Mmh, without a doubt." Caroline thought of Karen. Was she beautiful? Probably.

"Poor Peadar, he's looking a bit peaky these days. You never know what goes on behind closed doors, do you?" Rita said mysteriously.

"I think they're happy. Bridget's always in good form in work." Caroline couldn't let her mother-in-law away with that.

"Maybe so. But she's not a patch on Sheila. Now

John Harris. Why on earth did she break up with him? I never liked the fact that they were living together at all. It wasn't right. Too easy for the man. He went into that house and hung up his hat, so to speak. Sheila owned everything. Sure what man could stand a chance? A man has to be needed. Sheila likes her own way too much. But I never interfered, did I?" Rita gave Caroline a pointed look.

Caroline had to agree that she hadn't. Sheila wouldn't have stood for it.

"No, I never interfered. Kept my own counsel. But you see I was right. It didn't last. A relationship needs a solid foundation, I always said that. Marriage is the only solid basis for a good match. You know that, Caroline. Sure look at yourself and Seán, as happy as pigs in muck."

Caroline smiled. Not a very complimentary analogy. "We had our problems too."

"Of course you did. Everyone does. That's perfectly normal. None of us is perfect. But you didn't run away from your problems, did you?" Rita put down her cup.

"I did, if you remember." Caroline poured her another cup of tea.

Rita shook her head. "Not at all, you did not. You only did that to give him a fright and it worked, fair play to you. Men have to be guided by us. It's the women who really rule the roost."

Caroline didn't agree with her there.

"I wonder why he gave her up? I suppose we shouldn't be surprised. Anyone who'd leave a wife would leave a girlfriend, no problem. I'd say he had itchy feet. Too good-looking to be reliable." Rita tightened her lips.

Caroline couldn't let that go. "Apparently he wanted to marry Sheila."

"Marry her?" Rita's mouth fell open in astonishment.

"Mmh. Sheila didn't want to." Caroline said flatly.

That knocked Rita for six. "Well, isn't she a very foolish girl? A solicitor. I always liked him. He was the epitome of good breeding. A real gentleman. Where is she going to find another like him?"

"I don't think she wants to find anyone, Rita." Except Karen, Caroline said to herself.

"I know she's my own daughter and I love her dearly, but I have to say I think Sheila is a bit odd."

Caroline wished she had a tape recorder. Sheila would be highly amused by this.

"People want different things out of life. I don't think Sheila was ever interested in marriage."

"Ah, isn't it terrible? Having children is the best thing for a woman. It's natural. Where would you be without the twins?"

"I don't know," Caroline answered truthfully.

"And Sheila's so good with children. Sure she adores Colm and Ciara."

"It's mutual. They really love her. She's a great aunt." Caroline agreed.

"There you are. And she's very good to Mary's children too, isn't she?" Rita persisted.

"I believe so." This was getting awkward for Caroline. There was no way she could sit there and tell Rita that Sheila had never wanted children. Such a lie would choke her.

"I always imagined that some day Sheila would have a baby of her own. This Natural Woman thing is all very fine, but you can't cuddle up to a company, now can you?" Rita looked to Caroline for approbation.

"No, you can't," Caroline said sadly.

"I just pray she won't live to regret this. Imagine, he wanted to marry her. She's an awful headstrong girl. Did she seem upset to you last night?" Rita genuinely cared.

"A bit. It's a wrench for her, Rita. I think she loved John."

"Oh, Caroline. Could you not talk her into taking him back?" Rita took up her message bag.

"I wouldn't even attempt it. You know better than to ask me that," Caroline admonished her.

"No, you needn't look at me that way. I'm going to keep out of it too. I hate to see her hurt, that's all." Rita put down the message bag and sat down again.

"I know you do." If only Rita knew the extent of Sheila's hurt.

"She went off to Carrigeen this morning bright and early. Nothing puts her off her work. She's seeing Bridget about some big order. I can't get over this men's salon. A bit sissyish, don't you think? The men in Dublin must be a funny lot."

"Are you saying the men in Galway aren't?" Caroline grinned.

"No, wasn't I married to one for forty-five years? God rest him."

"You got one of the best, Rita."

"Don't I know it, love. Oh, here's himself. Dr Crosby Junior."

Colm gave his grandmother a kiss. "A bit early to say that, Gran."

"Ah, you flew through your Pre-Med just like your Dad," Rita said proudly. "There again, you didn't lick it off the street, did you?"

"He found the physics hard, didn't you Colm?" Caroline said to her son.

"Yeah, and the biology and chemistry, not to mention the behavioural science."

"Behavioural science? What's that about?" Rita wondered.

"Good question, Gran. Studying this family gave me a head start over the other students."

"Cheeky monkey." Rita smiled. "Are you going to go into practice with your father?"

Colm groaned. "I've at least six more years to do before I decide that. I'll probably specialise. Maybe paediatrics."

Colm went upstairs to change. He'd got a summer job as an orderly in the Regional Hospital. It was great experience.

"God, when you think of it." Rita got as far as the door and then stopped for another chat. It generally took her about a half an hour to leave. "Remember when he'd no interest in anything but football? Who'd have thought it? Another doctor in the family. Of course the Crosbys were very clever."

"Maybe he inherited my brains?" Caroline smiled sweetly at her.

"Oh? eh . . . maybe he did." Rita scurried down the path.

"Ciara, Sheila wants you to talk to you." Seán handed the phone to his daughter and went upstairs to Caroline in her workroom. She was working on a poster for a new aftershave.

"You never told me Molly was leaving the office in Carrigeen." He glanced at her work. "That's good. Eye-catching."

"Molly's going to the States with her boyfriend. He got a job in a big printing corporation. We'll miss her."

"Sheila's going to offer the receptionist job to Ciara. Why didn't you say anything?"

"Didn't know how you'd take it." She put down her pen and looked at him. "What do you think about it?"

"It's up to Ciara. She doesn't like the hotel. Maybe Carrigeen would suit her better. How would you feel about working with her though?"

"Great. We're on the same wavelength."

"That's for sure." He smiled. "From the time she started talking she sounded like you. I never stood a chance between the pair of you."

"Sheila's hoping she'll say yes. You know the way she likes keeping things in the family."

"Mmh. I'm not sure it's a good idea. Still, Ciara has to make up her own mind. She'll need transport. When is she doing her driving test?"

"Next month. I'll bring her until then." That would mean Caroline leaving early in the morning again. "It'll only be for a few weeks."

"Can she afford to buy a car?" Seán doubted it.

"She's been saving like mad." Caroline was proud of Ciara.

"The insurance will cost a bomb." Seán warned.

"I'll give her a present of that." Was he going to object?

Seán scratched his head. He couldn't really put up an argument. Ciara hadn't wanted to go to university. He was surprised. She'd been a brilliant student in school. She did the receptionist course and got a job immediately in a local hotel. She liked having her own money. He didn't argue with that. She was a good kid.

Ciara burst into the room. "Mum! Dad! Sheila's offered me a job." She hugged Caroline. "I can't believe it. I'm thrilled. I'll have to work out my notice and then I can tell that snotbag where to stick her job." Ciara waltzed around the room.

"Welcome aboard, love." Caroline was delighted.

"Are you sure it's what you want, Ciara?" Seán was still cautious.

"Oh Dad, I've always wanted to work for Sheila."

"You'll be working for me, darling," Caroline reminded her.

"Your mother's a hard taskmaster. She likes to crack the whip," Seán joked.

"You should be so lucky, Dad." Ciara laughed

and winked at him. "I'm off to ring Stephen. I can't wait to tell him." She ran out of the room.

"Did she say what I think she said?" Seán was shocked. "My God, she's only a child."

"She's nineteen, Seán. They're not as innocent as we were."

* * *

Sheila was very pleased. Ciara would be an asset to the company. She'd practically grown up with it. It was in her blood. She had a good manner too. She'd relate well to customers and clients.

Rita was sewing in the kitchen. "How did it go with Bridget today?"

"Fine." Sheila went to the fridge for a cold beer.

"I never liked that girl," Rita said bitchily.

"Mam, come on now. She's brilliant at her job. She's very creative. She's responsible for all the new ranges." Sheila sat down opposite her mother.

"Ah, she learned everything she knows from you." Rita was scornful.

"Me and Peadar. She was one of his brightest students. He always said that." Sheila tilted the glass as she poured the beer. That way it had a nice head.

"Oh, she's bright all right. And downright cute." Rita bit the thread off.

That always irked Sheila. Why couldn't she use a scissors? It was funny the way silly things could get on your nerves.

"When are you going back to Dublin?" Rita asked.

"In the morning. Would you like to come back with me for a few days?" God, that slipped out. Sheila hadn't meant to say that.

"Do you mean it, Sheila?" Rita's face lit up. "Oh, that'd be grand. I haven't been to Dublin for ages. Are you sure I wouldn't be putting you out?"

"No, you wouldn't. I'll have to work though," Sheila warned her.

"Oh I know that. Sure I can do the shops, as they say. I've a few old cronies left there too. Remember Annie Moore?" Rita put the thread back in the sewing basket.

"No." Sheila couldn't keep up with her mother's never-ending list of cronies.

"Ah, you do," Rita insisted. "She married that fella she was in digs with in the forties. He was a bit of an eejit but he left her very well off."

Sheila hadn't a notion who she was talking about.

"I'll give her a ring. And I'll have to visit Mary and Jim. I was always very fond of Mary. I'm dying to see her kiddies." Rita planned to make the most of her time in the city.

Sheila knew that Mary wouldn't mind. She liked Rita. "Right, pack a bag."

"I'm not bringing much stuff." Rita folded the pillowcase she'd been stitching.

"How long are you going to stay?" Sheila was almost afraid to ask that.

"A week, if that's OK?" Rita looked at her.

"Great. But you'll need a few changes of clothes if you intend to do all that visiting." Sheila smiled.

"I'm going to get myself a whole new wardrobe, my girl. The mother of Natural Woman has to keep up the side."

God help her, Sheila thought. It was easy to please her. "Right, Mam. You go up to bed and have a good night's rest." Sheila kissed her. "I want to leave at eight in the morning before the traffic."

Sheila didn't particularly like the thought of her mother spending a whole week with her, but the old lady needed a break too. She'd been very good over the past few years and Sheila appreciated her kindness. The older she got the better she got on with her mother. She'd bring her to the theatre. They could go for a meal another night. Rita loved eating out. She loved Sheila being recognised wherever they went. She was innocent in lots of ways. No, Rita wasn't the worst.

"Caroline?" Rita whispered into the phone. It was dead handy having this extension in her bedroom. Sheila had insisted on it for security reasons, but Rita found it useful for making secret calls.

"Is that you, Rita? I can barely hear you. Are you all right?"

"I don't want Sheila to hear me."

"Oh?" More intrigue. Rita loved these games.

"I'm off to Dublin tomorrow for a week. Sheila asked me up and I didn't like to say no." Rita confided to Caroline.

Caroline could believe that all right. Rita wouldn't pass up on that chance.

"Yes," Rita continued. "I think she's a bit lonely going back to that big barracks of a house on her own. It's understandable, isn't it? She'll be missing John and she could do with some company. We all need our families in times of crisis."

Caroline didn't think this was Sheila's motivation, but sure let the old dear think what she liked. "You're very good, Rita."

"Well if her own mother couldn't be good to her, I don't know."

"True." Caroline tried to sound sincere.

"Anyhow I can keep an eye on her, see that she doesn't work too hard. I can do some of the cooking." Rita said with great satisfaction.

Caroline could imagine Sheila's reaction to that. "Great. Well, have a good time. Let us know what train you're coming back on and we'll meet you at the station."

"Right. I'll phone you and let you know how things are going on." Rita stressed the last four words.

"Do that. Bye, Rita."

"Bye, pet." Rita was still whispering.

Seán got into bed and snuggled up to Caroline. "Was that Mam?"

"Yeah, she's going to stay a week with Sheila," Caroline murmured sleepily.

"What brought that on?" Seán put his arm around her.

"I'm not sure. Sheila must have asked her on the

spur of the moment." Caroline shifted her position. Seán's bony arm dug into her.

"Definitely." Seán moved back onto his own pillow.

"It'll leave us free at the weekend," Caroline thought aloud.

"Good point. Why don't we go away ourselves?" Seán propped himself up on his elbow.

"Where?" Caroline was getting interested.

"Anywhere. Somewhere relaxing and romantic." Seán leered at his wife.

"I'd be on for that," Caroline sounded enthusiastic. "Somewhere near. I don't want to have a long drive."

"Why not book in for two nights to the Ardilaun?" Seán suggested.

"Are you serious?" Caroline thought he must be joking.

"Yeah." Seán couldn't see why not.

"We'd keep bumping into people we know. It wouldn't be a proper break." Caroline was dismissive of the idea.

"We wouldn't bump into them in our bedroom." He leaned over and nibbled her ear.

Caroline pushed him away. "Seán Crosby, are you suggesting we stay two days in a hotel room?"

"Why not?" Seán smiled to himself.

"Ya randy old thing." Caroline punched him.

"Let's face it, Caroline. We don't get much privacy here."

"That's true." Caroline thought about it more seriously.

"It'd be like a second honeymoon," Seán said dreamily.

"Except for the varicose veins." Caroline laughed.

"We won't see them in the dark." Seán wouldn't let her ruin the image. He turned out the light. "Are you on for a practise run?" He reached for her.

Caroline pushed him away. "No, save your energies till the weekend."

Ciara couldn't sleep. She was too excited. She was actually escaping from that kip and the wagon of a manageress. Working in Carrigeen! It was a dream come true. It'd be a huge raise in salary too. Sheila was very generous with her employees. With Stephen's promotion in the travel agency they'd be earning good money between them. He reckoned they could get married on her twenty-first in two years time. They'd have to save like hell though.

Ciara imagined her future. Carrigeen and Stephen. They'd buy a nice little cottage somewhere. They'd have children. She wondered if twins were hereditary. She'd have to ask her dad. How would he react to her marrying Stephen? Her mother'd be all right but Dr Seán Crosby mightn't be impressed. He didn't think Stephen was good enough for her. He wouldn't relish the idea of being a grandfather either. Ciara giggled under the blankets. Gran would be a great-grandmother. That'd tickle her pink. Ciara fell asleep picking out names for her unborn children.

CHAPTER THIRTY-TWO

Sheila hadn't seen Mary for over two months, not since Rita spent her week in Dublin. She'd been a bit strange during their visit, not as chatty as she usually was. Even Rita noticed. Every time Sheila tried to make an arrangement to meet her since then, Mary put her off. She sounded edgy and short-tempered on the phone. Had Sheila done something to upset her? She couldn't think of anything. Perhaps Mary just needed a break. Sheila was due in Grasse the following week. Wouldn't it be brilliant if Mary could go with her? She'd phone and ask her now.

"Hi Jim. Mary in?" Sheila's tone was chirpy.

"Hi, Sheila. No, she's not here. She's gone to London to see Joanne," Jim replied.

"Oh that's good." Sheila couldn't make out his tone.

"Yeah, ah she needed some time to herself." Jim tried to keep his voice light.

"Mmh," Sheila agreed. "I was a bit concerned. She hasn't been in good form lately."

Jim hesitated, "No, she hasn't."

Sheila wanted to sound him out. "I was going to

ask her to come to France with me next week, but the holiday in London will probably be better for her. She hasn't seen Joanne for a long time."

"Yeah, she misses Joanne. To tell you the truth I think she's quite depressed." Jim was clearly worried.

Sheila tried to cheer him up. "So do I. A while away from the kids and the house will do her the power of good."

"Yeah." Jim didn't sound that convinced. "I think it goes deeper than that. Anyway Joanne might get to the bottom of it. How are you?"

Sheila answered quickly, "Oh, busy, you know." She hesitated. "Have you seen John?"

Jim paused. "Once or twice. He's OK I think."

Sheila had to ask this. "Does he ever mention me?"

"No." Jim coughed. He was embarrassed.

"Just as well. When will Mary be back?"

"The day after tomorrow. I'll get her to phone you," Jim promised.

"Thanks, Jim. How are you coping with the kids?"

"A bottle of vodka a day. No, everything's fine. My mother's staying," Jim explained.

"You have my sympathies!" Jim's mother was a terrible fuss-pot.

"Ah, she means well. The kids get on great with her except Davy hasn't had so many baths in his whole life." Jim felt sorry for the child.

Sheila laughed.

"Right, I'll get her to call you, Sheila. Take it easy," Jim said by way of goodbye.

"You too." Sheila hung up.

Jim sounded worried himself. What was up with Mary? She frequently gave out about being left on her own. She often cribbed about Jim. But he seemed to think it was more serious this time. He was doing the best he could by the sound of it. Hopefully Joanne would sort her out. Mary just didn't seem the type to suffer from depression. When things went wrong, she used to bounce back. Was it the thought of going back to school? Fourteen years in the one job might have taken their toll. Mary gave herself to others all the time. her students, her children, her husband. It was time she took something for herself. A bit of self-indulgence never did anyone harm. Sheila'd suggest that next year she should take a career break.

* * *

Sheila spent four days with Yves and Sophie. They gave her a huge welcome. Yves was very circumspect. It was seven years now since he'd tried to seduce her. Sheila still got a kick out of the thought of that. Sophie knew what her husband was like because she kept making jibes at him and winking at Sheila. But there was no sign of animosity between them.

Sheila had to increase her order for most of the essential oils. She was well known now in the area and had made good friends. Gaston and Claudette invited her to a large dinner party in their home in Cannes. The last time Sheila had met Yves's brother was on the yacht in Monte Carlo. Claudette was still trying to pair her off with one of the jet set. She invited her latest protégé, Pierre Thibaud, a shipping tycoon. Sheila was polite, but she wasn't interested.

On her third day Sophie drove Sheila to a beautiful place called Valensole. Fields of wild lavender stretched as far as the eye could see. Sheila was bowled over. Perched on long stems, the tiny purple-blue flowers were covered with star-shaped hairs and the narrow leaves were grey/green. What a sight! What a fantastic poster this would make for Natural Woman. When they got back to Antibes, Yves promised to get a professional photographer to take pictures. Sheila couldn't wait to show her find to Caroline. These photos alone would make her trip to France worthwhile.

* * *

Sheila had always used lavender oil for her massages. Lavender had a positive effect on psychological disorders as well as having marvellous skin healing properties. She remembered Mary's wedding morning when she gave the nervous bride a lavender massage. Mary said it had worked. Eileen used it in the male salon for burns and sunburn. She treated some of her customers for acne, eczema, psoriasis, others for abscesses, boils and fungal growths. One man told her it had cured a scar which he'd had for years. Bridget made up hair tonic from it which another customer swore improved his hair growth.

When she got the photos from Yves she posted them to Caroline. Her sister-in-law phoned back immediately.

"These are magnificent, Sheila. I've the art department working on them. We could use them for our outdoor advertising campaign, billboards and the buses."

Sheila pictured lavender buses zooming through the traffic.

"We've used the rose, the rosemary, the violet, the jasmine, the geranium and some of the others. Why did we never think of lavender for our advertising?"

"Usually our designs are small and simple. The sprig of rosemary worked very well. So did the single rose. But when I stood there gazing at that whole field of lavender, I was stunned. It's so rich and colourful. You can almost smell the fragrance from those pictures. They'll look wonderful on posters. We'll stick with the sprig motif for our jars and bottles." Sheila knew exactly what she wanted.

"Oh definitely. I thought the lettering on the posters should be in silver." Caroline could see it clearly.

"Perfect." Sheila agreed.

"OK. I'll send you up the designs next week at the latest. How's everything else?"

"Fine. Mary's coming over tonight." Sheila didn't tell Caroline how worried she was about Mary.

"Give her my best," Caroline said automatically. Her mind was already back on the posters.

Mary arrived at nine. Sheila got a shock when she saw her. She looked ten years older. She'd lost a lot of weight, but it didn't suit her. She was scrawny. Her hair was dull and her skin had a deathly pallor. Sheila hugged her. She felt so fragile that Sheila thought her bones would break.

"My God, Mary. What's happened to you?"

"I haven't been well." Mary took off her jacket and sat on the sofa. Without the coat she looked even smaller and more frail.

Sheila handed her a large brandy.

Mary lit a cigarette and exhaled loudly. She seemed distant. Unreachable.

"You look very run-down." Sheila couldn't keep the concern from her voice.

"I am. The doctor has me on a tonic."

"Jesus, it doesn't seem to be working."

Silence.

"How did you get on with Joanne?" Mary's sister must have got an awful shock to see her in this condition.

"She was very good to me." Mary's voice was flat. Sheila had to drag the words out of her.

"What did the doctor say was wrong?" Sheila had to know.

"Nervous exhaustion," Mary said almost dismissively.

Sheila nodded. She'd better shut up and not push on with this. It was clear that Mary couldn't discuss it.

"Thanks for the invite to France. I wouldn't have been up to it, though." Mary sighed.

Sheila brushed it off. "Oh, it doesn't matter. It was only a thought. You can come with me the next time."

Mary stubbed out the cigarette. "I'm sorry I'm being such a pain. I can't pull myself out of it. The doctor said it'd take time."

Sheila searched for something appropriate to say. How could she help if she didn't know what the matter was? "How are the kids?"

"Fine." Quite unexpectedly tears sprang to Mary's eyes.

God, Sheila thought. What is wrong? Why would the mention of the children upset her so much? "I hope you're not thinking of going back to school next week? You'll have to get a cert, Mary."

Mary shook her head. "No way. I'm looking forward to going back. School keeps me sane. I haven't missed a day in years and I'm not going to start now."

Sheila was appalled. How could she even think she was going to be able to stand in front of a class and teach? She could barely speak. She'd never cope with seven or eight classes of giddy schoolgirls. It was impossible.

"I wonder what Karen is going to do. Will she go to college?" Sheila thought a change of topic might ease things.

"Mmh. If she's as clever and determined as you, she'll do all right," Mary said but there was no real feeling behind her words.

"I hope she will. I've been thinking about starting the search for her." Sheila studied her friend's expression.

Mary perked up a bit. "Oh, I think you should, Sheila."

"Now mightn't be a good time. She's at a crossroads in her life." Sheila bit her lip thoughtfully.

Mary sat up suddenly. "There'll never be a right time. I think you should go for it. Where would you start?"

"I'm not sure," Sheila admitted. "The Adoption Board, maybe. They mightn't be able to help but it's worth a try."

"It certainly is. Seventeen years of not knowing . . . I don't know how you stuck it." Mary lit another cigarette. She was chain-smoking.

"Maybe she won't want to meet me?" Sheila said anxiously. "Maybe she resents me."

"Resents you? Why would she do that?" Mary got agitated.

"Maybe she thinks I abandoned her. I did, in a way," Sheila said sadly.

"Jesus, we've been through all this before. You did not abandon her." Mary was angry with Sheila.

Why was Mary so vehement? Sheila felt as if she were being told off. Mary had never treated her so impatiently before. Sheila tried to make light of it. "I'm not going to rush into anything. I wouldn't want to do anything to hurt Karen or her family. I'll just make some initial inquiries. I'm going to approach the whole thing very cautiously."

Mary raised her eyes to heaven. "Crap. Make up your mind and and do something. Fecking around won't help."

God, Mary wasn't herself at all. Sheila'd have to get off this subject fast. "Ah, I'll think about it for a while longer. As I said, Karen may not want to have anything to do with me and I have to be prepared for that. I know you think I'm being silly, but I still think she might feel as if I betrayed her. I gave her away. That might be all she sees. What did I ever give her in real terms? Nothing."

Sheila was about to put on a record when suddenly Mary jumped up off the couch. "You gave her a life, Sheila. You went through agony. You were frightened and alone. Then you made the bravest decision of all. You gave Karen a family. Will you stop traumatising about betrayal and abandonment. I'm sick of it."

Sheila nearly died. What the hell was going on? Mary started to pace the room, up and back, biting her thumb. "You gave her a life, Sheila."

"Sit down, Mary. I didn't mean to upset you." Sheila was actually getting frightened.

Mary sat down and took a long gulp from her glass. "I can't sit here and let you go on with this bullshit. I can't take it."

Take what? God Almighty, was she cracking up altogether? Sheila couldn't answer her. She thought Mary was losing her mind.

"There you are, saying the most stupid things. You betrayed your daughter. Bloody rubbish. You abandoned her. God, you haven't a clue, have you?"

Sheila stared at her in horror.

"You didn't kill your baby, did you? Not like me. I killed my baby; the slaughter of the innocent. Jesus, you don't know the meaning of guilt."

What was she saying? She'd definitely gone over the edge. Sheila thought she should ring Jim.

"No, don't stare at me as if I were raving. I'm telling you the truth. I hadn't intended to, but I've got to get it off my chest."

"I don't understand, Mary," Sheila said very gently. She felt thick, really thick.

"No, you wouldn't. I don't understand it myself, but it's quite simple really. I killed my baby. I'm a murderess. What do you think of your lovely friend now?" She defied Sheila to answer.

"You killed a baby? Mary, that's impossible. You wouldn't hurt a fly. You love kids. You've given your life to children, your own and other people's. Has the doctor got you on some medication? It must be the drugs you're on. They're making you confused." Sheila was clutching at straws. She'd try to get to the phone to ring Jim.

"Medication! I wish it were that bloody simple. No, I'm not confused, Sheila. Everything is as clear as crystal in my head. Unfortunately."

"Mary, if you'd rather not talk about this . . ."

"I have to talk about it. I'm tired of being in denial. I'm fed up with all the pretence and the sham. You thought I went to London for a holiday, right?" Mary stared at Sheila.

Sheila nodded.

"Believe me it was no holiday. It was a

nightmare . . . I had an abortion." Mary broke down and sobbed bitterly. Sheila ran over and cradled her in her arms. Mary cried for a full five minutes. It was harrowing. She accepted another brandy and wiped her eyes with the tissue she'd been clutching. Shakily, she went on. "When I found out I was pregnant, I panicked. I couldn't have another child."

Sheila still didn't get it. "I know you both decided on two children years ago, but surely Jim wouldn't have minded? He adores Davy and Maeve. He'd have welcomed another baby, Mary. I'm sure of it." Feck it, why had she said that? Mary turned to her. "Another man's baby? I doubt if he'd be that welcoming."

"Another . . . Mary, what are you saying?"

"Jim had a vasectomy four years ago. I couldn't have another child because *we* couldn't. Now do you understand?"

Sheila nodded blankly. Silence. Finally Sheila came out with the unmentionable. "An affair?"

"Hardly." Mary laughed scornfully. "It was that blasted night in Lesson Street. One time, I swear it."

No need to swear for Sheila. Once was all it took for her too.

"I know there's no excuse for what I did, but I never meant any harm. I was lonely and fed up. I wanted a bit of excitement. I sure got it. Selfish bitch, amn't I? They should have a government health warning on those places. They're dangerous. Drink is dangerous."

Amen to that, Sheila thought. "So, I thought I'd got away with my secret night of passion and then

. . . bingo. Pregnant. I couldn't believe it. At the start I toyed with the idea of leaving Jim. I thought I'd tell him the truth and accept the consequences. But I love him, Sheila. I know that sounds absurd after what I've just told you, but I do love him." The tears ran down Mary's face.

"I know you do." Sheila had her arms around Mary. She patted her shoulder, trying desperately to give her some comfort.

"And what about Davy and Maeve? What would happen to them? Why should they suffer? They're totally innocent. Jim was totally innocent. How could I break up my family?" Mary started to cry again.

Sheila could think of nothing to say. Abortion. The horror of it.

"So, I had to make a choice," Mary continued, her voice still shaking. "It was either the unborn child or the family I love. Joanne came with me. She didn't judge me. She didn't offer advice. She just stood by me and tried to piece me together. The place was clinical and efficient. They did the job. I was no longer pregnant. Problem gone. But it isn't gone, Sheila. I'll never be able to live with it. I butchered my own baby. Every time I look at the kids, I wonder would the baby have looked like them. I'm guilty of murder. My own child. I'll never forgive myself. Never."

Sheila hugged her and stroked her hair. Words would have been cheap at a time like this. Sheila wouldn't insult her by mouthing inane platitudes. Darkness fell, but Sheila wouldn't let her go, even to switch on the light. They sat in the glow of the street lamps for a long time. Finally Mary started to doze. She was exhausted.

Sheila rang Jim and told him Mary was staying the night. She put her in the lavender room and tucked her up like a child. Mary was as vulnerable as a child. She was broken by her horrific experience. She'd have to come to grips with what had happened and for that she'd need counselling. Tomorrow, Sheila would find out the name of a good psychiatrist. She'd insist that Mary went. It was going to be a long haul and it was going to be terribly hard.

Sheila went back to the sitting-room and put on a record. She'd never be able to sleep. She was drained. She pitied Mary from the bottom of her heart. To think of the way she used to envy Mary with her idyllic marriage and her beautiful children. It was such a shame. It was cruel. How would Mary ever get that closeness back with Jim? She was effectively living a lie now and she knew it. Lies and deception . . . how could a marriage survive? Mary was not the deceptive type at all. Quite the contrary. If guilt didn't destroy her, the deceit might. She'd have to be handled with kid gloves. Sheila thought of the tiny mite Mary had destroyed. Terrible images of pain and bloodshed flooded her brain.

A new life wiped out. Sheila sat and wept for the terrible loss. She walked over to the mantelpiece and picked up the photo of Mary's wedding. There they stood in all their finery in the grounds of Iona Church: Mary and Jim glowing with happiness, Sheila smiling for the camera, Paul, the proud best man. Sheila thought back to the joy of that day. Maurice O'Callaghan boasting proudly of his little girl. Emily O'Callaghan delighted with her new son-in-law. The Ryans drinking to the happy future of their only son and his beautiful bride. Everyone at that wedding was convinced that Jim and Mary were made for each other. They were deeply in love. They were young and full of hope.

Davy's birth. Mary and Jim surrounded by friends and family welcoming the new arrival. The marriage had been blessed. A year later, Maeve. The perfect family. Oh God, why did this have to happen?

Sheila didn't excuse Mary. There was no excuse. Mary said that herself. But she did deserve compassion. What was the point in judging her? She was hard enough on herself. She would punish herself for the rest of her life. Sheila couldn't harden her heart against her. How could she? Mary was her best friend. She was always there for Sheila or for anyone else who was in trouble.

What about the religious aspect? Sheila had given up on religion after the adoption, but Mary was still a practising Catholic. Abortion was what used to be called a mortal sin. Mary disagreed with the Pope on many issues, but not on that one. Human life had to be prized above all. Sheila agreed. Would Mary feel alienated from her Church now too? What about that friend of hers, Father

Lacey? Could he help her? Would she confide in him? Probably not.

Sheila thought about Karen. She saw everything in a new light now. Mary was right. She had given life to her child. She hadn't abandoned her. She had protected her. She had given her away in order to give her a better life. Karen would understand. She wouldn't blame her. Sheila would find her and try to make up for the lost years. It was true what they said, where there's life there's hope.

Where there's life . . . that was no consolation for Mary. She had wiped out that life, she had given her baby no chance. But Mary was thinking of other lives too. A lot of what she'd said rang true for Sheila. Mary was no coward. She'd have faced up to the situation if she'd been the only one to be considered. But she wasn't. There was Jim. He'd have been shattered. There were Davy and Maeve. How could she ruin their lives? Oh God, what a choice she'd been forced to make.

Tomorrow, Sheila would find help for Mary. Maybe some day she'd recover. She'd never be able to forgive herself or forget. She'd never try to justify her desperate act. But maybe she'd get the strength to accept it . . . deep down, Sheila doubted it.

CHAPTER THIRTY-THREE

Karen had a fantastic Christmas. There had been plenty of parties and socialising. Many of her new friends had flats in town. She had changed since her Leaving Cert three years before. She was certainly more optimistic because she was finally on the way to realising her ambitions. It hadn't been easy. Sheer determination spurred her on.

She'd done the interview for the journalism course in Rathmines. She was delighted with her Leaving results and took it for granted she'd be accepted for the course. She wasn't. At first she ranted and raved and felt sorry for herself, but Liz persuaded her not to give up. She could try again the following year.

Karen went to Paris for a year to work and to improve her French. She found a job in a café. She rented a tiny apartment with a Swiss girl and fell in love with Jean Luc. Where better to learn about love than in the romantic capital of the world? Jean Luc got rid of her inhibitions and her bitterness. They hung out together on the Rive Gauche. They ate in cheap restaurants in Montmartre. Jean Luc was studying literature at the Sorbonne. His friends were idealistic and full of life and new ideas. A new world opened up for Karen. She grew up. She realised how spoiled and peevish she'd been. How had her family put up with her?

She came back to Ireland in the summer of '85 a different person. Her biggest concern was how she could make it up to Liz and Frank. She'd been stupid and selfish, but it wasn't too late. She vowed things would be different from then on. She flew through the interview the second time. She remembered it proudly. She was assertive, but not aggressive, as she'd been the first time.

Now in '87 she'd finished her course and was free-lancing for a local paper. It wasn't the height of success, but at least she had her foot in the door. Who knew where she'd end up? In the meantime she was getting experience. God, she'd come up to tidy her room and here she was reminiscing! She'd better sort out all these papers and lecture notes. She'd file them neatly in order. She might need to consult them again and anyway, Karen hated throwing out things. She was a hoarder.

"Karen, Paula's on the phone." Liz came into the room. The floor was strewn with papers. "My God, do you want a hand?"

"I wouldn't say no," Karen replied as she went to talk to Paula.

Liz was dismayed. Where to start? She didn't want to disturb anything. She wasn't sure which bundle of notes went with the other. The problem solved itself when Karen came back.

"Here, Mum, all these here are the newspaper

law lectures. Jesus, the lecturer was a hoot! We'd a great laugh in his class."

Liz flinched at Karen's taking the name of the Lord in vain, but she said nothing. It was a terrible habit. "OK, I'll put them in this folder. How's Paula?"

"In great form. We're going to see a film tonight." Karen knelt down beside her mother.

"Good. What are these?" Liz picked up another bundle.

"My French notes and essays." Karen was proud of them.

"That was your best subject, wasn't it?" Liz put the pages in a neat bundle.

"Absolutely. That year away was a godsend. I've you to thank for that."

Liz smiled. "I regretted it for a while. I thought I was going to lose you to Jean Luc."

"No chance. Oh, watch out, don't step on the practical journalism lectures. They're the most important for what I'm at now." Karen retrieved her prize possessions.

"What are they about?" Liz asked.

"Writing skills, newspaper production, ethics . . . all that stuff." Karen didn't want to go into lengthy explanations.

"Remember you loved the radio journalism course? I could see you yet in broadcasting. You'd be a natural," Liz said proudly.

"God, I'd love that. The future Marian Finucane!" Karen said excitedly.

Liz couldn't see Karen in that role. "She's brilliant. She has a great way with people."

"Yeah. Blast her anyway!" Karen laughed.

"It's funny to think you've finished, Karen." Liz sounded sad. "You really loved Rathmines, didn't you?"

"It was brilliant. I'm sorry I dropped the central and local government course after first year. It was very interesting. The only subjects I didn't like were the shorthand/typing and the business and finance." Karen made a face.

"You hated business studies in school too, remember poor Mrs O'Loughlin?"

"I'd rather forget her, if you don't mind," Karen drawled.

"You're terrible!" Liz had to laugh. "Whatever happened to that nice fellow, Chris Moore?"

"Got into RTE, lucky beggar," Karen said enviously.

"They were all nice in Rathmines, weren't they?" Liz had met a few of them during the two years Karen was there.

"Yeah, we were all close. Much better craic being in a class of thirty than being anonymous in a huge lecture room in university." Karen had heard stories from other friends.

"I'd say so. You'd know each other very well after the two years." Liz filed the last bundle of notes.

"Yeah, warts and all." Karen smiled.

"There, finished at last." Liz stood up. "Will they fit in your press?"

"Yeah, I'll shove them up on top. Thanks, Mum. It would have taken all afternoon without your help."

"I feel like some air. I think I'll go for a walk in the park." Liz stretched.

"I'll come with you. Stick on the kettle first. We'll have a cuppa. I'll just change these jeans. I'll be down in a sec." Karen felt like a walk herself.

* * *

Paula and Karen went for a drink after the cinema. The Sackville Lounge was as handy as anywhere. It was small and friendly with long leather couch seats, wooden panelling and mirrors advertising Paddy. The pub sat about fifty people at the max. Karen got their beers.

"Janey, I needed that." Paula took a big swig. "I'm in bits after that film. I thought she'd never bloody die."

The film in question was *Fatal Attraction* with Glenn Close and Michael Douglas.

"It's a lesson for married men, isn't it? God, he was a terrible creep, but he didn't deserve that." Paula chewed her gum with gusto. "What did you think of it, Karen?"

Karen's lips were tightly set. "I didn't like the message of that film. I thought it let men off the hook."

"Off the hook? No way." Paula took another swig. "His poor wife was nearly killed. The little girl was kidnapped. Even the shagging rabbit ended up in the stew. God, it was disgusting."

507

"But what did it say about women? What are we meant to think? That men shouldn't have affairs because they might end up with a raving psychotic. It'd put any man off all right, but not for the right reasons." Karen thought the film was desperate. Cheap thrills. An unclear moral. Tawdry.

"Ah, I thought it was great. Real scary." Paula shivered.

"How's work going?" Karen thought this'd be a safer subject. Paula would know what she was talking about.

"Great. I had a few weirdos in today. One woman wanted a frizzy perm. She had dead straight hair and I warned her it mightn't take. She looked desperate after it, like a floor mop. But the customer's always right. Then a woman with curls wanted straight hair. Jesus, there's no pleasing them. They expect us to be miracle workers. And shrinks."

"Pardon?" Karen thought she'd misheard.

"Shrinks. They tell us all their problems. I swear if I'd a fiver for every bit of advice I dish out, I'd be a fecking millionaire." Paula secretly loved the chats.

Karen tried to imagine asking advice of Paula. She'd need to be desperate. Let's face it, Paula was nice, but she was no Anthony Clare.

"How's the writing going, Karen?"

"Ah, it's Mickey Mouse stuff I do. I was down in the courts last week. Boring." Karen didn't want to discuss it.

"I thought that'd be terribly exciting. One of the girls in work was called to jury service. She said it was really interesting. A stabbing case. Of course she couldn't give us any details. Sworn to secrecy and all that." Paula got two more beers.

"How's Steve?" Karen didn't really want to know but she thought it would be polite to ask.

"Great. There's a job for a buyer coming up and he thinks he might go for it. I mean he's in that shop now for four years. There's nothing he doesn't know about men's clothes. He's a real snazzy dresser, isn't he?" Paula thought that Karen would agree.

Karen gulped. Steve Clarke had no taste. He was all flash. Of course that appealed to Paula.

"Karen, you should come in for a trim. You've split ends. You're wrecking that gorgeous hair of yours. God, I'd kill to have hair like yours." Paula had always admired Karen's auburn tresses. Her own hair was a mixture of blonde, strawberry and brown.

She wasn't exactly a good ad for the hair colour industry, Karen thought. "I'll nip in when I've time. Maybe next week. I don't want it cut though."

Paula was horrified. "I wouldn't dream of cutting it. I'll just trim the ends, like I said. How's your ma?"

"Flying. I went to the park with her today." Karen handed Paula a cigarette.

Paula leaned over to light it. "You're getting on much better with your folks these days."

"Yeah, they're sound." Karen agreed.

"I always liked your parents. They're very good to you, Karen. My auld lad's not bad if he didn't spend all his time in the pub." Paula sighed.

"But you get on well with your mother, Paula."

"So, so. Not as well as you get on with yours. There are too many of us at home. I'd love to get a flat but I couldn't afford it," Paula said in desperation.

"What about sharing with Steve?" Karen suggested.

Paula was shocked. "No way. No way would I live with a man. Not till he signed the contract anyway. If he wants me he can bloody well marry me."

Karen could see her point. Too many people nowadays had a liberal attitude. "I'd like to share with you."

"You would?" Paula got excited. "Jesus, that'd be great."

"I can't afford to at the moment though. I've a chance of getting a sub-editing job at night in the *Press*. If that comes off I'd seriously think about it." Karen meant it.

"When'll you know?" Paula's excitement rose.

"Not till next month." Karen hoped she'd know by then.

"We'd need to save for the deposit," Paula said. "They usually ask for a month's rent in advance."

"OK. We're not in any rush. I'm not going to move into the first kip we see. And I'll have to prepare the ground at home. See how they take to the idea." Karen said.

"That's understandable. Janey, they won't even notice at home if I move out. The younger ones'll be fighting over the bed." Paula laughed.

"Well now we've something to plan for." Karen liked the idea more and more. She'd love to move out and be independent. "When I'm not living at home, it'll be easier for me to look for my mother."

Paula was surprised. Karen hadn't mentioned that in years. Paula thought she'd given up on the idea. "You're still going to go ahead? I think you're mad."

Karen stared at her. "Why?"

"Don't know. You might open up a whole can of worms. What you don't know won't hurt you, that's what I believe." Paula thought Karen was playing with fire.

"That's not always true," Karen said wistfully. "It's different for you, Paula. You know who you are, where you came from. You can trace your family back if you want to."

"Believe me I don't want to. I remember Granny Taylor and I don't want to go any further back. She was a right nutter. She drank Guinness all day and she smelt something awful. She was like that character in the story . . . remember?" Paula searched for the name.

"'The Confirmation Suit'?" Karen informed her.

"Yeah. Poor kid, I understood him completely. Relations can be an embarrassment."

Karen was amazed. Sometimes Paula could be very astute.

"I think you should leave well enough alone, Karen."

"Perhaps. But I can't stop wondering about her," Karen said softly.

"Yeah." Paula sighed. "I'd be the same, I suppose. Do whatever you think is right. But I wouldn't go expecting too much. You might never find her."

"I'm prepared for that," Karen said after some thought.

"What if you do find her and . . ." Paula stopped.

Karen said it for her. "She doesn't want to see me?"

"Well, it is a possibility," Paula murmured.

"I know. I'll have to cross that bridge when I come to it." Karen had considered the possibility herself.

"And then there's your parents. They might be hurt," Paula reminded her.

"They needn't know. It's not going to change anything between them and me," Karen argued.

Paula didn't agree. It would change everything in her opinion, but she wasn't going to say that to Karen. It wasn't her place.

"Drink up, Kar. We'll have to run for the last bus."

* * *

It was six months later that the girls found a flat they liked and they could afford. The flat, or apartment as Paula insisted on calling it, was in Glasnevin, just opposite the Tolka House pub. They were beautiful red-brick apartments set in landscaped grounds. The rent was high, but the owner had the flat nicely decorated and furnished.

Karen was highly excited the day they signed the papers.

That night Karen enthused about the flat when she got home. "We're moving in next week, Mum. I can't believe it. Paula let me have the big bedroom, but hers is a grand size too. We have a large living-room, a tiny kitchen and a good-sized bathroom. It's terrific. Our flat overlooks the Tolka river and on the other side of the road you can see the rose garden in the Botanics."

Liz tried to be pleased for her. "Dad and myself will help you move in."

"Thanks, Mum. Paula's Dad said he'd move some of our heavier stuff in his van. Not that I'll have anything heavy."

Frank put down his paper. "Have you given it to her yet?"

"No," Liz replied. "Will we give it to her now?"

"What?" Karen asked suspiciously.

"We've a surprise for you," Liz explained. "We were going to wait until your twenty-first in September but I knew you needed it now."

"What? What?" Karen got more excited.

"Here." Frank went to the sideboard and took out a slip of paper and handed it to his daughter. It was a receipt.

Karen stared at it in disbelief. "A computer? You've bought me a computer?"

Frank grinned. "The latest Macintosh. None of your old rubbish for our daughter. A printer too."

Karen hugged him, then her mother. "Oh God,

that's absolutely fantastic. My own computer. What can I say? You're both so good. It's what I've dreamed of for ages, but I'd never be able to afford one like this. Thanks so much." She hugged them again.

Liz was delighted with her reaction. It reminded her of how excited Karen used to get when she was a child. "It's really for your birthday, remember. But we thought since you were moving out this'd be a good time. They'll deliver and install it when you give them the word."

"Thanks, Mum. Oh, I can't wait to tell Paula. I'll put the computer in my new bedroom. I'll be able to work in peace. God, this is the best present ever. It must have cost a small fortune. Thanks again." She grabbed her jacket. "I'll call over to Paula's now. See you later. I'll never be able to thank you enough."

"Three times is quite enough." Frank grinned. "The fortune was well spent to see the expression on your face."

"Anything on the box?" Frank handed Liz a mug of coffee.

"Tch, nothing but tripe. I hate when the good programmes go off the air for the summer. There's only rubbish on."

"Mmh. Well, we certainly got it right this time, didn't we? She was ecstatic." Frank saw that Liz was lost in thought. "What's up?"

"Ah, you'll only laugh at me if I tell you." Liz was embarrassed.

"No, I won't. I think I know." Frank assured her.

"Do you?" Liz put down the mug. "You probably do. Sometimes I think you can read my mind."

"It's from living together for so long, love. It's the move that's upsetting you, isn't it?" Frank was expecting this.

"Yes. You think I'm overreacting." Liz knew the way Frank's mind worked.

Frank didn't dismiss her fears. "Of course I don't. It's an emotional time. Big change for us all."

"Why is she going, Frank?" Liz looked broken-hearted.

He put his arm around her. "She's going because she's an independent young lady who wants to make her own way in the world."

"It's not because of us? Because of me?" Liz had to know.

"Don't be silly." He ruffled her hair. "It's normal. It's time Karen spread her wings. She's not our little girl anymore."

Liz started to sniff. "That's what I'm afraid of."

"Oh Liz, come on. You wouldn't want to see her tied to your apron strings, would you?"

"No, no I wouldn't but . . . I can't help feeling that it's something we've done . . . or haven't done," Liz whispered.

Frank shook his head. "What we've done is a damn good job. She's able to stand on her own two feet. We helped her to be like that. You encouraged her to go abroad for a year. That was the best thing that ever happened to Karen. It gave her a taste of freedom. It let her be herself and not just our daughter."

"Yeah," Liz agreed. "I know. But she's very young to be moving out of home."

"We were married on your twenty-first. You didn't think that was too young." Frank reminded her.

Liz shrugged. "That was different. I had you."

"Well, she has Paula. She has us. It's not as if she were moving a million miles away. Glasnevin is only down the road. When we see the apartment you'll feel better about it." Frank was sure of that.

"You're probably right." Liz thought that made sense.

"I know I am. Some of the lads at work give out because their offspring won't move out!" Frank emphasised.

Liz laughed. "Yeah, that might be worse!"

Peter came in with his friend, Mark. They were both studying computers and languages in DCU. Mark was from Cork and he was in digs in Fairview. He shook hands with Liz and Frank. He was quite formal in his ways and Liz liked him.

"Hi, folks." Peter grinned. "Had a few pints in the bar. Is it OK if Mark kips here tonight?"

"No problem." Liz smiled. "I'll go up and put clean clothes on the bed."

"Please don't go to any bother, Mrs Shaw." Mark was embarrassed at the idea of putting her out. "I'll borrow Peter's sleeping bag."

"What were you two laughing at?" Peter sprawled in the armchair, his long legs draped over the side. He had a way of untidying a room in a minute.

"Karen's found a flat," Frank told him

"Cool. Where?" Peter was interested.

"Glasnevin," Liz replied.

"Couldn't be better." Peter was thrilled. "That solves our late night transport problem, Mark."

"Hang on a minute, son," Frank butted in. "You needn't think that you and your drinking buddies can bum free accommodation from Karen and Paula."

Mark looked pained. Peter shrugged off his father's warning and dragged the mortified Mark off to the kitchen to make chips. Two minutes later he was back. "I've a brilliant idea!"

"What?" Liz wasn't sure she wanted to hear this.

"Karen's room will be free, right?" He looked at both of his parents.

"Yes, from next week." Frank studied Peter. What was he plotting?

"Can Mark move in here next term? September?" Peter came straight out with it.

Frank looked at Liz. She seemed to be considering the idea.

"Can he, Mum? He'd be no trouble and it'd be a few bob for you."

"What does Mark say?" Liz asked.

"He'd be thrilled. We could get a motor bike between us. Deadly. He'd feel more a part of our family than where he is now. Go on, say yes," Peter pleaded with her.

Liz hesitated. "All right, if your father doesn't mind."

Frank had to smile. "Anything to keep you two happy. And Mark of course."

517

Peter bounded off to tell Mark the good news.

"Now, are you satisfied? In one fell swoop you've lost a daughter and gained a lodger." Frank kissed her cheek. "We're not destined to be alone."

"Lost a daughter?" Liz echoed nervously.

"I didn't mean that the way it sounded. We'll never lose Karen, Liz."

"I hope not." Liz turned the telly up again. Things were happening too fast. She didn't like that. How would Karen feel about Mark moving into her room? She mightn't like it. She might think she was being replaced.

Liz knew in her gut that Karen would look for her natural mother. The move out was a step in that direction. She couldn't help feeling sad. They weren't losing Karen exactly, but things were changing. Dramatically. She knew she couldn't do anything to stop the change. It wouldn't be right to even try. Frank was sure that everything would work out for the best, but Liz couldn't get rid of the uneasy feeling that was gnawing away in her stomach.

CHAPTER THIRTY-FOUR

"So, are you pleased with the cottage?" Seán asked his daughter over breakfast.

Ciara buttered her toast. "Yeah, it's just what we wanted. There are two bedrooms, a kitchen-cum-dining-room and a big bathroom. That's all we need for the moment. Stephen's planning the garden at the moment."

"I'm amazed that he agreed to live in Carrigeen," Seán said. "He'll have a long drive into Galway for work every day."

"Dad, he's delighted we've finally got our own place. Anyhow I used to be the one with the long drive. It's his turn now and he doesn't mind. We're both just glad that things are finally working out. We were supposed to be married two years ago." Ciara poured out more tea for the two of them.

"That'd have been madness. You're very young." Seán couldn't see why his daughter was so intent on marriage.

"I'm twenty-three, for God's sake," Ciara protested. "We've been going out together for eight years."

Seán nodded. No point in going against Ciara.

She was like her mother when her mind was made up. "So, have you decided on the big day?"

Ciara smiled. "November. We'll go to see Father O'Loughlin next week."

"Why couldn't you wait till the spring? It'll be freezing in November." Seán thought Caroline would be too rushed if she had to plan the wedding for two month's time.

"No, Stephen and I both want the wedding this year. No more postponements. We're going to honeymoon in the Canaries. Holidays are much cheaper in the winter."

She was right there, he had to agree.

"And we don't want a big fussy affair," Ciara continued. "Just family and close friends. Colm will be best man, of course. Stephen's sister, June, will be our bridesmaid. That's it."

"And the reception? Where do you want that?"

"We don't really mind. Gran suggested the Great Southern." Ciara looked at her father. What would he think of that? Would it be too expensive? To her surprise he seemed amenable to the idea.

"Well, at least it's central. I was hoping you wouldn't want the reception in the hotel in Carrigeen. Too far for the guests." Seán stood up and got his bag. "Is Colm up?"

"I heard him in the bathroom. He's a pathology lecture at ten, I think." Ciara buttered another slice of toast. She was very proud of her twin who was now in fourth year medicine.

"Bring your mother up a cup of tea before you leave," Seán told her.

"No need, I'm up." Caroline came in in her dressing-gown. She wiped the sleep from her eyes and sat at the table.

Seán went over and kissed her. "I'm off, love. I'll see you tonight. I'll leave you two in peace to plot the wedding." He left.

Ciara put on some toast for her mother. "It's great the way you still fancy each other, Mum. I hope Stephen and I will be like that when we're old."

Caroline spluttered her tea. "Old? Who's old? Your father and I are in our prime!"

Ciara laughed. The phone rang and she went to answer it in the hall. Caroline was amused by her daughter. Old. She was fifty-one. Middle-aged, she had to admit. The funny thing was that she felt better now than she had ten years ago. She had more energy. She was looking forward to this wedding. She loved organising things. She liked the excitement.

"Sheila wants to talk to you, Mum." Ciara called from the hall.

Caroline was anxious when she put down the phone. Sheila had sounded elated, but Caroline was very nervous about the whole thing. Sheila had rung the adoption board. They'd told her to contact the adoption agency for help in tracing Karen. Sheila had made an appointment for next week, the twenty-fourth of September. Karen's twenty-first birthday. Caroline prayed Sheila was doing the right thing. Anything could happen. It could be a disaster.

That night Caroline told Seán all about it.

Seán tried to take it in. "She's actually going ahead then?"

Caroline nodded. "She wants me to go up. We always go for a meal on Karen's birthday."

"I thought that was long forgotten." Seán couldn't believe it.

"By you, maybe. Not by Sheila. She used to come to Galway to celebrate Karen's birthday. It was our annual custom. You just didn't realise it." Caroline turned down the TV.

"You never said anything," he accused her. "Why was I kept in the dark?"

"Sheila thought you'd disapprove. You always told her to forget Karen and get on with her life." Caroline said quietly.

Seán puffed on his pipe. For a second he reminded her of his father. "Well, she did get on with her life, I grant you that."

"Yeah," Caroline agreed. "But she never forgot her daughter, Seán. It's not something she could forget."

Seán thought about it. He'd been blind all these years to Sheila's real feelings. How could she have pined for a child she'd never even seen? It didn't make sense to him. "I hope she's not building herself up too much. She could be in for another fall."

Caroline knew that was true. "She said something about a counsellor. Apparently they do counsel the mothers on what to expect."

"Do you honestly think she's going to find out

anything? What about privacy? I thought these things were highly secret." Seán sighed. "The adoptive parents have their rights."

"Yeah. That's what I thought. Let's just wait and see how she gets on before we jump to any conclusions," Caroline advised.

* * *

Paula was nearly finished curling the back of Karen's hair. The curling tongs were very hot and she almost burned her fingers. She stood back to admire her handiwork. "Beautiful. It looks fabulous. Bouncy and natural."

Karen wasn't so sure. She looked in her dressing-table mirror. She thought it was too much. "I'd prefer the front straighter, Paula."

"Nonsense. It's perfect. Put on your new dress." Paula handed her the black dress that Liz had bought for Karen's birthday.

Karen stepped into it and struggled with the zip.

"Here, I'll do it." Paula zipped her up. "Jesus, Karen. You look fantastic. Really glamorous. You're so tall and slim."

Karen grimaced. "Honestly, do I look OK? I feel a bit overdressed."

"Tch," Paula answered impatiently. "You're so bloody used to your jeans, that's all. I'm telling you, you look absolutely fabulous. Dead sexy. I hope Steve doesn't fall for you. You're only to dance with him once. I don't want him getting any ideas."

The thought of dancing with Steve didn't exactly

turn Karen on. If she had her way, Steve wouldn't be coming to her twenty-first bash at all. But she had to invite him for Paula's sake. They were an item, as Paula kept saying.

Their buzzer went.

"I'll get it. It's probably Steve." Paula pressed the button which opened the front door to the apartment complex. They heard footsteps on the stairs. Paula went to open their door.

"Hello girls, all set?" Frank kissed his daughter. "God, you look great." He put a pile of bags down on the draining board.

"What are these?" Paula looked into the bags.

"A few things Liz sent over." Frank explained. He couldn't get over how his daughter looked. She was stunning.

"Jesus, a few things?" Paula gasped. "There are rashers, sausages, pork steak, biscuits, coffee, sugar, brown bread. She's gas." Paula put the perishables into the fridge. "She mustn't think we look after ourselves at all."

"She doesn't," Frank agreed.

"Well, I'm not complaining!" Paula was delighted with the goodies. They'd keep them going for a week.

"We're waiting for Steve to come in from work, Dad. Would you like a beer?" Karen went over to the fridge.

"Don't mind if I do." Frank accepted the can of beer. "I hope Steve won't be long. I left your mother fussing in the tennis club. She's bossing everyone around."

"Poor Mum," Karen said. "She takes things too seriously. There's no rush. Most of the gang won't arrive till late. My work-mates will all be in the pub."

"Sure I told her that," Frank answered in exasperation. "But will she listen to me?"

"You were very good to come over to collect us, Mr Shaw." Paula poured beers for herself and Karen.

"Not at all. It's only ten minutes in the car. Well Karen, how do you feel? I wish I was twenty-one again." Frank smiled at his daughter.

"I feel excited. In case I don't get the chance to say it later, Dad. I'd like to thank you for everything." Karen hugged her father.

Frank hugged her back. "We'll all be expecting a speech, Karen."

"You're not serious?" Karen looked terrified at the prospect of that.

"Yeah, definitely," Paula chimed in. "You have to make a speech. Ah, you'll be fine after a few jars. You'll probably be in line for the bumps too."

"Oh no, Paula," Karen protested. She wanted her party to have some semblance of dignity.

"Don't worry, love." Frank put his arm around his daughter. "Anyone who puts a finger on you will have me to answer to."

"Jesus, Mr Shaw," Paula butted in, "if Chris Moore puts a finger on her, don't interfere!"

"Who's this Chris Moore?" Frank wanted to know.

"He's just a friend. Don't mind her." Karen gave Paula a dig.

The buzzer went again. "That's definitely Steve." Paula grabbed her jacket. "I'll meet him down in the hall. You follow on when you're ready." Paula slammed the door behind her.

"She's nuts about that guy," Karen raised her eyes to heaven. "There's no accounting for taste."

Frank sat on the tiny couch beside his daughter. "Karen, can I have a word now that we're alone?"

"Sure, Dad. What is it?"

"This is a very important birthday for you. You came into the world twenty-one years ago today. I know you must be thinking about your birth mother." Frank put his arm around Karen. "If you ever want my help or advice, I want you to know I'll support you in any way I can. Your mother finds it a bit difficult, but she's there for you too."

Karen gulped. "To tell you the truth, I've been wondering about her all day. Do you think she remembers, Dad? Would you say she knows it's my twenty-first?"

"She knows, pet." Frank looked into Karen's eyes. "I'm sure she knows. She loved you very much. You know she gave you your name?"

"She what?" Karen's mouth fell open. "My name?"

"Yes. We hadn't the heart to change it." Frank swallowed hard.

"But how did you know? You never saw my original birth certificate. Mum told me that." Karen was intrigued.

Frank took her hands in his. "When we got you, there was a little prayer pinned onto your vest. The name Karen was written on it. Apparently the people who fostered you for the first few weeks found it when they took you from the hospital."

Karen's eyes filled with tears. "Thanks for telling me that, Dad. It means a lot."

"I felt you should know that. It's your right. Liz and I discussed it at length and we both agreed we'd have to keep the name. It was her choice. It's a nice name."

"Mmh," Karen answered softly. "It means the pure one. I looked it up."

"Well then, you were aptly named. Come on, love. It's time to party, as you young people say." Frank pulled Karen up from the couch. "We're both very proud of you, Karen. Anything you decide to do is OK by us."

"Thanks, Dad." Karen slipped on her black suede jacket. "I might look for her sometime. But not yet. I'm not ready yet."

* * *

Sheila was in great form after her visit to the adoption agency. The counsellor had been very helpful, very understanding. There was no way she could give Sheila any information about Karen's whereabouts, but she did assure her that Karen had been adopted by a loving couple who had adopted a son the year after. That was always a good sign, the counsellor explained. Sheila was delighted.

Karen had a brother. A proper family. On the way home Sheila had her hair done. She persuaded Louis to cut it to shoulder length. He didn't want to, but she persuaded him that it was more appropriate for a woman of forty. Her beautiful auburn curls framed her face. He had to admit the new style gave her a girlish look. When she got back to the salon, Nuala gave her a massage to relax her.

Caroline arrived at about seven o'clock. Sheila could see that her sister-in-law was a bit on edge. Sheila kissed her. "Don't worry. Everything went very well."

Caroline hugged her. "God, I'm so relieved."

"Come on upstairs for a drink. I'll tell you all about it when you've put your stuff in your room." Sheila showed her up to her room. "Seán didn't mind your coming to Dublin, did he?"

"Not at all. He was a bit worried about you, though." Caroline dumped her case on the double bed.

"Do you want to unpack?" Sheila opened the wardrobe.

"No," Caroline said quickly. "I want a drink and I want to hear it all."

They came down to the sitting-room and Sheila poured the sherries. "Here's to Karen."

Caroline raised her glass. "Come on, Sheila. Tell me. Put me out of my agony."

Sheila told her what she'd found out.

Caroline was agog. "But did they tell you anything about how to trace her?" Caroline had to know.

"Mmh, it all depends on Karen really." Sheila lit a cigarette.

"What do you mean?" Caroline prompted her.

"I was able to leave my name and address with the agency. They have them on file now. If Karen tries to contact me they'll give her the details." Sheila smiled.

Caroline didn't know what to think. "Supposing Karen doesn't?"

"Then there's nothing else I can do, Caroline. I wouldn't want to, anyway. I couldn't force anything on her. She's a grown woman now. But I feel in my bones that she'll try to find me." Sheila had a dreamy look in her eyes.

Caroline didn't want to spoil the moment. "I hope you're right."

Sheila put down her glass. "The counsellor told me that not all adopted children try to find their natural parents. But that's OK too, you see. It means she's happy and well adjusted and getting on with her life."

Caroline looked disappointed. "But that means that you'll never find her."

Sheila nodded. "I know. I'll have to accept that. But if Karen does look for me, I've made her job much easier. Don't you see?"

"Yeah." Caroline didn't understand why Sheila was so pleased. Nothing much had really happened today, in her opinion. "It's still a long shot, Sheila."

"I know that." Sheila took another sip. "There's something else. I need your help with this one."

"Anything," Caroline said without hesitation.

"The counsellor said I could write a letter to Karen. Will you help me with it?" Sheila asked quietly. "I wouldn't want to put her off. I need to get it just right."

"A letter?" Caroline was confused.

"Yeah, a letter." Sheila said urgently. "I want to write it tonight. I want to explain everything to her. I want to tell her how much I love her and how badly I want to meet her." Sheila got more excited.

Caroline paused to think. "You don't want to be too gushing," she warned Sheila. "That could definitely frighten her off. I mean she doesn't know you from Adam."

"Don't rub it in." Sheila went over to the writing desk and pulled out a pad. "But you're right. I don't want to go over the top. You have to help me word it, Caroline. You're good at that."

They put their heads together and after a half an hour Sheila was fairly happy with the result. It was more of a note than a letter.

September 24th, 1988

My darling Karen,

As I do not know the name you were given at adoption, I have always thought of you as Karen. I am writing this note on your twenty-first birthday. What a pity that we couldn't have celebrated it together! I want you to know that I have thought about you every day of your life.

I wish you every success and happiness. If you would like us to meet please contact me. That would make my dreams come true.

God bless you, my dear daughter,

From your mother with all the love I can give,

Sheila Crosby.

"That's nice, Sheila." Caroline said approvingly.

"Tch, I don't know. It doesn't really say how I feel, does it?" Sheila thought it was too tame.

"I don't agree." Caroline read it again. "It's simple. I like that. As you've said yourself, you don't want to scare her off. It gives her the option to get in touch. She'll know from the note that you're dying to see her."

"Are you sure? This is vital." Sheila was nervous.

"I know it's vital. What about the letter your father wrote to Karen?" Caroline reminded her. "You could put that in the envelope too."

Sheila beamed. "Oh God, yes. Brilliant. That way she'd know her grandfather had accepted her. That's brilliant, Caroline."

"I'd love to know what's in Pat's letter." Caroline mused. "Is there no way we could steam it?" She looked eagerly at Sheila.

Sheila was appalled. "Caroline, shame on you. That's a private letter Dad wrote for Karen. I wouldn't dream of interfering with it."

Caroline was contrite. "Sorry. I don't know how you hung onto it for all these years without being curious."

"Of course I was curious," Sheila emphasised. "More than curious. But I could never open a letter that was meant for someone else."

Caroline wished she'd kept her big mouth shut. She felt like a criminal. "Right, go and get your dad's letter and put them both in a large envelope. When will you give it to the agency?"

"Tomorrow morning. I've delayed long enough."
Sheila hurried off.

She was someone on a mission, Caroline
thought. At least the visit today had given her hope.
But Caroline doubted that Karen would be in touch
that soon. In fact, although she'd only admit this to
herself, Caroline doubted that Karen would be in
touch at all.

They went around the corner to the Unicorn
restaurant for their meal. Caroline had mussels for a
starter and Sheila had melon. They both had the
duck à l'orange for their main course. The
restaurant was cosy and the food was excellent.
That's why Sheila liked it.

"How's Mary?" Caroline asked as she sipped her
white wine.

"All right." Sheila was a bit evasive.

"Still teaching?" Caroline studied the dessert
menu.

"Oh yeah, she took a career break for a year
back in '85." Sheila wanted to change the subject.
She guessed that Caroline suspected something. But
Sheila would never betray a trust. "But she's back
teaching full-time since then."

"She had some sort of a breakdown, didn't she?"
Caroline asked. It wasn't that she meant to pry. She
genuinely liked Mary.

"I wouldn't say a breakdown," Sheila said
slowly. "She was just tired out. Jim was away a lot
of the time."

"Does he work in England much now?" Mary

called the waiter and ordered the ice-cream. Sheila didn't want dessert. They both ordered coffees.

"No, he's mostly in Dublin now. He's very good to Mary. Very devoted." Sheila didn't mention the fact that Mary was attending a psychiatrist. Four years on and Mary was still suffering.

"What age are her kids now?" Caroline noticed Sheila flinch.

"Davy's eleven and Maeve's ten. They're lovely kids. Maeve's a wonderful little pianist." Sheila stirred her coffee.

"Mary was good at music too, wasn't she? Does she still play?"

Sheila shook her head. "I don't think so. I haven't heard her play in years. It's a pity."

"Yeah. It's hard to find the time to do everything," Caroline replied. "Do they still see John Harris?"

Sheila wondered why she'd brought him up out of the blue. Not that it bothered her particularly. "Mary says Jim does, when John's in Dublin."

Caroline was surprised. "In Dublin? Why? Has he moved?"

"He's in Waterford. He went back to his wife. Has his own law practice there."

"You're joking!" Caroline was flabbergasted. "Back with his wife!"

Sheila laughed at her reaction. "Hilarious, isn't it? Leaves his mistress to go back to his wife!"

"Tch, he didn't leave you, Sheila." Caroline said crossly. "That man would have done anything for you."

Sheila nodded. "Maybe. Anyhow it's all water under the bridge now. He's happy, I hear. They're fostering a child. A boy."

"Fostering? They're a bit long in the tooth for that aren't they? He must be what? Forty-five?"

"About that," Sheila agreed. "Not exactly in his dotage yet. No, they're not as fussy about the age thing when it comes to fostering, apparently. He wanted children so I'm glad for him. For them."

Caroline could see that she meant it. "Well, how did you celebrate your fortieth last month? Your mother was sure you'd come down for it. I think she wanted to have a party for you."

"Precisely why I didn't go down!" Sheila laughed again. "I went for a meal with the gang from the salon and the two shops. They made a big fuss. They say life begins at forty but I don't believe a word of it."

"I'm not too sure of that. You certainly look good on it. Your hair's lovely like that. You could pass for twenty-five, honestly." Caroline looked admiringly at her sister-in-law.

"Thanks." Sheila was delighted. "I don't feel forty, actually. I felt older at twenty-five. But I think you kind of take stock of your life when you get to forty."

"Yeah," Caroline agreed.

"That's why I set the wheels in motion to find Karen. It was hanging over me for years. Tonight I feel I've done something definite. The ball's in Karen's court now."

Caroline nodded. There was nothing she could add to that.

* * *

The party in the tennis club was in full swing.

"What do you think of Chris, Mum?" Karen asked her mother. "Isn't he divine?"

"He's a lovely chap," Liz agreed. She hadn't heard Karen mention a boy since Jean Luc. Maybe Karen was falling for this one. Liz could see why Karen fancied him. Tall, blonde and handsome. A good job in RTE. Very nice.

"We'll need a truck to get all these presents home, Karen." Liz was thrilled for her daughter. She'd got some lovely things: jewellery, clothes, vouchers.

"Is this what Paula gave you?" Liz examined the beautiful case of skin products. "Natural Woman. That stuff costs a fortune. It was very good of Paula, wasn't it? My God, there must be thirty things here. You can pamper yourself for months."

Karen smiled. Beauty creams were not high on her list of priorities. But she didn't want to be ungrateful. This case of muck must have set Paula back over a hundred quid.

Someone turned out all the lights and Frank wheeled in a huge cake with twenty-one lighted candles. Everyone cheered as Karen stood up to blow out the candles.

"Speech! Speech!" they all chorused.

Karen surprised herself. Suddenly she knew exactly what she wanted to say. She looked around the room. Her aunts and uncles were all assembled.

Her cousins smiled encouragingly at her. Friends from college and from work clapped. Neighbours cheered her on. Her brother Peter put his arm around her for moral support.

Karen wasn't a bit nervous. "I'd like to thank you all for coming tonight. You've been very kind and very generous. Thanks for the beautiful gifts. Thanks to Paula for putting up with me through thick and thin." Karen smiled over at her friend. "I'd like to say a special word of thanks to my brother, Peter, for always being there for me."

"Nice one, Peter." Mark wasn't as shy as he used to be.

"Ssh, let her speak," someone else shouted.

Karen took a deep breath. "I can't let this occasion pass without mentioning the two most important people in my life. They've been wonderful; understanding, loving and most supportive. I owe everything I have and I am to them. I just want to tell them I love them very much. A huge thanks to my Mum and Dad."

Everyone cheered. Frank and Liz hugged Karen. It was the happiest moment of Liz's life. Even Peter, the cynic, thought it was nice.

The music started up again and Karen found herself literally swept off her feet by Chris Moore. This was turning out to be a great party. Karen was giddy with the excitement of it all.

* * *

They didn't get back to the flat till three in the

morning. Paula put the kettle on. "That was one terrific party, Karen."

"Yeah, the best." Karen flopped onto the couch.

"I was chatting to your Mum at the end. You made her very happy tonight. Your speech was lovely." Paula said. "I was nearly in tears."

Karen scratched her nose. "I meant every word I said. They mean everything to me, Paula. I'm very lucky to have them."

"Sure I'm always telling you that. They idolise you, Karen." Paula poured the tea.

"I've been thinking about what you said. I think you were right." Karen took the cup of tea from Paula.

"About finding your other mother?" Paula asked her.

"Yeah, funny to think of her as that. I think I'll leave well enough alone. I've no right to go barging into someone's life and turn it upside down. I'll leave her in peace. She's probably suffered enough without me arriving on the scene and stirring up old memories."

Paula sighed. "It must be desperate for you, Karen. Anyone would be dying with curiosity. But look at what you'd be risking. You said tonight you had everything. You do, Karen. Be happy with the way things are."

Karen smiled at her. "I am. I honestly am. I realised that tonight. They're a great pair. By the way, Chris Moore has asked me out on a date."

"Whoopie!" Paula pulled her up and whirled her around the room.

* * *

Sheila had a very disturbed night's sleep. Distorted images invaded her dreams: parties in strange places, weird happenings, screams, laughter and tears. She actually woke herself with fright at one point. Sheila was in a lather of sweat. She'd dreamt she was meeting Karen on O'Connell Bridge. When she got there a tall red-haired girl turned and waved. Sheila waved back. Suddenly, Karen climbed up on the parapet and jumped into the murky Liffey below. Sheila screamed. She woke screaming. Caroline ran into her room and turned on the light.

"Sheila, Sheila, wake up. Wake up." Caroline held onto Sheila's thrashing body.

"Oh, Jesus." Sheila clung on to Caroline for dear life. "I'm sorry. It was just a nightmare. I'll be OK in a minute." Sheila's hair was stuck to her forehead. It was wringing wet. So was her night-dress. She pushed the bedclothes down to cool off.

Caroline soothed her. "Was it about Karen?"

"Yeah," Sheila took a long breath. "It was terrible. Before that I think I was dreaming about Donald Fagan. I'm not sure. Mary was in the dream too. I dreamt he was cutting up a baby. Mary stood there, laughing hysterically. It was horrible." Sheila was still shaking.

"I'll go down and make us both a cup of tea." Caroline puffed up Sheila's pillows.

Sheila sat up straight in the bed. "Could you pass

me my cigarettes, Car? They're over on the dressing-table. Jesus, I'm in bits."

Caroline handed her an ash-tray too. "You went through a big ordeal yesterday, Sheila. It's natural that you'd be a bit uptight. Dreams are nature's way of getting rid of tension."

Sheila nodded. She wished there was a less traumatic way. When Caroline left the room Sheila got out of bed and opened her window wide. The cool air soothed her somewhat, although she was still shaking.

She could understand why she'd dreamt about her daughter. Karen had been so much on her mind. But Donald Fagan? What the hell was Donald Fagan doing in her dreams? She hadn't thought about him in years. It was weird. It was like some sort of omen and Sheila didn't like it.

Maybe it wasn't him at all. Maybe she'd been dreaming about John Harris. That would make more sense. Caroline had asked about him during their meal. No, no, it was definitely Donald Fagan. The face was blurred in the dream, but the blonde hair was unmistakable.

Sheila slipped back under the sheets. Caroline came back with the tea. "Feeling better?"

"Mmh," Sheila said. But she wasn't.

CHAPTER THIRTY-FIVE

Donald Fagan was dozing off when the air-hostess came around with the trolley.

"Do you want anything from the bar, sir?" The attractive brunette smiled at him.

"No, thanks." He smiled back.

He was sleepy from so many hours flying. Jet-lagged. He didn't want to befuddle his brain with drink. It would be funny to be back in Ireland. Funny peculiar. He'd left in 1977. God, that was thirteen years ago. He'd only been back twice in all that time. Once for his sister's wedding and the second time was for his mother's funeral. The years had flown.

Four years teaching in Spain followed by five years in France. He'd hated Bilbao in Northern Spain. It was the largest city in the Basque Province, a highly industrialised place. He'd detested his pokey apartment with its grubby white walls, threadbare green rug, chipped wooden floor and the paint peeling off the walls. It was like something out of an O'Casey play. When he opened a window it literally took his breath way . . . and he wasn't talking about the view!

Bordeaux was a lot better. He preferred France. He loved strolling on a summer's evening watching the boats and ships in the harbour. Then into a nearby bistro for a glass of Sauterne, his favourite white wine. He lived in a nice area near the University. He liked wandering around this city with its wide streets, large squares and baroque churches. A lot of living and a lot of loving.

He grinned when he thought of the number of women he'd dated. He'd spent a fortune on socialising and making merry.

Then he'd decided he wanted to make some real money. He went to Riyadh. It was cheap to live there in the eighties and he'd been able to save. There was little you could spend your money on anyway. No pub crawls. Islamic law didn't suit Donald. The ban on alcohol and the segregation of the sexes were a real threat to personal freedom. Although they did manage to have a few jars in each other's houses. Still, he didn't really like the lifestyle. The Westerners stuck together socially. Living in such close proximity in the compounds bordered on mental incest, in Donald's opinion. He felt caged in. Trapped. He had to admit they lived the good life, but he wasn't happy despite the luxury of their villas and swimming-pools. Donald hated the way the women were so subservient. Even Western women had to wear long black shrouds once they left their compound. He'd met one girl who had her ankles slapped with a stick by the religious police, because her dress was too short. Incredible. Women couldn't drive either. He wasn't comfortable having underdogs from Sri Lanka, India or Pakistan wait on him hand and foot for a pittance of a salary. One law for the rich. It was quite sickening. Money was god in Saudi Arabia.

Then two years ago, he'd met Yvonne, an Irish nurse. She was young, attractive and full of life. He liked her a lot. When her contract was up six months ago, she'd come back to Dublin. He'd been lonely without her. He'd had enough of the heat. The Irish rain would be welcome at this stage. Anyhow, now in 1990 things had changed. His salary no longer seemed that attractive. The best money went to engineers on the oil rigs. So he'd finished out his year and followed her back. He'd be getting off the plane in one hour. What would Dublin hold for him now?

Would Yvonne still be interested? He'd soon find out. What about his old Uni friends? He should have stayed in touch with them. Making a new life mightn't be easy. What about a job? He was fed up with teaching. He'd given enough of his life to the brats. It was a thankless job in his opinion. He was bored with it. How could he motivate students when he wasn't motivated himself? No, time to retire from a life of drudgery and try something new.

Financially, he was in a good position. He'd saved quite a bit and the money from his share of the sale of the family home was substantial. That had been gathering interest. Must be a tidy sum by now.

Donald stretched his legs and yawned. They'd soon be approaching Dublin airport. He'd go and stay with Miriam, his sister, for a few days till he'd made some plans. No point in rushing into anything.

* * *

"I'm so glad you're back, Donald. I missed you." Yvonne leaned over and kissed him.

They were parked outside her parents' home in Drumcondra in Donald's new Corsa. He felt as randy as hell. He really wanted her. This was bloody frustrating. Forty-three years old and he was reduced to courting in a car. He'd have to do something about it.

"Yvonne," he whispered into her ear, "I've something to ask you." He'd have to broach the subject now. He'd have to squeeze the universe into a ball. Maybe it wasn't such an overwhelming question?

"What is it, Don?" She stroked the back of his neck which sent tingles up and down his spine.

"Let's get our own place." There, he'd come right out and said it.

She pulled away from him? "What? Do you mean live together?"

Jesus, maybe he'd gone too fast. "Yeah, what do you think?"

She paused for a minute. Then she smiled. "I think it's a great idea. I didn't think you were ready for that type of a commitment."

543

He grabbed her and kissed her full on the mouth. Her tongue pushed between his teeth. He felt himself getting hard. He broke away. "I was afraid you'd say no."

"Don, how could I refuse you anything?" She smiled seductively at him.

He breathed a sigh of relief. "Great, we'll start looking for somewhere tomorrow."

She put her hand on the door as if to go. Then she changed her mind and turned to him. "Do you want to come in?"

He shook his head. "Better not. Not after the last time. Your parents don't think too kindly of me."

The week before he'd started to make love to Yvonne on her mother's couch, but in the middle of their manoeuvres, he'd keeled over and fallen into the coal bucket. Her mother had come charging down the stairs, ready to confront the burglars! Not exactly conducive to romance, that house.

"No, I'm afraid they think you've corrupted me." Yvonne laughed. "It's because you're such a man of the world!"

Donald smiled, but he wasn't amused. She hadn't meant it as an insult, but the truth sometimes hurt. He was eighteen years older than she was. That was a fact and he didn't like it.

"You'd better go on in. I think I see your mother peeping out through the curtains. I'll head back to Miriam's. Jesus Christ, I can't wait to get out of there. It's driving me nuts."

"Ah, they were good to put you up for the last few weeks," Yvonne pointed out to him sternly.

"I know, I know. Miriam is grand. So is Harry. But those three savages of hers! I could strangle them."

"You've no patience, Don." Yvonne gave him one last kiss and slipped out of the car.

He rolled down the window and leaned out. "We're starting to look tomorrow night, right?"

She nodded. "Pick me up after work. I'm finished at six."

Yvonne ran down the steps of the Mater Hospital. Don was waiting.

"Where are you parked?" She pecked him on the cheek.

"Just over there." The car was parked in Berkeley Road. "Yvonne, how would you feel about living over a shop?"

"A shop? What kind of shop? What are you up to, Donald?" She gave him an accusing look.

"A newsagency. Right across the street. It's up for sale. Going for auction, next week. There's a large flat upstairs."

Yvonne gasped. It wasn't what she had in mind. "You're going to buy a shop?"

"Why not?" He grinned like an idiot.

"But you know nothing about shopkeeping."

"What's to know? I can learn." He slipped his arm around her.

He sounded as if he'd already made up his mind. Cocky as ever.

"Come on." He squeezed her waist. "I've called

there earlier. They said we could come back together and look at it."

Well, at least he was involving her in the decision. They crossed the road. She didn't relish the thought of living over a shop. But it wouldn't be any old shop. It would be Don's. Maybe she'd get used to the idea. There was one thing in its favour. She'd be three minutes from work. Ah hell, if it wasn't a complete dive, she'd agree. It wasn't as if she'd be married to the shop. She wasn't even going to be married to him. Not yet, anyway!

*   *   *

Mary was lucky to find a parking space at this time in the afternoon. Maeve undid her seat belt. "You'd better get Nana some sweets, Mum."

"No honey, not today. She mightn't be allowed after the anaesthetic. Anway, she'll probably be thirsty. Hospitals are always so hot. We'll get Nana some Seven Up and a few magazines." Mary locked the car.

"God, I'd hate to be in hospital. It must be awful," Maeve said passionately.

"Don't say that to Nana. We're here to jolly her along, right?" Mary guided her across the busy street. "Here's a sweet shop here. You choose a magazine for her, OK?"

They went in. Mary went to get the drink while Maeve examined the magazines. The shopkeeper had his back to them. He was sorting out newspapers. Mary coughed for attention. He turned suddenly. "Sorry love, did I keep you waiting?"

Mary froze. She stood there like a prat. She tried to answer, but no words came out. She was rooted to the spot.

"Here," Maeve took over. "Just the Seven Up and this magazine, please." The little girl handed them to the blonde man. What was up with her mother? God, she must be in one of her funny moods again. Maeve took the purse from her mother's bag and counted out the exact amount.

"Efficient, isn't she?" The man smiled. Then he took another look at his customer. "I know you from somewhere, don't I?"

Mary stuttered. "I . . . I don't t-think so." She felt the blush spread up her neck to her cheeks. "We're not from around here. We're . . . we're just visiting my mother in the Mater."

The shopkeeper shook his head. "No, no, I mean way back. I knew you years ago. I never forget a face."

Mary stuffed the bottle into her message bag. "I'm sure you're mistaken. I've a common face." She tried to laugh. She took Maeve by the arm and dashed out of the shop.

"What is it with you, Mum! Why're you pulling a freaker?" Maeve was mortified by her mother's behaviour. "He was nice. Real friendly. You could at least have been civil."

Mary didn't answer. She was still in shock. She'd just been talking to Donald Fagan! Sweet Jesus! Wait till Sheila heard this. The asshole was back in Dublin. A shopkeeper. A mingy little shopkeeper! And Sheila was the owner of a beauty empire . . .

queen of Dublin's glitterati! What a turn up for the
books. A shopkeeper. Bloody hilarious. He'd
vaguely recognised her. Maybe he'd figure it out
later.

"Mum, I left the magazine on the counter. We'll
have to go back," Maeve said in a panic.

Mary could have strangled her. Reluctantly she
walked back to the shop. She'd willingly have left
the bloody magazine there, but Maeve wouldn't
have stood for that.

"You're back!" he beamed at her. "You forgot
your magazine." He handed it to her. "I think I
know where we met before. You were in UCD in
the late sixties, weren't you?"

Mary was about to deny it when Maeve popped
in with, "Yes, my Mum's a teacher."

He smiled. "I used to be a teacher too. I was
abroad until recently. Got sick of the old classroom,
so here I am with this little business. It's a lot easier
on the nerves. You're Mary . . . eh. . . O' something-
or-other, aren't you?"

"Mary Ryan, now," she replied curtly.

He put out his hand. "Don Fagan. Remember
me?"

Mary shook his hand, but she felt like belting
him one.

"And your friend was Sheila . . . Sheila Crosby. I
dated her a few times. Ah, you wouldn't remember
that." He dismissed the idea as being of no
importance.

"I do remember now," Mary said pointedly.

"How is Sheila? Do you still see her?" The same
lop-sided grin.

"Yes, Sheila and I are still best friends." Mary glared at him. She hadn't meant to, but she couldn't help it.

"I suppose she's married too with children."

He was ready now for a long chat about the good old days, Mary saw. He could sod off. "No, Sheila's far too busy to even think of marriage."

"Oh? The career type, eh?" He smiled again. "Funny, I'd have sworn she was the marrying kind. Of course that was a long time ago. People change."

"Do they?" Mary arched her eyebrow. "Can't say I've noticed that." He bloody well hadn't changed anyway. Same smoothie.

A young girl in a nurse's uniform came into the shop. To Mary's surprise Donald Fagan put his arm around the girl. "This is Yvonne. Yvonne, this is Mary, an old mate from college."

An old mate, my foot! Bloody nerve of him! Mary smiled. "You're Donald's daughter?"

The girl howled with laughter, but Donald turned white. "Yvonne is my girlfriend, as it happens."

Mary should have apologised, but she didn't. She merely smirked. "Oh?"

"She keeps me young." Donald sneered.

"I must dash." Mary hurried to the door. She had to get out of there before she said something she'd regret.

"Tell Sheila I was asking for her," he shouted after Mary, but she'd already shut the door behind her.

Yvonne took a choc ice from the freezer. "Who was she?"

"I used to go out with her friend in college," Don replied absent-mindedly.

"Oh? Tell me more." Yvonne leaned over the counter and tickled his chin. "I want to know all about your glorious past."

"Ah," Donal said offhandedly, "it was nothing. Kid stuff."

"Who was she?" Yvonne wasn't going to give up.

Donald sighed. "Her name was Sheila Crosby. Still is, it seems."

Yvonne got all excited. "Sheila Crosby? Jesus, I wonder . . ."

"You wonder what?" Donald asked.

Yvonne went over to the magazine rack and picked up the latest Cosmopolitan. She flicked through the pages till she found what she wanted. She spread out the two-page article on the counter. "Is this her, by any chance?"

Donald was dumbfounded. He stared at the photo of the beautiful redhead under the caption: Sheila Crosby: Ireland's Natural Woman.

* * *

Mary was very quiet that evening. Jim had got used to that by now. There was nothing wrong with their marriage as far as he could make out. The kids were well and happy. Her job was fine. She still enjoyed teaching. He was working in Ireland most of the time these days. But Mary had definitely changed. She'd lost a lot of her spark. He knew something had happened to cause that change, but if Mary couldn't tell him, that was OK. People, no matter how close they were, had a right to their private thoughts and feelings.

"How was your Mam today?" Jim asked her.

"Quite good. She was sore after the surgery but that's to be expected. She was in great form though. Maeve entertained her." Mary was relieved that her mother had come through the hip replacement so well. It would take a few months for a complete recovery but these operations were usually a great success.

Jim went on reading his newspaper. Mary was busy correcting tests so he didn't want to disturb her.

"Jim." Mary put down her pen. "Something odd happened today. Do you know who I met?"

"Who?" He folded *The Irish Times*.

Mary sat back and folded her arms. "Donald Fagan."

"Who?" Jim didn't recognise the name.

"Donald Fagan. The shithead from college who got Sheila pregnant." Mary shuddered.

"You're kidding!" Jim exclaimed. "Where did he spring from? I thought he went abroad."

Mary nodded. "He did. But he's back. He bought a shop in Berkeley Road."

"What had he to say for himself?" Jim wondered if Mary had gone on the attack.

Mary lit a cigarette. "The usual bullshit. He's still a right pain. Looks very well, though. He hasn't aged a bit; same blond hair and he's bronze from all the travel."

Jim looked anxiously at his wife. "Are you going to tell Sheila?"

She shook her head. "No."

Jim thought that was wise.

"I was going to." Mary flicked the ash. "But on second thoughts I don't think it'd serve any purpose, do you?"

"No." Jim didn't have to reflect. "How long is it since Sheila contacted the adoption agency?"

Mary bit her lip. "Two years. I doubt if she'll ever hear from her daughter."

"So do I," Jim said.

"I could have spat on him today. He really gives me the creeps." Mary shuddered again.

"You didn't say anything about . . . Sheila, did you?" Jim asked. He hoped she hadn't, but with Mary you never knew.

"No, I was tempted to blurt out everything, especially when he asked if she was married, but . . . I managed to contain myself." Mary stubbed out the cigarette with venom.

Jim was getting really interested now. "Is he married?"

"No way. He has a girlfriend half his age. A nurse. She seemed nice. Poor girl." Mary stood up. "Do you want a coffee?"

"No, I'll get myself a beer." Jim went under the stairs and came back with two bottles of Harp. "I think we should keep this to ourselves. Although sooner or later, Sheila's bound to bump into him. Dublin can be very small."

Mary shook her head. "They won't be moving in the same circles, that's for sure. It's gas to think about it. Sheila's such a huge success. She leads such an exciting, glamorous life and he owns this little shop, real Mickey Mouse stuff."

Jim laughed. "Surely you mean Donald Duck stuff!"

Mary glowered. She was in no mood for Jim's feeble attempts at humour. "I'll say nothing to Sheila. I just hope Maeve doesn't blab it the next time Sheila's here."

"Ah, I wouldn't worry on that score. You know kids. In one ear and out the other. Maeve will forget about him by tomorrow."

Mary stirred her coffee. "Let's hope so."

PART FOUR

CHAPTER THIRTY-SIX

Karen woke suddenly. What time was it? God, eleven o'clock. She'd only had a few hours sleep. Creaks, bangs and thuds from next door. The new tenants moving in. She stuck her head under the pillow in an effort to blot out the noise. It didn't work. It wasn't fair. She was knackered. Working the night shift was a pain.

She shouldn't complain. She'd been delighted six months ago when she'd landed this job in RTE as a sub-editor. She loved working there. There was a terrific buzz in the newsroom. Some amazing stories emerged, but very few of them got into the news. Too sensational or gruesome.

Karen closed her eyes again. Maybe she'd get back to sleep.

"Kar, you awake?" Paula poked her head in.

Karen grunted. "I am now." Jesus, would she ever get any peace?

Paula came in and sat on the bed. "Steve and I are going to see the priest this morning to finalise the wedding arrangements. Afterwards, his parents are taking us for lunch, so I won't see you till tonight."

"I'm working tonight," Karen mumbled sleepily.

Another loud thud followed by a creaking noise.

"Christ, what are they at?" Karen sat up in a temper.

Paula laughed. "They're moving their furniture. They've bought the place. They're not renting like we are."

Karen got out of the bed, grumpily. "Well, I wish they'd bloody well pipe down. They're worse than a herd of elephants. No point lying there listening to them. I might as well get dressed."

"Have you any plans for today?" Paula asked.

"No," Karen lied. "I might go into town and browse around the shops."

"OK." Paula slung her bag over her shoulder. "I'll see you tomorrow."

Karen said goodbye and struggled bleary-eyed into the bathroom.

She lay back in the suds and thought about what she was going to do this afternoon. It was now or never. She hadn't confided in Paula and she felt a bit odd about that. But Paula was up to her neck in arrangements for her wedding. It'd be strange when Paula moved out. In one way she'd miss her, but in another way, she was looking forward to the freedom of being on her own even if it would be more expensive. Paula was grand but she wasn't exactly riveting company. She was no mastermind. And Steve was here all the time. That pissed Karen off. What went on in Paula's bedroom was her own business, but when Karen had to chat to him the next morning . . . that was a different ball-game.

No, she hadn't said anything to Paula. She hadn't said anything to anyone, not even Liz or Frank. She had to do this on her own. It was nobody else's damn business. She mightn't like what she found out. She mightn't find out anything. The adoption agency had told her to come in at four o'clock. She'd an appointment with someone called Niamh.

Up to two weeks ago, Karen had dropped the idea of tracing her natural mother. She'd got her life in order and she didn't want to disrupt her new-found peace. Then something odd happened. She'd developed a rash on her back and had gone to the doctor. He gave her a cream and he told her it was a type of eczema and . . . that it was hereditary. He asked her if her mother or father had ever had it. How the hell was she to know? It made her think about the fact that she knew virtually nothing about herself. Nothing about her history. All sorts of things occurred to her then. What about family illnesses? What about when she had children of her own? Heredity. It was important. Terribly important.

* * *

"I don't like leaving you with all this unpacking," Donald said as he looked in dismay at all the boxes and crates on the stitting-room floor.

Yvonne put her arms around his neck. "I don't mind, love. In fact I'd prefer to organise things myself. You go on back to the shop. I know you don't trust Barry."

Donald kissed the tip of her nose. "It's not that I don't trust him, but he's a bit dopey. If it gets busy, he's a dead loss."

She kissed him lightly on the lips. "Go on, then. I'll be fine. I'll see you later." She pushed him out the door.

Yvonne looked around her. God, this was great! A proper place to live in at last! The last two years over the shop had been hell. She hated the place. It was old and impossible to keep clean. Berkeley Road was noisy and the night-time traffic was a nightmare. It was impossible to sleep when the ambulance sirens blared up and down the street to the hospital. It had taken her ages to persuade Don to move. But this apartment in Glasnevin had been worth the wait.

She went over to the french window and opened it. They had a small balcony overlooking the Tolka river and the wigwam church. Very picturesque. She'd get some plants and terracotta pots. There was enough room for two patio chairs. The sun shone out here in the mornings if today was anything to go by.

She went into the small kitchenette and started to unpack the crockery and the cutlery. It was amazing how many presses there were in such a small space. She rummaged in the boxes till she found the transistor. Music while you work. She put the few groceries she had into the presses and the fridge. She arranged the pots and pans neatly in the press under the sink.

Next she made up the double bed in the bigger

of the two bedrooms and unpacked all her clothes. The wardrobe was big enough for her stuff, but Donald would have to use the wardrobe in the other room. No big deal. She arranged all her bottles and jars on the dressing-table. His shaving stuff could go in the bathroom. He'd moan about that but she was used to his complaints.

Great! She'd got loads done and it was only twelve. Now for a well-earned cup of coffee. She plugged in the kettle and spooned the coffee and sugar into her Bewley's mug. She opened the fridge and then remembered that she'd no milk. Damn! She hated coffee without milk. Should she knock on the door of the flat next door? Why not? She'd be able to introduce herself. It was nice to be neighbourly.

A tall red-haired girl opened.

"Hi! I'm Yvonne Monaghan. I've just moved in."

The girl nodded. No trace of a smile. "My name is Karen Shaw."

"Pleased to meet you." Yvonne shook her hand. "I'm sorry to be on the scrounge already, but could I borrow some milk? I haven't had time to shop yet."

Karen opened the door wide. "Come in."

Yvonne hesitated. "I don't want to disturb you."

Huh, Karen thought. She must be joking. What did she call the riot this morning if it wasn't a disturbance? "No, not at all, come in."

Yvonne followed her into the kitchen. Their flat was nice too. They'd lots of plants and wall hangings. "This is lovely," Yvonne said approvingly.

Karen took a litre of milk from the fridge and handed it to the girl. "Take this. We've loads."

Yvonne smiled. "Are you sure? Thanks. I'll pay you."

Karen shook her head. "You'll do no such thing. I'll be able to borrow from you when we run out."

"We?" Yvonne asked.

"I'm sharing for the moment," Karen explained. "I live with Paula, my friend. She's getting married soon so after that I'll be on my ownsome."

"Oh, I see. I'm living with Don, my boyfriend." Yvonne said. "We used to live over his shop. Dire. I'm looking forward to living here. It's a lovely area."

Karen nodded. "Well, I was just on my way out, so if you'll excuse me."

Yvonne felt rebuffed. This girl was not exactly friendly. "Oh, I'm so sorry to have kept you." She hurried to the door. "Thanks again for the milk. Maybe yourself and your friend . . . eh . . . "

"Paula," Karen said.

"Yeah, maybe yourself and Paula would come in for drinks one evening."

"That'd be nice," Karen replied stiffly, "but I work at night. Still, I'm sure we can come to some arrangement. We'll wait till you settle in."

"Right." Yvonne smiled again. She felt uncomfortable.

"Bye for now." Karen knew she'd been a bit abrupt as she showed her to the door. She'd better soften her tone a bit. "Welcome to River Gardens."

* * *

The 19 bus was packed with people coming home from work. Those standing lost their balance every time the bus lurched forward. Harrassed mothers hung on to their whinging children and their overcrowded shopping bags. A few, who had managed to get a seat, tried unsuccessfully to open out their evening papers. Most people were in foul humour. Not so Paula Browne. Paula was delirious with happiness. This time next month she'd be Mrs Steve Clarke. Ooh, little butterflies danced in her tummy when she thought about it. She was so lucky! They had their house in Bayside all ready. Her mother was delighted because she'd only be a stone's throw away from Clontarf. They had all their furniture. They had a new fitted kitchen. Paula was glad they'd decided to wait till they'd everything they wanted for their house. Too many people rushed into marriage and then found themselves in a financial strait-jacket, she thought. She'd known Steve for eight years now, but they'd only been going steady for five. Some people thought that five years was too long for an engagement, but Paula didn't. She'd wanted to wait and do it all properly. Now they'd enough saved for a decent wedding and a honeymoon in Torremolinos.

She'd left Steve and his parents at three and had a quick run around the shops. She bought a sexy négligé and underwear. She still needed some shorts and tops and a black bikini. She might invest

563

in some new jewellery. There was nothing like earrings and a neck chain to glamorise an outfit. She must buy a few sundresses too. She'd seen a nice navy one in Dunnes. All in good time.

Paula got off the 19 bus at Tolka House and crossed the busy road. Cars came flying up and down the hill. Bloody dangerous. She was tired and sticky from being in town all afternoon and was looking forward to a nice bath.

She foostered in her bag for the key. It was always in the last pocket she looked in. She fumbled with the key, trying to hang on to her parcels at the same time. She finally managed to open the door. Karen was sitting on the couch, reading a letter. She looked upset.

Paula hurried in. "Karen! What's up? What are you doing here? I thought you were working tonight." Paula glanced at her watch. It was nearly seven. It took Karen at least an hour to get over to Donnybrook. "What's wrong?"

Karen sat dumbly, staring at her letter.

Paula sat beside her. "Bad news?" It must be bad news. Karen never missed work.

Karen shook her head.

"Are you OK?" Paula asked anxiously.

Karen nodded again, but she looked pale and tired. Paula was dying to find out what was going on.

"Are you sure you're all right?" Paula asked more insistently.

Karen stared at Paula as if she wasn't there. "I know who my mother is." Karen's voice was a whisper.

"What?" Paula couldn't have heard properly.

"I know who my mother is. Here." Karen handed Paula the note that the counsellor had given her.

Paula read in silence. She reread it several times. "God, Karen. Where did you get this?"

Karen explained where she'd been that afternoon.

Paula tried to take it all in. "Sheila Crosby . . . Sheila Crosby . . . is that who I think it is?"

"Oh, it certainly is," Karen said bitterly. "You have my mother's products strewn around the bathroom."

"What?" Paula gaped at her. "Natural Woman?"

"Yeah, I checked out the address. Natural Woman." Karen laughed. It wasn't a normal laugh. "Natural bleedin' woman!"

"Oh, Jesus!" Paula gasped. "She was all over last Sunday's supplement. She's gorgeous, Karen. I always thought you looked like her, remember I said that to you when she was on *Kenny Live*? She's absolutely gorgeous."

Trust Paula to come out with something like that. Who gave a fuck what the bitch looked like?

"Sheila Crosby! I can't believe it! What are you going to do?" Paula was still perusing the letter.

"Nothing." Karen's voice was dead.

"Nothing?" Paula gaped again.

"Nothing." Karen repeated.

"Why not?" Paula exclaimed. "That letter says it all. She loves you, Karen."

"She doesn't know me." Karen took up the letter and tore it viciously.

Paula grabbed the pieces off the floor. "Don't do that, Karen. Don't. The woman loves you and she wants to meet you." Paula pleaded. "It's a lovely letter, Karen."

Karen glared at Paula. "Words are cheap."

Paula couldn't believe Karen's reaction. "Words are not cheap," she admonished her. "That woman probably went through torture writing that letter. It's not fair the way you've dismissed her."

"Dismissed her?" Karen shouted. "I didn't dismiss anyone," she said pointedly.

"Tch, stop being so ratty. What's got into you? I'd have thought you'd be thrilled with this news. You always wanted to know who your mother was. Now you know. You have some answers at last." Paula said.

"I have all the answers I need now." Karen's voice was seething with rage.

"What's that supposed to mean?" Paula retorted.

"Well, it's bloody obvious why she gave me away, isn't it? I'd have been an encumbrance." Karen sounded really bitter. "Who'd want a demanding baby around when a career, fame and fortune beckoned? Babies aren't glamorous, are they?"

Paula was very annoyed with Karen. She was being totally unreasonable. "I don't think you're being fair, Karen."

Karen jumped off the couch. "Oh, you don't think I'm being fair? That's a good one. That bitch gave me away and then went on to build a career for herself. Not just any old career, mind you. Oh no . . . She had to be the best. She had to be the toast of Dublin's jet set. I've met her type before. Ruthless business people, Paula. They don't care whose toes they tread on to get to the top. God knows who else she hurt to get where she is today. She's just another fucking gold-digger. Natural Woman. What woman who was natural would give away a child, for God's sake?"

Paula had to answer that. "She had you twenty-five years ago, Karen. Natural Woman didn't exist then. She must have been a young girl when she had you. She most likely couldn't keep you."

"What makes you such an authority on the subject?" Karen shouted. Why was Paula acting like this? Karen thought she could rely on Paula for a bit of moral support. Now, instead of understanding what Karen was going through, Paula was taking sides with that bitch.

"I've read all about her in those fashion magazines you're always giving out to me about," Paula said haughtily. "She started that company in 1972 in a very small way. You'd have been five by then. Her father gave her the money to start up, as I remember."

"Yeah, probably a pay-off for getting rid of me." Karen shuddered.

"Jesus, will you stop and listen to yourself, Karen?" Paula was disgusted with her friend. "Natural Woman had nothing to do with you. I'm telling you there was no such company when you were born. Your mother had probably never even thought of it at that stage. Sheila Crosby's in her

567

early forties, I think. You're twenty-five, Karen. She wasn't even twenty when she had you. Don't tell me she had any huge ambitions back then. Maybe she started up the business because she had nothing else. Did that occur to you?"

Karen ignored what Paula was saying. She shoved a page under Paula's nose. "Would you like to read what he wrote to me?"

"Who?" Paula asked.

"Her father." Karen hissed. "My dear departed grandfather. Jesus, I have relations crawling out of the bloody woodwork now."

Paula read the letter.

24 November 1967

My dearest Karen,

I should be writing this letter to you to welcome you as the newest member of our family. Sadly, this is not to be.

Your darling mother, Sheila, told me about you only last week. You are now two months old and I know I will never be able to meet you, my angel. You are with your new family now and I pray you will have a happy and a healthy life.

You will never know the pain and the anguish your mother suffered at giving you away. I am an unwilling witness to that suffering. Your mother loved you deeply. She wanted what was best for you, my dear granddaughter. It took a lot of courage to do what she did.

If I had only known of your arrival I'd never

have let her go through with the adoption. She, of course, doesn't know this and it's better she doesn't. Her sense of guilt and regret is bad enough as it is.

Someday I hope that Sheila will get over her tragic loss and make some kind of a life for herself. But no matter what happens in the future, Karen, I want you to know that your mother loved you.

Pray God, that she will find you. Pray God, that you'll understand and be able to love her. She's a wonderful person and my greatest treasure.

God bless you and keep you always,
With fondest love from your grandfather,
Pat Crosby.

Paula put the letter down. "Karen, this must mean something to you."

Karen sat down again. "Must it? I fail to see what."

"Oh God, it's heartbreaking. The old man wasn't told till you were gone. He sounded desperate in that letter." Paula read the last bit again.

"Desperate?" Karen said. "Yeah, he must have been desperate all right. Why couldn't she have confided in him when she was pregnant?"

Paula put her head in her hands. Karen was so pigheaded. "That was in 1967, Karen. Single girls didn't confide in their parents. She was afraid. Terrified. It's obvious."

"Well, it doesn't make any difference anyway,"

Karen said quietly. "The old geezer's dead by now. Probably her mother is dead too and she feels safe in contacting me. The shame is gone. Guilt is a thing of the past."

Paula got annoyed again. "That's not what he meant and you know it. She felt guilty because she gave you away, not because she had you."

"Sure," Karen said scornfully. "The woman's a saint."

"No," Paula argued. "She isn't a saint. She's just a normal woman who wants to find the daughter she had to give up. She sounds very sincere to me. Your grandfather seemed to be lovely too."

"I'm sick of discussing it." Karen put the letter back in its envelope.

Paula noticed that she didn't tear up this one. "So, that's it then? You're not going to do anything about her?"

"No." Karen pouted. "Let Natural Woman get on with her unnatural life. I'm not going to intrude."

Paula gave up. Karen was as stubborn as a mule. She wasn't as hard as she made out to be though. Paula had noticed that Karen's eyes were bloodshot when she came in tonight. Those letters had touched her despite what she said.

* * *

"You did a great job today, pet. The place looks lovely." Donald kissed Yvonne on the cheek. She turned her head to kiss him full on the mouth.

"Mmh," he mumbled into her ear, "let's go to bed."

"First I've got to have a shower." She extricated herself from his grasp and went off to the bathroom.

He poured himself a whiskey. He was thrilled that he'd let Yvonne persuade him to buy this place. She was right. It hadn't been a good idea to live over his business. He could never get away from it. Here, he could relax and unwind after a day in the shop. He put on his Classics By Moonlight CD and poured himself a large scotch. He lay back in the armchair, shut his eyes and relaxed. This was terrific.

Yvonne came back, draped in a towel. Her long brown hair was damp and curled around her face in a most appealing way. She looked dead sexy. "Ready, lover boy?"

Donald was turned on, but he was exhausted. He'd been on his feet all day. He wasn't ready for Yvonne. "Do you want a drink?"

She shook her head. No, she didn't want a damn drink. She wanted to go to bed and make mad passionate love. How long had it been since they'd had sex? Too bloody long. Donald was always too tired. It infuriated her. Maybe he was too old for her? Maybe she needed someone of her own age. Still, she really fancied him. She loved his tall bronzed body with its taut muscles. She loved it when he held her in his arms. She couldn't imagine being with anyone else. Donald was a part of her now. She wanted him so much.

Yvonne dropped the towel. She stood there

naked in front of him. Her milky white body was alabaster in the glow of the dimmed lamps. She was graceful, statuesque, at ease with her body. "No, I don't want a drink. I want you."

"Come here." Donald patted the couch.

Yvonne smiled her little cherub-like smile. She was incredible, a mixture of brassiness and purity. *"If you want, here it is, come and get it."* She lilted as she went off to the bedroom.

Donald smiled and followed her.

The glare of sunshine woke Donald early the following morning. Yvonne was already up. He could smell the coffee. He pulled on his grey slacks and white shirt and went out to join her for breakfast.

"Morning." He rubbed her neck and sat down at the kitchen counter beside her. "Sleep well?"

Yvonne poured his orange juice. "Mmh, like a log. There's nothing like exercise to make a body sleep." She winked at him. "I'm on at eight. I'll take a lift with you into work."

"Fine." He stirred his coffee.

"Oh, I forgot to tell you last night, I've met one of our neighbours. The girl next door." Yvonne put his boiled egg in front of him.

Donald cracked it open. "What's she like?"

Yvonne bit her lip. "Hard to say. A bit stand-offish. In the looks department she's a knockout."

Donald leered. "Must check her out."

Yvonne slapped his hand playfully. "Just you

dare! Her name's Karen. She's sharing with another girl who's getting married next month."

God, Donald thought. Yvonne had that dreamy look in her eyes again. Marriage. No way, baby. It wasn't that he had anything against marriage. He hadn't. It was what went with it. Babies. Donald was forty-five years old. He'd escaped all that and he didn't intend to get trapped now. But Yvonne's biological clock was ticking away. He knew she wanted children. Fine for her. She was young. He wasn't. "So, what does she do, this Karen?"

Yvonne shook her head. "I don't know. I suggested a drinks party here one evening, but apparently she works nights."

Donald sighed. "Why did you have to do that?"

"It doesn't hurt to be friendly, Don." Yvonne went off to get dressed.

Sometimes Donald made her mad. He was turning into a real fuddy-duddy. Didn't want to mix. She was damned if she was going to lock herself away. She wanted company. Her mother's warning kept going around in her head. *He's too old for you, Yvonne*. On the other hand, she grinned into the bathroom mirror, he was great in the sack when she finally managed to arouse him. Guess you can't have everything!

CHAPTER THIRTY-SEVEN

Sheila was due in the women's salon this morning as it was Nuala's day off. Phyllis, their new masseuse, had four of her regulars so Sheila would interview the new clients, advising them on skin care and which products would suit them best. Then she'd book them in with Nuala for their individual treatments.

Caroline phoned. The new hotel range of products was doing very well, she told Sheila. Ten of the top hotels in Ireland were now using Natural Woman and Natural Man soaps, shampoos, bath and shower gels in their en suite bedrooms for the use of their guests. The forty staff in Carrigeen were run off their feet with all the new orders.

"How's Ciara coping with motherhood?" Sheila asked.

"Brilliantly," Caroline enthused. "Caoimhe's a pet. She's adapted very well to the crèche. Conor's wife knew what she was doing when she set that up. She's looking after about eight babies now."

"Carrigeen is producing more than skin products." Sheila laughed. "And Seán? Is he enjoying his new role as grandad?"

"He doesn't know himself. He dotes on that child and she adores him. You'd want to see the way she smiles at him." Caroline sounded peeved. "He's much better with her than he was with the twins."

"They say that being a grandparent is easier," Sheila mused aloud.

"When are you coming down?" Caroline asked. "I want you to have a look at the new packaging for the autumn products."

"I'll be there next week for Mam's birthday," Sheila replied.

"Eighty-two years old and she's as feisty as ever. It's incredible." Caroline was full of admiration for her mother-in-law. "She's cracked about Caoimhe. It's a pity my own mother never lived to see her."

Sheila knew that Caroline really missed her mother who was now four years dead. The old lady had died in a nursing home at the ripe old age of eighty-eight. Although Caroline was very upset at the time, she had accepted the death as a happy release. Nobody would want to see a parent live on in pain or frustration.

"Does Mam want a party?" Sheila asked.

Caroline chuckled. "Don't you know bloody well she does! We'll have it here in my house. It'll be easier for me."

"OK," Sheila agreed. "I'll come down the day before and give you a hand. It's a pity Colm won't be back."

"Yeah, but this summer elective thing in Africa's very important. He says it's a great learning experience working outside his own hospital." Caroline sighed. "I miss him dreadfully."

"Not to worry," Sheila said consolingly. "He hasn't gone forever. Do you think he'll go into the practice with Seán?"

"For a while anyway," Caroline said. "I think he's going to go on to do paediatrics eventually."

"Ironic, isn't it?" Sheila remembered how Seán had wanted to do that.

"Yeah," Caroline assented. "I'll let you go. See you next week, then. Friday?"

"Yep, Friday night." Sheila hung up.

Sheila took Eileen Brophy out to lunch to Davy Byrne's.

"How's Kevin?" Sheila asked. She always took a great interest in Eileen's son.

"Just finished primary school," Eileen told her. "I can hardly believe it. He's a good kid."

"What would you do without him?" Sheila remarked.

"I don't know," Eileen confessed. "He's given my life a purpose. He's great company now. I have to admit I'm mad about him."

Sheila knew the child was crazy about his mother too. They had a great relationship. Eileen had always been open and honest with him.

"There were times when I wondered if I'd be able to cope on my own," Eileen went on. "It hasn't been easy, but it's been well worthwhile."

"You never considered marriage?" Sheila felt a bit of a hypocrite asking her that.

"Not really." Eileen finished her smoked salmon salad. "It's different once you have a child. You see men in a totally new way. You're not as free as they are. You have different priorities. The whole dating thing becomes irrelevant. Kevin came first. That's the way it had to be." She added by way of an afterthought, "I don't regret anything though."

"You've a done a great job, Eileen. The boy's a credit to you." Sheila smiled.

"Thanks." Eileen appreciated Sheila's compliment. Most people treated her with a certain amount of censure or suspicion. "I'm not advocating single parenthood, mind you," Eileen said thoughtfully. "Rearing a child is never easy. I still think a happy marriage is the best place for a child to grow up in."

Sheila nodded. Eileen was no fool. Nevertheless, Eileen and her son were right together. Sheila knew it had been difficult, but Eileen was a terrific mother. The little boy was happy. Well adjusted. He'd give her no problems, Sheila was sure of it. "What are you doing about holidays this year?"

"I've no plans for myself. Kevin wants to go to the Gaeltacht with a few of his classmates."

"Oh?" Sheila lit a cigarette. "Does he like Irish? That's great."

Eileen smiled. "I don't know if he's all that interested in Irish *per se*. He's a real Dub. He swears that he won't dance with boggers at the *céilí*! But the holiday will do him good."

"It'll give you a break too." Sheila paused. "I was wondering if you'd go to Grasse for me this summer? I'm thinking of opening a new store so I want to stick around here."

"Grasse?" Eileen beamed. "I'd love to. I really enjoyed it the last time. If I could go when Kevin's away, that'd be perfect."

"Good, we'll arrange it so." Sheila was pleased.

"Where are you opening the new store?" Eileen was surprised that Sheila was embarking on another venture.

"Galway. A friend of mine, who gave me my first job, is retiring and selling his chemist shop. He's given me first refusal on the property." The phone call from Liam O'Flaherty had come out of the blue. Sheila had jumped at the chance. It made sense to have a Natural Woman shop in her home town. "Galway is alive with tourists all summer. The shop will encourage them to visit the Carrigeen factory."

"Yeah," Eileen agreed. "It's a great idea. It'll mean a lot more work for you though."

"Not necessarily," Sheila said. "If I get the right staff and a good manager, it'll be a piece of cake. The essence of success in business is to know how to employ good workers and be able to delegate."

"True," Eileen agreed. "Why keep a dog and bark yourself!"

"Exactly." Sheila laughed.

"Patti said that there was a strange phone call this morning." Eileen stirred her coffee. "A woman rang looking for you and when Patti asked her name, she hung up."

Sheila dismissed it. "If it's important she'll ring back."

"Mmh," Eileen replied. "It happened last week too. It's a bit odd."

"What did Patti say?" Sheila was getting curious now.

"She said she was well spoken, youngish. She seemed very hesitant." Eileen thought about it. "I think she was hoping you'd answer the phone."

Sheila finished her coffee. "I'll tell Patti to try to get her name next time. It's probably a reporter. They can be shifty."

Nuala dashed into the men's salon. "Eileen, quick! Come over to my window. She's over there again."

Eileen followed Nuala across the hall, into the women's salon and peered over her shoulder. "Where?"

Nuala pointed. "There, on the other side of the street, by the lamppost. She's just standing, staring over here. This is the third time I've seen her. It's spooky."

"Ah, she's probably waiting for someone. Maybe she's a model from that agency up the street." Eileen didn't think it was that unusual. "Stand back or she'll see you."

"I hope she does." Nuala was angry. "What does she want? I think I'll tell Sheila when she gets back from Galway."

"Tch, don't go bothering Sheila. The girl's not doing any harm. She's very pretty, isn't she?" Eileen said admiringly.

"From this distance she is," Nuala agreed. "Tall and leggy."

"Look, Eileen! She's coming over. I'm going out to reception," Nuala said determinedly. "I've got to find out what she wants."

Nuala went out to brief Patti. There was something very odd going on and Nuala wanted to get to the bottom of it. She didn't like mysteries.

"OK, Mrs Lynch, we'll see you tomorrow." Patti hung up. "What's up?" she asked Nuala.

"That girl who's been watching the place is coming over." Nuala was excited. "Find out all you can."

The door opened. The girl walked in. She was wearing dark blue denim jeans and a jacket with a navy and white striped T-shirt underneath. Her long red hair cascaded in little curls down her back. She wore no make-up but she was strikingly beautiful. She approached the desk. She looked confident but her hands were trembling.

"I want to see Sheila Crosby." Her tone was imperious.

Patti smiled at her. "I'm terribly sorry. Ms Crosby's away at the moment. Would you like to make an appointment for a consultation?"

The girl shook her head. "When will she be back?"

Nuala pretended to be engrossed in the filing cabinet, but she was listening very intently.

Patti smiled again but she wasn't going to give any information to a total stranger. "I'm afraid I'm not at liberty to tell you Ms Crosby's arrangements. Perhaps you could let me know what it's in connection with?"

The girl froze. She bit her lip. "It's personal."

Patti nodded and took up her pad. "May I take a message?"

The girl frowned and walked to the door. She put her hand on the doorknob and turned back to Patti. "Just tell her that Karen called."

"Karen?" Patti asked politely. "May I have your last name?"

"Just tell her Karen. She'll know." The girl closed the door behind her.

"Weird with a capital W!" Nuala emerged from behind the filing cabinet.

"Isn't it?" Patti exclaimed. "Do you know what's even weirder? I recognised her voice. She's the one who's been ringing and hanging up."

"Did you notice anything else?" Nuala nudged Patti eagerly.

Patti nodded slowly. "She's a dead ringer for Sheila."

"That's what I thought!" Nuala said excitedly.

"Jesus." Patti scratched her head. "What are you getting at Nuala?"

Nuala smirked. They had all heard the rumours. "You tell me!"

"I don't know what to think!" Patti was totally flummoxed.

* * *

The party had gone really well and Rita was in her element on Sunday morning.

"I hope that photo will turn out well," Rita said

to her daughter at breakfast. Rita had insisted last night that Caroline take a photograph of herself, Sheila, Ciara and Caoimhe. Four generations of Crosby women. Strictly speaking Caoimhe wasn't a Crosby at all but you couldn't say that to Rita.

"Caroline's a great photographer, Mam. You can have it blown up and put over the mantelpiece!" Sheila was joking but Rita took her seriously.

"That's not a bad idea, love." She beamed with pleasure.

Jesus, how painful, Sheila reflected. The thought of it made her cringe. "I'm calling over to Kate and Liam this morning. He's signing over the shop to me."

"I never thought Liam O'Flaherty would retire," Rita said thoughtfully. "What'll he do with himself? That shop was his life."

"He's been working hard all his life, Mam. He wants to retire to play golf and look after his garden."

Rita guffawed. "And what about Kate? She's no golfer. She'll go mad without her daily chats."

"Yeah, that's what I thought." For once, Sheila agreed with her mother. Kate O'Flaherty would really miss work. "Maybe I can get her to manage the shop for me?"

Rita stared in awe at her daughter. Sheila was really astute. Kate O'Flaherty would be delighted to keep her job. Sheila had it all thought out as usual.

The phone rang.

"That'll be Seán." Rita went to answer it but she was back in an instant. "It's for you. It's Patti. What does she want with you on a Sunday? Can't they leave you alone for one weekend?" Rita was disgusted.

Sheila patted her head in a placatory fashion and went out to the hall to speak to Patti. Rita took the opportunity to wash the dishes in the sink when Sheila was out of the kitchen. Sheila had insisted on buying her a dishwasher but Rita hated the damn thing. It was more trouble than it was worth. By the time you had the plates scraped and stacked you'd have the wash-up done three times over. Rita had no truck with these so-called labour-saving devices. She was singing merrily to herself when Sheila came back.

"Well, what was the emergency this time?" Rita dried her hands on the towel.

Sheila had gone very pale. "I've decided to go back to Dublin today," she said suddenly.

"Tch, for God's sake, Sheila. Can't you relax here for a few days? We don't see half enough of you," Rita scolded.

Sheila was preoccupied. She didn't answer. The message went round and round in her head. Karen called. Karen called. Patti had tried to ring Sheila yesterday but she couldn't get her. Patti thought it might be important so she phoned today. Important. Yeah, it was important all right. Nothing in Sheila's life had ever been so important. Karen called. Karen. Her adoptive parents had baptised her Karen! Laura, the nurse, had pinned her name to her vest. That's what Caroline had told Sheila. Thank you, God. Karen. Her daughter was really named Karen.

She'd missed her. Why did she have to call the one Friday Sheila wasn't there? Why had Sheila come to Galway a day earlier than usual? She'd missed her. God, what a lousy break.

* * *

"Tell me again, Patti. What exactly did she say?" Sheila said for the umpteenth time.

Patti was fed up repeating the story. Her boss was driving her mad. She'd interrogated Nuala too. She was acting like a crazy woman.

"How did . . . " Sheila faltered, "how did she . . . look?"

Patti couldn't resisit it. "She looked like you," she said bluntly. "We all remarked on it. She's the image of you."

Sheila flushed and fiddled with her pen.

Patti couldn't stop herself. "Is she a relation?"

Sheila nodded. Tears welled up in her eyes. "She's my daughter."

Patti and Nuala bamboozled Eileen into going for a jar after work. Neary's was crowded and Eileen was sorry she'd come. The other pair were all into the gossip.

"God, I nearly died when she said, 'She's my daughter'. I mean I'd suspected something for ages, but all the same." Patti blew a smoke ring.

"Yeah, it's fecking hilarious. The virgin queen with a grown-up daughter!" Nuala grinned.

Eileen was raging. These two had short

memories. Where would they be without Sheila Crosby? It was indecent the way they were carrying on.

"Jesus, I always wondered why she broke it off with Cool Hand Luke," Patti said conspiratorially.

"Who?" Nuala laughed. "You mean the John Harris character? What a beaut he was!"

"Yeah," Patti agreed. "Wouldn't have kicked him out of the bed! I heard them arguing once. He wanted to marry her, you know."

"You listened in on their phone calls?" Nuala was full of admiration for the receptionist's gall.

"Only once or twice." Patti blushed. "She wasn't interested in commitment, she said. Did ya ever? Well she's got a bloody commitment now, what? The return of the long-lost daughter. Wonder who the father was." She winked at Nuala.

"Who knows? Probably a married man." Nuala sniggered.

"Or a priest!" Patti made the sign of the cross.

That was it! Eileen had had enough. "Shut up, both of you! You're nothing but a pair of spiteful bitches. All you're interested in is a bit of juicy scandal. You make me sick."

They both stared at Eileen in horror.

"Why can't you stop and think? Why do you get pleasure out of being so cruel? Do you not realise the pain Sheila must have gone through? Or the girl? How must she be feeling? Think about it." Eileen stood up. "Just because you two are happily married. What gives you the right to judge? I'm leaving. I'm going to pretend this conversation never happened." Eileen took her handbag and left.

"Sensitive bloody cow!" Nuala lowered her gin and tonic. "She's just reacting because she's a single parent herself."

Patti didn't answer. She felt too ashamed. Eileen was right. They ought to have been more sensitive.

Sheila gave Patti the next morning off. She wanted to man the phone herself. Every time the phone rang, Sheila jumped. Another false alarm. Karen didn't ring that day. Nor the next. Sheila had to attend to the rest of her business. She left strict instructions with Patti to get a number if Karen rang back or to give her Sheila's private number upstairs. She didn't ring until a week later when Sheila was doing a stock-take of the basement. Patti took the call and Sheila dashed upstairs.

"Hello, Sheila Crosby speaking," she said nervously.

"This is Karen."

The voice sounded small and fragile. Sheila nearly wept into the phone. "Thank God, you called back. I had no way of contacting you." Sheila's voice was breathless.

A long pause. Say something, Sheila screamed inwardly at herself, say something.

The girl seemed to be more in control. "Would you like to meet some time?"

Would she what?

"Yes, oh yes." Sheila almost sang into the receiver. "When?"

"Tomorrow night?" The girl suggested tentatively.

Sheila breathed a sigh of relief. Her long, long wait was nearly over. "Where?"

"I could call over to your house on my way to work. About five?" Karen's voice was getting stronger as she gained confidence.

"Perfect." Sheila was grinning like an idiot.

"OK. See you then." Karen hung up.

Sheila replaced the receiver, jumped off the chair and threw her arms around Patti. She ran out of the office like someone possessed, dashed up the stairs into the privacy of her bedroom. She had two phone calls to make. One to Mary. The other to Caroline. She jumped up and down on the bed with excitement. This was the happiest moment of her life!

* * *

Karen sat there, shaking. She'd done it. This time tomorrow she'd have met her mother. God, she hoped she wasn't going to regret this!

Paula had sat beside her when she'd made the call. "Come on! We're going over to the Tolka for a jar to celebrate."

Karen shrugged. "There mightn't be anything to celebrate."

Paula yanked her off the sofa. "There will be, come on, Karen. Naturally you're a bit apprehensive. It's taken you ages to pluck up the courage to do it. Now it's done. You've started the ball rolling. I'm glad."

"You're the one who always told me to leave well enough alone," Karen reminded Paula.

"I know." Paula sighed. "But I've watched you torturing yourself for months. I think you should see her. You'll never be able to get on with your own life till you do. Anyway, we've to celebrate our last free night together. I'll be gone in a fortnight and you're working most of next week. So, let's go."

The Tolka was packed. It had been extended and done up tastefully since the new owners took over. Paula preferred the bar so she steered Karen in there. They got a free table up in the far corner. Paula got their pints of Harp and she chatted away leaving Karen to mumble an answer every now and again. Suddenly, Paula stood up and waved at somebody. "Look! There's Yvonne from next door. She's yer man in tow. You've never met him. I'm dying to know what you think of him!" She beckoned the couple over.

This was all Karen needed. Now she'd have to make an effort to converse. She should never have come out. She wanted time to herself to get her thoughts together.

"Hi! Sit down," Paula gushed over the newcomers. "This is Karen. Yvonne, I think you two have already met."

Yvonne smiled and shook hands. She put her arm around the handsomest man Karen had ever seen. He was tall, blonde and tanned with the deepest blue eyes imaginable. A bit old for this Yvonne, but very sophisticated and debonair.

"Hello again, Karen. This is Don."

Donald Fagan stretched out his hand. He couldn't take his eyes off this beautiful girl. His stomach did a little somersault. He knew her! He'd met her before.

"Hi!" He smiled. "Let me get you ladies another drink." He went up to the bar racking his brains to try to remember. Her face was so familiar. He'd definitely met her before. But where?

"All ready for the big day?" Yvonne smiled at Paula.

"Nearly." Paula nodded enthusiastically. "There's a lot to be done though. Most of it has to wait till the last minute."

"Don't mind her," Karen said with a grin. "This is going to be the most perfectly planned wedding in history."

"Karen's my bridesmaid," Paula explained. "She'll be bossing me around all day."

Karen raised her eyes to heaven. "In my dreams."

Paula laughed. "You'll miss me when I'm gone."

Karen nodded. "I will, actually. I'll have no one to pick up after."

Donald arrived back with the drinks. "I can't help wondering where we've met before. I know your face," he said in a puzzled tone to Karen. "It definitely wasn't in the apartments. I'd remember that. You're not a model are you?"

Paula roared laughing. "Our Karen a model? She'd die first, Don! No, Karen is a real brainbox. She's a journalist."

589

Karen gave her friend a filthy look, although she knew Paula hadn't meant any offence.

"A journalist? That's very interesting." Don stared admiringly at her. He couldn't hide his interest. Yvonne was beginning to feel uncomfortable.

Karen said nothing. She just sipped her pint in silence.

"You couldn't have met Karen before, Don." Yvonne was sure of it. "She probably reminds you of someone else. Come to think of it, she reminds me of someone too." Yvonne studied Karen again. Karen was getting pissed off with this. She left her pint and stood up abruptly. "If you don't mind, I'll have to go. I've a lot of work to do." She was gone in a flash. Paula stared open-mouthed after her.

"Your friend's a bit rude," Yvonne said pointedly.

"Sorry about that," Paula apologised quickly. "She's a lot on her mind at the moment."

"Oh?" Don asked politely. "Hassles at work?"

Paula paused. Should she say anything? Ah, why not? They weren't going to blab, were they? Anyhow, it wasn't a state secret. "No, her work's fine. It's just that she's having a bit of an emotional crisis at the moment."

"Boyfriend troubles." Don nodded sagaciously.

"Oh no," Paula told him in no uncertain terms. "Karen never has boyfriend troubles. She's this guy, Chris, head over heels in love with her. The fellas at work are always asking her out. No, she's no men troubles. Not that she bothers much with romance anyhow. No, that's not it."

"It has to be family then." Yvonne groaned.

Paula looked at the two of them. "It is."

"It's none of our business, Paula," Yvonne interjected. "Karen's life is her own affair. It's got nothing to do with us." Yvonne directed the last remark to Don.

"No," Paula continued. "You deserve some explanation for Karen's extraordinary behaviour tonight. She's stressed out actually. She's just traced her natural mother. Karen was adopted you see."

Don felt the blood draining from his face. "Her natural mother?" His voice came out as a squeak.

"Yeah," Paula got excited. "And you'll never guess in a million years who her mother is!"

Don got a flashback. Newman House. 1967. That face. No wonder he recognised it. Long auburn curls, green eyes. The brush-off. The only woman who'd ever given him the big heave ho.

"Who?" Yvonne asked excitedly.

"Sheila Crosby. The owner of Natural Woman. Incredible, isnt it?" Paula said triumphantly.

Don felt sick. He looked at Yvonne. She stared back at him. She remembered that incident in the shop. "How old is Karen?" Yvonne asked quietly.

"Twenty-six next September." Paula said thoughtfully. "Imagine she's going to meet her real mother for the first time in her life tomorrow. It's like a fairytale, isn't it?"

Yvonne nodded dumbly. Don had said he knew her in college. What year was that? Jesus, Yvonne had to get him out of there. She had to get him home. She had to know exactly what had happened with this Sheila Crosby. Could he be the father of this girl? Dear God, it was unthinkable. What kind of a louse did that make him? What's this he'd said? Kid stuff? Christ, what was that supposed to mean?

Don excused himself and hurried out to the jacks. He splashed cold water on his face. Get a grip, he told himself, get a grip. It had nothing to do with him. Nothing. OK she was Sheila Crosby's daughter. OK, so he'd dated Sheila Crosby for a while. That meant nothing. She'd got herself up the pole with someone else. That's why she'd broken it off with him. That's why she left college, it suddenly dawned on him. The bitch had been two-timing him all the time.

But he'd seen that look on Yvonne's face. He knew she'd be looking for some sort of explanation. He'd tell her the truth. This girl Karen had absolutely nothing to do with him.

CHAPTER THIRTY-EIGHT

D-Day. Sheila was a bag of nerves. She took the whole day off work to get ready for this momentous meeting, the most important meeting she'd ever had in her life. Louis had done a great job with her hair. Soft curls framed her face. She stared into the bedroom mirror critically as she applied her make-up. Mustn't overdo it. What time was it? Four o'clock. One hour to go. She looked all right. Except for the navy suit. It was too severe. Too business-like. She took it off and threw it on the bed. She put on her white linen dress. No, definitely not. It was too glamorous for this hour of the day. God, what was she going to wear? She stared in dismay at all the dresses, suits, skirts and trousers hanging on the rail in her wall-to-wall wardrobe. There must be something appropriate here.

She rang down to Eileen in the salon. "Can you come up? I need help."

Eileen had just finished with a client. "I'll be there in five minutes."

Eileen poured Sheila a strong cup of coffee. "Here.

Drink this. Now, let me have a look in your wardrobe."

"It has to be right, Eileen. I don't want to overdress."

"I know. Leave it with me." Eileen went off on her mission.

Sheila lit another cigarette. Her stomach was upside down. She felt nauseous. She couldn't sit. She paced up and down the kitchen in her underwear. What on earth was Eileen doing? It was four-twenty now.

Eileen sauntered back with a dress hanging over her arm. "This is ideal."

Sheila grimaced. "The olive? God, I'm not sure."

Eileen ignored her doubts. "Put it on," she said authoritatively.

Sheila slipped into the simple olive-coloured jersey dress. The bodice was fitted but the skirt fell in loose folds to mid calf. It looked great on Sheila. Simple but sophisticated.

"That's it." Eileen said critically.

"What about shoes?" Sheila said in consternation.

Eileen went off again and came back with a pair of flat beige shoes. "Here. Put these on and stop fussing."

Sheila did what she was told. She was relieved that Eileen had taken over. She couldn't think for herself today. She was hysterical, she admitted to herself.

"Now," Eileen said confidently, "you look terrific."

"Are you sure?" Sheila was still not convinced.

"I'm positive." Eileen was firm. "Now, try to relax. This isn't a job interview."

"No, it's a million times worse." Sheila shuddered. "I can't foul this up. I want her to like me."

Eileen wished she could do something more to reassure her. Normally Sheila was so confident and self-assured. Now she was as jumpy as a kitten. "Take it easy, Sheila. Try to calm down. You don't have to prove anything to this girl. She's your daughter. She's not coming to criticise. She's coming to meet you. She wants to get to know you."

"Exactly. What'll I do if she doesn't like me?" Sheila wailed. "I couldn't bear that."

"It'll be OK, Sheila." Eileen put her arm around her boss. "She will like you. Don't try to impress her. Just be yourself."

Karen got off the 11 bus. Four fifty-five. Good timing. Or was it? Twenty-six years too late, maybe. She straightened her cream skirt and buttoned her navy blazer. Paula had persuaded her to wear these although Karen would've felt much more comfortable in her jeans. She crossed the street and walked slowly towards the house. She wanted to turn back but curiosity propelled her on. She walked up the front steps, her legs trembling. She pushed the big door open and walked into the reception. The blonde receptionist smiled at her.

"Ms Crosby's expecting me," Karen said nervously.

Patti rang upstairs.

* * *

Sheila came down to the second floor landing, her heart in her mouth. Karen walked up the stairs slowly. The *point de rencontre* was symbolic, Sheila thought. They were meeting each other half way. Karen reached the landing and stopped dead. She stared at this beautiful woman who was her mother. She wasn't sure what to do. Should she shake hands? She managed a small smile.

Sheila was overcome. Her daughter. A mirror image of herself at that age. Her heart swelled with pride. This gorgeous creature was her daughter. At last she was here. She couldn't help herself. Sheila rushed over and clasped the girl. "Karen, oh Karen."

Karen stiffened. Sheila pulled away, conscious of having made a *faux pas*. She shouldn't rush this. She smiled warmly at her daughter. "Come on up." She led the way up to the third floor and into the sitting-room.

Karen looked around her. The room was exquisite, like something out of a Hollywood set. The whole house was palatial but not homely. Karen felt uncomfortable. She didn't belong here. She was almost afraid to sit on the plush white sofa when Sheila invited her to take a seat. She watched closely as Sheila sat down gracefully on the armchair. The woman was the epitome of elegance and sophistication. Karen brushed imaginary fluff from her jacket.

Sheila couldn't take her eyes off the girl. She had

this desperate urge to run over and hold her daughter in her arms. She fought hard to control the rising tide of emotion. She couldn't frighten Karen off. She must remain demure. "Would you like a drink?"

Karen shook her head. "No thank you. I'd better not. I've to be in work at seven."

Sheila nodded. This was a good opening for her first question. "Where do you work?"

Karen told her.

"RTE? That's marvellous. Do you like it?" Sheila asked gauchely.

"Yes, I do." Karen replied. "Of course I'd prefer to be a reporter. That's what I'm aiming for."

Sheila was thrilled. The girl had ambitions. She had a determined way about her that Sheila recognised in herself.

"Would you mind if I smoked?" Karen asked hesitatingly.

"Not at all. I smoke myself." Sheila opened the silver cigarette box that lay on the coffee table and offered her one.

Karen refused politely. She took a packet of Silk Cut Blue from her handbag. "I prefer these. They're not as strong."

They lit up and puffed in silence. Karen still felt very awkward. She had so much to ask but she didn't know how to begin. Sheila sensed her agitation. It was up to her to put the girl at her ease. "Tell me all about yourself." Sheila smiled encouragingly.

Karen swallowed hard. "Where do you want me to begin?"

Sheila laughed nervously. This was ludicrous. How could she expect the girl to sit there and give an account of herself? It wasn't on. "I'm sorry, Karen. This isn't easy for either of us. Why don't we just chat and see what happens. Have you any questions for me?" Stupid, stupid, stupid, Sheila scolded herself. Of course she had questions. That's why she was here.

Karen shrugged. She bit her lip. She wanted to scream. *Why did you give me away?*

Instead, she just sat there and idly flicked the ash from her cigarette into the Waterford crystal ashtray.

Sheila leaned forward. "Tell me about your family." Oh Jesus, why did she say that? It was far too near the bone. Family. The girl was here to find out about her real family. Surprisingly, Karen seemed relieved at the question. "I was brought up in Clontarf." Her voice grew steadier. She was on familiar territory now. "My father's a bank manager and my mother's a housewife. Frank and Liz Shaw."

Father. Mother. Sheila felt crushed. My mother's a housewife. A good mother, in other words. Karen's name was Shaw. It sounded strange. Karen Shaw. Sheila couldn't get used to it. She should have been Karen Crosby. No, by rights she should have been Karen Fagan. No. Not that.

"I have one brother, Peter. He's working in Germany. I share an apartment with my friend, Paula. She's getting married next week." Karen stubbed out the cigarette.

"Will you live on your own, then?" Sheila asked.

"Yes, I'm looking forward to that. I like privacy."

Sheila nodded. They were very alike, she thought.

Karen glanced around the room. She took it all in. The expensive furniture. The luxurious carpet. The paintings. The wealth. "I think I will have that drink."

Sheila jumped up. It'd be a relief to go out to the kitchen. "What would you like?"

"Have you any beer?" Not very sophisticated, Karen knew, but she wanted a beer.

"Of course." Sheila hurried out to the kitchen.

Karen glanced at her watch. Five-thirty. Another half-hour to go. This was painful. She shouldn't have come. The whole situation was absurd. Like a scene from a Beckett play. What had she expected? What could they possibly achieve by this? They were strangers.

Sheila came back with the drinks. Karen noticed she had poured herself a large gin and tonic. Or was it vodka? It was large anyway. She sipped her beer thoughtfully.

Sheila spoke suddenly. She had to take the bull by the horns. "I'm sure you're wondering about me, Karen. Why I didn't keep you." Sheila's eyes glistened.

Karen was terrified the woman would burst into tears. She wasn't able for this. She didn't want any outpouring of feelings. She couldn't take it.

Karen put down her drink and took a deep breath. "I did wonder about you, of course. Especially during the last few years. I have my family and I love them. But I wanted to know about you because I wanted to know more about myself." There she'd said it. She thought that she'd managed to say it cooly and without rancour.

Sheila was grateful. Karen had spoken softly and without apparent bitterness. Sheila wanted to explain everything to her. She wanted to reassure her. But she didn't want to swamp her. This was only their first meeting. They had a lifetime left to get to know one another. Sheila would have to take things slowly. "I have something for you. Will you come upstairs?"

Karen followed her up to the bedroom. The first thing she noticed was the framed photo by the large double bed. She picked it up.

"That's you," Sheila said quietly. "A nurse in the hospital took it. It was the only thing I had to keep." Sheila's voice shook. "I never saw you, you know."

Karen stared at her in horror. "You never saw me?"

"No." Sheila went to the wardrobe. Her chest was heaving. She had to get control. She mustn't upset the girl. This was all far too emotional.

"You never saw me?" Karen echoed in a daze. "You never held me?"

"In those days," Sheila still had her back to her daughter, "it wasn't allowed."

"How cruel." Karen's mouth dried up. "How terribly cruel."

"Yes," Sheila said simply. "It was."

Sheila turned around. She had a large folder in

her hands. She handed it to Karen. "I kept this scrapbook for you."

Karen sat on the bed and opened it. It dated back to 1967. She flicked through it. There were newspaper headlines, articles, family photographs. "When did you do all this?" Karen was amazed.

"Every year on your birthday." Sheila ran her tongue over her lips thoughtfully. "I wanted you to know about me . . . my family . . . your family." Sheila looked down at the floor. "You have a right to know everything."

Karen was overwhelmed. "Is this my grandfather?" She pointed to a photo of Pat taken in the garden.

"Yes," Sheila smiled. "That's my father. He was lovely, Karen."

Karen examined the photo carefully. "He has a kind face."

Sheila nodded. "He died when you were six years old."

Karen remained silent. This was the man who'd written the letter. Her grandfather. She felt choked up. Finally she said, "And your mother?"

Sheila paused. "She's still alive. She lives in Galway. All my family are there. Maybe someday you'll meet them."

My God, that had never occurred to Sheila. Why hadn't it? Why wouldn't this girl like to meet her maternal grandmother? And her uncle and aunt? And her cousins? What was Sheila going to say next? *Of course your grandmother knows nothing about you.* God, she should have thought about that.

Sheila sat down on the bed beside her daughter. "You must be dying to know why I didn't keep you. Why I couldn't keep you."

Karen wanted to obliterate this moment. What could she say to that? She had to say something. "When I was younger I used to wonder. Now I don't. It was twenty-six years ago. You weren't married. It was difficult."

"Yes." Sheila sighed. "It was difficult."

Karen went back to the scrapbook. She didn't know how to avoid the next question. "Did my father abandon you?"

Oh God, Sheila nearly died. She should have expected this. "No, he didn't. I never told him about you." She tried to make out Karen's reaction. The girl's face was dead-pan. No expression. No obvious hurt. No blame.

"I see," Karen said softly.

Sheila felt she owed her a better explanation. "He was a student too."

"Right." Karen nodded as if she understood. But she didn't understand at all. He was a student. So what? What possible difference did that make? Did she love him or not? Obviously not. Otherwise she would have told him.

"We were very young, you see." Sheila avoided her eyes. "There was no question of marriage."

Karen said nothing. He wasn't even told. My God, he had a right to know, didn't he? How dare she not tell him! What gave her the right?

"I wanted you to have a good home. A proper start in life." Sheila prayed she'd understand. "A family."

Karen nodded. Couldn't fault her there. She did have a wonderful family all right.

"Thanks for the album. You went to a lot of trouble." Karen felt like an idiot. She was evading the issue. "I'll study it properly when I get home."

Sheila had to accept that that was the only answer she was going to get. "I've marked all the photos and dated them. You have two cousins, two years older than you are. You can read all about them in there."

"Thanks," Karen muttered. What did she care about cousins? She wanted to know more about her father. Who was the man who had made this woman pregnant? What was he like? Where was he? What was his name? Karen was burning to ask these questions but her nerve failed her. This wasn't the right time. It was too soon.

"I'll have to get going." Karen stood up abruptly.

"Oh no," Sheila said in alarm. "Already?" She didn't want Karen to go. She'd only just arrived. Sheila had waited so long for this moment and now it was over. She couldn't bear it. "Will you come back soon?" she pleaded.

Karen flicked her hair back. The gesture unnerved Sheila. She felt she was being dismissed.

"Sure." Karen nodded.

"When?" Sheila couldn't hide her anxiety.

"Next week, maybe. I'll call you." Karen headed for the landing. "You have a beautiful place."

"Plenty of room anyhow." Sheila smiled.

Jesus, Karen thought, let me out. Next thing she'll be asking me to move in. Sheila walked her daughter down the four floors to the front door. The salon was closed and locked up. "Would you like to see around?" Sheila was getting desperate. She couldn't let the girl go like this.

Karen looked apologetic. "I have to dash. Next time, OK?"

Sheila didn't want her to walk through that door. She was terribly afraid she'd never see her again. "I'll give you a lift out to RTE," she offered hopefully.

Karen looked annoyed. "I wouldn't hear of it. I can get a number 10 down the road."

Sheila was mortified. She was making a fool of herself. Never before had she felt so insecure. It was demeaning, she knew. "Whatever you say. I'll hear from you soon then?"

"Yeah." Karen made her escape.

* * *

For the next week Sheila was in a daze. She couldn't concentrate on anything. Mary and Caroline pumped her for information of course. Sheila told them about the meeting with Karen as best she could. The trouble was she wasn't sure herself how it had gone. She felt she'd overstepped the mark in some way. Mary said she was probably imagining that. Caroline, on the other hand, trusted Sheila's intuition. Maybe the girl had been scared off. When she heard nothing after a week, Sheila phoned RTE. Karen wasn't on that day so she left a message to ring back. Another week went by and there was no response. Sheila was up the walls. Caroline advised her to leave it for a while. Karen would get in touch in her own good time. Sheila had to make do with that. But she wasn't happy.

Karen spent a month pouring over the scrapbook. It told her a lot about her mother. Sheila had written copiously about her feelings. There was no way that Karen could ever resent her again. She'd been a victim, that was obvious. She'd been irresponsible in getting pregnant but she hadn't been irresponsible after. Karen realised that now. Sheila had given her away because she wasn't in a position to do anything else. Karen thought she'd done the right thing. The scrapbook was a testimony to Sheila's courage and determination. Once a victim was not always a victim. Sheila had got off her ass and made something of her life. Karen had to admire her. She even liked her. Sheila was likeable. But Karen wasn't ready for a relationship with this woman. She had a mother . . . a very good mother. She didn't need another. What could Sheila be to her now? Where were they to go from here? Karen honestly didn't know. There was no mention of her father. It was as if he didn't exist. He was a student too. Who was he, this mysterious man? The scrapbook filled in half the jigsaw only. For the moment that would have to do.

Karen got on with her life. Paula's wedding had a funny effect on her. A typical family gathering. Paula's father giving her away . . . a girl needed her father when she got married. Karen had a father.

She had Frank. Chris Moore was getting very serious. Paula's wedding had made Chris think. He started to hint about marriage. Karen wasn't ready for that commitment either. She'd still too much to sort out in her head. She'd laughed off his suggestion of getting engaged.

Liz was glad that Karen had confided in her. Her daughter was very mixed up. Liz had dreaded her daughter meeting her natural mother, but it hadn't turned out at all as Liz had expected. The name Sheila Crosby had struck terror in Liz's heart. How could she compete? Then Karen told her she was going to leave things where they were. Liz was shocked. She now felt sorry for this woman Sheila. Karen shouldn't just leave the poor soul dangling. She'd have to get in touch again and explain how she felt. She persuaded Karen to write to her mother.

It was a month before Sheila heard a word. Then, one fateful Tuesday, the note arrived.

> *Dear Sheila,*
>   *Sorry about the delay in getting back to you. I've been really busy. Thanks for agreeing to meet me and thanks for the scrapbook. It has helped me greatly. I'm glad we met. I'm not sure where we go from here. I think we both need time.*
>   *I'll be in touch again,*
>   *Love,*
>   *Karen*

Sheila was numbed. *I'm glad we met.* Full stop. Past tense. Was that it? *We both need time.* How much time? Wasn't twenty-six years enough? Sheila felt idiotic. What had she expected? Weekly tête-à-têtes? Cosy monthly dinners? A family reunion? Sheila didn't know, but she'd expected more than this. She was shattered.

CHAPTER THIRTY-NINE

That summer was a scorcher. Ireland was not used to this. The price of foreign holidays plummeted. The sales of garden furniture and barbecues soared. After two or three weeks, you couldn't buy an electric fan for love or money. A doctor on the radio advised everyone to drink more liquids to avoid dehydration. People were warned about not wasting water. Hilarious in a country which teemed rain for most of the year. It was desperately hard to work in the heat.

Yvonne Monaghan was exhausted. She'd hardly slept at all. The heat was unbearable even with the window open. More than the heat was bothering Yvonne. Last night's row with Don had left her tossing and turning all night.

She heard Don pottering around the kitchen. Could she face another scene this morning? She'd have to. She couldn't go through another day on the wards with her mind not on the job. It wasn't fair to her colleagues or the patients. She'd have to have it out with Donald. Again. She dragged herself out of bed, threw on her cotton dressing-gown and went into the bathroom. He'd left a wet towel on the tiled floor. She was damned if she was going to pick up after him. She splashed cold water on her face and squinted into the mirror. Big bags under her eyes. Jesus, thirty years old. Depressing. She picked up the toothpaste. He'd left the top off as usual. That infuriated her. She brushed her teeth vigorously till her gums began to bleed. Stupid. Why take out her anger on herself?

She stormed into the kitchen. Don was reading the morning paper. He didn't look up.

"Donald, we have to talk." Yvonne poured herself a cup of tea and sat down stiffly at the table. "Now."

He grunted from behind the newspaper.

"We have to talk!" He wasn't even listening to her! She grabbed the paper out of his hands and threw it on the floor. Aggression was out of character for Yvonne, but she was raging. His indifference was really getting to her.

He stood up angrily. "Don't ever do that again." He picked up the paper and went back to the sports page.

Yvonne fumed. He needn't think he could ignore her like this. Who did he think he was? "Listen to me, Donald." Her voice was shrill.

Listen to me, Donald. Christ, nag, nag, nag. He was sick of her. Don glowered at her over the paper. Not a pretty sight! She looked a mess. Her hair was tangled. He noticed the lines around her mouth and eyes. When had they appeared? Her neck was scrawny too. She wasn't ageing well, that was for sure. "Stop whining," he commanded.

That did it! Yvonne was fit to be tied. "How dare you," she screamed at him. "How dare you say that to me."

Donald groaned. Not another bloody tirade. Not after last night. "Shut up, will you? I have a headache listening to you. Just shut up!"

"No, I will not shut up, Donald. You have to listen to me." She spat the words. "Last night you were too drunk to reason with. You wouldn't listen to me then. You've got to listen to me now. I can't go on like this. We have to discuss it."

He laughed and folded his arms. "Have to? Have to? Listen sweetheart, I don't have to do anything I don't want to."

Sweetheart. It sounded like a bad word coming from his mouth. How could he sit there, grinning in that supercilious way of his. He was actually laughing at her. Nothing that she'd said last night had made any difference. Nothing. "Don, let's not fight again today," she implored him.

"Suits me." He went back to his reading. He wished she'd get dressed and go to work. He'd had enough of this haranguing last night before he'd escaped to the pub. Then another onslaught when he came home. He regretted the punch but it had been the only way to shut her up. This wasn't working out. Too much hassle.

Yvonne sighed. "We can talk without arguing, Don."

"I'm not sure if we can, my sweet," Donald drawled. "It seems to me we're at cross-purposes."

He wasn't going to get involved in another futile discussion about marriage.

"How long are we together, Don?" She went to take his hand, but he pulled away.

Too bloody long, he thought to himself. "Forever," he smiled a sickly smile. It was beginning to feel like forever.

"Five years, Don. It's a long time." Yvonne tried to sound calm. Shouting and arguing were getting her nowhere. She'd try to be rational this time. "What do we have to show for it?"

What did she want to show for it, for God's sake? A bloody ring on her finger, that's what she wanted. No way.

Don stood up slowly. He had to get out of there before he really lost his temper. He'd go into the shop early . . . anything to get away from her. "I told you last night, Yvonne. Marriage isn't on the cards for us. It never was. When we moved in here three years ago, you understood that."

"But things change," she argued. "I've changed."

"Yeah," he agreed, "that's the understatement of the century." He thought back to their early years together. She was very attractive then. She was fun. She was full of life. Of course, she was young five years ago. Young and fresh. Look at her now, lined and haggard. She should look after herself more.

"Look, Yvonne," he said coldly. "I like it the way things are. That is, I did before you turned into this snivelling moan. We agreed we'd live together, that's all. I'm never going to get married, you'll have to accept that."

"Do you love me, Don?" She had to ask. That was the crux of the matter.

"Yeah, in my own way, I guess I do." He shrugged. He wasn't sure anymore. Funny, he used to be mad about her. It was true what they said: if you want to know me come and live with me.

In my own way . . . Yvonne felt sick. What was his own way? "People who love each other want to celebrate their love," she said softly. "I want to share my life with you, Don. I want us to be married. I want to have children. That's what love is about."

"Jesus, not the baby routine again." He walked to the door. "Will you get it through your thick skull, I don't want children. I don't want my life wrecked by squalling, smelly, snotty-nosed brats. Not now . . . not ever. I'm forty-eight years old, Yvonne. I'm past all that."

"What about me? What about what I want?" She followed him to the door. "What about me, Donald?" She pleaded with him and she was angry with herself for doing that. She felt demeaned. She tried to hold him back, but he went out to the landing.

"You know the score, Yvonne. You'll have to make up your own mind."

"Maybe I should leave?" She stared into his eyes, hoping for some reaction. Some flicker of concern or doubt.

"You'll have to do whatever you think is best for you." He turned away and walked down the stairs.

Chris brought Karen breakfast in bed. "Wake up sleepy-head." He kissed her cheek.

Karen opened one eye and smiled. "Mmh." She yawned and stretched and slowly sat up.

"I'm off to work." He put the tray on the bedside table. Orange juice, cereal, toast and tea.

"Aah." Karen was disappointed. "Can you not come back to bed for a while?" The heat was having an effect. She felt randy.

Chris chuckled. "I've just had a cold shower. You temptress, you're not going to have your wicked way with me!" He walked to the bedroom door. "Kar, will you think about what we discussed last night?"

"Yeah, I will," Karen promised. "Last night. God, don't mention the war. Will you ever forget it? That pair next door need to be locked up. Did they realise we could hear every word?"

Chris frowned. "If it went on any longer, I'd have gone in there and told him to lay off. I think he actually hit her at one point. He's a right bollocks. She seems nice enough. What does she see in him?"

"I don't know," Karen said. "There's no way we could end up like that, is there?"

"No earthly way. We love each other, remember?" He smiled.

He was lovely when he smiled, Karen thought. He was lovely full stop. He came back and kissed her tenderly. Then he left.

Karen drank her orange juice and poured milk over her muesli. *Will you think about what we discussed last night?* She'd have to do more than think about it. She'd have to do something. Today. They'd decided to get married. Liz and Frank were charmed. Paula was ecstatic. Everyone liked Chris.

Karen loved him. He was her best friend. Of course she fancied him like mad too. Who wouldn't? She thought back to the day he walked into their class in Rathmines. Chris Moore . . . tall, dark and handsome. He had longish dark brown hair and beautiful big brown eyes. All the girls on the course fancied him. When the gang went to the pub, he'd always sit beside Karen. She smiled when she thought about how they used to argue over politics, mainly about Northern Ireland. Chris was intelligent. He was compassionate too. He was a brilliant reporter. They had a lot in common . . . peas and carrots, as Forrest Gump would say. Most important of all, they were good friends. She'd wanted them to be more than that. But he'd never asked her out on a proper date . . . not until her twenty-first birthday party.

Then things changed. They started to see each other twice a week for drinks or the theatre. She loved being with him. The first time they'd made love, Karen knew he was the one. He was gentle and passionate . . . a wonderful combination. But it wasn't just sex with them. Karen reckoned that it was their friendship that made their relationship special.

Karen had lived on her own for a year after Paula got married. She discovered she didn't like being on her own. She wasn't as independent as she'd thought. When Chris moved in it seemed like the most natural thing in the world. They got on brilliantly from day one.

Karen was now twenty-eight. Marriage was the inevitable next step. Children. Karen had never stopped thinking about Sheila. She hadn't met her since that first meeting two years ago. She'd exchanged Christmas cards and holiday postcards. That was all. Karen couldn't face seeing her again. That diary made her realise how much Sheila had gone through. She didn't want to have to deal with Sheila's suffering. So, she'd deliberately dropped contact. She didn't like complications. At times she regretted ever having looked for Sheila Crosby at all. It had opened up too many wounds.

She'd avoided meeting Sheila again but . . . she wasn't able to avoid her thoughts. She thought about Sheila all the time. She worried about her. It seemed absurd to be worrying about a woman like her, a woman who had it all. The diary had told a very different story. Sheila had pined for her for all these years. Jesus, it was pathetic. But it was overwhelming too and Karen couldn't face it.

How could she marry Chris and have kids of her own when she hadn't sorted out her own feelings? What about the man who had fathered her? Where was he now? What was he like? Should she try to find him? Oh God, she just wanted the whole problem to blow away. She loved Liz and Frank and Peter. They were her real family. Why couldn't she be content with that?

But she couldn't. She had to know everything.

Sheila Crosby had given birth to her. It was Sheila's blood running through her veins. Sheila's and . . . whose? That was the question. Whose? Who was her father?

Instead of heading straight for RTE, Chris drove over to Clontarf. He had to talk to Karen's parents. Karen was tearing herself apart. He couldn't stand idly by and watch that happen. She was too dear to him.

He drove into the Shaw driveway on Mount Prospect Avenue. The sitting-room curtains were open. Good, Liz must be up. Chris knew that eight o'clock in the morning was a bit early for a visit but needs must.

"Mornin'." The milkman smiled pleasantly.

Chris smiled back. He rang the bell.

"Chris?" Liz was in her dressing-gown. She was taken aback. "Is anything wrong?"

Chris followed her into the kitchen. "I think we should have a chat. Is Frank up?"

Liz put a cup of coffee in front of him. "He's shaving. He'll be down for his breakfast in a minute. What's up? Is it Karen? "

"Yeah, it is." Chris stirred his coffee. The kitchen door opened.

"Morning, Chris." Frank Shaw, his tie askew, sat down for his breakfast. If he thought it odd that Chris was there at this hour of the day, he made no comment. Liz gave her husband a boiled egg and sat down with her cup of tea.

"I'm sorry to interrupt you both," Chris began. "I think we need to clear the air a bit."

"Clear the air?" Liz was surprised. "Is it about the engagement?"

Chris nodded. "In a way it is."

"Well?" Liz spooned sugar into her cup. "What's on your mind? You haven't changed the arrangements, have you? Everything is going ahead as planned, I hope. I was talking to your mother on the phone, Chris. We thought an engagement party might be a nice idea. Of course we'll have to see what Karen thinks. Everything's OK, isn't it?"

"He'll tell us, dear, if you give him half a chance." Frank gave his wife a look. "Go on, Chris." Frank nodded encouragingly at the young man.

Chris paused. How to put this without causing offence? "It's Karen. She's upset and confused. The idea of marriage is scaring her." He stared down at the red check tablecloth.

"Oh, sure we were all like that," Liz interrupted again. "Marriage is a terrifying prospect for the best of us. I remember my own mother saying . . ."

"Liz," Frank admonished her. "Let Chris talk. Please. Go on Chris, we're listening."

Chris was grateful to Karen's father. Her mother was making this difficult. "The reason Karen's so confused is . . . she needs to come to terms with . . ." he had to say this, "who she is."

Phew! He'd managed it. Now, how would they take it? He looked at each of them. Frank was nodding, but Liz looked uncomfortable.

"Who she is?" Liz repeated. "I don't know what you mean."

617

"You do know, Liz." Frank poured his wife another cup of tea. "Chris is talking about Karen's birth mother. Karen's feelings are very mixed up. I wanted to talk to you about it before, but you wouldn't." His wife's hurt expression crushed him.

Chris went on, although the tension at the table was palpable. "Karen's afraid of upsetting everyone. She doesn't want to hurt either of you. One minute she wants to get in touch with Sheila Crosby, the next minute she doesn't. She looks on you as her real parents but she worries about her other mother all the time. She wants Sheila Crosby to be a part of her life, I'm convinced of that."

"No, no, you're wrong there, Chris." Liz stood up and went to the sink. She spoke quickly and her voice was shaky. "I had it all out with Karen two years ago. She only met Sheila Crosby once. That was all. She didn't want to meet her again. She told me that herself. She decided to leave well enough alone. She told me. She said I was her mother, the only mother she'd known." She sounded panicky.

Frank stood up and put his arms around Liz's shaking shoulders. "Sit down, love. Don't be upsetting yourself. We have to listen to Chris."

Liz didn't want to listen. This boy was going to say something she didn't want to hear. Who the hell was he to be coming in here and disturbing them at this hour of the day? What gave him the right?

"You know how much I love your daughter," Chris said pointedly.

Karen couldn't move forward if Liz kept dragging her back. He took a deep breath and continued, "She loves you both, she loves Peter. She's always saying that. But meeting her other mother like that . . . it raised all sorts of questions for Karen. She needs to get to know her. She needs to know what Sheila's really like. She's dead curious about her. I can't blame her for that."

"Nor I," Frank agreed. "None of us here in this kitchen know what it's been like for Karen."

"How can you say that, Frank?" Liz had tears in her eyes. "I know what it was like for her. She told me."

"She told me too, Mrs Shaw," Chris said quietly. "She was terrified that you'd be upset. She didn't want you to think she was throwing your love for her back in your face. As I said, she'll always look on both of you as her real parents but . . . Mr Shaw is right. None of us here know what it's like to be adopted. Always wondering who your parents are . . . who you really are. It must have been desperate for Karen."

Liz started to sob. "We were here for her. I did my best to tell her the truth . . . always."

"Yes, we did try, Liz, but the problem is we didn't know the full truth. We had no real answers for Karen. We couldn't tell her about her mother." Frank took his wife's hand. "We knew nothing about her or . . . her father either."

"That's it," Chris butted in. He was glad Frank was the one who'd brought it up. "She has to know about her father too. I think she'd like to look for him. Karen says she can't have children of her own till she knows more about herself. It's understandable." Chris looked at Frank. How would that go down?

"Mmh," Frank said quietly. "I think Karen's right. There's been too much bloody mystery and secrets. That's what's wrong with her, Liz. You're dead right, Chris. It's time for everything to be out in the open. That's the only healthy way." He paused. "What's she going to do?"

Chris folded his arms. "I've persuaded her to go back to see Sheila Crosby today. Of course she's worried about that too. She wants to ask Sheila about her natural father, but she doesn't want to embarrass her. Honestly, she's so bloody sensitive about everyone else's feelings."

"Karen was always very sensitive, very deep," Liz said with a sigh. "I hope the two of you are right. I hope Karen knows what she's doing. I couldn't bear to see her hurt anymore. All I ever wanted was for her to be happy." Liz began to cry again. "I don't want to lose her. I couldn't bear that either."

Chris hugged his future mother-in-law. "That won't happen, Liz. I can guarantee it."

Liz sat alone in the kitchen after the two men left. She was utterly miserable. She knew she had to get over her deep-rooted animosity to this woman, Sheila Crosby. That name sent shivers down Liz's spine. She still felt threatened by the woman who had played a shadowy part in her life for so long. She knew she was paranoid. Overreacting. Karen was her daughter. She was Frank's daughter. They had raised her, loved her, nurtured her. Nothing could wipe out those vital years. So . . . why did she feel so insecure?

Was it insecurity or jealousy? Liz had to admit that she didn't want to share Karen with this woman. It wasn't fair. Liz was the one who had walked the floor at night when Karen had colic. She was the one who got up at ungodly hours to give Karen her bottle. She was the one who'd helped with the homework, met the teachers, brought Karen to school. She was the one who was there for Karen all the time. She was still there for her daughter. Twenty-eight years of motherhood . . . she wasn't going to be brushed aside. This woman couldn't breeze in now and expect to take on the mother role. Could she?

Karen got up. She'd do it now before she changed her mind. She went out to the sitting-room and picked up the phone. She dialled the office of Natural Woman. The receptionist put her through.

"Thanks, Patti. Sheila Crosby speaking." The tone was detached. Remote.

"It's Karen."

Silence.

"Sheila, this is Karen." She felt like a complete idiot. Why didn't her mother answer? Oh God, she shouldn't have rung like this, out of the blue.

"Karen?" Sheila's voice quivered. "How are you?"

"Fine." Karen wished she wasn't so damn nervous.

"It's great to hear your voice." Sheila grinned down the phone. At last . . . Karen on the phone. She was actually speaking to Karen.

"I'd like t-to . . . to meet you."

Sheila was ecstatic. "When? Oh when?"

"As soon as possible? Today?" Karen hoped she wasn't being too pushy.

"Great!" Sheila nearly dropped the phone with excitement. "Are you working today?"

"Not till tonight. I could come over to your place this afternoon, if that's all right."

"Perfect," said Sheila. "I was supposed to go down to Galway this evening for the races but that doesn't matter. I can cancel it."

"Oh no," Karen said hurriedly. "There's no need for that. I can see you when you get back."

No way was Sheila going to put off this visit. For two years she'd been praying for a call. She wasn't about to let Karen slip away again. Not if she could help it. "Look, I don't give a damn about the races. I'd much rather see you."

"Well, I can come this afternoon. That way you needn't upset your plans," Karen insisted.

"OK," Sheila agreed. She could take this afternoon off work and drive down after. God, she didn't give two hoots about work or the races or any damn thing. She'd take the whole day off. All she cared about was seeing Karen again. "I hadn't planned on going until about five. Can you come over before that?"

"Sure, I'll be there at three." Karen hesitated,

"Sheila . . . there's something I want to tell you . . . I'm engaged."

"Engaged? Oh Karen, that's . . ." Sheila was all choked up. "Who is he?"

"His name's Chris Moore. I'll tell you everything when I see you."

"Oh Karen, I'm so pleased for you. That's the best news ever." Sheila couldn't believe it. Her little girl was engaged. That's why she'd rung her. She wanted to tell her her news. Sheila was overjoyed. Karen wanted to share her happiness with her.

Karen bit her lip. She was glad Sheila couldn't see her expression. "I need to talk to you about . . . about my father." She blurted out the last bit.

Sheila drew in her breath. She started to shake. She sat down. Karen's father . . . Christ, Sheila hadn't given him a thought in years. He was totally irrelevant. Long forgotten . . . but obviously not for Karen. Of course she wanted to know about her father. Why hadn't Sheila recognised that? She was an idiot.

"Sheila, are you OK? I didn't mean to startle you."

Sheila shook herself out of her stupor. What was she going to say? She tried to keep her voice steady.

"Right, Karen," she managed to mumble. "We'll talk later. See you at three."

* * *

Sheila was up the walls. Two long years had passed. Now this. Two years of disappointment and frustration. Two years of waiting. Waiting for the postman . . . waiting for the phone to ring . . . waiting for the day Karen would unexpectedly walk in the door. It hadn't happened. Sheila had finally accepted that she mightn't ever see Karen again.

She'd filled those two years with work. She'd got on with her hectic social life: parties, dinners, fashion shows, launches of her new products, opening nights at the Gate and the Abbey. Finian O'Toole was happy to be her escort. He was even happier to be her accountant. Natural Woman was a goldmine! Two years of living a full life . . . a busy life.

Now this. When she least expected it, her daughter telephoned. She should be over the moon! When she first heard Karen's voice on the end of the line, she was. Then the bombshell. *I want to talk about my father.* Of course she did. Why wouldn't she? It should have occurred to her that her daughter would want that. She'd been living in cloud-cuckoo-land. Karen only wanted to see her now because she was getting married and she wanted to ask about her father. Naturally. What the hell was Sheila going to say to her?

What words would make sense of the whole mess? Sheila couldn't think straight. She had to talk to Mary. She rang the salon to tell them she wouldn't be in today. She tried to give instructions to Patti about rescheduling her clients, but she got confused. She'd much more important things on her mind. She poured herself a strong coffee. Then she rang Mary.

Mary dropped everything and dashed over to Sheila's. They sat in the pristine kitchen and talked for two hours. Mary to the rescue again. At twelve o'clock Sheila opened a bottle of wine. Mary knew she needed a drink. Sheila was like a herring on a grill.

"Sit down, Sheila. Try to calm down." Mary poured her a glass of the Chardonnay. Her own hands were shaking. Mary had a terrible sense of foreboding. This was like a bad dream.

Sheila gulped down half a glass of wine. "Jesus, Mary, what am I going to do? What am I going to do?"

Sheila got hysterical as the time crept by and Mary felt sorry for her. But what use was that? Who was she anyway to be feeling sorry for Sheila, in the name of God? She had to take charge and calm her down. She had to be the voice of reason. She had to be careful what she said. "Take it easy, Sheila. It's not as bad as it seems."

"Not as bad as it seems? Are you nuts, Mary? It's dire. She wants to know about her father. Her father. What do I know about him after all these years? God, how am I going to explain everything? What do I say?" Sheila was frantic.

Mary sighed. "Look, Sheila. Karen isn't a fool. She must know something."

"What? What could she know?" Sheila shouted at Mary.

How was Mary going to say this? "OK, let's look at this logically . . . "

"Logically!" Sheila nearly had apoplexy. "There's nothing bloody logical about any of this. What do you mean, logically?"

Right, it had to be said. "Karen must know that you weren't . . . in love with him." Mary took a quick glance at Sheila. So far so good. "I mean she must realise everything wasn't rosy between the two of you or you . . . or you would have married him."

Sheila nodded slowly. Did Karen know that?

"This was inevitable, wasn't it?" Mary handed her a cigarette.

"What? Karen asking about her father?" Sheila fiddled with the lighter.

"Yeah." Mary looked at her. Had it really never occurred to Sheila that this would happen?

"I . . . I don't know . . . I hadn't thought about it quite honestly." Sheila stood up and started pacing.

Mary poured her another glass. "Sheila, I can't believe that's true. She wanted to meet you so it stands to reason she wanted to meet her father too."

Sheila bit her lip. "Yeah, I know. I just hadn't thought about it. It seems ridiculous, but it's true. I didn't want to think about it, I suppose."

Mary didn't know what to say.

Sheila sat down again. "What am I going to tell her?" She flicked her ash nervously in the overflowing ash-tray.

"The truth," Mary said starkly. "You've already told her that you never said anything to Donald Fagan. She won't be under any illusions, Sheila. Just give her his name and let her take it from there. It's out of your hands after that. Karen's a grown woman. She has the right to do whatever she feels is right. To tell you the truth I thought she'd have asked ages ago. Funny how she waited so long."

"She's getting married." Sheila was on the verge of crying. "I don't even know her yet and now she's getting married. I'll probably never get to know her properly at all. She's going to have more on her mind now than getting to know me. I thought she'd want me in her life, Mary. How could I have been so stupid? She's a stranger to me. I don't know anything about her at all really, do I?"

"Tell her the way you feel," Mary said. "Tell her you'd like to meet her fiancé. That's great news. Getting married. She's got her life together, Sheila. You must be glad about that."

"I am. Oh, I am," Sheila said tearfully. "OK. I'll give her his name. That's all I can tell her anyway. What do I know about Donald Fagan now?"

Mary nodded guiltily. Should she tell Sheila that the bastard was back in Ireland? Should she? That he had a shop in Berkeley Road? Should she tell her that? Should she say blithely, Oh, by the way, I bumped into him a few years ago. Lord, she felt like Judas. But if she told Sheila that now, it'd make it worse. She should have told her when she met the bum five years ago. But then how was she to know this would happen? That Karen would turn up asking about him? Should she tell her now, this minute? Should she? No. Better not. Sheila would go mad. She had to change the subject before she blurted out something she'd regret.

"I've news myself," Mary said suddenly.

"Oh?" Sheila asked. She'd been so wrapped up in her own problem she hadn't even asked Mary how she was.

"I'm going back to college," Mary announced triumphantly. "Psychology."

Sheila was stunned. "You're giving up teaching?"

Mary shook her head. "No. I've taken a three-year career break. I'm going to Trinity as a mature student."

"Brilliant!" Sheila was amazed.

"Yeah." Mary laughed. "Wouldn't it be a scream if Davy gets in too. He wants to do business studies with German. We have to wait till August the 17th for the Leaving results. I'm always anxious the day the results come out. Teachers really do care how their students get on. But being a parent is much worse. You want them to get on for their own sake. You don't want to pressurise them. You have to be there to pick up the pieces if they don't do as well as they expected. It's hard." Mary knew she was rabbiting on, but this was safer territory.

Sheila was convinced that Davy would get what he wanted. He'd worked very hard. He was highly motivated. She pictured Mary and Davy in college together. "Daily lunch in the Buttery with your son."

"I'm sure he'd be thrilled at that prospect," Mary drawled.

"What does Jim say about all this?" Sheila asked. She was glad to be able to talk about something else. Even for a minute.

"Jim's all for it. He thinks going back to college will be the making of me. He's very supportive."

Sheila was pleased for Mary. It was eleven years since the abortion. It had taken Mary ten years to come to terms with it. Not that she'd ever really come to terms with it, but she had learned to let the past go. That's what she'd have to do today. Tell Karen the truth and accept the consequences. What other option had she?

"I'd better go, Sheila." Mary took up her bag. "Good luck this afternoon." She didn't envy Sheila. This would be very dicey. "Let me know how it goes."

"Yep. God, Mary, I didn't even offer you lunch. I'm sorry. I'm in such a tizzy I don't know what I'm doing."

"Don't worry about it." Mary dismissed the notion. "I don't think either of us could have eaten. Maybe you should have something now though, soup or something. Those two glasses of wine might go to your head."

"No," Sheila said despairingly, "I might as well have been drinking water. I'm too uptight to be tipsy. I have a headache actually."

They stood there staring at one another. Mary grabbed Sheila and gave her a big hug. "You'll get through this, Sheila. You'll know what to say when the time comes."

"I hope you're right." Sheila shuddered.

"I am. Think back on how you coped with much worse than this." Mary hugged her tighter. "Much worse."

Sheila walked her down to the front door. "It's like you said. I can only tell her the truth. She'll probably never find him at this stage. Don Fagan could be anywhere."

Mary had a sinking feeling in the pit of her stomach. She felt like a right heel. A coward. She walked down Sheila's steps and turned back. Sheila looked forlorn. Mary tried to smile.

"Good luck, Sheila. It'll be fine."

Would it be fine? Mary prayed it would be. She waved and got into her car. She felt like a rat deserting the sinking ship.

* * *

Karen arrived at three o'clock on the dot. Patti showed her up to the sitting-room where Sheila was waiting for her. Sheila looked causal in her blue sundress – an act of bravado. She felt anything but casual.

Karen hadn't dressed up this time either. She wore white shorts and a black T-shirt. Sheila smiled and ushered her to a seat. "You look well, Karen. You've a nice tan."

"I cheated," Karen admitted with a grin. "I used your self-tanning gel."

Sheila laughed. "It looks great. You're a good ad for Natural Woman. I can't take the sun myself, my skin's too fair."

"Mine too." Karen smiled. This conversation was a bit trite, but Karen didn't mind. At least they had something in common even if it was only the state of their skin. Sheila seemed very jittery.

"Will we have something to celebrate your

engagement?" Sheila went to the drinks cabinet. She'd have a soft drink herself or she'd be in no condition to drive to Galway.

"I'd prefer a coffee actually," Karen told her.

"Grand. I'll go and make it." Sheila put back the glasses.

"I'll come with you," Karen said.

She followed Sheila out to the kitchen. God, it was like an operating theatre, antiseptic. It was scrubbed clean, white and a cold green. Karen didn't like it at all. It certainly wouldn't be her idea of a cosy family room. It was far too stark. But then, domesticity wasn't what Sheila Crosby was about. This elegant four-storey building was more like a showhouse than a family home. It was sort of sad, really.

Sheila gave her a mug of coffee. "No point standing on ceremony," she said glibly.

"No," Karen agreed. This was bloody embarrassing. They were each trying to put the other at ease.

Sheila put a plate of biscuits on the table. "Would you like a sandwich or something?"

"No, no," Karen assured her. "This is fine." Karen didn't like biscuits but she took one anyway.

"So you're engaged," Sheila began. "You must be very excited."

"Mmh," Karen muttered between mouthfuls. "Chris is lovely. You'll have to meet him."

Sheila smiled with delight. "I'd love to."

Karen nodded. "He wants to meet you too."

"This is for you both." Sheila handed Karen an envelope.

"What's this?" Karen took the envelope.

"It's an engagement card. No, don't open it now." Sheila poured more coffee.

"Are you sure you wouldn't prefer a drink?"

Karen took another biscuit. "No, this is grand." She put the envelope into her bag. "Thanks. We're hoping to get married next spring."

Sheila smiled. There was no mention of an invitation coming her way. She didn't really expect one.

"So, you're off to the Galway Races?" Karen asked for something to say.

"Yeah." Sheila offered her a cigarette. "I go every year with Caroline, my sister-in-law. I think there are some photos of her, in the scrapbook I gave you."

"Yeah, there are. She's married to Seán, the doctor, right?"

Sheila nodded. She felt she should suggest that Karen would come to Galway some time to meet her cousins, but that was impossible. Ciara and Colm didn't even know Karen existed. And as for Rita . . .

Karen sat there puffing away. She didn't know what to say next. She could see that Sheila was on tenterhooks. She'd have to say something soon. How to broach the subject, that was the problem. She couldn't just come out with, tell me about my father, could she? She couldn't help thinking about that programme she'd seen recently on TV about artificial insemination. In a way, this was like that. Her father was merely a sperm donor when she thought about it. She couldn't put a face or a name to him. That's why she was here with Sheila now. For information. Information of the most intimate nature. She'd have to ask sooner or later.

Sheila could see that Karen wasn't going to come out with it. It was up to her to put her daughter out of her misery. "You want to know about your father?"

Karen looked Sheila straight in the eye. "If that's OK with you."

Sheila tried to keep her expression neutral. It wasn't OK with her at all. It was mortifying. She smiled at her daughter, a sad smile. "To tell you the truth, I haven't been looking forward to this. I'd like you to try to understand my position. You know, why I didn't tell him about you."

Karen grimaced. She pitied Sheila. This was embarrassing. "I think I do understand, Sheila." She felt funny calling her Sheila but she couldn't call her Mum or Mam or Mother, could she? "Were you afraid he'd dump you?"

Christ, she hasn't a clue. Sheila hesitated. She wasn't sure how to say this without hurting the girl. "No, Karen. I wasn't afraid of that. He might have rejected me all right but, to be frank, I wouldn't have married him. He was nice, don't get me wrong, but he was young . . . a bit come-day-go-day."

"Irresponsible you mean?" Karen suggested.

"Yeah, a bit. Not that I was very responsible myself, was I?" Why had she said that? Did she need Karen's approval? This was impossible. "Anyhow, I thought it better not to say anything to him. He couldn't have helped . . . not in any real way."

What the hell did Sheila mean by that? Why couldn't he have helped? He was the one who got her pregnant. He hadn't needed any help with that, Karen thought snidely. He should have been told. She didn't understand this at all. If she got pregnant, and there was no chance of that, Chris would be the first to know. "Don't you think he had the right to know?"

Sheila shrugged her shoulders. "I'm not sure. Perhaps. But rights always lead to responsibilities, don't they?"

Karen scratched her head. She wasn't about to argue, but she thought Sheila was wrong. He should have been told. "Can you tell me more about him?"

Sheila shifted in her seat. "I can tell you what he was like then. He was bright, witty, popular. He was very handsome, tall and blond. He hung around with a big gang of blokes. They liked to party. They used to go off to England every summer to work. He didn't take things too seriously, not even his studies. It was different in the sixties."

Karen smiled wanly. She knew all about the sixties. Flower power, free love, peace on earth. San Francisco with flowers in your hair. She imagined Sheila in long floral skirts and beads. Different times all right, but free love was a slight misnomer. "When did he break it off with you?"

Sheila lit another fag. This was the pits. Donald Fagan was a ghost from the past. She had loved him for a short time, or she'd thought she loved him. But it was years since she'd thought about him at all. She'd only thought about Karen. Donald wasn't part of the equation. She'd dismissed him from her mind years ago. Until now. She couldn't say that to Karen. Children wanted their parents to be in love. They wanted to be the result of that love.

But Sheila had always thought of her daughter with love. She wanted Karen to know that. But she couldn't say the words . . .

"He didn't break it off with me. I finished with him when I knew I was pregnant."

It sounded so callous. So cold-blooded. But that wasn't the way it had been. Sheila couldn't find the right words. She had nothing against Donald Fagan, she realised now. He was irrelevant. But to say that to Karen was unthinkable. She tried to soften it. "Neither of us was in a position to get married, as I told you before. There was no point going on with it. I finished my year and left college. After . . . after you were born, I lost interest in everything."

Karen could believe that. She tried to imagine what it must have been like for a single woman to go home to her parents after a trauma like that. "And you've never seen him since?"

"No." Sheila said ruefully. "I don't think he was too upset. I heard he had a replacement for me very soon after." Damn, she hadn't meant to say that. That made him out to be the villain of the piece. Sheila didn't want to blacken his name. She didn't want Karen to resent him. He was her father, after all.

Karen didn't like the picture that was emerging. The guy sounded like a typical womaniser.

"We were young, Karen." Sheila tried to undo

the damage. "I'm not blaming your father for any of this. We were foolish . . . " God, she nearly said, we made a mistake. How would that have sounded? Sheila didn't think of Karen as a mistake . . . Not then. Not now. The mistake was in giving her away.

Sheila didn't trust herself to say any more. "I know nothing about him since then, Karen. I believe he went abroad."

Karen finished her coffee. She was still missing the vital piece of the information. "All I need to know now is his name."

Sheila sighed. His name. Of course. "His name is Donald Fagan."

* * *

Karen staggered into Fitzwilliam Square. She didn't know how she'd got out the door. She was in shock. She'd tried to keep her cool. She'd tried to appear normal, but Sheila must have noticed how oddly she'd behaved. Karen knew she'd gone white when she heard that name. She'd stood up abruptly and left in a hurry. God only knew what Sheila thought.

She stumbled down Sheila's steps and rushed down the street. She crossed over at the junction of Baggot Street and Pembroke Street. She stepped out blindly and barely missed being hit by a car speeding around the corner. The driver rolled down his window and screamed at her. Karen hardly noticed. She was in a daze.

There was no way she was going to get a bus

back to the flat. She hailed a passing taxi and mumbled her address.

Karen sat back in the taxi. The driver turned on the radio. Good, even inane conversation was beyond her. She had to think.

Donald Fagan! Donald Fagan was her father! It had to be him. Sweet Jesus! Mr Smoothie . . . living right next door to her . . . her father . . . who would believe it? It was incredible. Ghastly. No, it wasn't possible. It was someone else with the same name. That silly ass couldn't be her father. Could he?

The description fitted. The age was right. He'd been abroad. Sheila was right there. Oh God, it must be him. But Sheila didn't know that he was back in Ireland. Back in Dublin. Living in Glasnevin. Living right next door to the daughter he never knew he had. Should she go to see him now, tonight? Should she knock on his door and reintroduce herself. Hi, I'm Karen. Remember me? Yeah, your neighbour. Your daughter. Jesus, it was far out.

Maybe she should wait. It would be madness to go rushing in. She'd discuss it with Chris first. What would Chris think? He wouldn't believe it. Donald Fagan! She hadn't talked to the creep since that night in the pub two years ago. What had he said then? He'd thought he'd met her before. *I know your face*. Yeah, he damn well did. It was Sheila's face he'd remembered. He probably knew! He probably had already guessed. That was why he kept avoiding her. He barely nodded at her when they met on the stairs. That had suited her fine. She preferred to keep herself to herself too. The girl, Yvonne, was friendlier. What was Yvonne going to say when she found out her boyfriend had a daughter, practically the same age as herself?

Was she going to go ahead with this tonight? Should she stop and think about it some more? It hadn't been a good day for Karen. Work last night had been particularly unpleasant. She'd had a run-in with one of the reporters. Karen arranged the timing of his report, checked the script and made the inevitable cuts. The reporter had a stand-up row with her about it in front of the whole newsroom. Karen was pissed off with this particular character. He was full of his own importance. The report was too wordy. Verbose. Try telling that to motor-mouth! She got her way. The editor agreed with her. She got a certain amount of satisfaction from that, but she didn't want to make too many enemies among the reporters either. After all, she was going to join their ranks one of these days. She'd make bloody sure of that. But she was still in bits after the episode. Now this. It was too much. She'd need time to digest the news, try to get used to the idea first.

She paid the taxi driver and got out. She went up to the flat and poured herself a beer, cold from the fridge. Damn! She'd left all the dirty breakfast dishes in the sink. She wasn't going to do the dishes now. She turned on the TV. Oprah Winfrey . . . Jesus, no way. She'd enough traumas of her own. She went to telephone Chris in RTE. He'd left her a message on the answering machine. He'd be late.

Damn. She needed to talk to him. No point in phoning him now. He'd only tell her to wait anyhow. She heard the TV on next door. Somebody was in. To hell with it, she'd worked herself up to this now. Her adrenalin was flowing. She was ready. It was now or never.

Don opened the door. His face fell. Her. What did she want?

"Is Yvonne in?" Karen asked.

Did he imagine it or was her tone threatening? "She's not here." He felt flustered. This girl made him nervous. "She's gone to see her mother." He was about to close the door when Karen stopped him. "Good. I need to see you alone."

Alone. Why did she need to see him alone? What the hell did she want? "Sorry. This isn't a good time."

Again he moved to close the door but Karen refused to be put off. "It won't take long."

Reluctantly he let her in. He didn't ask her to sit down but she did. She looked around her. His apartment was the pits. No taste at all. The yellow dralon three-piece suite was a monstrosity. It swamped the room and screamed at the floral green carpet. How did Yvonne stick living here? Still, she wasn't here to criticise his sense of decor, or the lack of it. She took the remote control and turned off the TV.

Donald seethed. She had some nerve! She looked self-possessed. Triumphant even. He was annoyed. This was his home. His sanctuary. This girl was invading his space and he didn't like it. "What do you want?" His voice was gruff.

Karen was furious. What did she want? Yeah, that was the question. She didn't think she wanted anything from this sleazebag. There he was in his white shorts, T-shirt and sneakers, looking like an ad for Reebok. Fecking idiot.

"I've just come from a visit with my mother, Sheila Crosby." She stared at him.

Donald flinched. "Bully for you!"

"You used to date her," Karen accused him.

Donald sniggered.

"Are you denying it?" Karen challenged him.

"I dated a lot of women. Is that a crime?" He grinned.

Karen glared at him. "It depends. In Sheila's case maybe it was a crime. You got her pregnant."

Donald snorted. "Ha! Is that what she told you? She's a great imagination."

Karen clenched her fists. "I'm no figment of her imagination, believe me. You got her pregnant. I'm the living proof." Now, let him sit there and grin if he dared. She hoped she'd shocked him.

Donald sat back on the sofa and laughed. A horrible laugh. "Don't delude yourself my dear. Sheila Crosby is, shall we say, mistaken. I dated her a few times but I didn't really know her. Not in the biblical sense, if you catch my drift." He leered.

Karen was mortified. He was such a cretin. He was smarmy. Karen was beginning to see why Sheila had never told him. "I didn't come here for a debate about the bible."

Donald licked his lips. "Why did you come?"

Karen took a deep breath. "To tell you that I'm your daughter. In my naïveté, I thought you'd want to know."

"That was very considerate of you, my sweet."

Karen squirmed in her seat.

He eyed her up and down. "But a bit naïve, as you said yourself. Did you think I was going to fall for this? Did you think I'd give a fuck one way or the other? What did you expect? Open arms and a welcome to the paternal bosom?"

"I'm your daughter!" Karen shouted.

He roared back at her, "I have no daughter. I never wanted a daughter. I certainly don't want one now."

Karen was appalled. He looked . . . mad. "But Sheila . . ."

"Sheila Crosby is your mother, fine. I'm very happy for the two of you. But you can't drag me into this. I'm not your father. I'd know if I was."

"Not if you weren't told," Karen protested.

"Exactly. Why wasn't I told?" he asked cynically. "Sheila Crosby never said a word to me about being pregnant."

"Because . . ." Karen blurted, but he interrupted again.

"Because it had nothing to do with me. That's why." He smirked at her.

Karen shook all over. Was he right? Was Sheila bluffing? God, what was the truth? Had Sheila sent her off on a wild goose chase? Had she lied to protect someone else? Sheila thought he was still abroad. Had she come up with his name because she thought it was safe? Jesus, what was going on? Who was telling the truth?

Her stunned expression had some effect. He softened his tone. "Look, I'm sorry for you. You're the innocent party here. But so am I. This woman can't get away with this. She's lying to cover herself. You have to face the truth. Sure everyone knew she was sleeping around. She probably doesn't even know who your real father is."

A blinding pain seared through Karen's head. Her mouth had dried up. She felt dizzy. He was lying. He had to be lying. "What if she'd told you? Suppose she'd proof?"

"Proof? Like a blood test?"

He arched an eyebrow.

"Yes, a blood test. Suppose it was indisputable that you were the father of her baby. What would you have done?" Karen pleaded with him.

Donald stood up. "It's lucky for you that didn't happen, my pet. I would have insisted that she got rid it. An abortion would have been the easiest option."

Karen shuddered.

"Of course the question is purely academic now. She didn't tell me because she knew I wasn't responsible. I'm not your father." He went to open the door. "A word of advice. You can't go around accusing every Tom, Dick and Harry of being your father. Your mother was obviously a whore, that's not your fault. Forget it and get on with your life." He opened the door wide. "Goodbye."

Karen stood up shakily from the sofa. The room was beginning to spin. She stumbled to the door.

Donald breathed a huge sigh of relief. It was over. He'd been dreading this for the last two years. It'd been easier than he thought. It had only taken ten minutes. The girl was a pushover. She'd believed him. Poor fool. Who gave a damn whether he was her father or not? Donald didn't.

He remembered hazily one drunken night of so-called passion. That hadn't been his best performance. A touch of brewer's droop. Sheila Crosby hadn't been terrific either, if he remembered correctly. She'd put up a bit of a virginal front, he smiled to himself. Still his manly prowess had won the day. He'd eventually persuaded her to succumb. Another conquest.

So, she'd got a bun in the oven for her trouble. Tough. He opened a can of cider and switched the telly back on.

CHAPTER FORTY

Chris got home from work at about eleven. The flat was empty. Strange. He was worried about Karen. She hadn't shown up for work and she hadn't answered the phone all evening. Where on earth was she? He looked in the sitting-room and the bedroom. She hadn't left a note. Most unlike her. He'd ring the Shaws. Maybe she was there. If not, he'd try Paula. He went to the phone in the sitting-room.

There was a message on the answering machine. He pressed play.

Chris, this is Frank. Karen is here with us. She's dreadfully upset. Could you phone as soon as possible?

What was going on? Why had Karen left the flat and gone home to her parents? What had got into her? He dialled their number.

"Frank? I've just got in from work. I got your message. How's Karen? What's going on?"

"We're not sure, Chris. She rang here about two hours ago. She was hysterical, screaming and crying into the phone," Frank said. He sounded worn out. "I drove over to Glasnevin and brought her back here."

"But what did she say? What happened?" Chris asked hurriedly.

Frank paused. "I'm trying to piece it together. It was impossible to understand her. She wasn't making sense. She screamed at us, she ranted and raved. Something about her mother and her father. We couldn't make it out. She was really hysterical. She screamed at Liz. Said it was all her fault. Liz ended up in tears. Then Karen ran up to her room and locked herself in."

"Where is she now?" Chris kept his voice steady.

"She's still in her room. She won't come out. Liz has pleaded and pleaded with her, but she won't even answer. I rang Peter at his flat. He came over immediately. She won't talk to him either. He tried to force the door but that made Karen worse. She screamed the house down. She's in her bedroom, sobbing her heart out and she won't let us in. Liz is frantic."

Chris took a deep breath. "God almighty."

Frank took the phone out into the hall. He didn't want his wife to hear. Peter had taken his mother into the sitting-room and forced her to drink a brandy. Frank lowered his voice. "I'm really worried about the two of them. Could you come over?"

"I'm on my way." Chris put down the phone and grabbed his jacket.

Karen lay face down on the bed. The tear-stained pillow stung her face. Her body heaved with sobs. She wanted to die. *It has nothing to do with me . . . I'm not your father . . . Sheila Crosby must have been sleeping around . . . An abortion would have been the easiest option . . . Your mother was a whore . . . I'm not your father . . . Forget it . . . I'm not your father.* Karen saw his face, his leer, his ghastly grin. She heard his raucous laugh. *I'm not your father.* Oh God, she wanted to die. Who was she? Why had she ever been born? Why? *An abortion would have been the easiest option.* Would it? Would it have been better than this? He was right. An abortion. A sharp pain and then obliteration. No more suffering. No more pain. She should have been aborted. *Your mother was obviously a whore.* Was she? Was she sleeping around? Donald Fagan. He didn't want her. He denied her. Sheila Crosby. She gave her away. They didn't want her. They abandoned her. Both of them. *I'm not your father. Your mother was a whore.* What did that make her? Unwanted. A mistake. A mistake to be got rid of. An unwanted pregnancy.

Karen sat up and looked around her room. The teddies, the dolls, the childhood books . . . old friends. The patchwork quilt made by her mother. No, not her mother. Liz Shaw was not her mother. The bookshelves made by her father. Frank, the man who posed as her father. She'd loved this room . . . her room as a child and a young adult. Her room where Peter used to come for late night chats. Frank and Liz and Peter. Her Family. No, no, no. They weren't her real family. They'd adopted her. They took her on. They took her in. Yeah, they'd taken her in in more ways than one, hadn't they? Why had they taken her as their own? She wasn't theirs. She didn't belong to them. They only took her because they couldn't have children of their own. They'd chosen her the way you'd pick something from a shopping catalogue. They were just as bad. She hated him. Donald Fagan. He'd denied her, rejected her completely. She hated her. Sheila Crosby. She'd given her away. She'd rejected her too. She hated them. Frank and Liz Shaw. They'd reared her as their own. But she wasn't theirs. She wasn't and she never would be.

Karen got up and walked unsteadily to the shelf. Her legs were wobbly. She was dizzy. She grabbed her teddy bear and crushed it to her breast. She crawled back into bed and pulled the covers over her head. She was going to stay here and never come out. She'd lie here and sleep. Sleep. Sleep would take away the pain. She'd lie here forever. They could all go to hell.

Bang, bang, bang at the bedroom door. Chris could hear her moaning softly. "Karen. Karen, it's me. Let me in." He knocked again.

"Go away, Chris." Her voice was muffled.

"Karen, please. Open the door. Let me in," Chris begged.

"I can't. I don't want to see you." The voice was stronger, but choked with sobs.

"Karen, please," Chris implored her. "I want to talk to you. I love you."

"Go away, Chris. Leave me alone," she shouted angrily. "I don't want you here. Go home."

Chris softened his tone. "Please, Karen. Open the door. I just want to talk to you. I need to see you. I love you. I can't go home without you. It's not home without you there."

No reply. He put his ear up to the door. He could hear her sobbing quietly. "Come on, Karen. Whatever it is, we can talk about it. You can talk to me."

"I can't talk to anyone," she said slowly. "Go away."

Chris knocked again, this time more gently. He didn't want to frighten her. "What's wrong, love? Please talk to me."

Another stifled sob.

"What happened, Karen?" Chris was getting desperate. "What happened, love? Please open the door and let me in. You can tell me. You can tell me anything. Whatever it is, it doesn't matter. I love you. Nothing else matters. I love you and I'm here to help you."

More sobbing.

"Karen." His voice was firmer. "Open the door."

"GO AWAY!" She screamed back. He could hear the hysteria in her voice. "Go away, PLEASE."

"I'm not budging till you open this door." He had to be tough with her. "Think about your mother and father. They're downstairs waiting to talk to you, Karen. They want to help you too."

A choked laugh was his response.

"Karen, your mother and father love you. They want to know what's wrong. They want to help."

"Help," she shouted back at him. "They've left it a bit late for that."

"Open the door, Karen." Chris was frustrated now. "I can't help you till you open the door."

"You can't help me, Chris. They can't help me either. Nobody can." Her voice was strange, removed.

"But I love you," he persisted. "We love each other. You do love me, don't you, Karen?" This was his last shot.

Silence.

"You love me, don't you?" he repeated despairingly.

Her voice was a whisper, a little girl's voice. "It's too late for us, Chris."

Chris came down to the sitting-room. Liz looked up anxiously. "Well?" She'd aged in the last two hours.

Chris sat down on the sofa. "No luck. She won't open the door." He felt defeated.

"What the hell happened today?" Peter poured a whiskey for Chris.

"I'm not sure," Chris took a large gulp. The whiskey burned his throat. "I presume she went to see Sheila Crosby."

Liz said nothing. She didn't remind them of their morning conversation. She didn't want to say, I told you so. But she'd been right. She'd been dead set against Karen going over there. They hadn't listened to her. Whatever happened today was Sheila Crosby's fault.

"There's only one way to find out," Frank said suddenly.

"What?" Peter looked at his father. He looked at

649

his mother. They were like two old people, vulnerable and afraid. He wanted to do something to help.

"We'll have to ring Sheila Crosby." Frank looked at each of them in turn.

"We don't have her number," Liz said quickly. Ringing Sheila Crosby was the last thing she wanted. That woman had done enough damage.

"Her salon number must be in the telephone directory." Frank was resolute. "What do you call it?"

"Natural Woman," Liz said scornfully.

"It's too late to get a reply there," Chris said. "We need her personal number. Have you got Karen's handbag? I think she has the number in her diary."

"Yeah," Frank replied. "She flung it in the hall on her way upstairs." He went to get it.

"Chris, I don't think this is a good idea." Liz glanced anxiously at her future son-in-law. "It'll make things worse. Karen's in an awful state. That woman can't help. She probably caused all this."

Frank came back with the bag and handed it to Chris. He rummaged through it and found the diary. He also pulled out an envelope. "What this? It's addressed to Karen and me."

"Open it," Peter came over and peered over Chris's shoulder.

Chris opened the card. A cheque fell from the card onto the floor. Peter picked it up.

Chris read the card aloud. *Congratulations. I couldn't be happier for you both. Please accept this with all my love, Sheila.*

"Jesus," Peter exclaimed. "Look at this! It's a cheque for a hundred thousand pounds!"

Chris was stunned. Frank looked at Liz. She'd turned white with annoyance. "There you are, that says it all. That woman with her bloody money. She tried to pay Karen off. No wonder the child's so upset."

"No, Mrs Shaw." Chris shook his head. "Karen doesn't know about this. The envelope was sealed, remember? Karen didn't open it. But it proves one thing."

"Yeah," Liz said smugly. "It proves that that woman thinks she can buy Karen's love. That's what it proves."

"Not now, Liz," Frank begged his wife.

"It proves Karen was there today." Chris ignored Liz's bitter retort. "Here's her number. I'll ring first thing in the morning."

"What good will that do?" Liz raised her eyes to heaven.

"None of us was able to get through to Karen tonight," Chris said firmly. "We don't know what happened today. How can we help when we don't know what's wrong?" His desperation made him shout. "Sheila Crosby might have the answer. She'll have to come over here."

"No," Liz stood up. Her eyes flashed angrily. "I won't have that woman in my house!"

Frank went over to his wife and put his arms around her. "Liz, we have to. We have to help Karen. This woman is the key to it all. She'll have to come here and sort it out."

"Huh! What makes you so sure she'll want to help?" Liz pushed her husband away.

"I think she'll come, Mum." Peter pleaded with his mother. "I think she loves Karen."

"So do I," Chris agreed.

Frank nodded. "I know she does. So do you, love. We've both known that from the beginning."

Liz was shaking. They were all trying to manipulate her. She was worn out.

"May I stay here tonight?" Chris asked. He wanted to be near Karen. She might yet open the door.

"Sure, I'll stay too. We can bunk down in my old room," Peter suggested.

"I'll ring Sheila Crosby first thing in the morning." Chris finished his whiskey. "I'll go up to Karen and give it one more try."

"She's probably asleep by now," Frank said sadly. "She's cried herself out."

"Yeah." Chris nodded at Frank. "Hopefully she'll sleep for the night."

Liz looked at her husband. He was distraught. Chris was too. Poor Peter. What must he be thinking? What had happened to cause Karen so much misery? Liz had never seen her like this. If she didn't come out of that room tomorrow, Liz would have to ring the doctor. They'd have to force the door. What if Karen did something desperate?

What if she came downstairs when they were all asleep and tried something? A knife? The oven?

"Frank, lock the kitchen door and take the key," Liz whispered to her husband.

Frank stared blankly at his wife. What did she mean? Oh God, surely not?

But he went and did as she asked. This was very frightening. He came back with a jug of water and a glass. "I'll leave this outside her door. She must be thirsty."

"Give it to me." Chris took the jug. "Maybe we should take turns keeping watch?"

"Right." Frank thought this was a good idea. "We'll let Liz sleep though. She's on her last legs."

Chris and Peter nodded agreement.

"I couldn't sleep," Liz insisted. "Call me if Karen opens the door. I have to talk to her. I won't be able to sleep till I talk to her."

None of them would get any sleep tonight, Liz thought. And tomorrow, that woman would come here. She'd come into their home and shatter their family circle forever.

CHAPTER FORTY-ONE

The Galway Races . . . the crowds . . . the
atmosphere . . . the style, the smiles, the fun. Huh,
some fun, Sheila thought. The thunder storm that hit
Ballybrit that Tuesday night was freakish. Caroline
and Sheila ran, with the rest of the crowd, under the
stand for cover. The sky darkened and torrential
rain beat down. Thunder growled overhead and
spectacular flashes of lightening terrified the crowd.
There was a huge explosion. Later they found out
that lightening had struck one of the pylons. The
computers went out and the races had to be
suspended for half an hour. The heat was
unbearable.

They decided to leave.

Sheila had parked near the entrance gate so they
had to slither down the hill through mud and wet
grass. Caroline's white shoes were ruined. Sheila
was in foul humour. She'd left Dublin immediately
after Karen had gone. She'd got into her car and
driven down to Galway at breakneck speed, but still
arrived too late for the first race. That had annoyed
Caroline. To make matters worse, Sheila had bad
period pains and her feet had swelled in the heat.

She hadn't won anything either. Then, despite the warm evening sun, the storm had struck with a vengeance. That had put the tin lid on everything. A bad omen.

Wednesday, August the 2nd was another hot sunny day. The temperature was up in the thirties. Sheila gave the races a miss. She couldn't get Karen out of her mind. She drove her mother to Barna to visit an old friend who lived in a hideous new bungalow. The two old ladies chatted over cups of tea and scones. It reminded Sheila of a scene from *Arsenic and Old Lace*. They bitched about some of the golf crowd, caught up on local scandals and complained about the heat. Sheila couldn't get over her mother. Eighty-five and still a gossip. *Plus ça change.*

Caroline called in after tea. She was in better form than she'd been the night before. She'd won a substantial sum on Life of a Lord, the unexpected winner of the Galway Plate.

"Seán backed the favourite, Postage Stamp, but it fell." Caroline laughed. Then she noticed Sheila's worried expression. "What's up, Sheila?"

Sheila gave her mother a cup of tea in the sitting-room. "Come on out to the kitchen," she whispered to Caroline.

"What are you two up to? Why can't you talk here?" Rita eyed them both. She hated to be excluded.

"Oh, just talking shop, Mam," Caroline replied quickly. "The new ad campaign. You watch the telly. We'll be back in a minute."

"Where's Seán?" the old lady asked. "I thought he went to the races with you."

"He did," Caroline told her. "He decided to go for a drink with Peadar and Bridget after the races."

"Where they did go?" Rita didn't like missing a trip to the pub.

"To the Corrib Great Southern."

"Oh, I'd loved to have gone." Rita was disappointed. She should have been asked, shouldn't she? She liked the Corrib Great Southern. The hotel was plush. The racing crowd always thronged the bar. There was a great atmosphere. Outside you could see the helicopters landing, bringing back the richer punters from Ballybrit. Definitely the way to travel, Rita thought. She liked watching the race-goers and criticising the style. It wouldn't have hurt Seán to ask her.

"Seán should have come over for me," Rita scolded Caroline.

Sheila handed her mother the remote control, made a face behind her back and ushered Caroline out to the kitchen.

"Look, if you're that concerned, Sheila, why don't you ring Karen?" Caroline suggested. Caroline could never understand why people caused themselves so much unnecessary worry.

Sheila was exasperated. "I still haven't got her phone number. I was going to ask her but she left so abruptly. We were getting on fine and then . . . when I gave her his name, she froze."

"Well, I suppose it was difficult for her," said Caroline.

"Mmh," Sheila agreed. "But I think it was more than that. She got a fright. It was as if . . . as if she knew him."

"Tch, that's hardly likely, is it?" Caroline said dismissively.

"I don't know," Sheila said thoughtfully. "I'm telling you, Caroline, she practically fell out the door. I got into a flap then and left myself. God knows what happened to her after. Maybe I should ring Patti? The salon would be closed by now but I could ring Patti at home to see if there were any messages for me. I have her home phone number in my address book."

Caroline thought she was overreacting but, if it made her feel better, she might as well. It was better than sitting there fretting. Caroline joined her mother-in-law in the sitting-room while Sheila made the call. Rita was beginning to doze off. She didn't even notice when Caroline changed the channel to RTE 2. Caroline didn't like missing *Coronation Street*.

"Sheila? Thank God. I was trying to get you all day." Patti was relieved to hear her boss's voice. "I rang and rang but there was no answer."

"I took my mother out," Sheila explained. "What is it?"

"Someone called Chris Moore rang the salon early this morning. He'd been ringing your private number but you weren't there. I told him you were in Galway. He said he had to speak to you urgently. It's about Karen."

"Oh no," Sheila groaned. "Did he leave a number?"

"Yeah, hang on."

Sheila drummed her fingers on the hall table. She knew it. She'd sensed there was something terribly wrong.

Patti came back on the phone and called out the number Chris had left.

"Thanks, Patti. I'll ring it straight away." She replaced the receiver before Patti could say goodbye. She dialled the number.

It was answered on the third ring. "Hello, Frank Shaw speaking."

She was on to Karen's father! This was the Shaws' house she'd rung. Her stomach muscles tightened.

"This is Sheila Crosby. Chris rang and asked me to phone." Sheila's voice shook.

"Hello, Sheila? I'm Karen's father." He had a deep mellow voice, but Sheila could hear the anxiety. "Karen's in trouble. Chris told me you were in Galway. I don't want to alarm you, but it'd be great if you could come here. Maybe you could come home tomorrow?"

"Mr Shaw," Sheila said nervously, "if Karen needs me I can be there tonight. I'll leave straight away. I could be at your home by half ten." Thank the Lord for all the by-passes. They cut the journey by at least an hour.

"That's very good of you. Have you the address?"

He was embarrassed. Of course she didn't have the address. Karen would never have given her their address.

"No, I have a pen here. Could you call it out to me, please?" This was awkward.

Frank called out the address and Sheila took it down.

"Is s-she bad?" Sheila stuttered.

Frank paused. "She hasn't left her room since she came home last night. She refuses to open her door. She won't talk to anyone. Not even Chris. I'm afraid she's been like this since her visit to you yesterday." He hoped he didn't sound as if he were blaming her, but that's the way it was. "Liz, my wife, sent for the doctor this morning but she refused to see him. What could he do? He suggested forcing the door, but we don't want to do that if we can avoid it. The doctor left some sedatives. A lot of use they are with her door locked. We just can't understand it. We thought you might be able to throw some light on it. Karen's never acted like this before. We don't know what's got into her. My wife is up the walls with worry." So was he, but there was no need to rub it in.

"I think I might be able to help," Sheila replied slowly. "That's if Karen will let me talk to her."

"We have to try everything," he said in despair.

"Yes." The blood had drained from her face. "I'll see you soon."

"Thanks." He hung up.

Sheila replaced the receiver. She was trembling. What had happened to her daughter? Sheila thought

about the visit again. *All I need now is his name.*
That was it! Everything had changed the minute
Sheila had told her his name. Donald Fagan. It had
something to do with him. Sheila knew it.

Sheila was ashen-faced when she joined Caroline in
the sitting-room. Her mother was snoring loudly in
the armchair. That was a blessing. It gave her the
chance to speak to Caroline. She told her about the
phone call to Karen's father.

"I'll have to go immediately. He sounded really
distracted on the phone. Will I wake Mam?"

"No," Caroline said decisively. "Go and pack.
Just leave, Sheila. I'll stay with her."

"But sure you can't stay," Sheila protested. "Seán
will be expecting you home."

"Just go. Don't worry about your mother."
Caroline pushed her upstairs.

"What will you tell her? How will you explain?"
Sheila turned on the curve of the stairs.

"I'm going to ring Seán. He can come over here.
This farce has gone on long enough. Your mother
will have to be told."

"Told? Told what?" Sheila asked in consternation.

"Everything," Caroline said determinedly. "All
about Karen. The whole story. Honestly, Sheila. All
the secrecy has caused nothing but trouble for you.
And for Karen. Sure it's bloody ridiculous. No
wonder things are screwed up. Lies, half-truths,
secrets. It's no way to live. The truth often hurts, but
hiding it hurts worse in the long run." Caroline was
never surer of anything in her whole life. She

looked intently at Sheila. A middle-aged woman still afraid of her mother. Still dreading her mother's criticism. It was insane.

"But it'll kill Main." Sheila was horrified. "She'd die of the shock."

"No, it won't kill her," Caroline insisted. "Even if it does, she's had a long life!"

Sheila laughed. But it was hysteria rather than amusement.

* * *

"I'm not going to see her," Liz argued. "You invited her here, Frank. You deal with her."

Frank was losing patience. This was no time for histrionics. "We'll have to pull together, for Karen's sake."

Chris made tea and brought it in on a tray. He'd sent Peter out for a drink with his friend, Mark. No point in having a crowd waiting when Sheila Crosby arrived. It'd be hard enough for the poor woman. He didn't envy Sheila. Frank was trying to talk sense to his wife, but Liz wouldn't budge. Chris understood Liz's anxiety up to a point. But this was no time for self-indulgence. Nobody mattered now but Karen.

"She sounded very nice on the phone." Frank took a cup of tea from Chris.

"Tch, very nice my foot," Liz retorted. "Look at the state of your daughter. Very nice! I ask you!"

Frank looked pleadingly at Chris.

"Mrs Shaw, she'll be here soon," Chris said

gently. "Please try to get on with her . . . for Karen's sake."

Liz sipped her tea in silence. Nobody spoke. You could cut the atmosphere with a knife. Chris wanted to go up to Karen's door again, but what was the point? Last night at least she'd answered him. Today nothing . . . nothing.

Sheila put the boot down. Luckily the traffic was light. It was still bright. That helped. The drive back to Dublin gave Sheila time to think. Karen needed her. That thought was uppermost in her mind. She'd have to be strong. She'd have to help Karen come to terms with whatever it was that had upset her so much. Karen's visit to her yesterday had been polite and friendly, but it had been superficial. Karen had been too together, too balanced. Underneath her emotions must have been on the boil. Sheila had tried to be honest, to be caring. But each of them had been too wary of the other's feelings. Too afraid of saying the wrong thing.

The time for politeness and formality was gone. Karen needed all the answers. The truth. She needed to be able to express all her feelings, her pain, her anger. Bottling up her feelings had probably caused this breakdown. Sheila had to have a proper heart-to-heart with her. She'd have to let her daughter get it all off her chest. And she'd have to be prepared for a final rejection herself. For the first time in her life, Sheila would have to be a mother. A mother . . . she prayed she'd have the strength and the courage. She reached Clondalkin at ten o'clock. She'd easily be in Clontarf by half past. She'd faced ordeals before in her life. But none as big or as important as this one.

* * *

She pulled up outside the house. She got out and locked the car. She tried to stop shaking. She had to be in control. She stared at the house. This was where Karen had grown up. She imagined her playing here in the front garden. Someone had planted a lovely shrubbery. She didn't quite know why, but that pleased Sheila. The house was lovely. They had new white PVC windows and door, but they'd kept the beautiful stained-glass tops of the bay windows. But this was no time to be surveying the property.

Sheila walked to the front door. Before she could ring, a young man opened the door.

"Sheila?" He smiled, a big warm smile.

He was gorgeous! Sheila went to shake his hand but, to her astonishment, he hugged her tightly. "Thank God, you're here." He stood back and looked at his fiancée's mother. She was a knockout. What a thought to have at such a time, but he couldn't help it. The woman was a beaut! More like Karen's sister than her mother. "Come in!"

Sheila stepped into the hall. Maybe this wasn't going to be as bad as she'd feared. A tall grey-haired man came out of the front room. "Sheila." He shook her hand. A good strong handshake. "I'm Frank Shaw."

Sheila smiled.

"Come in and meet my wife." He opened the front room door and showed her in. The room was large and simply furnished. The brown leather couch had seen better days but the room looked lived-in. Cosy. The bookshelf was bursting at the seams. The fireside rug was worn. A petite red-haired woman sat stiffly on the couch. She got up and shook hands. "Ms Crosby, I'm Liz Shaw."

Nothing more. No smile. No pleased to meet you. Just an icy stare. Polite but cold.

"Would you like to sit down and have a drink?" Frank took her arm.

Sheila hesitated. She didn't want to be rude but she was dying to talk to her daughter. "Could I go up to Karen first?" she asked nervously.

"Maybe we should talk first," Chris suggested. "Whiskey all right?"

Sheila nodded. She sat down reluctantly. Was this going to be the third degree?

"You got here very fast," Frank remarked politely. "You must have driven like a madwoman." Not very tactful but he was doing his best to be friendly.

Sheila nodded again and gratefully took the drink from Chris. "Your phone call frightened me. I was worried."

"We're all worried," Liz said crossly.

"Of course." This woman despised her. Sheila would have killed for a smoke but she couldn't see any sign of an ash-tray.

Chris wanted to move things along. "Sheila." He

felt he could call her Sheila. "What happened yesterday with Karen? I knew she was going to visit you to find out . . . " He couldn't finish it.

"Her father's name," Liz interrupted abruptly. "I might as well tell you that I was dead set against that. My daughter has been through enough, in my opinion." Liz refused a drink from Chris. This was not a social occasion.

Frank was furious with his wife. There was no need for this. Sheila Crosby was here in their home. She was trying to help. She deserved some courtesy at least.

"We know this is very difficult for you, Sheila. We wouldn't be asking you such personal questions if it weren't for Karen's sake."

"I realise that," Sheila said. She gave him a grateful smile. "I think you do have a right to know." She took a deep breath. "Karen called over to me at three o'clock. We were getting on well, I think." Sheila tried to ignore Liz's look of disdain. "I was thrilled to hear about your engagement." She smiled over at Chris.

"Listen, thanks a million for the cheque," Chris butted in. "We didn't expect anything so generous. Of course Karen doesn't know anything about it yet."

Liz groaned loudly. "The money's irrelevant," she snapped. "Could we just get on with this charade?"

Sheila looked down at the floor. She'd have to make a clean breast of it. The quicker she told the story the quicker she'd be out of this room and up to Karen. "I told Karen her father's name and she reacted very oddly. She panicked, I think."

"Well, I'm not a bit surprised. Sleeping dogs should be let lie," Liz said crossly. "The whole thing was a big mistake. Karen was mad to think she could manufacture a happy family. Things just don't happen like that."

Sheila tried to ignore that dig.

"I don't get it." Frank shook his head. "Why should she panic? Unless . . ."

"Unless she already knew him?" Sheila stared at each of them in turn. "I don't know," she said softly. "But his name came as a shock to her." Her voice was barely audible.

"What is it?" Chris's curiosity overcame his embarrassment. "What is his name?"

"Donald Fagan," Sheila whispered. "But he knew nothing about Karen. I never told him." She thought she'd have to elaborate, but Chris jumped up.

"Jesus!" His face turned white. "You're not serious!"

"What? What is it?" Liz cried in dismay.

"He's our next door neighbour. Good God! He's lived in the flat beside ours for the past three years." Chris rushed to the door. "I have to see Karen immediately. No wonder she's . . ."

Frank stopped him. "No, no, wait Chris. Let Sheila go. She's the right one to talk to Karen now."

He looked at his wife. She sat there, staring into space.

Sheila stood up slowly. "Will you show me up to her room?" she asked Chris.

He led the way upstairs. When they reached the landing, he took Sheila's hand. "Karen has known him for the last three years. I'm sorry if this sounds rude, but I have to tell you, neither of us could stand him. He's not nice." That was putting it as mildly as he could. "It's no wonder Karen's reacting like this. It must have been an awful shock for her."

Sheila was in shock too. "I had no idea. I thought he was abroad. This is awful. Do you think she might have confronted him?"

"I hope not," Chris replied gravely. "I sincerely hope not."

Sheila's heart was pounding. "I'd better try to talk to her."

Chris bit his lip. "I don't envy you, Sheila. If you need me, I'll be just downstairs. I'm sorry we had to meet like this."

"So am I," Sheila said. She meant it. "If things work out, maybe we can meet again?"

"I'd like that."

He doubted if things would work out though. The situation was dire. He wanted more than ever to see Karen now. He wanted to be the one to rescue her but he had to let this woman try first. She'd suffered too. Chris thought she was lovely. She'd a nice manner. She was sophisticated and yet there was something very vulnerable about her. It was an appealing mix. "I'm sorry that you had to go through that downstairs. Karen's mother . . . I mean Liz . . . finds it difficult."

"I gathered that," Sheila said sadly. "I'm not here to cause trouble, Chris. That's the last thing I want."

"I know." If only Liz could understand. "Good luck with Karen. And . . . try not to take it personally if she gives you a hard time. She's hitting out at us all. She can't help it."

He patted Sheila's arm and went downstairs.

"Liz, I'm surprised at you," Frank scolded. "You'd want to get a grip."

"Don't lecture me," she retorted. "I didn't do anything to cause this. That woman is responsible. Not to mention you and Chris."

Frank lost his temper. "You still don't get it, do you? We have to get it together for Karen. There can be no more us and that woman. We're all in this together, Liz. Do you hear me? Together."

Chris came in. He refused to be embarrassed anymore by his future parents-in-law's tiffs. Frank was right. They were all in this together. He wondered what was going on upstairs.

Sheila knocked on the door for the third time. "Karen, please. Open the door. We have to talk."

Silence.

"Please, Karen. I love you." There, she'd finally said it. She prayed it wasn't too late. "I love you. I want to help you. We can help each other."

A scornful laugh.

"Karen, open the door. Let me in, please. I've waited so long to meet you, to get to know you. Please don't shut me out. I can't bear it. I love you."

There was an unmerciful thud. Something hit the door. "Go away!" Karen screamed. "How dare you come here! Go away. I don't want you here. I hate you."

Sheila stiffened. "I don't blame you, Karen. You've every right," she said softly. Sheila heard her getting out of the bed. That was some progress. Now, if she could only get her to open the door.

"I love you, Karen. I've always loved you." Sheila repeated it over and over again.

A small voice came back through the door. "You'd a funny way of showing it."

Sheila took another deep breath. "I want to show it now, if you'll let me."

Karen snorted. "Oh? This is a convenient time for you, is it? I'm glad. But it's not exactly convenient for me. Sorry about that. Maybe you could call back some time when I'm not having a nervous breakdown." She shouted the last bit. "On the other hand, you're far too busy, aren't you? I'd almost forgotten. Listen, thanks for coming. You're very kind. You've done the mother bit now, so you can go. Of course you've left it a bit late, but better late than ever, isn't that what they say?" She laughed caustically.

Sheila cringed.

"Are you still there, mother dear?" Another bitter laugh.

"Yes, Karen." Sheila's voice cracked. "I'm sorry. I'm so sorry. I never meant to cause you this pain. My coming here was a mistake. You don't want to see me. I can understand that. I'll go, if that's what you want. But please open the door to your parents, Karen. They're in an awful state. Chris is too. They love you."

Sheila thought she heard her crying quietly. "Goodbye, Karen. I'm sorry things didn't work out between us, but I do understand. I won't bother you again. I'm glad I met Chris. He's a wonderful person. He needs you, Karen. Don't shut him out."

Karen sobbed on the other side of the door.

Sheila's heart was breaking. She wanted to take her child in her arms and comfort her. She wanted to kiss her and hug her and hold her. But much more than a thick wooden door stood between them.

Sheila was beaten.

"Bye, Karen. I'll think of you often . . . " Sheila broke down. She stood helplessly. She didn't belong here. She couldn't help her daughter. She was a complete failure.

Inadequate.

She turned away in despair and started for the stairs.

Now she had to face the others. Another grilling session.

Then she heard it . . . the sound of a lock turning . . . the creak of a door opening.

"Mum?"

Sheila thought she was hearing things.

"Mum."

Oh, God. Sheila turned back. Karen was standing in her bedroom doorway. Her hair was matted, her eyes were red and swollen, her T-shirt was crumpled and stained.

"Don't go, Mum!"

Sheila ran to her and crushed her in her arms.

Chris was standing in the hallway below. He'd heard Karen's door opening. He couldn't believe it. He dashed into the sitting-room. "She's done it. God almighty, she's done it!"

Frank and Liz stared dumbfoundedly.

"Sheila's done it! Whatever she said . . . she got Karen to open the door!" He whirled Liz and danced her around the floor. "I could kiss her! She got Karen to open the bloody door!"

"I'm going up there this minute." Liz broke away from Chris and made for the hall.

Frank pulled her back. "No, Liz. Leave them. This is Sheila's moment. We have all the time in the world."

"You sound like the Guinness ad." Chris grinned at them both.

Sheila held Karen tightly. They sat on her bed, arms around each other. Neither of them spoke. Their physical closeness was enough for the moment. Sheila stroked Karen's hair and looked around the bedroom. It was cosy and warm. The old mahogany wardrobe and dressing-table gave a homely feel to the room. Sheila tried to imagine Karen as a little girl growing up here. The make-shift bookcase and shelves, the dolls, the teddies, the books. This room had the same lived-in atmosphere as the rest of the house. Her home was a mausoleum by comparison, Sheila realised.

Karen stopped crying. She stretched over to the bedside locker and grabbed a pile of tissues. She blew her nose and then smiled at Sheila. "Do you want one?"

Sheila took a hankie and dabbed at her eyes. "We're some pair, aren't we?"

Karen nodded. "Did they send for you?"

"Chris rang me. God, they were so worried about you, Karen. So was I. Can I ask you . . . what made you open the door? I was blathering on and I knew I wasn't saying the right things. I didn't know what to say. I know I was like a crazy woman. Then I was afraid I was going to bawl . . ."

"It wasn't anything you said . . . it was that you came. I heard your voice . . . the words didn't matter . . . you were here for me . . . that's what mattered . . . I knew that you did love me."

Sheila hugged her again. It was ironic. Sheila had done her dead level best to stay cool, to be in control. It was when she'd lost control that she'd got through to Karen.

"What happened, love? What happened after you left me yesterday?"

"I can't talk about it," Karen whispered.

"Karen, I know it's very hard, but I honestly think it'd be better if you tried. I think I can guess anyway. You found him, didn't you?"

Karen nodded. She stared at the floor.

"He was my next door neighbour. Incredible, isn't it?" Karen still didn't look at her.

"You told him?" Sheila held her breath.

"Yes." Karen looked up. She shuddered. "He didn't want to know."

Oh God, Sheila thought. He'd rejected her.

"He told me in no uncertain terms that he'd never had a daughter, he'd no wish to have a daughter. Not now. Not ever." Karen's eyes filled up again.

"I suppose it was difficult for him, Karen. You turning up like that, out of the blue. He must have got a terrible shock." Sheila tried to soften it.

"No, it wasn't a shock, Sheila. He knew. He'd known for the last two years. He just didn't think I'd ever find out."

He must have recognised her, Sheila told herself. After all, Karen was the image of her. Sheila wasn't sure how to handle this. She couldn't say anything against him. He was Karen's father.

Karen screwed the hankie into a ball. "I hate him," she said venomously.

"Give him time, Karen. He may come around." Sheila took hold of Karen's hand.

"Come around?" Karen exploded. "You don't know what he said? He said you were a whore. That you didn't know who had fathered me. That you slept around." Karen raged on, unaware of how her words might be hurting Sheila. "He denied it, Sheila." She inadvertently slipped back into calling her Sheila, but Sheila didn't care what Karen called her now. It was enough that she was talking to her.

"He denied me, totally. He told me to forget it and get on with my life. Can you imagine? It was horrible. It was the worst moment of my life. I hate him. He's cruel and heartless."

Oh, sweet Jesus. What kind of a man was he? Why did he have to turn on her like that? His own flesh and blood? It was appalling.

"So, what do you think of Donald Fagan now?" Karen looked at her for an answer.

"I pity him," Sheila said gently.

Karen stared at her in disbelief. "You pity him? Save your pity for me." She started to sniffle again.

"I can't pity you, Karen. Why would I pity you? You're a beautiful girl. You've a wonderful family. You have me, I hope. You have a good man who loves you. God willing, you and Chris will have a family of your own. Why should anyone pity you?"

"Because I'm his, that's why. That despicable excuse for a man is my father. I have his genes, I have his blood running through my body. I probably have his character too. Oh God, it makes my flesh crawl. I'm his."

"No, Karen." Sheila knew the answer to this one. She'd thought about this for twenty-eight years. "You're not his. You're not even mine. We don't belong to our parents. We belong to ourselves. Each of us is unique. You're your own person. You belong to yourself."

Karen blew her nose again. "You're beginning to sound like a religion teacher!"

Sheila smiled. "Maybe so. But they do say some things that are true, don't they? Think about it. Sure, Donald Fagan and I created you. But you're not us, Karen. You're you. Your mother is downstairs at this minute, worrying about me. She thinks I want to take you away from her. I couldn't do that, even if I wanted to. You don't belong to Liz or Frank either, you see. You're not a piece of property. You won't belong to Chris when you marry him. Can't you see that? You'll share your lives and your love. That's the ideal for all of us. To share our lives and, if we're very lucky, our love."

Karen suddenly understood. She didn't belong to anyone but herself. It was a liberating notion.

"But why did you say you pitied him?" Karen still didn't understand that.

"Because he must be afraid of love . . . of commitment. That's the only reason he'd have to reject you, Karen. He never married, did he?"

"No, not to my knowledge," she said disdainfully. "He has a girlfriend of my age."

"Don was never long without a girlfriend." Sheila sighed. "We're only speculating, we don't know anything about him, really. But I never felt guilty about not telling him about you. It was as if I instinctively knew what his reaction would have been. He'd have run away."

"Worse. Much worse than that." Karen's face contorted. "I asked him. He said that he'd have insisted on an abortion." She turned her face away. Her throat tightened. She couldn't breathe.

Sheila pulled her to her breast. "That would never have happened, Karen. Remember? You were safe and snug inside me. I loved you from the moment I found out about you. I called you Buggins and I used to sing to you. I knew everything about you. I knew when your eyelashes grew. I knew when your nails grew. I knew about every part of your development. I read my manual. I used to talk to you all the time. For those months we were truly together. When I was convinced you could hear outside sounds, I played classical music for you. The day I felt your first kick I cried with joy."

"Did you really?" Karen's face lit up.

"Yeah." For a second Sheila was transported back in time to that beautiful house in Howth. She saw in her mind's eye two little imps running around the garden. Whatever happened to Tom and Julie? Maybe she'd get in touch with Susan.

"Sheila . . . Mum, what am I to call you?" Karen asked.

"Whatever you want. Whatever makes you comfortable."

"Maybe I'll stick with Sheila. It'll be easier for Liz."

Sheila thought that was very wise. "What were you going to ask me, Karen?"

"Ah . . . it doesn't matter." Karen brushed her hair back from her forehead.

"No," Sheila insisted. "Ask away. No more secrets or silences. Agreed?"

"Agreed." Karen smiled. "OK, here goes. Why did you never marry?"

Sheila smiled back at her. "I thought you'd ask me that. Well, it's not difficult to answer, really. After I had you, after . . . I had you adopted, I couldn't ever think about having other children. I just couldn't. I resented having lost you, Karen. If I'd married and had a baby, they'd have brought presents, had a party, cooed and gushed over the child. I couldn't have faced that. All I'd have thought about was how I'd felt so lonely and abandoned in the hospital when you were born. A ring on my finger would have made everything all right for everybody else. I'd have been allowed to have my baby then. I'd have been congratulated. I just couldn't have faced that. I only wanted you."

Karen felt a surge of love for this woman. "Well, you have me now." She jumped up off the bed. "Not that you I belong to you, of course."

"Of course not," Sheila agreed with a grin. "Karen, do you feel any better about things now?"

"Yes. I still hate that bastard though. But you're probably right. Maybe he is to be pitied. But that's his problem, as he'd say. He was right too, in a way. He told me to get on with my life. I'm going to do just that. I'm sorry I behaved so childishly. "

Sheila thought Karen had behaved childishly, but it was understandable.

"At first I resented you. I thought you got rid of me to be free."

"No, no. That wasn't it at all," Sheila protested.

"I know that now. I think I really do know how you felt. But you fought back. You showed them all."

Another childish reaction, Sheila thought.

"The business was my life until now, Karen. I won't pretend I didn't enjoy every minute of it. I'm a bit obsessive, I have to admit."

"Chris is always telling me that I'm obsessive. Maybe I inherited more of your personality than Donald Fagan's. Maybe daughters get the mother's genes."

"Perish the thought! If I thought I'd my mother's personality I'd do the world a favour and slit my throat!"

"Why? What's she like, your mother?" She had a new granny too. That suddenly occurred to her. "She looks nice in the photos."

"Let's just say the camera sometimes lies." Sheila laughed. "Ah, she's not that bad. She's a domineering, interfering old biddy but . . . she's my mother."

"I'll have to meet her."

"One step at a time, eh? I'll have to work on your mother first. She doesn't exactly approve of me," Sheila said. "This mothering business is more complicated than they'd have you believe. I hope you're learning from all this."

"Yeah, how not to be a mother," Karen groaned. "Jesus, I can't imagine it. But I'm glad we had this talk. You know, I lay here in this bed for the last twenty-four hours convincing myself that I couldn't marry Chris. I was afraid I'd turn out like my father. The thought of having children terrified the wits out of me. I wondered if I could be a good mother. Do you still regret having had me adopted?"

"Until tonight, I did," Sheila confessed.

"What do you mean?"

"Until I walked into this house, Karen. Do you know the first thing that struck me when I came in tonight? Struck me forcibly?"

"What?" Karen asked eagerly.

"Love. There's such a huge sense of love in this house, Karen. You can feel it everywhere."

"Didn't Mum freeze you out?"

"Well, she was a bit cool, I'll give you that. Don't worry, Karen. We'll sort it out. No, when I met your parents, I couldn't honestly say that I was sorry anymore. They adore you. Anyone can see that. They gave you a good life. A lovely home. They gave you a brother, a proper family. How could I regret that?"

Karen nodded. "Maybe you could have done the same."

"We'll never know now, will we? I'd have tried, that's for sure. But we'll never know. At the time I wasn't in a position to offer you much. The business was a life-line for me. I never dreamed it'd snowball like it did. I'm quite chuffed with myself, to tell you the truth. But I have to say this. Having you was the best thing I did in my whole life. I mean that."

"Thanks." Karen smiled. "Here." She handed Sheila a photograph album. "Look through that. I've read your diary. It's time you got to know about my life. There, that's me on Frank's knee after my bath. Oh, look at this one. It's Peter and me playing in St Anne's Park."

Chris peeped his head around the door. "Anyone for tea?" He grinned at the two of them . . . the two auburn heads together, bent over the photos.

* * *

Liz gave Sheila tea and salad sandwiches. She seemed to be friendlier . . . more thawed out. It was obvious that Frank had had a word with her. Sheila was exhausted. The night had been extremely emotional. She was burnt out.

"We'd like to thank you for all you've done," Frank said. "We know it wasn't easy for you, coming here like this."

"It wasn't easy for any of us," Sheila replied. "I don't think this is the right time, but I think it's important that we get together soon. It's important for Karen that we try to get on."

"I couldn't agree more." Frank looked at his wife. "Liz?"

Liz Shaw frowned. "I'm finding this very difficult. I'd prefer if we had it out some other time. I need to talk to Karen too."

Sheila sipped her tea. "You're right. We all need time to adjust. I'd like to have you all over to my house for dinner one night, if you both think that'd be OK."

Liz stared at her. The miracle-worker in her designer jeans.

"Liz," Sheila said suddenly, "I'd like us to be friends. It'll take time. But I want you to know that I didn't come back into Karen's life to cause you pain. Tonight I got a strong sense of what this family is like. I couldn't be happier for Karen. She's a lucky girl. You've done a wonderful job."

Patronising bitch. Liz had enough friends, thank you very much. She stared icily at Sheila. "We did our best."

"Karen loves you," Sheila said quietly. "Liz, you're her mother in the real sense of that word. Nobody knows that better than I do. I'd like to thank you both for all you've done for her. She's a lovely girl. You should be proud of her."

"We are," Frank answered her. "We're also very grateful to you, Sheila. You'll never know how grateful. You gave us the most precious gift anyone could ever give . . . you gave us our daughter."

Sheila was deeply moved. Against her will, tears sprang to her eyes again. It was a painful moment.

Liz saw her pain. But she still resented this woman. Sure, she was the one who'd brought Karen into the world. Without her, there would be no Karen. No Karen. But Sheila Crosby had no rights now. She'd given them up.

Liz had invested her whole life in her children.

Sheila Crosby was not part of their family. She never would be. She'd come here tonight and had succeeded where they hadn't. The heroine of the hour!

Bull! She was the one who'd caused all this grief. Frank could fawn on her all he liked. She had no intention of joining the Sheila Crosby fan club.

Frank knew that expression well. Liz was about to have another outburst. Best to get Sheila out of here as soon as possible. His wife felt threatened. She thought she was angry. He knew better. She was afraid.

CHAPTER FORTY-TWO

Sheila slept late the following morning. She was exhausted. The shrill ringing of the bedside phone woke her. She stretched out her hand and groped for the receiver.

"Sheila? It's Patti."

"Mmh." Sheila was still half asleep. "What time is it?"

"It's gone eleven."

"What!" Sheila opened her eyes with a start. "Oh my God, I slept it out."

"It's OK," Patti reassured her. "We weren't expecting you back to work for days. Is everything all right?"

"Eh yeah," Sheila mumbled. "I meant to get up early to ring my mother."

Patti hesitated for a second. "That's why I phoned you. She's here downstairs."

"Who is?" Sheila couldn't take it in. She was groggy.

"Your mother. She's down here in the waiting-room with Caroline."

"Jesus!" Sheila swung her legs out of the bed. Suddenly she was wide awake. "Send them up."

She banged down the phone and leapt out of the bed. Her mother was here! With Caroline!

Sheila dashed into her bathroom and splashed cold water over her face. She brushed her teeth hurriedly and combed her hair. As she was pulling on her dressing-gown, there was a knock. Sheila ran out and unlocked the bedroom door. Caroline stood there, smiling. "Hi!" She kissed Sheila. "She's here. I put her in the kitchen. Come on, it's time to face the music!"

Not again, Sheila thought.

She followed Caroline into the kitchen. Her mother was making coffee. To Sheila's dismay she spotted two suitcases on the floor. Her mother was here for a stay.

"Hello, Mam," Sheila said cautiously.

Rita turned around. She opened her arms for a hug.

Sheila was grasped to her mother's breast. How long had it been since they embraced? Not since her father's funeral. They weren't a demonstrative family at the best of times.

Rita sat down at the kitchen table. She ignored Caroline. "A granddaughter! I should have been told, Sheila. What kind of a monster did you think I was?"

Caroline sighed and Sheila lit a cigarette.

Rita talked on. "It should never have happened. That adoption. She was your baby. Your flesh and blood. You should never have given her away. I'd have cherished that child. When Seán came over last night and told me the whole story, I was devastated." She looked to Caroline for confirmation. Caroline tried to signal to her to shut up. Didn't she know how her words must be hurting Sheila? It was futile.

Rita went on and on. "When I think of it. A lovely baby girl! Oh my God, it's shocking. Why didn't you tell me? I'd have helped."

She didn't give Sheila the chance to answer.

"I'd have loved that child. I'd have accepted her into our family. And what about your poor father? He'd have understood. You didn't think he'd have rejected your own little baby, did you? You know how much your father loved you, Sheila. He went to his grave, never knowing. It's such a terrible shame."

Sheila didn't put her straight on that one.

Rita paused. "You did it for us, didn't you dear? You didn't want to upset us?"

Sheila nodded.

"But you see you were quite wrong now, don't you?" Rita looked at her daughter imploringly. "The baby was my flesh and blood too. My granddaughter. I'd truly have loved her."

Sheila didn't know whether she wanted to hug her mother or throttle her.

Caroline had to intervene. "There's no point in going over it all again, Mam. What's done is done. The main thing is that Sheila has found Karen again. We have to be thankful for that. We must look forward, not back."

Thank God for Caroline, Sheila thought.

Rita poured out coffee for the three of them.

"Anyhow, it's Seán I blame. He shouldn't have done what he did. He'd no right to interfere. He should have come to us, your father and me."

Caroline looked at Sheila. Let Rita blame Seán if it made her feel better. She was ready to blame everyone but herself.

The phone rang. Caroline picked up the kitchen extension.

"Yes, she's here. Oh? Hi! I'm Caroline. That's right. Yes, it is strange. Strange but lovely. I hope we can meet soon. Hold on, I'll pass you over to Sheila." She put her hand over the receiver. "It's Karen."

Sheila jumped up and grabbed the phone. "Hi Karen, yeah, I'm fine. You OK? Good. Yeah, my mother's here too. What? Now? Right, OK. No, no she'll be thrilled. Honestly. Right, see you then."

Sheila put down the phone and smiled at them. "Karen's coming over now. She wants to meet you both."

"Oh Sheila!" Rita hugged her daughter.

* * *

Yvonne trundled up the stairs to the flat. Chris Moore was coming out of next door with three large suitcases.

"Hello," she said cheerfully. "You're not moving out, are you?"

Chris put down the cases. "I'm not, as least not yet. This is Karen's stuff. She's gone back to her mother's."

Yvonne looked embarrassed. "You haven't broken up, have you?"

Chris ran his hand through his hair. Should he tell her? "No, no, nothing like that. You obviously haven't heard what happened the other night?"

"Sorry?" Yvonne was puzzled.

"Look, Yvonne, there's no easy way of saying this, but I think you should know." He noticed her blush. "Donald is Karen's father."

She stepped back. "What? What did you say?"

"Donald is Karen's father." Chris took her arm to steady her.

"Oh . . . oh no," she stuttered. "Karen's father?"

She wanted to dispute it . . . to protest that it couldn't be true. Instead, she stared dumbly at him.

"Of course he denies it. But Karen spoke to him the other night and, to be honest, he was very brutal with her. She can't face him again. She'll never come back here. I'll be moving out myself soon."

Yvonne froze. "I . . . I don't know what to say. I'm so . . . sorry. Please tell Karen I'm . . . I'm so sorry."

"It's nothing to do with you, Karen knows that. It's not your fault." He looked at the girl. She was as white as a sheet. "I'd better go. Good luck." Chris struggled down the stairs with suitcases. He wondered how he'd get the computer out.

Yvonne put her key in the door. She'd meant to go straight to bed. She was exhausted after her night shift in emergency. But this couldn't wait. Funny, she was in shock and she wasn't. She'd vaguely guessed this all along. She'd known it to be true, but she hadn't wanted to believe it.

She picked up the phone and rang the shop.

"Donald, I'm leaving you." Her tone was emotionless.

"Yvonne? Stop dramatising. What's wrong now?" He sounded bored.

"I've just met Chris Moore. He told me what happened. I've had enough, Don."

Silence. He was thinking what to say.

"No, don't try to deny it, Don. I've known the truth for too long. So have you. Did you honestly think you could get away with it?"

Donald got mad. "Get away with what? OK, so I'm her father. Who gives a damn? It's nothing to do with you. It was twenty-eight years ago, for God's sake. I never pretended I'd lived a monastic life. Of course I've a past. But that's nothing to do with you. There's no reason for you to be upset about it. I've no intention of having anything to do with her. She's nothing to me. I don't give a damn. Why should you?"

Yvonne bristled. That was exactly the point. He didn't give a damn.

"Don, it's not Karen's existence that I object to." She sighed.

Who was she to be objecting to anything? She had no right. "So, what's your problem?" he asked, but he didn't particularly care.

"My problem . . . my problem is the way you

treated her. She's your daughter, Don. That counts for something."

Donald cackled. "What do you think this is? Bleedin' Little House on the Prairie? Don't be ridiculous."

"Don, I've had it. I'm ringing to tell you that I'm leaving. Today. My father will pick up the rest of my stuff at the weekend."

"Ah, cop on, will you? I'll be home at about seven. I'll bring home a bottle of wine. This will all blow over."

"Good bye, Don." Yvonne replaced the receiver.

Rita gazed fondly at her granddaughter. The girl was gorgeous, the image of Sheila at that age. Same translucent skin, same green eyes, same beautiful long auburn hair. She had the Crosby looks!

"And you're getting married next spring, my dear. How lovely. We'll have a great day."

Sheila looked in horror at Caroline. Caroline stared down into her glass.

Karen smiled at her new-found granny. She had a distinct Galway accent but she tried to disguise it with what she thought was a cultured tone. Hilarious!

"When are we to meet your young man?" Rita poured her granddaughter another sherry and helped herself to her third. She was getting a bit tipsy.

"Tomorrow night, if you're all free. Dad wants to invite you all out for a meal." Karen looked at Sheila. Was that in order?

Sheila nodded at her. Frank was wise, she thought. They'd all meet again on neutral territory.

"Oh, I'll have to go in to Grafton Street and treat myself to a new outfit," Rita exclaimed. "Must make a good impression on your . . . your . . ." Rita got flustered.

"Your parents." Caroline smiled at the girl. Honestly, she'd thought it more often than she'd admit. She'd swing for her mother-in-law!

Caroline took a photo from her bag and handed it to Karen. "There's your cousin Ciara with her little daughter, Caoimhe."

"She's lovely," Karen said sincerely. "They're both lovely."

"Mmh," Caroline said proudly. "Ciara's expecting again."

Rita sat up proudly. "Two great-grandchildren. And when you have a baby, my dear, that'll be my third. Oh, it's wonderful, isn't it?"

Jesus, Sheila thought. How would Karen react to that? The poor girl must be overwhelmed. She glanced at her daughter but Karen was beaming.

Happy families, Sheila thought wryly.

"I'd like to meet everyone in Galway," Karen said suddenly. "Maybe I could go down for a visit?"

"Wonderful, my dear. And you can bring your fiancé with you, can't she, Sheila? We've loads of room." The old lady was elated.

* * *

Yvonne looked around the flat for the last time. Her father had brought her suitcases down to the car. He was waiting for her. Five years of her life wasted with Don. How had she been so blind?

She'd imagined herself as his wife, for God's sake. The mother of his children. She'd thought they'd have had a family, a real home, that they'd have grown old together. But that was the problem. Donald was old. Too old for her. Yet, in the most important ways, he'd never grown up at all. He'd still be chasing women in the Leeson Street clubs when he was sixty. Pathetic. She'd had enough. He'd never be able to make a commitment. That was his tragedy.

She checked the bathroom. She wouldn't leave any trace of herself in this flat. She had to wipe the slate clean. She left her keys on the kitchen counter and closed the door behind her.

* * *

Donald got home at seven, armed with a bottle of rosé and a bunch of flowers. His peace offering. No sign of Yvonne. She must be sulking in the bedroom. No, no she wasn't there. An empty wardrobe. The bare dressing-table. The bed neatly made. He wandered into the bathroom. No knickers hanging over the bath. No creams, oils and potions on the shelves. He came back to the sitting-room. The bookshelf was half empty. The coffee table was cleared. No women's magazines, no nail polish, no tissues.

Typical of her. She'd cleaned and scrubbed before she'd left.

Don went to the fridge. He cleared out all the rabbit food: the lettuce, the chives, the cucumber, the radishes, the carrots. Tonight, he'd send out for a Chinese.

He opened a can of beer. He slipped off his shoes, went back to the sitting-room and settled back into his favourite armchair. He took the remote control and flicked on the telly.

He'd put his aftershave and stuff into the bathroom later. He'd move his clothes out of the spare room and back to the wardrobe in his own room, where they belonged. This was his pad now, all his.

He might go out for a pint later. He might and he might not. He could do whatever the hell he liked now. He was free. FREE!

CHAPTER FORTY-THREE

It was a crisp spring morning. Karen's wedding morning. Sheila was up at the crack of dawn. She was highly excited. She had her shower early. It was just as well as the phone never stopped ringing.

Mary and Jim rang to wish her good luck. Ciara rang. She couldn't make the wedding as her second baby was due any minute. Rita rang. Thank goodness, she'd decided not to come. Her arthritis was playing up and Seán had advised her not to travel! Sheila was grateful to her brother. He knew that the old lady's presence might cause Sheila one or two awkward moments.

The phone rang for the fourth time in twenty minutes. Must be Karen.

"Hello, Sheila Crosby here."

An embarrassed cough on the other end.

"Hello?" Sheila repeated.

"Sheila, this is John . . . John Harris."

Sheila sat down. "Hi! How are you?" She knew her voice was unsteady. She tried to get her thoughts together. John Harris!

"Jim told me your great news. I just rang to say I'm very happy for you."

"Eh, thanks," Sheila murmured.

"What's she like?" he asked.

"She's lovely." Sheila had a catch in her voice.

"Yeah, she would be," he said pensively.

Sheila couldn't get over it. He still cared about her, she could hear it in his voice. "How are you, John?"

"Fine. We're all fine."

An awkward silence. There was nothing left to say. It was strange.

"Thanks for thinking of me today, John."

"I often think of you," he said ruefully. Then he hung up.

Sheila was very moved.

She was about to go into the lavender room to wake Caroline and Seán when the phone rang again.

"Sheila? it's Peadar."

"Peadar!" Sheila was delighted.

"I'm just ringing to wish you all the best today. I'm sorry I missed you on the last visit. I'd love to have met Karen."

"Not to worry. We didn't have much time. I think Karen enjoyed it though. They made a great fuss of her in Carrigeen."

"Bridget said she was gorgeous, Sheila. The image of you."

"Tell her thanks. And thank you for your thoughtfulness." It was typical of Peadar.

"We're all rooting for you down here. Maura's even planning free drinks this evening in the pub!"

"Jesus!" Sheila laughed. "That is something. Tell them I'll bring Karen and Chris down again when they get back from their honeymoon. And tell Conor the vases are beautiful. Karen was thrilled. She'll write to thank him herself."

"So, I'd better let you go. You must be up to your neck in it."

"Ah, not really. Karen's family are the ones who have all the hassle."

Peadar hesitated. "Are you all right? Caroline's with you?"

"Yeah," Sheila said. "And Seán. I've plenty of moral support."

"Good. Jesus, Sheila. I'm so happy for you . . . it's . . . "

"Thanks, Peadar."

Sheila put down the phone. He was so nice. They all were. All the gang in Carrigeen had been great.

What time was it? She'd have to wake the others.

They were already up. Seán rang Colm to check that everything was OK in the surgery.

"This is it, Sheila." Caroline hugged her. "I'll go and make some breakfast. You do your make-up in peace. Then I'll help you to get dressed."

"Caroline, can you believe it? I'm so happy. I just can't believe it."

Caroline smiled. "You deserve it, Sheila. If ever anybody deserved to be happy, you do."

694

They sat in the second pew, Caroline on one side of Sheila, with Seán on the other. St Gabriel's Church looked lovely with all the flowers and the lighted candles. Peter Shaw turned around to shake hands. He was nice, Caroline thought.

Liz nodded formally and stretched out a gloved hand. Caroline could feel Sheila stiffen. Caroline could understand how this woman must be feeling. It wasn't easy.

Chris winked over at them. He looked a bit nervous. Caroline liked him. The bridesmaid waved from the alter. This must be Paula. Sheila had told Caroline about her. She was now a weekly visitor to the gym in Fitzwilliam Square. She looked very pretty in her peach matron of honour's dress.

Caroline saw the guests stare in awe at the lovely woman in her elegant cream suit and wide-brimmed cream hat. Everyone recognised Sheila Crosby, the owner of Natural Woman. Why was this celebrity at Karen Shaw's wedding? What was the connection?

The ones who mattered knew, Caroline told herself.

The wedding march sounded. Caroline squeezed Sheila's arm. Everyone turned around. Karen walked steadily and confidently up the aisle on Frank's arm. She looked radiant. She wore a long flowing white dress, exquisite in its simplicity. Tiny pearl buttons decorated the empire neckline and the puffed sleeves. The delicate wreath of white flowers owed her long auburn curls off to perfection. She wore no veil.

Sheila gulped hard as her daughter smiled over at them. Tears pricked her eyes. She wasn't ashamed of them. She'd resorted to the stiff upper lip for far too long. From now on, she'd cry when she bloody well wanted to. Liz turned around again. She managed a small smile.

Caroline was moved by the gesture. Each of these women wanted what was best for Karen. But they were still very wary of each other. Caroline thought that Liz was making a brave effort. It was obvious that there was no love lost there, but that was OK. It must be hard for Liz, having Sheila here today. Bloody hard. It was a good job that Rita hadn't come. She'd have been bound to put her foot in it one way or another. They'd Seán to thank for making her stay at home.

Caroline glanced at her sister-in-law as Karen and Chris made their solemn vows. What was Sheila thinking?

Seán took his wife's hand. Marriage vows. He cast his mind back to his own wedding day. Caroline had been a beautiful bride. She was still a beautiful woman. They'd had some sticky patches, but they were still together. Time to count his blessings. He glanced down the church. Wasn't that Mary Ryan at the back? She must have slipped in. Sheila would be thrilled . . . Mary Ryan. He remembered the first time he'd met her. That awful day in Sheila's flat. God, the way he'd acted. All he'd wanted to do was to get shot of the problem.

The problem. He looked back at the alter. His niece. His beautiful niece. He was deeply saddened.

Mary watched the scene from the back of the church. The wheel had come full circle. Sheila Crosby . . . her friend of thirty years. The woman who'd built an empire. The woman who'd lived the good life. The woman who had wealth, success and fame. The woman who'd suffered in silence through a lifetime. The woman who'd helped Mary through her own tragedy. At last Sheila had found peace. What must she be thinking now?

Sheila closed her eyes and tried to imagine the years ahead . . .

Natural Woman would expand even further, opening up stores in London and New York. Rita would slip away peacefully in her sleep. Seán would retire and hand over to Colm. Colm would marry a beautiful Asian doctor who'd share his practice and his life. Caroline would run the factory and help to raise her five grandchildren. Mary would get her psychology degree but she'd return to teaching, her first love. Karen would get her wish and become a successful reporter. She'd be a loving wife and mother.

And Sheila? What about Sheila?

Sheila would walk on the beach in Salthill, the wind blowing in her hair. She'd sit on the rocks, like she used to do. She'd look out to sea and think of all that had happened. This time, she wouldn't be sad. Two little auburn-haired kiddies would run up to her calling her name. "Nana. Nana, come on in. The waters's lovely."

Such things were to be.

Could Sheila know all that? No, of course she couldn't. Which of us can see into the future?